ZARA ON ARRAN

Cicely Gill

Mallard Publishing

First published in Scotland by Mallard Publishing 2017

ISBN 978-0-9531014-8-1

Printed by Merchant City Print Ltd

Also by Cicely Gill

Ivory

The Trees of Childhood (poetry)

Acknowledgements

Many thanks to Elanor MacNamara, Stuart Gough and Louise Hope for close
reading and useful feedback and to John Weir for help with covers.

Chapter I   Strands

The day before Zara left Glasgow she bumped into D.I. Des.

'They need your help over there, do they? Serial sheep killer on the loose, Zara to the rescue?' Zara ignored the sarcasm.

'I need a break. This' — she circled her arm to embrace Glasgow — 'all this is getting to me.'

'Where are you staying? I'll look you up if I'm down for the day with the wife and the wean.' Zara smiled.

'It's the North Crag hotel, Brodick.'

'Sounds a bit bleak?'

'It was George's favourite climb before he had his stroke. Can't do heights any more.'

Now Zara stood at the deck rail of the *Caledonian Isles.* She had chosen Arran because of George and Kirsty who fortuitously had bought the hotel when George had been made redundant aged thirty-five. Shortly after, he had had a stroke. Zara's plan was to pay for her bed and board by working for them. She knew they could not afford staff but she was helping herself, because she needed time to assess her relationship with Barney.

She shifted her position until she was facing the island directly and not facing Barney and Glasgow. She wondered if she would ever be able to make up her mind about him. It was now over ten years since they had met and Zara was still unsure. At least, some days she was absolutely sure and some days totally doubtful. Sometimes she wished Barney would do something completely uncharacteristic so she could point to it and say to herself, Well I always knew there was *something* wrong with him. Barney, she knew, was taking her extended absence on Arran as a direct rebuff but he had phrased his objections indirectly:

'Ben will really miss you.'

To which Zara had replied, 'He can come down whenever he likes, weekends till the holidays start and then...' She had tailed off. Barney's son

Ben, her godson, was one thing but she didn't really want Barney down for an extended stay: she was trying to sort out her feelings in his absence.

She intended to do this by focusing on the hotel. Photos Kirsty had sent showed a very challenging garden. It had been thought that George working gently in it would have been a way of recuperating, but instead he had sat on the dilapidated garden seat and watched the brambles advance across what had once been lawn.

Zara had helped her dad garden as a child, until he died. She had been ten when she and her mother had moved to Glasgow. She was confident: what she did not know, she was sure people would soon tell her.

She tried not to think about Ben. She was not going to feel guilty about him. Even though she saw him most days, she had never committed herself to being part of the family. That's what her head told her but her heart took a punch every time his name crossed her mind.

Zara turned as if to shake off unwelcome thoughts. There was that man again. The man on the train. He was still deep in his book and frowning with concentration. The name of the book was *Murder not Proven* by Jack House. Zara knew she had seen the book before but she could not remember who it was about. Leaving Glasgow was partly about leaving criminal investigation behind, she told herself. But this is just a story, the voice inside her said. No harm in satisfying your curiosity.

'Sorry to disturb you but can I ask who your book's about?'

'One of the cases is the Goat Fell murder of 1889.' He sounded as if he found Zara's question perfectly ordinary so she continued:

'And is there any special reason why you are particularly interested in it?'

The man looked amused 'I'm a mountaineer. I've just come to live on the island and I've joined the Mountain Rescue team. The Goat Fell murder has always been a talking point for local mountaineers. No one really knows what happened, but it's always interesting to speculate.' He paused and looked at Zara.

'You're wondering why *I* am particularly interested,' she responded. 'I'm a crime journalist,' she stopped, 'but I'm on holiday at the moment.'

'Hence the interest,' said the man smiling. 'I'm Ronnie by the way. Pleased to meet you.' He held out his hand.

'Zara,' said Zara. The hand she took was warm and felt capable. 'Tell me about the murder. I'm sure I knew the story once but I've forgotten it.'

'Briefly,' began Ronnie, 'Edwin Rose, a clerk from Tooting in London met John Watson Laurie when they were both on holiday on the Isle of Bute. They weren't staying in the same accommodation there, but one day they found themselves on the same day excursion round the Kyles of Bute and they got talking on deck. Edwin Rose saw Goat Fell rising up before him in an inviting sort of —'

'How do you know that?' asked Zara

'Story-teller's licence. You bored? You want it quicker?' Ronnie was smiling at her.

'Sorry. Go on.'

'John Watson Laurie offered to take Edwin Rose up the mountain saying he knew the path well, and so, a day later they left Bute, stayed the night in Invercloy, now known as Brodick, and the next day they climbed Goat Fell.'

'The vessel is now arriving in port. Will all vehicle drivers and their passengers please return to the car deck and occupy their vehicle.' The tannoy had interrupted them.

'Listen, I'm sorry but I'll need to go. My parents are on the boat with their car. They've come over to check up on me. See if I'm eating breakfast,' he said.

'What about the rest of the story?'

'You'll have to buy the book. Or look on the internet. Lots of stuff there.'

'I'm staying at the North Crag hotel. Working for friends,' said Zara. 'Call in if you're passing. I'll make you a coffee.'

'I'm in Corrie at the moment but...'

'Whatever,' said Zara as if she didn't really care. Ronnie put his book in his rucksack and swung it over his shoulder.

'Bye then.' He walked away quickly and then stopped and turned back. Simultaneously a man in a red jacket and white trousers strode past the open doorway. 'Nice talking to you!' Ronnie smiled at Zara and then turned again, entered the doorway looking right and left before proceeding.

***

Zara waited until the last moment before leaving the deck. She looked up at Goat Fell and tried to picture Edwin Rose. She wondered if he had seen the mountain for the first time in sunlight as she was doing now. It looked beneficent, as if it were protecting the village that lay beneath it.

Zara had to search back in her memory to find the one and only occasion when she had climbed the mountain. She looked hard at the trees patched over the foothills and tried to imagine the path. She had been on a youth club trip. She remembered the leader, Andy, as an adventurer. They had sailed over, sixteen of them, on the seven o'clock boat from Ardrossan, having stayed the previous night in a school hall there, and, fortified with a Cal Mac full Scottish breakfast, they had set out for the mountain, taking the bus as far as Cladach. Zara thought she might have been thirteen. Her memories were clear but of odd things. Susan McKyntyre falling and scraping her elbow so badly that you could almost see the bone. Zara hadn't looked but Shona Scott had and then promptly fainted; Hamish MacNab dropping his sandwiches in the burn. He'd managed to fish them out but they were completely soggy. He still ate them. Andy had said to him, 'I'd take you to Antarctica with me, Hamish.' Zara had fleetingly wished she'd soaked her sandwiches.

These pictures, rather than those of the terrain were what had remained with her. She only recalled the long path of mud and stone stretching out ahead and always up. She had been quite a fit girl but had found herself wondering just how fit you had to be to stride out unflagging and without pause as Andy did, his black hair tied with a spotted scarf like a happy pirate.

The reason for the very early start was only made clear when they had made their first stop. Instead of returning the same way, Andy had told them, they could choose either to descend into Glen Easan Biorach and walk down to Lochranza where they were all to stay at the youth hostel, or go back via the Corrie path and catch the bus to Lochranza. The first option had an obstacle: the mountain Cir Mhor, which they would need to scale before reaching the glen. There were three other adults so no problems about dividing the party. Most of the girls chose the Corrie option but Zara had felt it was mostly because they fancied Duncan who was too attractive for anyone's good.

The sight of the horseshoe made up of Cir Mhor, A' Cir, Ben Tarsuinn and Ben Nuish released Zara from her reverie. Formidable. She thought again of Edwin Rose, his expectations. At what point she wondered did he have doubts, if at all? If the murder was not proven, then had it been an accident? As if in answer, a cloud appeared covering the Goat Fell summit and Zara, still thinking of the youth club trip, remembered a moment when, on the descent from the mountain, clouds had appeared from nowhere and Andy had shouted, 'Stay exactly where you are! It will pass'.

Zara had sat still watching the cloud move towards them all. Then there was a sudden breeze and Andy's spotted scarf went fluttering past and landed on a rock about three feet below her. She began to bend to retrieve it but then stopped remembering what Andy had said. She felt dizzier for having thought about leaning out. She could have been sitting on the edge of a twenty-foot drop. After the cloud had gone Andy came over to her. 'Well done', he had said. 'Always respect the weather. Now if I anchor your foot I think you could easily stretch down and get my scarf for me.' Zara smiled thinking about how she had enjoyed the praise. Then she saw an image of Edwin Rose — there had been a picture in Ronnie's book — had he had a moment like that, dizzy and suspended with an enveloping cloud separating him from the rest of the world?

Zara waited, still dreaming, in the crowd assembled to disembark. She noticed that the man in the red jacket was ahead of her, and thinking back, Zara wondered if Ronnie had been trying to avoid him: had there been something odd about his turning back to her? Then she was on the gangway taking her first breath of Arran air, and scanning the waiting crowd on the pier for Kirsty who loved meeting the boat even though the hotel was only five minutes away and Zara could easily have walked. She had just decided that Kirsty had not made it when she was seized in a great bear hug.

'Are you blind? I've been waving at you ever since you set foot on the gangway. Great to see you. Come on. My car's over there.' They dodged through the traffic now streaming off the boat and Zara threw her rucksack into the back of Kirsty's four-by-four.

'Don't ask,' said her friend. 'I hate driving a gas-guzzler but it is really convenient when we have to get guests from the boat with their luggage.' Zara laughed and settled back into the old relationship: it was good to be with someone who could read her mind.

'How's George?' she asked.

'He's good. Day to day, he's fine. Just not very strong. Doesn't have the energy he used to have. It's not fair at his age. He hates not being able to do things.' There was a silence as Zara digested this. She'd known of course but it was different hearing it face to face. 'He's taken up riding. You'll see Riga in a moment.'

They had turned off the Shore road and were driving along a higher parallel. Kirsty turned left and soon stopped. The hotel was on the left, a red sandstone building with an art deco porch and a roof with Chinese proportions. A whinnying sound took Zara's attention away from the house to the field opposite. A black horse with a white star was looking straight at them.

'That's Riga,' said Kirsty. 'Isn't she beautiful?' Zara was about to go and say hallo when George appeared. Zara hadn't seen him for months as he didn't like leaving the island now. At first she didn't think he looked ill but she soon realised that it was the pleasure of seeing her that was fuelling him and that underneath there was a chronic lassitude. She saw at once how challenging the garden would be for him.

Zara's room was in the roof.

'Used to be one of the maids' rooms,' Kirsty told her. It was small but the skylight gave a view across the bay towards the mountains.

'I bet the maid didn't have a double bed though,' said Zara, grateful for the luxury but regretting the lack of floor space.

Zara had managed to pack two changes of clothing in her large rucksack and these she quickly put away in the chest of drawers under the skylight. Beside the bed there was only a small table with a reading lamp. An easy chair was strategically placed next to the heater. There were bookshelves attached to one wall. The books were old: the ones Kirsty knew she would never read again but was unwilling to be parted from, thought Zara. She was reminded of the book belonging to Ronnie. She wondered if Kirsty and George had a copy.

Before going down to eat, Zara took a last look out of the window. Goat Fell loomed up mysterious, though its cap of cloud had gone. Or am I making it mysterious she wondered.

The hotel had guests, but none of them had wanted an evening meal that night, so Kirsty was quite relaxed, chattering non-stop about the season and un-tackled repairs. Zara watched George's face become sad as Kirsty listed jobs for which they would have to pay tradesmen whereas before…

To change the subject Zara told her friends about Ronnie and the book.

'We used to have a copy,' said George at once but it's probably in one of the attics in a box. I'll try and look it out for you.' Zara realised as she thanked him that even this might prove too onerous a task. She turned back to Kirsty:

'You must tell me exactly what my jobs are to be. I really want to be useful to you. George can give me orders for the garden but you'll have to be specific about the house. I don't mind what I do — cleaning, shopping, sous chef.'

Kirsty found a piece of paper and talked through her requirements as she wrote. She was particularly happy to be able to put Zara on the car insurance, because it meant she could pick people up from the boat, leaving Kirsty free to cook dinner. George could have driven but he couldn't lift luggage without getting tired. Zara herself felt exhausted, but she knew it was just the sea air.

'I don't think he did it,' said George as Zara stood up to go to her bed.

'Who didn't do what?'

'Laurie, John Watson. 'Didn't murder Edwin Rose.' Zara went up to her attic with that thought in her head. Holiday reading, she thought. More like a hair of the dog.

Chapter II   At sea

Zara was up early next morning. Two guests wanted breakfast at seven o'clock as they were catching the ferry at eight-twenty. Zara served them with the usual fried egg, sausage and bacon and listened to them sing the praises of Kirsty and George:

'We always came this time of year and we were nervous when the hotel was bought over but the previous owners assured us it would be all right and it's been wonderful, hasn't it Bernard?' Bernard nodded: he was completely deaf.

Zara ran them to the boat and picked up some messages on the way back. When she returned Kirsty was waiting in the hall.

'Problem, Zara. I think you might be able to solve it for us. One of our guests has a spare ticket for the *Waverley* for this afternoon. He was going to take his mother who lives in the care home but she's not well enough. You wouldn't need to pay for the ticket. He just doesn't want to see it wasted.'

It was a beautiful day and Zara could not think of a better way of spending it. Kirsty assured her she would manage. Zara, anyway, would be back in time to help with the evening guests.

'What's his name then and how old is he? You're not sending me off to spend the afternoon with some old codger I can't relate to are you?'

'He seems very nice,' said Kirsty. 'Maybe a bit older than you. Barney's build. Quite fit-looking. Name's John Smith.'

'Really?' said Zara. 'I can usually tell a lot from a name but John Smith! Is he here now? Can I meet him?'

'He's gone out. He said he didn't know if he would be back before getting the *Waverley* but I'm to phone his mobile to tell him if I found anyone. He'll meet you at the pier. He said he would just give you the ticket. He's not expecting you to be his companion or anything.'

'Sounds good,' said Zara, envisaging an afternoon at the rail watching gannets dive, uninterrupted by human conversation.

***

During the morning Zara changed the beds of the guests who had just left, and cleaned their rooms. Before leaving for the pier she had a bowl of soup in the kitchen with Kirsty. John Smith had been phoned and he'd told Kirsty he would be standing beside the red-painted mine, on the south side of the pier office. Zara smiled. An odd choice but it appealed to her sense of the practical.

The sunny day was holding up as she set out. The sea was a dark but definite blue, with small white waves which slid lazily towards the shore on the incoming tide. She watched as seagulls flew through the path made by the sun's rays, their bodies shining so white against the sky.

The *Waverley* had already docked and was disgorging passengers who would promenade along the front and seek postcards, coffee, tea and cake until it was time to regain the ship in two or three hours. Zara would be on that ship sailing south down the Clyde as far as the island of Pladda and then back. She dimly remembered a trip taken when she was six. She had been fascinated by the engine room, the beautiful pistons whose steady movements turned the paddles that kept the ship ploughing through the waves. She hoped the engine room was still accessible and not closed off because of some boring health and safety regulation.

As she rounded the corner of the Cal Mac building, she saw a figure dressed in white trousers and a t-shirt, complemented by a red baseball cap, and a red striped jacket. It had to be John Smith. She realised also in the same instant that this was the man who had been ahead of her getting off the boat the previous day. She noticed he looked at her twice but perhaps he did that with all females under forty. She walked up to him confidently.

'I'm Zara. I believe you are the man who is so kindly —'

He held out his hand: 'John Smith,' he said smiling. He had very even teeth except, Zara noticed, his canines had not grown to maturity. This factor enhanced his smile. 'Look,' he said, 'I don't want to impose on you in any way so here's your ticket and don't feel obliged to pay' — Zara had opened her purse — 'or even chat to me on the boat. I'm just pleased someone is getting the benefit'. Zara thanked him profusely and felt that politeness demanded that she asked after his mother. There was the minutest of pauses:

'Oh, she's okay but she's been ill and she gets disoriented easily. Early stages of dementia probably. She's better where she's familiar with her surroundings, though she always did love a trip on the *Waverley*. She likes the sentimentality, you know, — "the last ocean-going paddle steamer in the world"— she has a postcard of it in her room.' Zara nodded and the man took this as an invitation to go on. 'I live in Glasgow and I don't get much holiday. It's difficult for me to visit. Mother moved back to the island when my father died. She'd inherited a small cottage from an aunt. She was born here though.' Zara nodded again wondering how much longer he was going to go on. 'Unfortunately the location was too remote' — he *was* going on! — 'and she found it too lonely and it was difficult accessing the shops. Then she had a fall and although she recovered well, she decided that she would be better in a home. So she sold up.' A pause.

'What a sad story!' said Zara.

'Yes. Well, there's lots of things in life that are outwith our control.'

Zara sensed that this was the moment to leave, otherwise, in spite of what John Smith had said, she would end up being in his company all afternoon. She backed slowly, waving her ticket as an extra thank you and followed the crowd boarding the boat. She stood at the rail looking back at the shore and thought it weird to be heading away so soon after reaching the island. She watched idly as people streamed on; there was a happy atmosphere and she felt part of it.

When the boat pulled away and the paddles started churning the water in earnest, Zara realised she had not seen John Smith board and she felt a tiny pang of disappointment. Not that she wanted his company, but she had a curiosity about him which had not yet been satisfied. She circled the boat and stood for several minutes at both bow and stern before seeking the engine room. She had forgotten how noisy it was, but she still felt the magic of the sleek metal cylinders working so steadily, so accurately in their housings. She stood looking down, mesmerized.

'Amazing isn't it?' It was him. She raised her head in the direction of the voice.

'I was wondering if you were on the boat. I didn't see you board,' said Zara, realizing too late she must sound as if she had actually been looking for him.

'Easy to hide in a crowd,' he answered smiling. This was so patently untrue in relation to the white and red figure that stood before her that she assumed he must be making a joke.

'Oh sure,' she said, 'I always wear bright colours when I'm trying to conceal myself. She saw him hesitate before recognizing her sarcasm and smiling again.

'I interrupted your engine meditation,' he said. 'I'll leave you to it'. And he was gone. He was quite mercurial the way he was there one moment and gone the next. Zara had a fleeting feeling of something having slipped from her grasp. She studied the pistons again but could not regain her contemplative mood. She wanted suddenly to breathe fresh air.

She went back upstairs and onto the deck at the offshore side. She took deep breaths as the water frothed over and over in a white wake, the gulls following, gliding upwards in the thermals and then diving on abandoned crust and crumb. Zara walked along to the stern and watched the cliffs, dark and sunless at this time of day and she felt glad to be in the warmth and the light.

'Ice cream?' Here he was again holding out a cornet for her.

'Thank you!' Zara loved ice cream. She would probably have accepted one from her worst enemy. 'How did you know I liked vanilla?'

'They only had vanilla.'

It was now impossible not to stand together licking the cool sweetness in the heat.

'It's not often you feel too hot in the west of Scotland,' said Zara.

'And on a boat with a breeze and all,' he offered. The ensuing silence was not uncomfortable but John Smith broke it: 'Can I ask you, since we're talking, what you are doing on the island?' Zara explained briefly and the man listened. 'You are a good friend then. I like to hear of that. Are you staying all summer?'

'I may,' said Zara and suddenly she was not sure she wanted to tell this man everything. 'But I may not.' He nodded.

'Depends how things turn out,' he said. It was something between a statement and a question.

'Yes,' said Zara. 'It depends.' There was a pause then while Zara weighed up what she might lose or gain by asking a question. 'And you?' she asked, taking the opportunity to look him fully in the face.

'Me? I'll be leaving soon.'

'Mum happy about that?'

'Mum? Oh Mum, yes, well, she doesn't remember what happened yesterday anyway.'

'I'm sorry.' Zara thought she'd heard a sadness in his voice.

'But I would like to climb Goat Fell before I go.'

'I want to do that.' Zara said the words before she thought.

'Well, are you a climber? Do you love dangerous places?' Zara found these questions strange and was about to say so when a cry went up from a passenger standing ten feet from them:

'Look! Look!'

The rush towards where the man was pointing was immediate. Zara wondered if the boat minded having so much weight on one side, but then she was carried away by the sight. Six dolphins undulated through the water, each following the other, leaping and diving in a spell-binding symmetry. Like creatures from another world, thought Zara.

'The world beneath the sea is revealed,' said John Smith as if reading her mind and Zara suddenly felt as if everything was in harmony. There was an excited buzz resonating through the crowd. People with binoculars gazed at the very last sight of the vision. There was a sense of incredulity in the air. 'I feel really blessed,' Zara heard one woman say to another: 'It were worth the eighteen quid just for that'.

John Smith had turned back to her:

'So will you come?'

'Come where?'

'Up the mountain. We could go tomorrow. After you've done your chores. Back in time to serve dinner if needed'. Zara said 'Yes'. It was the dolphins. She was in a mood to agree with anything. She was still scanning the horizon for a last glimpse. She did not want to believe they had gone.

After, the sun went in and Zara went with John Smith to have tea in the café. Her companion seemed elated. He talked about the mountains; about the adrenalin rush he felt from perching in high places; how he liked to poise himself till he sensed his balance to the last millimetre, so he had to think himself into the idea of leaning inwards, although the sheer rock to one side of him was vertical and the rock on the other side non-existent.

'Do you belong to a mountaineering club?' Zara asked They were back on deck and the subject had not changed.

'No, I like to climb alone.'

'But —'

'I know what you're going to say, that it's dangerous. I love the danger. It's a love that keeps me alive.' While Zara privately thought this sort of talk was unhinged, she was intrigued. People's personal passions fascinated her. Even so, she replied calmly:

'Well don't be leading me into any dangerous places. I don't want to end up like Edwin Rose.' John Smith laughed:

'No chance of that: I'm no John Laurie.'

'You know the story then?' asked Zara .

'No not really. Two men went up a mountain. One came down. That about sums it up, doesn't it? Look there's a gannet about to dive.' They watched the bird hover, then plummet head first into the water making its own small splash and they waited for it to surface, a small fish in its mouth.

'I wouldn't mind being a gannet, if I had to be a bird,' said Zara.

'Get preyed on by gulls.' Zara shrugged. Gulls, men what was the difference she thought but didn't say.

***

For some reason best known to the captain, the boat turned round before Pladda, the original destination, and headed back to Brodick. John Smith asked Zara about her work, her upbringing, where she'd been and what she'd done and she answered him honestly but without reference to things that really mattered to her. She did not mention Barney and Ben. For his part John Smith regaled her with stories from his youth. He appeared to have worked in many different spheres and places. He had been a tram driver in Budapest, learning Hungarian in six months; he had been a motor mechanic's assistant in Australia, a safari guide in Kenya and any number of things in the UK.

'Have you ever been married?' asked Zara suddenly, realizing as soon as she the words were out of her mouth that it was an unguarded question — she didn't want him to ask her that.

'No, not the marrying kind, but I once tried to write a book. That's us now. We're docking.' They watched as one of the crew failed to catch the rope thrown from the shore. Zara wondered how it felt to miss in your one moment when the crowd is focused only on you. John Smith accompanied her down the gangway and then stopped.

'I'm just going to the tourist information office.' He muttered something about a map. 'I'll see you later about tomorrow.' Abruptly he was gone. Zara was left feeling a wrong-footed by his departure. She hadn't been able to say a proper thank you.

***

Because the trip had gone well, Zara felt excited about the next day. She had cleaned her walking boots and packed light waterproofs in her rucksack. She had a flask and even a packet of plasters. She felt equipped.

However, she did have a feeling of guilt to be going off again the very next day.

'I won't go if you need me,' she said to Kirsty, having told her friend about the projected trip even before commenting on the *Waverley* afternoon.

'It's okay, Zara. No worries. No dinners tomorrow anyway. Our guests are all at a wedding. Think of it as data collecting: you'll be primed to tell our guests about the easiest route and what to take et cetera. You might even have a story about seeing a stag at ten feet or...' Kirsty spread her arms wide to indicate anything was possible.

'I haven't found that book yet,' said George when they had settled down in the snug behind the kitchen after all the guests had been seen to. 'I did look, but I keep getting waylaid by other books. There's an awful lot of stuff up there. I can't think why we brought it all.' Kirsty looked meaningfully at George and then at Zara.

'You wouldn't part with anything, love, remember? You said you'd already lost part of yourself and you didn't want to lose any more.'

'Ye', ye', okay. I did say that. I wish I could find that book though. It's irritating. I thought I could go straight to it.'

'Do you want to talk about the garden?' asked Zara seeing George begin to look distressed. They drew a plan of the area and then went out and discussed what was needed in the way of pruning and chopping and then what George wanted new. Zara soon realised that the plan was going to be no-plan. George felt he wanted a cherry tree *here,* but he would need to see it in place before he could decide what flowers might be near it and whether they would be random clumps or in a bed. They did decide that a reasonable-sized rectangle by the back wall of the garden could be assigned to vegetables. George had a catalogue and started becoming enthusiastic with the thought that there was still time to plant peas and beans, not to mention lettuce, carrots and courgettes. It would be Zara's task to dig the plot over.

Chapter III   Choppy waters

Zara was just thinking about the fact that John Smith had not communicated with her about their proposed trip when there was a ring on the bell. Kirsty went to see what was wanted.

'A word with Zara,' she said on returning. 'John Smith.'

'I've ordered a packed lunch for two. We won't be able to leave till eleven when you'll have finished your chores. Have you a flask? Something hot and a bottle of water too, although there is plenty of water in the burns. You have boots?' Zara had only been able to nod assent at intervals as this stream of orders and information hit her.

'You seem to have it all organised,' she said when he at last drew breath. She noticed he was no longer wearing his white t-shirt but a green one. However, it still matched his trousers. She wondered if he would have yet another outfit on next day. Zara said goodnight and went back to the kitchen.

'So that's another chore for you tomorrow, Zara. Packed lunch for two. You'll be able to choose your own fillings and decide between a Kitkat and a caramel shortcake. You can make yourself a wee bowl of salad if you like.'

'You're all right thanks,' said Zara. Much as she liked salad she couldn't see herself eating it on a mountain. 'I'll take a couple of tomatoes,' she said noticing Kirsty's face.

***

The next day Zara was up at six-thirty. There were seven guests for breakfast including John Smith and three were catching the eight-twenty boat. Zara set the tables in the dining room, changed the flowers in the hall and the sign that said 'No vacancies' to 'Vacancies'. She took a brush to the front step and shook the door mats. Kirsty was in the kitchen grilling bacon. After breakfast Zara would be running a couple of guests to the boat and then be coming back to hoover and dust the dining room and hall. Kirsty had a rota of which rooms were cleaned when and although it seemed super-pernickety, Zara could see that the just-polished look of the

North Crag hotel contributed greatly to the welcoming feeling she experienced every time she came through its front door.

John Smith did not talk much when she served him his breakfast. He was reading a mountaineering magazine. The only thing he said that had a bearing on their projected trip was that he would be going to visit his mother briefly beforehand, to take her a new postcard of the *Waverley*.

'I'll probably go in afterwards as well,' he added. 'She likes hearing a story and something worth telling is bound to happen.'

Zara was finished by ten-thirty having hoovered a couple of rooms and changed the bedding. New guests were coming that evening. In her own room she gathered up her boots — to put on on the doorstep — there was no notice saying 'No boots beyond this point' but the whole tenor of the hotel announced it. Zara was wearing knee-length trousers and long socks. She had a fleece over her t-shirt and her waterproofs were neatly rolled inside her rucksack.

She went downstairs. John Smith was already there, sitting on the sofa at reception reading his magazine.

'I'll just get the packed lunches,' she said.

'Great', he answered hardly taking his eye from the page. Zara fleetingly registered something odd about this but she was in action/holiday mode so she let the thought go.

When she returned, he was standing by the door. She handed him his package and began to put hers in her rucksack. Consequently, it was John Smith, not Zara, who took in the figure coming up the steps, a man whose face was all smiles as he lighted on Zara, who said,

'Zara! Surprise!'

Zara looked up to see Barney and behind him his dog, Nessie. Before she could stop herself, her face fell.

'What on earth are you doing here?' she said in disbelief. 'Shouldn't you be working?'

'Had some time off in lieu. Lovely day and all that and...'

'Well you should have phoned.' Zara's sharpness came as much from embarrassment as anything else. 'What about Ben? Who's getting him from school?'

'His Gran. It's her birthday. They're going to the pictures and he's staying over at hers.' A long pause. 'I was going to suggest,' said Barney with the look of a man who knows he is wading in deeper, 'that we spent the day together'.

'But I've arranged to go up Goat Fell with —'

'John Smith,' said John Smith stepping forward and holding out his hand. Barney took it but with no semblance of pleasure. The other man smiled. 'This looks like a situation I should bow out of. I had no idea I was stepping on... or not even that... could be seen to be...'

'You're not,' Zara snapped. 'Give me two seconds,' and she propelled Barney through the front door and onto the grass out of John Smith's earshot. 'Barney! I came down to Arran to have time on my own. I just don't understand.' Barney looked contrite.

'I'm sorry. The idea occurred to me yesterday evening. I'd taken the day off anyway but suddenly — I think it was when I heard the weather forecast — I thought it would be a great idea to come.' Zara didn't help him. 'I didn't think you would be that displeased to see me.' Silence. 'Who is that guy anyway? I don't like the look of him.'

Barney had probably said the worst possible thing he could have thought of.

'Go Barney. Just go. What right have you to question me about whom I see? Just go!' Barney turned and left and Nessie who had been jumping up and down doing an I'm-pleased-to-see-you routine with Zara who, even though she was angry couldn't help absently patting her, Nessie followed Barney without looking back.

Zara went straight back into the hall where John Smith had been standing.

'Right,' she said as she entered. 'You ready?' But John Smith was no longer there. A quick word with Kirsty informed her that he had left by the back door and headed over the fence into a field. His body language spelled 'escape', Kirsty had been sure of that.

Zara hesitated for perhaps ten seconds then she threw off her rucksack and ran, down the lane and round the corner. No sign of Barney. Had he run too? Had he thought he might catch the 11.05 boat? She thought he would be hard pressed. She had to slow down, she had a stitch but she had to run till she could see the gangway. She hit the shore road. No Barney in sight but the boat was ready, the gangway lowering away from it. Where was Barney? On the boat or off it? Maybe he hadn't intended to catch it. Maybe he was even now sitting in a café enjoying a latte and a dough-nut before setting off on a walk on the shore or... She reached the pier.

Walking slowly along by the bus stance eyes on the ground, the noise of an engine made her look up and she caught sight of Barney staring hard at her from the north-end bus. It was difficult to read his expression. Zara sprang at the door as the bus began to back, and beat a fist against it. The driver stopped. The door slid back and the driver looked at her with a professional patience:

'Where to then?' Zara then realised she had left her purse in her rucksack at the hotel:

'Barney,' she said, 'where are we going?' He understood her predicament at once and threw her his wallet.

'Lochranza,' he said.

***

All the long way through Corrie and Sannox, Barney did not say a word. Zara spent the first mile recovering her breath. When she had exclaimed, 'Oh look, a seal' as they passed along the Merkland shore and Barney had not responded, she began to wonder if she had made a mistake joining him. She glanced at his face surreptitiously but it remained impassive. Her heart dropped.

'I'm sorry Barney. Really. I'm very sorry.' Barney's face did not alter and she saw his right fist was balled up and completely white.

'Not now, Zara,' he said. 'Wait till we get off the bus.' The bus was now climbing up the Boguille and Zara looked left to the mountains; the Witches' Step, a black silhouette against the blue sky, seemed to remonstrate with her. She wondered suddenly if Edwin Rose and John Laurie had quarrelled, as some thought, and whether either of them had felt as she did now as if she were on one side of the Witches' Step and Barney was on the other.

They left the bus at Lochranza castle and walked silently over the green grass to stand looking up at the walls.

'I'm sorry Barney,' Zara said for a second time. Barney looked at the water and at a solitary sailboat speeding across the expanse before them.

'Okay Zara.' He held out his arms and she stood within them feeling at once safe.

'That man, that John Smith, he means nothing to me.'

'Don't spoil things by protesting. I don't want to know anything about him.' Zara nodded. 'I shouldn't have come. You are absolutely right. Or I should at least have phoned.'

'No,' said Zara, 'because I would definitely have put you off and then we wouldn't have been here now'.

They set off back along the way they had come on the bus and took the narrow road which led to a junction; they could choose to go round the Cock of Arran or up over the hill to the right and thence down to the shore to follow the path back to Sannox. The latter was one of Barney's favourite walks and he wanted very much to show it to Zara.

'I don't mind,' said Zara. 'It's your day.'

For miles they let the wind talk as it blew over the rough grass and they uttered only what seemed necessary regarding an uncommon flower or a bird's song. They stopped while they still had height and ate some of Barney's rolls and chocolate. The sea seemed far away in the distance.

'So different today from yesterday,' said Zara, 'or is it just that the colours are affected by the direction of the light? This is north-east we're looking isn't it?' Barney nodded. 'Yesterday Brodick Bay was an entirely different blue.'

'And I was imagining you hard at it with a mop and bucket, 'Barney smiled across at her, 'but you were what, strolling along the front with an ice cream?'

'You're right about the ice cream,' Zara answered at once, without thinking. 'I had one on — she made the minutest hesitation — on the *Waverley...*'

'Ah, the *Waverley*,' Barney's voice seemed to Zara to come from very far away. 'I don't know why but somehow when you say the word *Waverley*, the name "John Smith" jumps into my mind.'

'It's not what you think,' said Zara.'

'And what do I think?' asked Barney, looking at Zara as she looked out to sea.

Zara's first instinct was to be angry but the feeling seemed to rise and die with the breeze. She put her hand to the grass and let the coolness blow over it.

'If I tell you exactly what happened, will you believe me?'

'Okay,' said Barney, still looking at her, watching her face.

She proceeded to give him a detailed account of how the *Waverley* trip had come about and what John Smith had said and what she had said, and the dolphins. She found the dolphins tricky because they were the reason she had said 'Yes' to Goat Fell and it was hard to explain the mood, the exultant mood which had encompassed everyone on deck and made her decision possible.

'Fine,' said Barney when she had finished, 'but why were you so angry when I turned up? I can see the part to do with me coming when I had said I wouldn't but it wasn't just that, was it?' Zara was silent. She couldn't explain to Barney that she'd felt he was assuming a commitment to their relationship which the encounter had brought sharply into focus. She had felt trapped. So she'd beat her wings: it was as simple as that. She didn't feel at all attracted to John Smith but supposing she had? Barney's behaviour would have seemed entirely inappropriate.

'Do you know,' said Barney, 'the thing which makes me believe you?' Zara shook her head. 'The way you always refer to him as 'John Smith'.' Zara laughed. Barney pushed her unresisting body down onto his waterproof jacket and suddenly they were together.

***

The day mellowed for Zara and Barney from then on and by late afternoon they had walked back as far as the Sannox burn. Zara had been quiet. The shape of Cioghe na h-Oighe seemed to tower above her and reminded her of the Goat Fell murder.

'Barney, do you know anything about Edwin Rose, the story?'

'Not much,' Barney answered 'but as it happens I do know that he's buried in a little graveyard just down the path to Glen Sannox. We could visit it if you're interested.'

He turned to her expecting her to say no but her face had lit up.

'You're not joking?' she said.

Barney crossed the road from the shore side and took the path beside a rose-covered cottage. Not far down, they came upon the small graveyard in which Edwin Rose's bones now rested. Zara stood and looked at the grave in silence. Barney was mystified:

'Why this sudden interest in the murder?' Zara explained about the guy on the *Caledonian Isles* reading *Murder not Proven*.

'It's intriguing,' she said, 'the whole story. It sounds as if it might have been a miscarriage of justice'. A robin sang from a nearby tree. 'See', said Zara, 'the robin agrees with me'.

'That's the other thing I remember,' said Barney. 'Laurie has the record for being Scotland's longest serving prisoner. He did forty-one years. Most of it in a mental wing I might add.'

'My God!' said Zara. 'How bad is that?'

'Even then,' said Barney, 'in 1889, he might not have been found guilty if the trial had gone on longer. It only lasted two days. It's thought that someone had the judge's ear, someone in whose interest it was to control the amount of information that came out.' Barney had Zara's full attention. 'It seems that the doctor who was expert witness for the prosecution, also Lord Provost of Linlithgow — a man of big status —by a strange coincidence had entertained Rose and Laurie in his house for tea the day before the murder. His son was friends with two guys Rose had got to know. The doctor had not declared this salient fact before or during the trial. Apparently there were rumours that Rose had come on to Laurie. They did share accommodation in Brodick. The doctor would not have wanted his good name besmirched by such a story.'

'Dark,' said Zara gazing down the glen at the mountains rising on either side. 'What a waste of two lives.'

And with that, her mood seemed to change. She put the murder out of her mind and became focused on getting back to Brodick. She had to be on hand in case of unexpected guests she told Barney, so she would not be able to eat with him. She did not want him to come back to North Crag and risk him bumping into John Smith again. She realised Barney did not know he was staying there and she didn't want him to know.

Back on the road they started thumbing lifts. Almost at once a car that had shot past them shuddered to a halt.

'What do you think?' said Barney. 'Will it make it to Brodick?' They hurried forward. The driver held the front passenger door open for Zara.

'Hi Zara. It's Ronnie, remember me. Not my car but would you like a lift?' Barney climbed into the back with Nessie.

'Barney,' said Zara, 'this is Ronnie, the guy I met on the ferry.'

'Pleased to meet you,' said Barney. Zara didn't think he sounded a bit pleased but Ronnie didn't seem to have noticed anything untoward. He chattered away. He had been helping someone cut down an unsafe tree. Zara remembered he'd said he was staying in Corrie, the next village.

'I'll be round to the North Crag for that coffee!' he shouted after Zara as he dropped them in

Brodick.

'I'll look forward to it,' Zara shouted back.

'I'm starving,' said Barney.

'So am I,' said Zara. 'I'll ring Kirsty and see if she needs help.' Barney nodded in the direction of Ronnie's car.

'An improvement on John Smith anyway.' Barney had meant the remark as a slightly bitter joke but Zara took him seriously.

'Don't start, Barney. You'll be giving me reasons not —'

'to marry you? Hm.'

'You've never seemed the jealous type before.'

'Maybe I've never had cause before.'

'What about DI Des? You never seemed jealous of him and he's an old flame.'

'Should I have been?'

'Barney please! Don't spoil things just when we're on an even keel. Why don't you go down to the pier and get something to eat at the restaurant?'

'You not joining me?' Zara phoned Kirsty turning away from Barney as she did so.

'She sounds a bit flustered. I think I'd better check in. I'll join you for a coffee if I'm not really needed. I'll phone you anyway,' she added as Barney looked likely to object. 'And Barney, you can put Ben on the boat any time but please don't come yourself until I give you leave.' She looked fully into his eyes and he searched hers for signs of genuine feeling.

'Okay,' he said at last. 'It was a lovely day we had though, wasn't it?'

'A wonderful day, Barney.'

She watched him make his way along the front, strolling, waiting for Nessie but never once looking back towards Zara. She felt sad. She did not want to upset him but she was adamant she was going to have her time alone and the more she thought about the day the more she felt she hadn't really made up her mind about him.

Reaching the hotel, Zara made for the kitchen to find there were no bookings for dinner at all.

'But I thought there must be a whole party in, you sounded so un-calm,' said Zara.

'John Smith,' said George who was sitting on a stool stirring a pot on the stove. 'In a nutshell, John Smith appeared about half an hour after you left and offered to dig the vegetable patch we planned. No word of climbing or not climbing Goat Fell.' Zara looked from one friend to the other:

'So, what did you say?'

'George was about to say "Yes" but I said "No."' replied Kirsty.

'Why?' asked Zara.

'I don't know. I just did. The idea seemed a bit left field but it could just have been a generous offer ...'

'I felt a complete fool,' said George.

Chapter IV   Rocking the boat

Over the next days, Zara contrived not to think about Barney at all although she did text him after she received a thank-you postcard from him. She threw herself into life at the hotel. The weather continued fine, so she made a start on the garden, beginning by cutting the grass. There was a patio outside the French windows which opened from the dining room and she encouraged George to come out and hoe between the paving stones. Although he sat down every ten minutes or so, by lunch time he had made a visible impression and was, of his own volition clearing various tubs of weeds and talking about what to put in them. They went for a trip to the garden centre and returning, together filled the tubs with petunias, lobelia and alyssum. Later George was pleased to hear a couple of the guests commenting on how beautiful they looked.

Zara had not seen John Smith again. He had left the day after the Barney encounter and without taking breakfast. Kirsty had had a strong feeling that if she had not happened to come into the hall as he was passing through, he would have left without paying.

'I don't quite know why I'm saying that,' she said to Zara.

'Maybe you think he resented you not taking up his offer to dig the garden,' said Zara.

'He was very polite.'

'Good con-men always are,' said Zara. 'He bought me an ice cream on the *Waverley*. Without asking me if I wanted one. He was a bit odd. Not that it wasn't a generous gesture. On top of the ticket as well.' We rubbish the man and then feel guilty thought Zara. What's that about I wonder, but she didn't wonder long: there were other things to occupy her mind.

For one, Ronnie came by to claim his coffee, bringing with him his copy of *'Murder not proven'*. He said Zara was welcome to borrow it, but that he would like it back after she'd read it.

They took their mugs out onto the patio and sat with George among the flowers.

'I was all set to go up Goat Fell the other day but… the plan fell through.' Zara wondered why she was always starting sentences which she then found difficult to finish.

'Rained off?'

'No.' Zara couldn't think of a way of explaining so she asked a question:

'Have you been up? Since you've been here I mean?'

'No. I hope to, soon. Would you like to come? Maybe later this week?' Zara saw George hide a smile. 'I can show you exactly where the murder happened.' Zara stopped hesitating. The investigator in her said,

'Yes, that would be great.'

'What about you George?' Ronnie, Zara noted saw no reason not to be inclusive.

'I'm afraid I'm not able to. Thanks for asking though. Someone has to stay at the hotel.' He looked at Zara and she saw he was teasing her to get himself out of having to tell the truth.

'Hey, I was up at six this morning. You weren't even awake!'

'Zara's amazing,' said George seizing the opportunity to change the subject. 'Works like a Trojan. Transforms things in an instant.' He opened his arms to embrace the patio. 'You should have seen this two days ago.'

'You did a lot too George. Don't put yourself down.'

'You were the driver though, Zara.' George saw Ronnie look at Zara even more speculatively than before.

***

'So what's with this Ronnie guy,' Kirsty was asking, and it was obvious to Zara that George had reported the scene on the patio in detail. Zara intuited a heavy subtext: What are you thinking of going up the mountains *with this guy Ronnie* when you have a wonderful man called Barney who is dying to marry you? Even though Kirsty was an old friend, Zara made a point of avoiding the subtext.

'I told you. I met him on the boat when I came over. He had the book about the murder. I invited him to drop by for a coffee and that's what he's done.' She tried to face Kirsty with a completely impassive expression.

'And the mountain?' said Kirsty as if Zara hadn't spoken

'It's a molehill,' said Zara holding her hair down in front of her nose in a characteristic gesture.

'I hope you know what you're doing.' Kirsty looked resigned.

'When have I ever?' said Zara getting up from the kitchen table to sling some pieces of carrot into the soup pot. 'Thanks for asking though.' Zara's mother had always quipped that Zara's middle name was 'incorrigible' but exasperating though this often was, nobody loved Zara any the less for it.

***

Zara had arranged to meet the man in question at Cladach at twelve noon on the following Saturday as Ronnie had found work which kept him busy during the week. Zara had cleared it with Kirsty and had risen early to make sure she did as much as possible in the hotel before she left.

'I do appreciate all you're doing,' said Kirsty when they sat down for what had become a regular coffee break. 'You've no idea how much less stressful it seems since you've been here. I'm not continually looking at chores needing to be done. I'm looking and they've been done! It's wonderful and George loves you being here. I even think he's been eating better since...' George entered at that moment.

'Don't leave your lunch behind this time, Zara,' he said, squeezing her shoulder as he sat down beside her. Zara's lost lunch had become a standing joke. 'Or perhaps you're taking the one you left. I expect it would still be edible.'

'I thought I saw you eating it George,' said Zara. George shook his head.

'Maybe Riga ate it. I wondered why there were hoof marks in the hall.' It was good to hear George making jokes. 'So you're going to have a guided tour of the Goat Fell murder scene,' he went on. 'Marvellous. Everyone's idea of a good day out. And cheaper than the Chamber of Horrors.'

'Maybe this Ronnie guy is planning a visitor centre up there,' said Kirsty.

'That's really macabre,' said Zara. 'You're only saying that because you've taken against him for some reason.'

''I haven't taken against him. I was just making a joke. I'd rather you went with him than with that John Smith.'

Zara made up her rolls in silence and nothing Kirsty or George could say would bring her back into the conversation.

'Have a lovely time,' they shouted after her.

'I'll try,' Zara muttered as she closed the kitchen door.

Once outside in the fresh air though, Zara looked only forward. She'd even waxed her boots. Her rucksack felt light enough on her back and contained the necessary and no more. It would be exhilarating to climb upwards away from people and into the wild spaces where sanity still reigned. Or so she hoped.

If Zara thought about Ronnie, it was as of a friendly stranger still: she had no fixed idea of him. Like the mountain itself, he was an unknown quantity and she was happy to let things take their course. Yes, he was an attractive man but she had not as yet consciously compared him to Barney.

The first thing Zara noticed when she reached Ronnie who was standing waiting on the side of the rough Cladach road, was his huge rucksack.

'You going for a week or have you got a body in there?' Ronnie smiled from under a straw hat.

'I do happen to have a small tent with me and various useful accessories. I was considering staying up there — unless the weather turns. You could come down yourself I daresay...' He stopped as Zara's eyebrows started to rise. 'You seem such an independent sort of person I thought... but if it worries you being alone, I'll bring you down and go back up.'

'That fit,' said Zara. 'I suppose I don't have to decide now.'

'Course not,' said Ronnie.

They walked on in silence, the odd start causing both of them to want a little time for digestion. Zara was reflecting that the one thing Ronnie hadn't suggested was that she might want to stay up there as well. But then she thought it would have seemed pushy and she might well have not been at all sure she wanted to say 'Yes'.

Zara was glad she had been out running the last couple of days. Ronnie had a long stride and his attempts to accommodate her shorter ones were intermittent. He would find himself ahead and then stop and look at the view until she caught up with him.

'I'm sorry,' she said when this had happened for the seventh time. 'It must be tedious for you trying to go at my pace.'

'It beats bringing someone down on a stretcher,' he said.

'I haven't read much of the book yet,' said Zara. 'I fell asleep over it in bed last night. Not that I wasn't enjoying it, if enjoy is the right word.'

They had stopped where the path led over a small bridge. There were flat boulders, dry above water.

'A good place for a wee break,' suggested Ronnie. Zara had thought he was going to go relentlessly to the summit:

'Great idea,' she said. 'I have some rather rewarding chocolate in my bag.'

'Good-oh!' said Ronnie, picking up on her Famous Five imitation. He produced a flask of coffee and they sat opposite each other on different rocks. Zara felt the water just on the off-chance it would not be as cold as she might have imagined. Then she bent over and tasted it as it trickled over a rock beside her.

'What flavour is it today?' said Ronnie.

'Sunshine with a hint of peat,' said Zara. 'Why, what is it usually?'

'Well, I've known it to be ginger and lemon and once, on a rare day in October it was pure strawberry.'

'And what kind of whisky were you drinking it with?' asked Zara.

'I wouldn't drink on the mountain… except perhaps weak beer,' he added as if he realized his answer sounded unlikely. Zara laughed out loud and then stopped when she saw he had been serious.

'Have some more chocolate,' she said to get over her embarrassment. She liked Ronnie, she felt, but he seemed to have a bumpy personality: things appeared to be relaxed and then suddenly she'd said the wrong thing.

There was a slight breeze which prevented Zara from feeling too hot and she felt quite pleased with her fitness level though she did wish she had longer legs. The shoulder and the steeper part of the mountain were on their left. If the sun were not shining thought Zara, the scene would be gloomy in spite of the heather. Lone rocks stood about randomly: Zara would have liked them to get into huddles and have a silent conversation.

'Would you leave your hat here, in the middle of a burn?'

'I'm not wearing a hat,' said Zara puzzled.

'You haven't got to that bit then? Rose's hat was found on a rock, anchored by a stone. It's one of the mysteries. One, why would you do that with your own hat? Two, why would anyone do it with someone else's hat? On a rock possibly, where it could be seen but not in the middle of the water where it might get washed away.'

'So there's a possibility that Rose somehow left it there himself…' Zara pondered this for a minute or two, then she reached Ronnie's hat from the bank where it sat on top of his rucksack, and placed it on a rock beside her. Then she anchored it with a round stone. 'Sorry. All in the interests of science.'

'That's my best hat. My only hat in fact.'

'I thought if we had the real thing in front of us we might get some ideas about how it could have happened.'

'One of us is Laurie and one of us is Rose you mean?'

'Yes,' said Zara. 'Which do you want to be?'

'I'm not particularly superstitious but neither of them really appeals to me.'

'So you wouldn't play 'Macbeth' if it were offered to you?

'That's hardly an analogy!'

'I don't know: in both cases there is murder and victim.'

'Maybe I'm just superstitious,' said Ronnie. 'More coffee?' Zara held out the plastic cup he'd given her earlier.

There were people heading up the path and they called out to Zara and Ronnie about the loveliness of the day and the last one said,

'Where's the next picnic spot?' and Ronnie replied,

'It's about half a mile...'

'...by the burger stall!' added Zara. Ronnie smiled and the words seemed to hang on the air long after the walkers had become dots.

'Did you come to Arran as a boy then? On holiday?'

'Often.'

'Which village did you stay in?'

'Lamlash, Corrie, Whiting Bay...'

'And what did you do? Did you have brothers and sisters to play with or did you make friends on the beach?'

'I can see why you became a journalist.'

'Except my questions don't seem to be eliciting any answers. Am I being too curious?'

'Sorry. No. I don't know. I just find it hard to give pat answers. I begin to feel as if I'm in one of those train encounters. You know... Going far? Student? On your own?'

'My questions weren't like that!'

'No they weren't.' Ronnie's fingers stroked across his chin and down as if he were smoothing a beard. 'Okay. It's just that I'm in a bad patch just now and I don't feel like talking about myself.'

'Someone die?' It was a shot in the dark but the effect was instant. Zara saw Ronnie's face change and then become expressionless.

'Yes... well someone tried.'

'I'm sorry,' said Zara wishing she could bite off her tongue. 'I didn't mean to upset you.' She noticed his fists were tight and he almost forgot to uncurl them to aid his balance as he stood up on his rock.

'It shouldn't have happened,' he said, 'but it did. Come on. Let's go. I'm okay. Let's talk about something else'. Zara hopped onto the bank and put the remainder of her chocolate away in a safe pocket in her rucksack. Ronnie put away his flask and then hoisted his pack on his back. He turned towards the path. 'Let's go,' he said again striding out as before.

'Haven't you forgotten something?' Zara couldn't resist the tease even though she knew Ronnie was under pressure. When he stopped and turned round she looked back. The hat was still anchored under its stone. 'That easy,' said Zara. 'Interesting.' All it took was for you to be focused on something else she thought but did not say. Was that what had happened to Rose and Laurie?

Ronnie stood still and Zara realized he was waiting for her to go back for the hat: you put it there, you fetch it were his unspoken words.

'Why do you need it anyway?' asked Zara. There was something about Ronnie that made her want to get under his armour.

'Sensitive skin,' he said taking the hat from her and ramming it onto his head. 'Can't be too careful.'

After that Zara chattered as she walked, uncaring as to whether Ronnie answered. It was a way of trying to keep up and she found she was getting a second wind. She told him about the youth club trip up Goat Fell. He asked her if she had been born in Glasgow. She told him about her childhood in Ayrshire and how she and her mother had moved to Glasgow, after her father had died in a train accident, falling onto the track from the embankment at the bottom of their garden.

'How terrible for you!' Ronnie said. She felt his empathy touch her.

By the time Zara and Ronnie reached the shoulder they were on much easier terms. Zara couldn't help comparing her present companion to her *Waverley* companion, John Smith. She had been quite sure she did not want to get to know John Smith as a friend although he had been perfectly amicable — and generous she added to herself remembering the ticket and the ice cream. Ronnie was completely different. She felt curious about both men but with John Smith it was an objective analysis where with Ronnie she could believe they might become friends, even though...

Here Barney's image reared up in the forefront of her mind and she felt momentarily guilty. But, argued another part of herself, maybe getting to know Ronnie will help me decide about Barney: he'll either come out much better or much worse. She didn't consider Ronnie in all this. What she did know was that he was attracted to her and oddly, the way she knew this was through the ironic and slightly abrupt way he spoke to her.

They had stopped to gaze back down the glen. They could see boats in Brodick Bay.

'Fishing boats,' said Zara idly.

'But no fish,' said Ronnie.

'What?' said Zara but then she heard voices and turned. 'My God,' she said. 'What a coincidence!'

Ronnie had stopped and was looking towards a couple that had materialized in front of them. She could not see his expression. The man was John Smith.

'Hi there,' Ronnie was saying. 'You decided you were up for it then? You came up from Corrie?' There was a slim brunette standing some way behind John Smith.

'Daffodil?' said Ronnie. 'It is you, isn't it? What are you doing here?'

'Yes, it's Daffodil. Call me Daffie,' she replied looking back at him steadily. Ronnie just nodded and turned to Zara who was wondering why the woman had not answered the question.

'Zara, meet Daffodil and John...'

'We already met,' said Zara colouring in spite of herself. She shook hands with Daffodil and nodded to John Smith who seemed completely unfazed by the reunion. Zara was focusing on whether Daffodil was his girlfriend or someone he'd picked up in the way she'd been picked up, although it wasn't till now, faced with another instance of such behaviour, that she wanted to call it that.

The two men were discussing the climb. Daffie stood looking down at her boots. Zara wondered if she felt double-crossed. John Smith had given the briefest of explanations of his previous acquaintance with Zara — we met on the *Waverley* — but Zara felt that if she herself was curious probably Daffie was too. She plunged straight in:

'Is John your boyfriend then?' Daffie looked as though it was a question she had not yet considered.

'We met in the pub,' she said. 'I was with my girlfriend Emma-Rose. She was going to come too but then she had a phone call her mum had gone to hospital so she went home. I stayed on because she said she'd come back and anyway another friend is coming at the weekend. Her cousin, Marra, that's short for Marradonna in case you were wondering, he's got a caravan in Lamlash we can stay in.' She stopped as if she felt she'd said too much.

'So John told you he was going up Goat Fell and you sounded enthusiastic and he invited you to join him?'

'Sort of,' Daffie said. She sounded disconnected from her voice. She was shy Zara concluded. Perhaps more John Smith's type.

They began to climb the last rocky stretch, the men ahead, the women following.

'John says there this cave where a body was found. He wants to sleep in it tonight.'

'You're joking?' said Zara pulling up short. She wondered if Ronnie and John had actually set all this up beforehand but why she thought, involve her and Daffie and theoretically, Emma Rose: if they wanted to experience a night on Goat Fell, they could just have gone themselves.

'Was Ronnie there last night then?' Zara asked

'Didn't see him,' said Daffie.

'Has John got a tent?'

'No, just a sleeping bag. He says he'll make a heather bed and we can put the sleeping bag over us in this cave where the body was found.'

'You quite happy with that?' Zara felt like Daffie's mother.

'I suppose. Do you think it might be cold then?' Zara looked harder at Daffie. Maybe she was younger than she appeared. Did she really have no other qualms about staying the night in a corrie which had held a gruesome corpse — murdered or not — with a man she hardly appeared to know, except as to whether she was going to be warm enough? Zara made up her mind on the spot: she was staying on the mountain too. John Smith and Ronnie were waiting up ahead, obviously thinking Zara and Daffodil might need help but both women managed without. The rocks were what Zara liked best, testing her muscles and sizing up which part of her body she should use to lever herself onto the next stone.

'You okay?' Ronnie had let the other two go ahead and stood waiting for her, towering like a giant on the next rock.

'Fine', said Zara understanding the subtext to be *haven't forgotten that you are with me.* 'By the way,' she said, climbing up beside him, 'if I wanted to stay on the mountain with you, would that be all right?' After a millisecond hesitation Ronnie said,

'Share my tent do you mean?'

'I didn't bring a tent,' said Zara.

'Nor you did. Sleeping bag?'

'I've got a fleece in my rucksack,' said Zara. 'It's not going to be that cold is it?' Ronnie looked amused. 'I might roll against you inadvertently,' said Zara. 'Would you mind?'

'What and suck all my warmth away?' He put his arm around her waist and squeezed her. 'I think we'll find some way of managing.'

Zara was on the point of mentioning her doubts about Daffie and John Smith when there was a shout and she looked up to see them waving madly from the top. Daffie was standing on top of the triangulation point and John Smith was taking her photo. Then they heard him shout,

'We won, we won, we won!'

'I wasn't aware it was a race,' said Zara.

'Mountains have strange effects on people, don't you think?' said Ronnie.

'Looks like it,' Zara muttered, still thinking about John Smith and Daffie.

At the top, besides themselves, there were the three people who had passed Zara and Ronnie on the bridge. They were having a picnic and sitting looking towards Glen Rosa and arguing about what they could see in the distance.

Because of the other party, Zara's party did not spend long on the top, though John Smith got the picnickers to take a photo of them silhouetted against the sky. The woman who took the photo inadvertently used her own camera and had to take another with John Smith's. Zara wondered quite why it had been assumed the four of them were now together. She resented the intrusion but the others seemed fine with it so she said nothing. They agreed a picnic spot below the summit and shared all their remaining sandwiches and rolls. John Smith produced a battered gingerbread and some apples.

'Three course meal in there for supper?' asked Ronnie nodding towards John Smith's rucksack. 'Looks kinda heavy to me.'

'I have a little stove on which to cook some sausages and beans. Also soup and bread,' said John Smith. Ronnie's imagination had stretched no further and Zara only had chocolate left.

When it was decided — John Smith seemed to have a knack of propelling things forward without appearing to have done so — that they would push on until they reached the col at the bottom of which Rose's body was found, Zara fell behind as they walked. She was trying to work out whether there were any grounds for thinking Ronnie and John Smith had met before their encounter in the pub the previous evening. They weren't behaving like long lost buddies, yet there seemed to be *something* between them. Maybe thought Zara it was just a love of the mountains. Maybe it was quite the thing for people to join forces casually: after all that's what Rose and Laurie had done. This thought was not at all heartening and Zara hurried forward to join the others.

'Are you going to join us in the corrie?' John Smith was asking and Zara was glad when Ronnie shook his head.

'The tent wouldn't fit inside,' he said. John Smith, Zara noted, did not take this for the obvious joke that it was.

Chapter V   Unknown waters

They were high up at eight hundred and ten metres but it was still very warm and so clear they could hear, from far away, the voices of the other party. They reached Coire nam Fuaram about six o'clock and by this time they were all hungry again and tired, but more relaxed with each other, though Zara did keep wondering how on earth she'd come to be there, even though she'd made all the requisite decisions herself.

John Smith cooked his sausages, fastidiously, turning them every few seconds to make sure they were evenly browned. As he worked he talked and Zara was surprised at his ability to make everyone laugh.

'I don't know how they manage Mother in the home,' he began. 'Do you know when she first went there she was always wandering into the kitchen and starting to prepare meals?'

'Would the kitchen have been left unlocked?' asked Zara.

'She was cunning,' said John Smith. 'She would creep in after one of the cleaners and hide in a broom cupboard — one not much used — and then come out when the coast was clear. Once she managed to fry herself eggs, bacon and mushrooms with fried bread in the middle of the afternoon.'

'Didn't the staff miss her?'

'She probably said she was going into the garden. Anyway her downfall was a tin of Devon custard which she loves. She saw it on a high shelf and unfortunately took a high stool to reach it, my mother only being five foot nothing. And she fell off but not before knocking down a whole shelf of tins. The noise was like a machine gun going off. I believe at first people thought they were under attack.

'Was your mother okay?' asked Daffie.

'Amazingly she got away with a bruised thigh. Tough old boot my mum. They asked her if she wanted me to come over but she said, 'No, his breakfast is spoiled now.'

'She was thinking she was cooking for you?' asked Daffie. John Smith thought for a moment:

'I'm not sure about that,' he said, 'it might have been her cover. She loves a fry up and she's not allowed, because of her stomach'.

The beans had been previously heated in the tin and John Smith poured them into cups for him and Daffodil and onto a plate for Ronnie and Zara to share and gave two sausages to each person. Ronnie was to do the second round after. When she was given a roll, Zara sawed into it with her own penknife and put her sausages inside. No one spoke for a minute or two. The sun was beginning to go down. Zara wondered whether she had made a good decision about staying.

Ronnie managed to burn his sausages and his beans stuck to the bottom of his pan but no one refused them and Zara was sure she could have eaten the same again had it been available.

Coire nam Fuaram now looked grim as the light faded. Zara went and stood about a foot from the edge.

'Imagine being Edwin Rose down there then.' Zara jumped: she hadn't heard Ronnie approach.

'What a place to fall from, pushed or not,' she replied.

'Accidents are so easy,' said Ronnie. 'People must nearly die all the time. Sometimes it will be murder that goes down as an accident and sometimes the other way round.'

'And sometimes something in between,' added Zara.

'If you were going to murder someone, how would you do it?' John Smith's voice. 'I often wonder whether John Laurie went up with murder in his mind or whether it was unpremeditated.'

'I'm sure Edwin Rose just fell,' said Daffie, joining them but staying away from the edge.

'Is that because you don't want Laurie to have done it?' asked Zara. 'Tragedy rather than treachery?'

'I can think of a brilliant way to do it,' said John Smith. 'You suffocate your victim like this.' He suddenly made a grab at Zara and she felt his thumb close over her windpipe. 'And then let them fall over.'

'Let go of her for God's sake,' shouted Ronnie as Zara quickly changed colour. John Smith released her.

'Well you try it on me then,' he said. Ronnie seized his neck and squeezed until he felt the man start to let go. He released him abruptly and John Smith made as if to fall towards the edge. 'See. It's easily done and I'm a big person. Daffie would go over like a straw in the wind.'

'Try me,' said Daffie. Zara thought to herself as she recovered her breath that the woman must foolishly be imagining that she was missing out but then Daffie said, 'I used to do judo. I could stop you no bother'. Ronnie stepped forward and encased her neck with his hands but gently. Zara wondered if he was doing it so that John Smith couldn't. Up came Daffie's hands, fingers strongly linked. The suddenness rather than the strength broke Ronnie's grip. Daffie laughed nervously.

'Well done,' said Zara, 'but somehow I don't think this was the game Rose and Laurie were playing'.

'They may have been playing some game though,' said John Smith.

Zara had read enough to know that there was a school of thought that believed that Rose might have approached Laurie sexually. She met Ronnie's eye.

"If that had been the case would he not have tried something on at the boarding house?' he said. 'And if he had been knocked back, would they have gone up the mountain together the next day?'

'Who knows' said John Smith. 'Sexual decisions aren't made in the head.' There was a silence while Zara at least tried to think of a new topic of conversation.

'My mother,' John Smith began, 'once nearly had the gardener at the care home dismissed because she said he was flirting with her. Poor guy didn't stand a chance. Mother is a terrible flirt even now.'

'How old is she?' asked Zara.

'Eighty next birthday.'

'When is her birthday?' asked Daffie.

'June the nineteenth,' said John Smith. Zara had started to wonder if the guy was on something or whether if he weren't, he should have been.

And as if this wasn't enough, he brought a penny whistle out of his pocket and began to play Burns songs. They made Zara feel sad. She had to admit he played beautifully though.

'Can you not play something more cheerful?' Zara couldn't help her voice sounding snappy.

'Sorry. Come on Daffie. We'll make a move. Thank you for your company.'

'Where are you camping?' asked Zara, thinking of the woman. 'You can't start going down to the corrie now. It's too dark.'

'Dawn,' said John Smith. 'We'll go at dawn.'

'I'm not sure I want to,' Daffie said.

'Don't worry.' John Smith smiled as if switching his affability back on. 'We don't have to. We can see how we feel in the morning. I know a brilliant overhang just round the corner from here. We'll be really sheltered under it.' Zara suddenly felt tired and irritated. Daffie was at least twenty-five and old enough to look after herself. Zara wanted Ronnie's tent to be up and her in it. She was past caring about anything else.

John and Daffodil disappeared and Zara and Ronnie found a suitable place for the tent from where neither of them was going to wander out in the middle of the night and meet their death over a sudden edge.

***

'How about some hot chocolate?' said Ronnie as he finally made the tent secure.

'You haven't?' said Zara. 'How wonderful.' Ronnie immediately lit his primus and added water to his saucepan. Then he put the chocolate ready to stir in.

'Do you think they'll be okay?' Zara asked.

'Aye surely. I think John knows what he's doing, even though he seems a bit strange sometimes.'

'Do you think he lived with his mum too long?'

'Could be that. Could be he's not the world's best conversationalist and when you get in the mountains, it shows. The mountains always seem so wise, even though they don't speak. I always feel put in my place. Not put down but... you know...'

'Humbled,' Zara supplied.

'I wasn't wanting to sound spiritual about it.' He handed her a cup. 'Here's to Goat Fell anyway. May it teach us compassion!'

'That's a very strange thing to say,' said Zara as Ronnie let out a long breath. 'Do you know John from way back or did you just meet in the pub?'

'I met him once years back. Then again... in the pub...' Ronnie was suddenly concentrating on his hot chocolate.

'Look... do you mind if I tell you about what happened? It's just that for some reason I'm able to talk about it today.'

'Is this about John?' asked Zara. Ronnie changed colour.

'My sister,' he said. I was going to tell you about my sister.'

'I'm sorry. I misunderstood you. I can't promise I'll be anything but an ear though.'

'That's okay,' said Ronnie. 'I understand.' He looked into the western sky where there were still vestiges of light. 'It was like this.' He lapsed into silence again before he seemed to gather himself together. 'My sister Gina tried to take her life.' Zara nodded and waited. 'She took an overdose,' he continued, 'but fortunately she was found before it was too late... she had the stomach pump.'

'And how is she now?' asked Zara when she felt she had to break the ensuing silence.

'She's doing well. Back home. Talking about going back to work but...' Again silence.

'How old is she and has she tried before?' Zara was hoping to get more of a picture.

46

'She's twenty-two. The baby of the family. There's three of us plus Mum and Dad. Everyone's rallied round.'

'Any idea why she...?

'Not really. She says now she was depressed about work and about not having friends. Not having boyfriends. She has got some friends and they've been great.'

'And what else?' asked Zara feeling the repeated silences held something missing.

'They blame me. They all blame me. My brother's in Australia and he blames me! That's why I came away. I couldn't stand it anymore. It makes me sad but it also makes me angry. They've even got Dad on their side — Dad, who never takes sides!'

'How can it be your fault?' asked Zara.

'Her last boyfriend, someone she thought she might form a long-term relationship with, took a scunner to me. I was not living at home but near enough that he would see me quite often when I visited my parents. He thought I didn't like him; that I didn't think he was good enough for my sister and suddenly he went and took a job up north and left Gina in the lurch. She became depressed and was off work for weeks. But that was three years ago. And now she takes an overdose and they all say it's because the guy left and he left because of me. I don't know what to do. I love my family but... at the moment... they are difficult to love.'

'I'm sorry,' said Zara.

'The mountain brings it up in front of me. Makes it seem stark and unmanageable. I can't see any solution.'

'And you can't talk to them about it?' asked Zara.

'I've sort of been sent to Coventry. If I go round, they offer me tea and I sit in my usual seat but they don't begin any conversations. If Gina is out and I ask after her, they close up. If I get Gina on her own she becomes hysterical as if I were going to harm her in some way. Then I start feeling guilty and that makes it harder and harder to visit.' Zara couldn't think of anything useful to say so she said nothing. In spite of the coolness of the night, she was falling asleep. Ronnie heard rather than saw her yawn. 'I'm sorry,' he said. 'I shouldn't have burdened you with all this.'

Zara didn't know why but she began telling Ronnie about the previous year when she had been inveigled by her own stubborn personality to track down the perpetrator of a brutal death. It didn't feel relevant but she kept going, Ronnie listening intently. After a while he interrupted:

'You are telling me not to give up, is that it? However black things look, somewhere there's a way through?'

'You make me sound like a bad American film,' said Zara 'but yes, I suppose that is what I'm saying'. She was surprised at Ronnie's perception.

***

The tent had a waterproof base and when they had both laid their jackets on top of it for Ronnie, because he had given Zara his foam mat, they spread Ronnie's sleeping bag opened out over both of them. They lay for some time in complete silence. Zara began to wonder if Ronnie had fallen asleep when he said,

'Zara?' She grunted. 'Zara, I'm really very attracted to you.' He sounded so tentative Zara was more amused than apprehensive.

''That's nice to know,' she replied, turning slightly towards him.

'It's just that I don't want you to think I'm suddenly going to pounce on you. I know that you being here with me in this tent could just be a practical move on your part...' His voice tailed off. Zara felt he was waiting for a response.

'Absolutely practical,' said Zara, 'but it doesn't mean I don't find you attractive.' They moved towards each other in the darkness. Zara felt more awake again. She did not tell Ronnie about Barney but to cover up told him about her affair with Des which was in the past now but which showed her to be a person of normal relationships.

He told her about a couple of his relationships and about his family and his job. He was a qualified carpenter and thinking of setting up his own business. This was another reason for him being on the island. He needed to think out his plans.

'You're not thinking of setting up here though?'

'No definitely not.' Zara was about to ask him why when she nodded off and then woke to find it was after midnight: they had been talking for hours. There was a sudden movement from Ronnie and she felt herself enveloped in his arms. She said nothing. He lay stroking her back but it felt dreamlike to her: she was unsure it was happening, she was so tired.

Then all at once, there was a loud shriek and both Ronnie and Zara sat up in alarm. They were both fully clothed; Zara was the first out of the tent and she quickly pulled on her boots. There was no moon but, because of the time of year, it was not wholly dark. They stood still getting their bearings.

'Perhaps it was a bird,' whispered Zara. Ronnie shrugged.

'We'd better go and see though, don't you think?' They set off in the direction taken by Daffie and John Smith, making no attempt to hide themselves. They came round a corner made by a huge rock and there on the path was John Smith, standing facing away from them. He seemed perfectly calm.

'We heard a shriek,' said Zara.

'Sorry to wake you,' John Smith replied. 'It was Daffie. She got up for a pee and somehow found herself near the edge of the gully. I was asleep when she went but, you know, you sense a person's absence. I leapt up and went to her. She was shaking and shivering, poor soul.'

'Shall I go to her?' asked Zara.

'No, that won't be necessary. I only left her to have a pee myself.' Zara noticed then his flies were not done up properly. She looked across to the overhanging rock which was John Smith's shelter and could just make out the huddled figure of Daffie in her white jacket. Zara suddenly did not know what she was doing out there in the cold when she could be under a sleeping bag. Ronnie noticed her shivering:

'You go back. You'll freeze to death.' Ronnie seemed to be about to engage in a discussion with John Smith on the subject of what parts of the Highlands could be seen from North Goat Fell. Zara felt daylight would give better answers. She turned abruptly and said goodnight. Despite the relative discomfort of the bumpy ground, she fell asleep in a matter of minutes and only stirred when Ronnie joined her sometime later.

Once, she wakened and sat bolt upright hearing another bloodcurdling scream but when she looked out of the tent, everything was calm. She was disoriented and spooked by the looming rocks. Nightmare she decided. Result of earlier shriek. She snuggled back down, her breathing slowly going back to normal.

Chapter VI   Lethe

When she next wakened it was still early morning and, unzipping the tent she looked east to watch the sun rise. It was another clear day. She spoke to Ronnie:

'Going to be another...' She was aware then of an absence behind her. Ronnie was not there. Although the simplest explanation was that he had gone out to relieve himself, Zara felt a sense of foreboding. She pulled on her boots and started off towards John Smith's shelter. After two or three steps she faltered and decided to be more circumspect. She stood and looked at the terrain and worked out that if she climbed the rock in front of her she would be able to look down on the shelter and not be seen. She had no idea however of what she expected to see.

She saw nothing. The rocky shelter was uninhabited. There was not one piece of evidential litter in the whole visible area. Did they know about some cold mountain pool and had they gone off madly at dawn to plunge into it? The more Zara thought about it, the more likely it seemed. When something is completely lost, there is usually a simple explanation she thought. The same for people surely. Why hadn't they wakened her she wondered. Maybe there was a note. Maybe Ronnie and John Smith had decided on some dawn exploit when they'd been talking after the first shriek. Ronnie came back, found her asleep and thought he would write her a note telling her where they had gone. It would be somewhere obvious. She just hadn't looked. He wouldn't have just gone off. He wasn't that kind of person. She felt happier as she clambered off the rock and wandered back to the tent.

The gully did not look so menacing in the early light and she was drawn to the edge, reminded again of Rose and Laurie and remembering that Ronnie had been going to show her exactly where Rose might have fallen to his doom. She half lay as she peered over. The steep sides looked difficult to scale and there, as her eyes travelled over the gully bottom she saw there was a boulder. Someone on it. She had found them. She shouted down.

'Hey you might have waited for me!' But the figure on the boulder was not moving. Where were the men? It had to be Daffie bundled up there. Was she asleep? She didn't look very comfortable.

Zara remembered that Ronnie had had binoculars in his rucksack. Maybe her eyes were playing tricks and it was not a person at all: she just wanted it to be. She went back to the tent, looked summarily for a note but found none. The binoculars were in a pocket of Ronnie's rucksack. Ronnie had used them once on the way up when he thought he had seen an eagle but it had flown off out of sight whatever it was before he could adjust the lens. She picked up her fleece from under the sleeping bag.

She walked back to the side of the gully and looked down through the binoculars. It was definitely a person. A tied up person, unconscious or dead she could not tell. Her first instinct was to go down but almost immediately she realized she had no idea what was happening down there. She'd best phone the police. She made herself scrutinize the person. No use pretending: it had to be Daffie, her head at a funny angle. She looked all around but there were no signs of life anywhere. She hurried back to the tent: a helicopter? Was that what was needed? She felt confused. Ronnie, if only Ronnie were here. He was in the Mountain Rescue. He would have known what to do. She did not want to believe he was involved in something nefarious with John Smith.

Her fingers hit 999 and she heard herself try to explain the situation. It all sounded very implausible but at last she seemed to get her message through to the man on duty. He told her to stay where she was till someone came, to ring again if anything else happened and to avoid exposing herself to unnecessary danger.

Zara clicked off her phone and sat looking at it, her head not working properly. She dialled Kirsty at the hotel and then realized it was still only five-thirty in the morning and terminated the call. She started back to the tent and then she realized Kirsty and George might worry about her if they saw a helicopter heading for Goat Fell: they might think an accident had befallen *her*. I must go to them she thought, grabbing her rucksack and starting off back and then stopping just as suddenly. That man has no idea where I am she thought. Probably thinks I'm on the A77. She stood rigid, not being able to decide whether to go or stay but after a few minutes she began to think more rationally. She found half a sandwich in her rucksack and an apple. She thought about making tea but drank some water instead. Every so often she looked about her, half expecting to see John Smith or

Ronnie but some part of her brain knew this was unlikely. She had to go back and look over the gully again: had she really seen what she thought she'd seen? She did not even know if the person were dead or alive. Daffie she corrected herself. She didn't like putting a name to... she might be alive. Zara was suddenly very near convincing herself of it.

And here I am wasting time she thought and looked wildly round for the best route for descent. She scrutinised the rocks with the binoculars and thought she saw a diagonal path sloping down not too steeply and then away. She swung the binoculars back to the figure on the rock. No movement. But now she noticed something she'd missed before: the rope around Daffie was not just a short length such as you might use to truss up a chicken, it had a long end reaching upwards. It came to Zara that Daffie had been lowered down into the gully. By whom? By John Smith? He was probably strong enough. If he had a rope that long, did that mean he'd planned ahead? Or had he just packed it because he saw himself as a mountaineer? The rope was secured around a rock. To get to it Zara would have to walk around the top of the corrie but she would have to walk round anyway as the route she had selected started from there too.

She made her way round to the rope, trying to concentrate on each step, knowing that if she allowed herself to think about anything except the job in hand, the horror of the situation might knock her off balance. Her hands were cold on the stone not yet warmed by the sun. Everything was still. Zara did not allow her mind to puzzle over where Ronnie and John Smith were. Thoughts of them coming back would fill her full of fear. As it was, any small sound made her jump, even the sounds she was making herself, like the small stone she dislodged from its bed which found its way over the edge falling interminably till it hit the bottom of the gully with a sharp lonely sound.

At last she reached the rope. It looked new and very sturdy. She tested it between her hands. Then pulled on it. It was secure, tied around a pillar rock with a professional-looking knot. Zara wondered whether John Smith had shinned down it himself. It made sense. She wasted no time. There was no point worrying about whether the rope would hold. She had to get down to Daffie as quickly as possible and this seemed to be the best way. The rope was very slack. Zara climbing down was not going to make it tighten around… the person at the bottom. She faced the rope and took hold of it with both hands and, gripping tightly, let her legs swing until they were clear of the edge. She looped the rope over one foot and held it in place with the other and then, not daring to look down, slowly eased one hand till it was below the other. Who would have imagined the climbing ropes in the gym at primary school would have afforded her such a useful lesson she thought.

Once she had the hang of it, she found she went down quite fast, soon reaching the point where, with the next step she would have to circumvent the figure of Daffie. There was some swaying and swinging before she managed to set a foot on the boulder. She stood for a moment, uncertainly balanced and then let go of the rope. It was definitely Daffie. How could it have been anyone else? She searched in vain for a pulse. Kept trying because she wanted so much to find one. She felt Daffie's neck. It seemed warm but perhaps she was imagining that. She noticed bruise marks on the windpipe. Asphyxiation? Daffie's hands were tied and then the rope tied round her ankles so she had ended up in a foetal position. She was not marked in any other way. There were no signs of a struggle.

Zara took off her fleece and covered Daffie with it. She sat silent and shocked. Too shocked to feel fear or cold. She looked at the time. It was now six and Kirsty would be up. She phoned her.

'Just to let you know I'm okay,' she said when her friend answered. 'Spent the night on Goat Fell. Yes… *I'm* fine but there's been an accident. A girl found at the bottom of a gully. I need to wait until the Mountain Rescue come. No, I'm perfectly all right. I just wanted to let you know so you didn't worry if you saw the helicopter. Look, I'll tell you the story later, okay. I can't really explain on the phone… Yes, of course I'm telling the truth: I'm absolutely fine… Yes, yes.' Zara sounded resigned. 'I'll phone Barney later when he's up. No of course I don't want him to hear it on the news.'

Barney would be furious with her thought Zara but only because he cared for her. He would see the whole adventure as an avoidable act on the part of someone who was too much of a risk-taker. Zara knew he was right; she was often unable to predict the danger but often the risk-taking paid off. At what point in this trip for instance should her alarm bells have rung? One of the reasons why Zara could not make up her mind about making Barney her permanent partner, was the fact that he hated her investigations. He was constantly amazed at the alacrity with which she seemed to land bang in the middle of other people's misfortune and then feel duty-bound to do something about it.

She must have dozed off. She jerked awake at the sound of the Mountain Rescue vehicle. Two grim faces were gazing down at her, nonplussed. They made their way down to the boulder.

'Dead?' asked one man. 'I'm Davy by the way. This is Tom.'

'Zara,' said Zara. 'Dead I think,' she faltered. It was too real to say out loud.

Tom drew back Zara's fleece and felt for a pulse. He shook his head.

'Some time ago I reckon.' His eyes took in the bound feet and hands and the secured rope. He shook his head again. 'I won't ask questions. You look all in. The police are just behind. Would you like some tea?'

Zara found herself shivering and shaking so much she could hardly hold the cup offered to her.

'Been here all night?' ventured Tom. Zara nodded.

'Saw your tent,' said Davy.

'Not mine,' said Zara. The men were immediately alert. 'Ronnie's,' said Zara. Ronnie that's just come to —'

'That's why he didn't answer the call-out! Where is he?' asked Davy.

'I don't know,' said Zara.

'We'll wait for the police,' said Tom, drawing the fleece back over Daffie's body. 'Biscuit?'

Davy had relayed the information that the person they were looking for was found and no longer alive.

'Takes the pressure off a bit,' he said by way of explanation. 'For us,' he added, 'not for anyone else. Blanket?'

Wrapped inside the blanket Zara momentarily withdrew, feeling cocooned in a world of her own. She could hear the voices of Davy and Tom but not their words. She had no idea if it had been a few minutes or much more than that when she was roused by the sound of different voices and opened her eyes to see two police officers.

'I'm Sergeant McSorley and this is Police Constable McCash.' Zara was glad the police constable was a woman. 'Are you up for answering a few questions?' Zara nodded and they looked at her more closely. 'It's just that it's better if you can tell us as much as you can as early as possible. I can see you're tired though.' Zara nodded again. 'Name?' asked MacSorley. 'Age? Address? Was it you that found the victim? At what time? When did you come up the mountain? Were you with others? What were their names? Is that your tent? Whose tent is it? Did you know the deceased?'

Everything went fine until Zara attempted to explain her relationship with the other members of the 'party' as Mac Sorley insisted on calling it.

'Ronnie had invited me to climb Goat Fell with him,' began Zara. We'd met on the boat last um… Wednesday and I'd invited him to drop into the hotel where I'm working, the North Crag. Kirsty and George McNay's place.'

'And who invited the other people, John Smith and Daffodil?'

'Nobody,' said Zara. 'We met on the shoulder and sort of joined up. Ronnie had met John Smith in the Ormidale and…' Zara saw she was going to hesitate and then, in trying not to, did so. 'I had met John Smith on the *Waverley* last Thursday.'

'And he didn't ask *you* to go up Goat Fell with him?'

'Well, yes he did but…' Both officers were listening very intently. 'It didn't work out. I couldn't go.'

'I know you are very tired and very stressed, Zara, but I'm sure you'll agree your testimony is of the greatest importance. Someone has died here. The fact that they are tied up seems to suggest foul play. You say you were not present at the time of death but it appears you have a lot of circumstantial evidence in your head which may be extremely useful to us in helping determine exactly what happened here.' Zara nodded.

'Zara, can you explain in a bit more detail how you came to be on the *Waverley* with John Smith?' Police Constable McCash spoke for the first time. As she explained, Zara felt increasingly uncomfortable. No one was accusing her of lying or suggesting she might have had some involvement in what had happened but as things stood and until forensics had examined the physical evidence and a pathologist had pronounced the cause of death, Zara realised there was no reason not to place her in the frame with the others if there were to be a murder charge.

Sergeant MacSorley asked her to describe the two men.

'Ronnie seemed very friendly and pleasant. Genuine. Not a great talker.' She stopped remembering the conversation about his sister. 'But he did talk at length about his sister who attempted to take her life recently. He was sore because for some reason the family blamed him.'

'Did he come on to you?' asked PC McCash. Zara almost jumped.

'Yes, well no, not exactly. We were sharing a sleeping bag but...' Zara was embarrassed, 'we fell asleep anyway.'

'Anyway?'

'And then there was the shriek,' Zara suddenly remembered this gratefully.

'What time was that?'

'Not sure. Maybe about midnight.'

'And did you or Ronnie investigate?'

Zara recounted John Smith's explanation of the scream.

'This was the last time you saw John Smith?'

'Yes,' said Zara

'And did you see Daffodil?'

'I did,' said Zara. 'John Smith said not to go over, but I looked across and she was definitely there, in the shelter of that rock, the one they were sleeping under.'

'Not just some clothes that looked like a body?'

'I saw her white jacket,' said Zara pointing at Daffie's body, 'and I saw her arm rise up and cross her face.' The officers wrote in their notebooks.

'And,' said MacSorley, 'then you came back to the tent. What about Ronnie?'

'He followed later. I was asleep but I woke when he returned... I think...'

'But then he wasn't there in the morning?' Zara was silent: she was recalling her nightmare.

'Something you've just remembered?' Zara couldn't tell whether there was any irony in PC McCash's voice.

'Sorry. I don't think my mind's working properly. I had what I thought was a nightmare. I thought it was because of the shriek we'd heard earlier. I sat up suddenly but everything was calm and still. I could hear nothing. I assumed it had been a dream.'

'And was Ronnie there at this point?' the sergeant asked.

'I don't know. I thought he was. There seemed to be warmth but...'

'But what?'

'It may just have been the sleeping bag. I went back to sleep after my heart stopped racing.'

'You didn't think of getting up? Having a look?'

'I thought it was a nightmare. I'm sorry. I'm sorry!' Zara began to see lots of implications in her words and behaviour: it doesn't matter if you go to sleep after an alleged nightmare, as long as nobody's found murdered the following morning. Zara looked at Daffie's body and then away. Tiredness overwhelmed her. She wanted her mind to take in the fact that Daffie was dead but her mind said, 'Sleep'. She could summon up no detachment which would have enabled her to think rationally.

'Okay,' she heard Sergeant MacSorley say. 'We'll leave it there for now, except, I'd just like to ask, did you have any idea as to where John Smith and Ronnie might have gone? Or whether they went together?' Zara shook her head.

Chapter VII   No Trace

Zara stood up to leave. The police were talking into their radios about scene of crime officers and about identification. They had not found anything in the rock shelter that identified Daffodil.

'Did you see her use a mobile? We can't find one,' said MacSorley.

'No,' said Zara, screwing her face up with the effort of thinking, 'but she said she was going to stay with friends in Lamlash. Her friend had a cousin with a caravan. His name was Marra, short for Marradonna.'

'Aye well, not too many of them to choose from in Lamlash. Should be able to track him down,' said PC McCash. The two officers smiled. Zara was glad she'd been able to say something useful.

Zara assured the police she would be all right to return on her own and promised them she would come to the station later to make a statement and answer further questions. It was the ropes she thought as she walked past the tent. If they had been tied differently it might have looked as if they were supporting Daffie but they were... She could not get the image of a trussed up chicken out of her mind. She wondered if Daffie's personality had made her a more likely victim. She had seemed so innocent and gentle — though she had managed that judo move very well. It all went round and round in Zara's head but she could make no sense of it. She climbed carefully down from the Goat Fell summit. At least Daffie was found soon, not like Edwin Rose she thought. And then mused on the aftermath of that, Rose's brother coming up from London to find him, not knowing for two whole weeks where he might be, the inexplicability of his disappearance and the inadequate piecing together of a story which never revealed its mystery.

***

Zara was fortunate enough to pick up the boat bus on its way from the north end when she finally reached the shore road. She didn't think she would have made it to the hotel otherwise. She phoned ahead to Kirsty.

'I'll start running you a bath,' her friend said. By the time Zara reached the hotel she could hardly speak. She sank into the bath and closed her eyes, not heeding Kirsty's admonition that it would be better not to fall asleep there. She was so unconscious that when Kirsty knocked on the door half an hour later, she cried out in alarm convinced she had heard a shriek. However, having woken up she felt hungry and dressed quickly in clean clothes to find George making her a special breakfast.

'You'd better get out there, you're late. Joke,' he added as he saw from her face she was believing him. 'Sorry Zara.' He went over and gave her a big hug. 'Course you must be feeling fragile. Sit down and eat. Don't try and talk. Plenty of time for that.'

Zara did try but found she could not string a sentence together properly.

'John Smith,' she said. 'On the mountain. But where is he now?' and 'Daffodil's mobile was missing. But not her bag. Behind a boulder. And her purse. It was the ropes. Sorry George I don't think I can finish this egg.'

Kirsty came in from the dining room.

'You still look rough,' she said 'but the police want you at the station as soon as.'

'As soon as what?' asked Zara.

'They are expecting CID off the next boat. They want your fingerprints and DNA. And they want to interview us about John Smith.' The three of them sat in silence. No one wanted to express the possibility that someone who had slept under North Crag's roof would go on to do a murder.

'Perhaps it was that Ronnie fella,' said George.

'No, not Ronnie,' said Zara. 'Not a chance.' George and Kirsty looked at her expecting an explanation but she couldn't say to them, No, because I shared a bed with him, because I liked him. It made her head swim, the idea that she might have been taken in. Or worse, it struck her, taken out. Perhaps Ronnie and John Smith had planned the whole operation from the start. Ronnie had been reading that book. Asking her to come up the mountain might have been a cover or did something go wrong? Did Ronnie and John Smith quarrel? Perhaps. Resulting in what happened on the mountain with Daffie? Perhaps it made sense to their convoluted minds and the world was meant to understand.

As she spun this story to herself, Zara became more and more certain it was rubbish: Ronnie did not have anything to do with the murder: she had no evidence, she just felt it.

***

The men from CID were unsmiling and Zara was glad to be innocent in the face of their interrogation but first they listened and recorded a chronological statement of what had happened from when Zara started up the mountain with Ronnie. They appeared to be comparing what she said now with what she had said on the mountain. Zara thought they looked satisfied but then the questions began.

'Could you tell us all you know about 'John Smith'?

'Why do you say it like that, as if it's not his real name?' asked Zara.

'Because it's not his real name,' said the Detective Sergeant. 'He booked into the North Crag as John Smith but John Muirhouse is what's on his birth certificate. He gave a false address as well. Wilton Street in the West end of Glasgow.'

'Everyone's lived in Wilton Street at some time or other,' said Zara hoping to raise a smile.

'Everyone else maybe but not John Muirhouse. He has always lived with his mother in Govanhill.

'How did you find that out?'

'We found a receipt for a pair of trainers in a trouser pocket. Shop remembered him. Regular customer. Why am I telling you this? Look Miss MacDonald, just stick to answering my questions, will you? Then you can go home and sleep. Recover the good temper I'm sure you possess. Or did you leave it on the mountain?'

'And did your sense of humour go overboard before you reached Brodick?' The words were out of her mouth before Zara could stop them.

'Another hot sweet tea for Miss MacDonald,' said the DS giving Zara a hard smile. Now he thinks I'm snappy because I'm worried and he thinks I'm worried because I'm hiding something thought Zara.

'Where do you think John Muirhouse went?'

'I've no idea. I hardly spoke to him yesterday.'

'And on the *Waverley*, between bites of ice cream, did he mention any places he was fond of? Anywhere he was planning to visit?' Zara told them he was visiting his mum who was in the Brodick care home. The DS raised his eyebrows. 'Except, as you will have realised if you can put two and two together, he was lying. As I told you, his mother lives in Govanhill.'

'But,' said Zara, her mind replaying everything John Smith had said, all the stuff about the kitchen, 'I see'. Pause. 'Does he have any previous?' she asked.

'It seems he's been in court a few times but he's always got off.'

The words hung in the air. Zara felt a subtext: let's hope he doesn't get off this time.

'He's not gone home then?'

'Not been seen in Govanhill since he left for his holidays a week ago. We've appealed for information. He's maybe spoken to someone in a pub.'

'He was in the Ormidale the night before last. That's where he met Ronnie.'

'We know that. We're hoping he spoke to more people in more pubs. The rope,' said the DS suddenly. 'Do you remember him talking about climbing at all? That was a fancy rope he used on Daffodil Brown. From a sports shop.' Zara nodded.

'Sorry. That's a bit I forgot... I think it's because I only heard the tail end of the conversation. He was talking about when he climbed K2.' The DS pursed his lips and screwed up his nose at the same time:

'John Smith,' he said, 'whose mother is in a care home in Brodick may have climbed K2, but John Muirhouse whose mother stays in Govanhill, has never been out of the UK. He doesn't even have a passport.'

'Ah,' said Zara, 'I see.'

By the time they had finished, Zara felt guilty, not of murder obviously but because it seemed to her that the officers thought she could be an accessory to the crime. Or maybe she thought, they were just pushing her because she was at least there and they had so little to go on. They'd taken her fingerprints and DNA sample and said they would most likely need to speak to her again, adding the usual, 'Don't hesitate to get in touch if you remember anything that might be useful to us'.

***

When she arrived back at the hotel, Kirsty and George were both in the kitchen drinking coffee. The police had been to examine the room John Muirhouse had slept in, which had not been touched because Zara the chambermaid had been absent and Kirsty had had too much to do to get round to it. George silently passed Zara coffee, in her favourite mug with the words, 'I am the mug, not you' written on it.

'Well,' said Kirsty, 'I don't think they learnt much. When he was staying here I didn't think of him as particularly taciturn but when the police asked me to remember everything he'd said I couldn't think of anything. Well, nothing that would point to anything, like what he might be going to do. It's not as if murderers go around saying, 'Who is it today? Oh well, since I'm in Brodick...'

Zara could see Kirsty's attempts at black humour were meant to lighten the atmosphere and that she was worried about George's reaction to it all but George seemed energized. He turned to Zara and asked,

'Could you tell me exactly where it all happened — only if you are ready of course. I want to be able to visualize it.' Zara shivered and saw Daffie tied up and on the boulder but she knew George was not being ghoulish, merely curious because he was familiar with the terrain.

Once she began, Zara found the whole story spilling out and realized as it progressed just how bizarre it all appeared. Bizarre, yet if there had been no grisly outcome, how ordinary. She might have been sitting in the kitchen merely apologizing for not being there to perform her early morning duties and telling her friends how beautiful the sunrise had been.

'They are talking to Ronnie's parents as well,' Kirsty was saying. Zara had forgotten: of course Ronnie had mentioned on the boat that they were with him.

'I wonder where they are staying,' said Zara.

'The Rosa guest house,' said Kirsty. The police asked us where it was.'

'Did they ask you if you knew Ronnie?'

'We said he'd had a coffee on the patio with you but that we hadn't really spoken to him much. Why do you ask?'

'I'm just wondering whether they believe I had nothing to do with it all,' said Zara.

Kirsty and George were quick to pooh-pooh the idea but Zara was wide awake now and, using the excuse that if you've not slept properly, it's better to stay up and go to bed at the normal time, she decided, once she had changed some beds and done some hoovering, she would go and visit Ronnie's mum and dad.

***

She walked along recalling what Ronnie had said about his parents; the stand-off regarding his sister. She wondered if they might think Ronnie bad enough to have been involved in a murder. Zara found the Rosa easily and as she rang the bell she spotted a couple sitting half-hidden in a shrubbery. They were talking quietly to each other. A woman in her thirties opened the door and smiled.

'What can I do for you?' she said. 'I'm afraid I've no vacancies till next week but...'

'It's okay,' aid Zara. I'm not wanting a room. It's just that I believe Ronnie's parents are staying here and...'

'You're a friend of Ronnie's?' Zara nodded.

'Sort of,' she amended. 'I was with him on the mountain...'

'I'll go and ask them,' said the woman softly.

The Balfours were only too pleased to talk to someone who had been with Ronnie and who wasn't a police officer.

'It must have been terrible for you,' said Margaret Balfour. Her eyes were full of suffering. Zara put her hand on her arm.

'I'm really sorry about what happened. I really have no idea where Ronnie's gone.'

'He's a good climber,' said his father,' but anyone can fall and lie undiscovered...' Like Edwin Rose thought Zara.

'Those officers were very polite,' said Margaret. 'They said the whole mountain would be searched but they did ask lots of questions about how well Ronnie knew John Muirhouse. I suppose they want to find him to see if he has any clues about what happened.' Harry Balfour looked cynically at her.

'He may be in the frame, Margaret. From the police perspective, it could have been either of them.'

'Not our Ronnie,' his wife said.

'Of course not,' said Harry. 'Of course not.'

'You're the girl that asked him about his Jack House book, aren't you?' Margaret suddenly remembered. 'Funny that...' Harry shook his head at her. 'Don't start getting morbid, Margaret. He'll probably walk in the door by lunch time.'

Zara felt on the whole, they had been glad to talk to her. She promised to return and gave them her number at the North Crag. The part of her mind that was used to investigation was starting to kick in and she knew the police wouldn't tell her more than they had to. She needed to cultivate anyone in the least bit involved.

There was nothing odd about Ronnie's parents thought Zara as she walked back along the beach. Nothing there that would induce you to doubt Ronnie's sanity or his capacity for — Zara still didn't like saying the word 'murder'.

On the other hand, the more she thought about John Muirhouse, the stranger he appeared. She went over her knowledge of him: dominant was his predilection for fantasy. Why would he pretend his mother was in a care home in Brodick when she was in reality living in Govanhill? And if he had no mother on Arran, then the 'spare ticket' story didn't hold up. But had he bought two tickets on spec, relying on his charm to reel in a companion? Or had he had someone in mind from the start: Zara herself or someone else? Maybe he'd had a few refusals before her.

It came over to Zara in an overwhelming wave of clarity: if she had not had the showdown with Barney — if Barney had not appeared — she might now be in Daffie's position. She had reached the front and sat down hard on one of the seats facing the sea. On what basis had John Muirhouse chosen his victim? Would Zara have done just as well?

And then another thought struck her: was this merely his first? Would he be back for more or would he seek out another island with mountains and another corrie, earning himself the title of Gully Murderer? As if to bring her back, her mobile rang. It was Barney whom she had texted that she was safe but to phone her as soon as.

Barney sounded agitated but Zara was relieved to find he wasn't angry; she didn't have enough energy to defend herself. She gave him a skeletal account of what had happened and he listened patiently to the end.

'Thank God you are safe, Zara,' he said. 'This is... I don't know what to say. I'm coming down, as soon as I finish work tomorrow. Will that be okay?'

'Yes, of course,' said Zara, realizing as she spoke how much she wanted to see Barney now. 'Will you be bringing Ben?'

'What do you think? It will be difficult keeping the whole situation from him.'

'We can try,' said Zara. 'I'm only a circumstantial witness, after all. There must be a limit to how many times they'll want to interview me.'

'I'll bring him,' said Barney'. He'll cheer you up.' Zara suddenly felt overcome with emotion.

'That would be great,' she said.

She arranged to meet the two of them off the six o'clock boat the following evening, closed the call and walked back to the North Crag feeling much better. Kirsty and George were warm and sympathetic but their anxiety at being involved inhibited Zara from showing all her feelings. She didn't want to risk breaking down in front of them.

When she reached the front door of the hotel, there was a woman hovering.

'I was wondering if you served coffee to non-residents,' she said. Zara didn't like the way her eyes darted in at the windows.

'I'm afraid not,' she said smiling but not feeling friendly. 'You could try along at —'

'This is where John Muirhouse stayed isn't it?' the woman cut in.

'We don't discuss who is and who isn't a resident at the North Crag.' Kirsty had appeared and stood on the top step looking down on the woman whose question she must have heard through the open window.

'Well that's what it said on Twitter,' said the woman huffily. 'I just wanted to take a picture of the room he stayed in.'

'Are you from the press?' asked Kirsty.

'No, I'm a holiday-maker'.

'Well I suggest you go and buy an ice cream, and then sit on the beach in the sun.' The woman tossed her head and turned away.

Chapter VIII   Avoidance impossible

'Go to bed now,' said Kirsty to Zara. 'Just for a couple of hours. Set your alarm if you like but you are so tired you'll do yourself an injury if you try to stay on your feet any longer.' Zara found herself unable to put up any resistance and went slowly up the stairs to her room. She lay there calmed by the cool sheets and also by the knowledge that Barney was coming. Funny she thought as she drifted off, I came here to get away from him and if I hadn't I wouldn't have been on the mountain. 'Barney' and 'Ben' were comforting names she felt but was asleep before she managed to tax her mind as to why.

***

Meanwhile all ten beds at the North Crag were filling up. Kirsty and George could not believe it. They actually had people asking if the room John Muirhouse had stayed in was available. The police had not given the all-clear so it had been unoccupied but this was more than compensated for by the sudden flood of bookings not only for the week to come but for the whole of the rest of the month. Kirsty found it ghoulish, especially since people began to ask over breakfast whether John Muirhouse had had the full Scottish or whether he was a vegetarian — like Hitler, one guest said meaningfully.

George joked that they should quickly have invented a Gully Surprise ice cream and served afternoon tea on the front lawn with a prize for the person who could sit the longest in John Muirhouse's chair. But both of them were relieved when Friday came and with it, Barney, Ben and Nessie. Ben had been given the attic next to Zara and he was enchanted by the skylight view of the mountains.

'I want to climb the highest one,' he said at once. Zara looked at Barney.

'I think Aunty Zara has a special trip planned for us down the other end of the island,' he said. 'We're going to hire bicycles and —'

'But I want to climb —'

'You'll love cycling here. Sometimes you can go downhill for miles and miles,' said Barney, 'and you might be able to ride a horse.'

'We'll have a picnic?' Ben was beginning to be mollified.

'A huge picnic and we'll probably stop at a café too.'

'Okay and can we swim in the sea?'

'Of course, Ben.'

'You are coming too, aren't you, Aunty Zara?' said Ben as Zara had done nothing but nod her head occasionally as Barney improvised.

'You bet,' said Zara 'I shall have to get up very early and do my hoovering and dusting and then when I've helped with breakfast and making packed lunches — big call for packed lunches this week for some reason. Everyone going up —'

'— everyone going up the mountain,' finished Ben. 'Who is John Muirhouse, by the way? Is he a very important person?'

'Why do you ask?' said Zara.

'I heard someone say, "This is where he started out to do the deed?" Was it someone in history? Is Arran famous?'

'George has a horse here at the hotel, did you know?' said Barney desperately. 'He's called Riga. Isn't that a beautiful name? We could go and talk to him after we've eaten if you like.'

'Can I ride him?' asked Ben.

'He's too big for you,' said Zara, 'but we can certainly go and give him some carrots'.

Ben went out with Nessie to explore the garden leaving Zara and Barney alone.

'I don't think this is going to work, keeping Ben in the dark,' said Zara.

'Well I don't want him over-excited about a terrible crime like last year,' said Barney. 'It's not natural for a boy his age to be discussing a murder at such close quarters. And he'll be pestering us to go and see where it happened. You wouldn't want that.'

'We'll play it by ear. You're only here for two days. We'll try and keep ourselves to ourselves.' Zara went over to Barney where he stood by the skylight and slid her hand round his waist. 'Not my favourite view any more I'm afraid.'

'What is it about you, Zara that seems to attract bad things?' said Barney hugging her to him.

'You're not a bad thing though, Barney,' said Zara kissing him. Barney smiled, recognizing Zara's remark for the backhanded compliment that it was.

***

Fortunately, Goat Fell was shrouded in mist when the three of them set off southwards on their hired bikes the following day.

'I wouldn't want to get lost up there,' said Ben looking towards the mountains. George had offered to look after Nessie. Kirsty approved; two short walks were good for the convalescent.

Where they could, they abandoned the road for the cycle track and reached Lamlash without incident. When Ben saw Holy Isle he said at once,

'Can we go there? It's a wee island. Maybe when we get there, there may be an even smaller one the other side.'

'We'll see what time the boats go,' said Barney. They ate ice creams from the Pier café while waiting.

'What about the bikes?' asked Ben.

'No roads on Holy Isle,' said Zara.

'I want to climb to the top,' said Ben. 'We can eat our picnic there.' Barney and Zara exchanged glances: the plan seemed to be working. Ben was enthusiastic about the day and there were not so many people about that Zara felt someone was going to pounce on her and ask her about the murder.

The boat trip went without incident.

***

Zara climbed slowly. She wasn't sure how tired she was but she found Ben wanted to stop and ask questions all the time so she relaxed and sometimes just let Ben and Barney go on ahead. The sun had come out and as they climbed there was a little breeze. Ben loved the way things became smaller as they climbed higher.

Perched on convenient rocks, they began to eat their picnic.

'Do you think if I jumped from up here I'd land in that boat?' asked Ben. The gannets made an almost continuous background noise but it only served to enhance the silence when it came.

'It looks quite dangerous going down,' said Ben.

'It's okay,' said Barney. 'Just have to be careful.'

'We're a third as high as Goat Fell.' Ben threw an apple core into a tiny gully. 'Can I have more juice?'

Zara wanted to lie back but she wanted to stay responsible for Ben, not leave it all to Barney. Even so, she must have nodded off because the next thing she knew, she heard a voice saying,

'Excuse me, but was it not you that was on Goat Fell with John Muirhouse?' A man of about fifty stood in front of her, perfectly pleasant as if his question was of the most ordinary kind. Barney had risen and was moving between him and Zara.

'I think you've made a mistake, pal. Would you mind just leaving us to our picnic?' Zara's face had completely changed colour and that together with Barney's stance, drove the man into flight. He waited a few yards further on and when his companions came into view he beckoned nervously to them.

No sighs of relief from Zara and Barney. The damage had been done.

'I thought you said you didn't know John Muirhouse,' said Ben when the party had disappeared.

'We didn't actually say anything about him,' said Zara.

'Well I asked a question and you didn't answer. But I know there was a murder, wasn't there? The body was at the bottom of a gully. Like Edwin Rose.'

'How do you know about Edwin Rose, Ben?' asked Zara.

"From your book, '*Murder not Proven*',' said Ben looking at Zara as if she were stupid. Barney glanced at Zara resignedly.

'Okay Ben. It's just that we didn't want you worrying about Aunty Zara like last year.'

'Is she in danger then?'

'She went up Goat Fell last Wednesday and camped.'

'I wanted to camp. You might have waited for us, Aunty Zara!'

'And in the morning,' Barney went on, 'she went for a little walk and unfortunately saw this figure in the gully. She phoned the police and it turned out the person wasn't alive anymore.'

'Where was John Muirhouse? Was it him that did it?'

'We don't know. We don't really know anything because John Muirhouse disappeared and hasn't been seen since.'

'So did you have to talk to the police, Aunty Zara?'

'Yes, I've done that. I've told them everything I know.'

'So that's why you didn't want to go up Goat Fell again. There might have been another body.'

'Hopefully not,' said Barney.

'Do you think we can talk about something else now?' asked Zara. 'It's just that I'm a bit sad about what happened, Ben, if you don't mind.' Ben nodded. But all the way down, intermittently he would turn to his father with a whispered question like, 'Are there any big gullies on *this* mountain?' Only the excitement of the motorboat back to Lamlash and the return cycle ride to Brodick successfully quietened him down and by the time he had eaten his tea his eyes were drooping.

'Tomorrow I want to ride a horse,' he said to Barney who was making sure his son was happy about his bed in the attic. 'I want Aunty Zara to come and say goodnight,' he murmured but by the time Zara entered the room, he was fast asleep.

Barney found Zara sitting on a window seat in the dining room looking out over the water. She told him the whole story and Barney listened without interruption.

'What I don't quite understand... don't understand at all actually,' said Barney, 'is why Ronnie disappeared. Did he have some role in the murder, did he just maybe think it would look as if he'd had a role? It's very odd they've both disappeared unless they are involved with each other in some way.'

'Ronnie's parents think he went for a walk and fell somewhere. There is a search going on.'

'His parents aren't going to believe he had anything to do with it.'

'He didn't have anything to do with it.'

'You'd put money on it?'

'You bet I'd put money on it.'

'How can you be so sure? You can't know him that well.' Zara looked at Barney to see if the remark was barbed. She had told the camping story fairly truthfully but not dwelt on the intimacy of the tent. Barney had not pressed her. He was not by nature a jealous man; would buy the idea of closeness for the sake of warmth on a cold mountain.

'No I don't know him well. You're right. It's impossible to be sure. I wouldn't have clocked John Muirhouse for a murderer either. I wouldn't have accepted a ticket for the Waverley from him if I had. He was odd but he didn't seem malevolent. He was considerate.'

'You mean he bought you an ice cream,' said Barney. Zara's mouth set in a grinning rictus.

'Yes. Well.'

'That wasn't considerateness, it was him trying to charm you.'

'Probably,' said Zara.

'Sorry,' said Barney, 'It must be frightening to imagine —'

'— that I might have been the victim,' Zara finished the sentence for him. She reached for his hand. 'Thanks for coming, Barney. 'It's better with you here.'

'Why don't you come back to Glasgow with me? For a bit at least?' Barney added seeing the hesitation in Zara's face.

'I can't let Kirsty and George down. George really can't do much. He does what he can but anything physical really tires him and then Kirsty starts worrying.' Barney acquiesced with a shrug and then he said,

'But Zara, you don't have to be involved. Don't for God's sake get involved. The guy might be a serial killer.' Pause. 'Did you mean it when you said you wouldn't have to talk to the police anymore?'

'I think so. They said the usual like… if I remember anything else et cetera… Unless the forensics turn up something untoward.'

***

The next day was bright and sunny and Zara, Barney and Ben took a cycle ride to Sannox, Nessie running all the way and they all took a welcome dip in the sea. After, they walked down the glen. Zara thought of Edwin Rose again and how strange it was that he was buried in a graveyard there when his family were in London. I would have wanted him back she thought and her mind went to Daffie's relatives, realizing she hadn't thought of them before. She wondered what they were like. No one could cope well with a murder. They would be spending the rest of their lives wondering how it had all happened.

Zara began to speculate about the two screams she had heard. They'd sounded disembodied. She imagined that that was why she had thought the first was a bird. What had Daffie and John Muirhouse been doing to elicit a sound so tortured? And why had she and Ronnie been so easily reassured? Why had she not followed her first instinct to go across to Daffie and see if she were all right? Daffie must have been petrified thought Zara to sit there under the rock and not move, when she could hear us talking to John Muirhouse.

When Zara saw Ben and Barney off at the pier it was not a sad occasion: they were coming back the following weekend. Ben was ecstatic.

Chapter IX   Letters and Knives

Zara had been wrong. The police called her the next day and demanded she come in at once. She thought they were just being officious. No leads, so interview everyone again. Sure enough DI McGilroy asked Zara to go over her story another time, leaving nothing out.

Every time she told the story, she was gripped by fear. It was peculiar how there seemed to be more fear in the story now; that had all come afterwards with retrospection. When she had finished the DI looked at her grimly.

'I'm going to ask you to remember anything you might have left out at the point where the four of you were together after the sausages.' Zara went cold. She was sure she'd said everything. There was a long pause.

'I've nothing to add,' she said at last. The DI's eyes gleamed.

'The forensic evidence,' he said, 'shows us that there are fingerprints on Daffodil Brown's neck. We know one set belong to John Muirhouse but the other ones belong to someone else — not you, we know that — so probably Ronnie Balfour.' Zara remembered Ronnie's hands, not large for his height and compact: she could see them round Daffie's neck. She put her hand to her head: she had forgotten the asphyxiation incident. 'This puts Ronnie Balfour firmly in the frame, unless you maybe have anything to add to your story…?' The DI waited.

Zara began speaking, realizing as the truth came out how macabre it sounded but also how it fitted beautifully into what happened later.

'So you were discussing the Goat Fell murder case of 1889 and you experimented with asphyxiation. John Muirhouse tried to asphyxiate you, then Ronnie Balfour tried to asphyxiate *him* and then had a go at Daffodil Brown. Ever thought of taking up dancing?'

'That's what happened,' said Zara. The DI looked at her sardonically.

'Really? Then can I ask you why you managed to miss it out of your original statement. Or is it such a commonplace activity for you that you overlooked it? Even if what you say is true, it points to your involvement. We can't rule out the possibility that you were an accessory to the murder.'

'An accessory?' Zara was furious. 'But it was me that told you what happened. Why would I have done that if I were involved?'

'Speaking in general terms,' said the DI, 'it's quite usual in some types of murder for someone's role to be that of the discoverer. Especially murders that contain ritual.' Zara was doing all she could to stay calm.

'Are you suggesting I witnessed what happened?'

'I'm suggesting nothing,' said the DI. 'Did you? Is that what you want to tell us? It would make things a lot easier if you could tell us everything you know. Maybe you were just meant to keep watch. Maybe it was important to Muirhouse and Balfour that they had an observer.' Zara's stomach lurched as she heard Ronnie's name again: she could not believe he was involved. That was not how things had been. And yet... what *had* happened while she was in the tent? She did not know.

'We haven't enough evidence to hold you,' the DS was saying 'but I can't stress too highly that your evidence may be key to this enquiry. Please don't do a disappearing trick like the others. And Miss MacDonald, do dredge that memory of yours, just in case you've forgotten a few more nuggets which might help us.'

*****

Zara spent the rest of the day with George in the garden clipping the edge of the lawn, discussing whether it would be good to have a pond and whether if they did, it would contain lilies or goldfish or both.

'Can a goldfish sense when a hawk is about to dive on it, and go under a lily leaf?' asked Zara, doing her best to concentrate. George didn't know the answer.

Kirsty came out to say someone had rung from the *Record* but she'd told them Zara wasn't allowed to say anything to the press because it might prejudice the search for Muirhouse and Balfour. Zara noticed that Ronnie had reached surname status. She still refused to believe he had had anything to do with the murder. Yet he had not been found. Nothing had been found to indicate the direction the two men had taken in leaving. Had they walked for miles down a burn? And which burn? There were tens of footprints going up Goat Fell and several taking the path the alleged murderers had taken to Coire nam Fuaram. The police had compared prints they'd found in conjunction with those of Zara and Daffie but there was no sign of these being carried on and no prints of Muirhouse and Balfour going from the location of the tent and the rock. Had John Muirhouse changed his boots? For something lighter? It was as if both men had disappeared into a time warp. A bit like Rose and Laurie thought Zara and wondered if Muirhouse, like Laurie was going to pop up somewhere unexpected. At least Daffie's body had not been found riddled with maggots, though that was a small comfort, a whole dead body instead of a living woman.

Zara had heard a news item where Daffie's aunt — her parents were dead — had been interviewed. She had been struck by her outburst:

'People always say how wonderful their children are when they die like this or in a car accident or a drug overdose. How bright and friendly and talented as if they would miss them less if they had been ordinary and dull. She was my niece. She was my niece.'

***

And so the week went on with rescue attempts dwindling as the idea of Ronnie Balfour lying injured or dead became more and more remote. People went on looking but increasingly the view was that he had left the island although no one could give a good reason why. In the pub and the tea-rooms the consensus was that Ronnie would not have had anything to do with the murder. All who had met him testified to that. In fact, most of the discussion centred on anecdotes where Ronnie figured positively, as if these somehow proved that he could not possibly have been involved. He was a well-kent face even though he had only just started staying on the island, since he had been a frequent visitor from childhood.

About John Muirhouse less was known. People had sighted him and noted his elastic stride and how his height seemed to lift him out of the orbit of other folk. He did not bend to speak to you. One man recounted how he'd ended up arm-wrestling him after a couple of drinks. Mikey thought he could arm wrestle for Scotland 'But this fella,' said Mikey, 'he could lay your arm down as soon as look at it. It was... I couldn't believe it. Like it wasn't the surprise factor or anything like that. It was like my arm was just made of straw.'

Then after the long silence, everything changed. John Muirhouse came, verbally at least, out of his hiding place and rang the police. He wanted to report a murder, he said but he thought he'd leave it till tomorrow. The duty officer got the GPS of the mobile but then Muirhouse rang off. The officer swore blind the man had identified himself by name 'which would mean he was talking about the Goat Fell murder, wouldn't it?' When some uniforms went to the spot they found the mobile, obviously left for them. There was a draft message on it: 'I have the right answers but do you have the right questions?' The police reckoned the message was for them. The next day, Thursday the 10th, a letter arrived at Stewart Street police station in Glasgow:

'Dear CID,

You will be glad to discover that I know the name of the man who murdered Daffodil Brown. A flower in your name is not very auspicious when it comes to murder is it? I can deliver the man to you but first I want your assurance that I myself will not be hunted down or charged. The man is dangerous. I know where he is. We can work together on this. I saw him kill Daffodil Brown with my own eyes. He used my climbing rope to truss her up. It was night. He must have lured her out from our shelter. Maybe they had made a tryst earlier and were waiting for me to fall asleep. I am a light sleeper but I woke too late. I followed at a distance. Why did I not stop him? I hear you ask. Officers, I hope you will believe this. I could not move. At first the sight paralysed me completely. Anyway there was no time. What I saw was a folded shape and the rope — I missed the point where the lady went over the edge but we're talking about a fit man here and Daffodil Brown was a mere wisp of a thing. I pulled myself together and ran to a place where I could see the action. The figure dropped inertly down and came to rest without moving on the boulder. My reading of this, if I may make so bold as to offer an unprofessional opinion, is that he had asphyxiated her previously till she was unconscious, then trussed her up the easier to lower her into the gully.

He left the rope secured to a rock and, I thought, began to make his way towards the path down into the gully. I started to follow meaning to intercept him, not wanting to get trapped myself at the bottom but unfortunately I stumbled and alerted Balfour with the ensuing sound of a stone falling and bouncing off rocks on its way down. The perpetrator looked my way, saw me and fled. Here endeth the lesson. Broadcast your assurance for me and I will tell you what happened next and lead you to your man.

Yours sincerely,

John Muirhouse.

There was no doubting the source of the letter — unless someone else had written it and planted Muirhouse's fingerprints all over it. Fingerprints bearing signs of toast with soft-boiled egg. Forensics were very certain in their report. The letter was postmarked in the city centre and thought to have been posted somewhere neutral like Central Station.

As they imagined Muirhouse had intended, the letter raised as many questions as it answered, but at least DI McGilroy felt it was now worth stepping up the search on the mainland, revisiting Muirhouse's mother in Govanhill, Muirhouse's place of work, his acquaintances — he did not seem to have any friends.

Regarding Ronnie Balfour, thinking had now to be re-thought. Up till then there had been a consensus on dual involvement after Balfour's fingerprints were found on Daffodil's neck but now there was the possibility that Balfour had been the sole perpetrator. There was no way on present evidence to rule it out. McGilroy was frustrated and annoyed, feeling he was waiting for another letter from Muirhouse, but a letter that might, even so, just be a tissue of lies.

He did not have to wait long. The next day brought a second letter in different handwriting with different ink, paper and envelope and posted from another part of town. Read too many Famous Five books as a child thought McGilroy.

The writer sounded as if he wanted to confuse:

'Dear CID,

Further to my letter of the 9th June, I want to explain a theory I have about the killer of Daffodil Brown. When I saw him head towards the bottom of the gully, my first thought was that the killer wanted to approach the body from below — as if he were coming on it by accident. This seems to indicate a ritualistic bent, a way of detaching himself from the act but at the same time gaining a sense of drama.

This may sound quite crude to you but there have been other murders that have shown the same complete insensitivity. But you, at the CID will know all about this, having been well-versed in experiences of this nature since when you first picked up the detectives' handbook.

The other thing I would like to say which I omitted to say yesterday is that, although you may believe the contrary if you wish, I did not walk cold-bloodedly away from the victim thinking she might be alive. I have seen dead people and I know that Daffodil Brown was one such. I thought the pursuit of Balfour would be a more useful occupation and I was fairly certain the dark-haired female who thinks she's Wonder Woman would find Daffodil soon enough.

Lastly, I imagine you are wondering why Balfour took Wonder Woman, up the mountain. Well you can wait. The best parcels are always the small ones.'

Muirhouse had signed off and then added a post script:

'You lot are *so* easy to hide from.'

McGilroy's first impulse was to tear the offending letter into little bits but he knew that would give endless pleasure to Muirhouse were he ever to get to know. He wondered briefly if there was a mole in his force but then thought again that that was the way Muirhouse would want him to think.

McGilroy pondered the letter and then pondered some more on yesterday's letter but came to no conclusions. He gave copies of both to his team and told them to try and read between the lines but since this was one of his favourite diktats they merely nodded and went on with what they were doing. McGilroy, feeling the lack of something concrete to do, decided to talk to Zara again.

By this stage in the week, Zara had recovered some of her equilibrium. Partly, the structure of the day at the hotel was conducive to calm thinking and calm behaviour: if she felt at all glum she took herself into the garden and did some hard physical work.

When Kirsty called her to the phone she was outside planting red geraniums and had, up till then been feasting on the intensity of their colour. She was thinking about the number of vibrations of the colour 'red' and wondering whether it was the number that elicited her response or something else. When Kirsty said the name 'McGilroy', Zara's geraniums turned blood colour.

Zara went through to the kitchen sink to wash her hands. Ever since she had known the possibility that Ronnie might be implicated she had felt her hands were not clean. She kept trying to remember the occasions that his fingers had contacted hers, giving or taking a torch, a piece of chocolate. She could if she isolated one guilty finger, feel a tingling there. She made herself dab her hands dry, not rub them; she knew the feeling she had was an invention of her mind.

Passing through the summer crowds on the Shore road — the *Waverley* was in — she wondered just how many people were thinking about the murder. Every day there were headlines in the tabloids and she'd seen people sitting on the beach soaking up the news or non-news as it often was, as they soaked up the sun.

'I'd like you to read these, Miss MacDonald and tell me if you can throw any light on them.' McGilroy put the two letters down in front of Zara who physically jumped in surprise when she saw the signatures. The tabloids had not had access to the letters. Zara read through both and then she read them again with McGilroy and one of his team sitting silent opposite her. She felt the DI was watching her for any change in her expression but when she looked up he was staring out of the window.

'Well,' he said. 'Anything?'

'You just want me to say what comes into my head?' He nodded trying to stay patient. 'Well,' said Zara, 'a flower in your name', that bit, he's obviously referring to Daffodil and Rose as in Edwin Rose but I expect you sussed that.' McGilroy nodded again.

'And?'

'Perhaps he's referring to the Goat Fell case when he says he doesn't want to be hunted as John Laurie was.' McGilroy's expression altered but he just said 'And?' again.

'If you're asking me if this fits with the man I met on the *Waverley* I can only say he was quite dismissive when I mentioned the story after he had invited me to...' Zara's head swam for a second '... go up the mountain with him. "I'm no John Laurie," he said. Then he started talking about gannets.'

'Thank you,' said the DI. 'Go on.'

'This bit, 'Maybe they made the tryst earlier', I couldn't swear to it but I cannot think where there was an opportunity for that, on the mountain at least.'

'You're assuming that Muirhouse believes what he's saying?'

'Is that relevant?' asked Zara 'He could be making it all up, like the story about his mother or he could just have that detail wrong; after all he says himself he is hypothesising.'

'Um,' said McGilroy in a voice which his team would have recognised as having a degree of positivity in it. 'And the second letter?' Zara thought hard but eventually shook her head. 'Nothing. Nothing at all,' she said.

Zara walked away from the interview wondering whether one could assume John Muirhouse knew where Ronnie Balfour was. Although there was nothing in the letters that evidenced that.

There was no letter the following day and McGilroy didn't know whether to feel disappointed or relieved. He was not sleeping well and missing his wife and children back on the mainland. When his daughter Susie phoned him early that day, at first he felt a flush of pleasure but then he heard something in her voice:

'What is it, sweetheart?'

'Daddy, someone tried to kill my rabbit in the night.' McGilroy was at once full of dread.

'Is he all right? Tell me what happened,' he said.

'Danny was going fishing. You know how he gets up really early. He opened his curtains and saw a movement by the hutch. The hutch door was open and he saw a dark hand reach forward and something glinting.'

'He didn't kill Peter though?'

'No. Danny shouted and the man jumped away and was over the hedge, running away. Danny couldn't get down quick enough. He was gone.'

'I'm glad Danny didn't get there,' said McGilroy, 'the man might have been armed'.

'He dropped his knife!' McGilroy who had been standing up to this point, sat down heavily on his hotel bed.

'Nobody's touched it?'

'Danny's got it in a polythene bag.'

'Where's your mum?'

'I'm here.' Shona had taken the phone from Susie. 'She wanted to tell you herself.' McGilroy heard his wife tell Susie to go and get dressed.

'You've phoned the local station?'

'Of course. They should be here any minute.' Pause. 'It's maybe nothing.' She wanted it to be a statement but it was more of a question.

'I'll be interested to know if we have the fingerprints already,' said McGilroy. 'Is Susie okay? I wish I'd been with you.'

'We're fine. It could have been a prank. Let's not get panicky before we have to.'

'Did Danny get any idea of what the guy — I'm presuming it was a guy — looked like?'

'Not really. It was only half light. There was cloud.'

***

It was Sergeant MacSorley who had suggested there might be a connection to the Goat Fell murder. He had noticed McGilroy looking preoccupied. This was unprecedented in the time he'd spent in Brodick. When McGilroy told him, with reluctance, what had happened MacSorley said,

'Not another message then?' and McGilroy jumped visibly.

'Surely not!' but his exclamation echoed uncertainly in his head and the more he thought about it, the more anxious he became. The rabbit incident had hit him at his weakest point and he had lost his detachment. He became convinced that John Muirhouse was the man in the garden, the man with the knife and that he was threatening McGilroy's family.

MacSorley couldn't believe the change in him. His concentration had gone to pieces and he was almost completely ineffective. At the end of the day, McGilroy said to MacSorley,

'This is ridiculous but I'm going to have to go home. I need to see them. See them with my own eyes, that they're all right.' MacSorley thought of saying that he'd been joking about the message but then he realised that he hadn't.

'I think that's a great idea. I'm sure we can hold the fort till you get back. Your team that is, of course.'

'I'll be back on the first boat,' said McGilroy to his team, 'so no slacking'.

'Of course not, sir,' replied one of the detective constables unsmiling. After the DI had gone MacSorley realised both men had been joking.

The next day McGilroy was back, much relieved. His family were treating the business calmly. Apparently there had been one of two other weird incidents involving pets in the area and the local police were of the opinion that this was another one.

Until the next day, when forensics told them that the fingerprints on the knife handle matched those of various items on the mountain which Muirhouse had come in contact with.

Chapter X   Unexpected faces

Zara had not been able to make sense of the Muirhouse letters. As far as she could see, they only provided one solid piece of information: Muirhouse was alive and active. The letters themselves could be complete lies or part lies, but not she imagined, the complete truth. But even though she told herself this, she could not help wondering, totally against her instinct, if Ronnie Balfour *had* been involved, after all.

She went over and over the evening and the night on the mountain. The fingerprints on Daffodil's neck she could account for because she'd been here and taken a part in the whole, as it seemed now, ridiculous game. Muirhouse had not been clever enough to orchestrate the incident so that it would be Ronnie's fingerprints only on Daffodil's neck. They now knew the official cause of death. There had been pressure specifically on the windpipe but the hand of the perpetrator had been gloved in plastic. This pointed to a strange degree of compliance on Daffodil's part.

The biggest problem was Ronnie's disappearance. She didn't think he was lying at the bottom of a ravine. She didn't know why. It would have been too ironic, him reading about Rose and Laurie and then ending up in a similar situation. But if you looked at it all from the outside, Ronnie's reading *Murder not Proven* could also point a finger of guilt. Or had he had an argument with Muirhouse and was Muirhouse now trying to blacken Ronnie's name to deflect the truth?

After ten minutes or so of this type of thinking, Zara would feel confused and on the edge of dizziness. Then she would think of going back to Glasgow and Barney but there was her obligation to Kirsty and George and she was really enjoying her time with them — whenever she could forget about the mountain.

However, when Barney phoned on the Thursday and said that Ben had a commitment at school which meant they would not be able to leave till Saturday morning, Zara said suddenly,

'I'll come up. I'll come up Friday lunchtime after I've done my chores and just stay twenty-four hours.' Kirsty conveniently, had a seventeen-year-old cousin staying for the weekend whom she thought she would have difficulty getting out of the house. She can stay in and help thought Zara, imagining the universe had put the cousin on Arran for her benefit.

On the boat over Zara considered what she was doing and reflected that it was the absolute opposite of what she had intended. She was not really giving herself the chance of experiencing life without Barney: why was she running back to Glasgow if he didn't mean anything to her? But that was too harsh. Of course he meant something to her: he was her best friend, but Zara was worried that if they became a partnership she would lose that. Also Ben. She had to be sure. Ben had lost one mother: she couldn't be responsible for him losing another. How often did she tell herself this?

Barney and Zara spent the late afternoon in the park waiting for the time to collect Ben. After, they were going to McDonald's — Ben's favourite — and then back to Barney's. It felt odd to Zara not to go back to her own flat but there was no point, she would just have cut down the time spent with Ben and Barney.

Ben was on a high since his team had won the competition and he was loth to sit down in the restaurant for any length of time. When he had finished eating he went and stood by the window hopping up and down, looking at the cars and the people.

'I've seen two lemon-coloured cars, one man in a pink turban, two women in long black clothes down to the ground and a man with eleven plastic bags — I don't think he'd just been to Asda.' He waited for a response.

'You don't often see even one lemon-coloured car,' Barney got up and walked over to him. Zara was still finishing her food and looking down when someone tapped her on the shoulder. She turned and found she was looking into the face of John Muirhouse.

'Been on the *Waverley* recently then?' He was crouching beside her now and she could see those even teeth though his eyes were not managing to smile.

Zara hesitated a moment too long. She should ring the police but she was thinking of Ben. She did not want to catapult him into a violent scene or even one requiring too many questions asked. Worst a scene where it might become evident that she and Ben were connected. In that moment John Muirhouse read her mind.

'I won't forget that ice cream we shared,' he said.' He rose to his feet and walked swiftly to the door. Zara's fingers found 999 but she knew it would be too late unless by some miracle there were a couple of officers just perambulating in the immediate vicinity.

'I've just sighted John Muirhouse'.

'What?'

'He's wanted in connection with the murder on Goat Fell, Arran.'

'What? My name? You're going to lose him. He was in McDonald's on Sauchiehall Street. He's walking west at this moment.' Zara was on her feet and half out of the door. 'He's tall, wearing a green cap. Black sweatshirt. Black trousers. Not jeans. Trainers.' This was taking for ever. She wished she'd phoned Arran. At least they'd have understood her. 'I'll be back in a minute. I've just seen someone I know,' she called to Barney. Barney did not look pleased but Zara was away before he could respond.

Zara could still see the green cap ahead of her and she began to run, dodging through the Friday crowds. She followed it all the way down the street to the lights at Charing Cross. Where was it? She looked all ways, panicking. Then she saw it to her left and saw a hand reach up and whip it off and into a pocket. She stayed back. There were less people here but John Muirhouse did not turn round. She watched him cross Bath Street and disappear into the train station. 'Yes, I'm still here. He's gone into Charing Cross station. No cap now.'

***

Barney was not in the best of moods when she returned but he said nothing about where she'd been beyond,

'Manage to catch up with them then?'

'Sort of,' said Zara, making a not-now-later gesture with her head behind Ben's back. Zara began to feel depressed and when Barney started laughing and joking with Ben she found it hard to match their mood. She knew

Barney was covering up his curiosity. The joking continued all the way back home. Zara remained quiet.

While Barney was saying goodnight to Ben, Zara rang the Arran police. Sergeant MacSorley answered.

'I wondered if they caught John Muirhouse,' Zara began.

'They stopped the next four trains either way but he wasn't on any of them.'

'Doubled back then,' said Zara. She found her hand was trembling: talking about it made her realise the horrible reality that John Muirhouse had discovered her in the middle of Glasgow. Did that mean he knew about Barney and Ben? She re-connected to the sergeant's voice:

'Must've. Unless of course he suddenly got a lot shorter or put on a blue cap.' Zara didn't remember MacSorley having a sense of humour.

'Oh well,' she said, 'it was him. He came and spoke to me!'

'I daresay there will be another letter in the post,' said MacSorley.

***

Barney came back into the living room and accepted the glass of wine Zara had poured for him. They sat together on the sofa and a not entirely relaxed silence ensued.

'Have you got something on your mind?' asked Zara at last.

'I don't know if you will believe this but I was going to ask you...' said Barney, '...to ask you if you would be willing to think seriously about making our relationship permanent but' — he held up his hand as Zara was about to interrupt — 'I've decided not to.'

'Why is that?'

'It was when you went out after that... person.'

'But you know who it was!'

'Of course I know who it was!'

'I didn't want to involve Ben.'

'Okay but Zara it was just another example of how you jump headfirst into situations. You just don't think about the danger. Muirhouse must have followed you. That means there is a good chance he knows there is a connection between me and you and, worse, between me, you and Ben. 'Zara nodded, not trusting her voice. 'I've decided,' Barney went on, 'that I can't live with someone who is so willing to sacrifice her own safety and possibly the safety or at least the well-being of other close family members.'

'I'm sorry you feel that way,' said Zara, 'but I'm not at all certain I would have said "yes".' Barney did not flinch.

'Well that's good news,' he answered. 'No broken hearts then.'

'You're such a friend Barney. I don't ever want to lose you.'

'Don't worry, Zara, you won't. I'll always be there for you. I'll always love you.'

'I'm sorry Barney. I know I'm impossible but you know I'd do anything for you and Ben.'

'Everything except,' said Barney. 'Another glass of wine?'

Because they both wanted to feel at ease it was not long before they had both slipped into their usual way of being with each other.

'What did the guy Muirhouse say to you?' asked Barney, giving Zara permission to talk about the incident in McDonald's.

'He mentioned the Waverley expedition and sharing ice cream. I could have thrown up. It felt as if he were imagining we'd actually shared the same ice cream!' Barney reflected her disgusted expression. 'But the strange thing is,' Zara went on, 'he didn't mention the mountain. It was as if he didn't remember I'd been there.'

'Or he wanted you to forget,' said Barney. 'Or he has a mental condition where he forgets what he's done.'

'Don't think so,' said Zara. 'There was something arrogant and jeering about him, the way he crouched down. It was like catch-me-if-you-can but as soon as he saw I was thinking "police" he just melted away.'

'Some people are good at Houdini,' said Barney.

'It makes me doubly certain it was him that did it.'

'And not Ronnie?'

'You don't think it was Ronnie do you?'

'I don't know Ronnie.'

'Neither do I,' said Zara.

'But where is Ronnie?' asked Barney.

'Where indeed?' said Zara. 'It's as if there is a hole in the middle of this case, an exasperating hole — with Ronnie in it.'

'Loads of people go missing every year,' said Barney.

'You're not suggesting it has nothing to do with what happened on the mountain?' Barney was silent for a moment, then he said,

'It's a bit like when you lose something: the answer is either very simple or very complex. If it's complex you find the object after a year at the bottom of the clothes basket or under a very large pile of newspapers.'

'And you think that's where we'll find Ronnie?'

'That's not funny, Zara,' said Barney, trying not to smile.

***

When Zara returned to Arran the next day she was surprised by a phone call almost as soon as she walked in the door.

'Des!' she shouted. 'To what do I owe this? I've assaulted nobody. My record's clean.'

'Hang on, Zara. This is a serious call. I'm now in charge of the new Goat Fell case or Goat Fell Twice as the operation has been named.' Zara groaned silently: knowing a D.I. could often be useful, as she had found when she had been investigating the criminal machinations of Malloch in Glasgow last year but Des would not want her having anything to do with this present case, *his* case it would be from now on.

'But what about McGilroy?'

'He's off the case. Woke up yesterday with a blinding migraine. Couldn't stand. He'd been frightened by a rabbit. Or rather, someone trying to kill his daughter's rabbit. Fingerprints on the knife left behind turned out to be —'

'Muirhouse's?

'Sadly, yes but I think that was just the proverbial straw. Good man. Too much stress. If he takes a break now, he's more chance of coming back.'

'I can't believe you're on the case,' said Zara. 'Just my luck.'

'That might well be, petal. With me on it, you won't need to do a thing. Just enjoy the summer. Keep the bathrooms clean.' Des had a not very subtle way of irritating Zara and though she knew it was deliberate she could not help rising to it.

'So what's new?' she said. 'Warning me off your patch from the get-go. You'll come crawling when everything begins to look cold. You'll find you can't get along without my razor-sharp brain. Who ran Malloch to ground? Who was instrumental in getting Jack Deakin charged? Not you,' said Zara. Not DI Des.'

'Okay, Zara. Let's be serious for a moment. I was actually calling you in regard to the evidence. I want you to come to the station. And give us a proper account of what happened yesterday when you met John Muirhouse.' Zara almost slammed the phone down. It only took her a moment to realize why she was so annoyed: faced with opposition she knew she wanted the liberty to pursue the case. She hadn't consciously made up her mind to do this but the more Des took control, the more she felt she did not want to be left out. She knew she'd come to Arran to forget about being an investigative journalist for a while but she was itching to do something, find something out that was new. I'll give it a week she thought and then review the situation, remembering for once, Barney's words about her rushing into things on an impulse. I'll wait for a sign, something that tells me it's important I'm involved.

Des listened carefully to Zara's account of the encounter with John Muirhouse. She was brief during the interview and behaved as if she hardly knew Des but she did start the exchange with 'How's Pam? And how's the baby... Lallabelle is it?'

'Lalage,' said Des.

'I knew it was something with a tune in it,' said Zara.

'Thanks,' said Des, when she had said everything she could remember. 'You've been most helpful. Now if you don't mind casting your eyes over this,' and he slapped down two sheets of paper. Zara could tell at a glance it was another letter from John Muirhouse.

'Oh my God,' said Zara, 'the Daily Racket', but she could not deny her interest. John Muirhouse had changed his handwriting yet again. Why thought Zara. He's signing his name. Maybe it's all a game to him. Maybe the next one will be written in orange juice.

'Dear CID', the letter ran,

'You will be glad to hear that I'm about to write to my MP about stepping up numbers in the police force. There I was, as large as life in the middle of town. I WALK to a station and AM I caught? Well you know I wasn't caught obviously.

That woman. Is she an informer? She's obviously not a cop. You've no idea how safe I feel. Not that I have any need to fear. I'm not the guilty one. All you have to do is give me an assurance I'm not going to be charged and I'll tell you where the murderer is. Come to my mother's house and give her the message. Obviously I'm not going to appear in person. Better still, what about a written assurance signed by the officer directing the team? Go on. How about it? You're going to have to do something. Stalemate, that's what you have now.

You've only got so long though. Sorry but that's the way it always goes. If you don't come to me, I may leave for North Africa or Thailand. And then what will happen? You will never be able to solve the mystery.' Zara looked up.

'Does that imply,' she pointed, that he knows where Ronnie is? And if he knows, does Ronnie know he knows?'

'Good question,' said Des but in a tone which told her he wasn't going to start discussing that point with her. She continued reading:

'Just do this and we'll be able to wrap up the whole thing. Don't you want to see the headline: It was Ronnie Balfour — murderer confesses his part in heinous crime? Or abominable crime if you like.' Zara shook her head as she came to the end and the inevitable 'Yours sincerely'.

'So, are you going?'

'Haven't decided yet,' said Des. 'Is there anything there that links with anything he said on the mountain?'

'McGilroy asked me the same question regarding the first two letters. No. No comment. Except, he uses the word 'obviously' too much, obviously.'

'He never mentioned North Africa or Thailand to you on the mountain or on the *Waverley*?'

'Nope.'

'Do you think any of what he says is true?'

'Yes, no, I don't know,' said Zara. 'I think this interview is over. Can I get back to my cleaning now?'

Walking back to the hotel, Zara thought hard about what she had said to Des, going over the Muirhouse letter in her mind and also her encounter with the man in Glasgow. She did wonder how Muirhouse had happened to be at McDonald's. Had Muirhouse known she was in Glasgow? Had he got someone shadowing her on Arran? She must become more aware.

Zara went back further and started thinking about Ronnie Balfour and John Muirhouse. A sentence came back to her: you decided you were up for it then? — Ronnie to John Muirhouse. Zara was not sure she was quoting Ronnie verbatim. In her mind the subtext had merely been that they'd met the previous night in the pub, talked about going up Goat Fell and well, well, here we are but what if, she wondered now, the remark had been a code and the two men really were well-acquainted. She went back over all the conversations.

On the premise they were in it together Zara thought to herself, where is the supporting evidence? She cast her mind back to the sausage fry. John Smith, as he was then, had entertained the rest of them with various tales which seen in retrospect were probably false. He had not at any time behaved as if he knew Ronnie.

But what about later, the shriek in the night? Zara had at first thought it was a bird. Supposing it had been John Smith imitating a bird as a signal to Ronnie? Maybe if Daffie had not made the cry but was just awake, the shriek had been a gambit for the two men to get together and discuss what they were going to do. Ronnie had suggested too that Zara should go back to the tent. Could it have been set up so she would assume the whole meeting innocent, a bland encounter in the night, forgotten in the morning?

The second shriek, the one Zara thought she had imagined to be part of a bad dream, that one could have been real. That could have been Daffie. What would have happened she wondered if she had responded that second time?

Zara turned round and started walking back to the police station. She found Des sitting in the same chair in the same position. She blurted out what she had just surmised, not caring whether he thought she was exaggerating.

On the contrary he was at once very interested.

'I was coming to the conclusion just before you walked in that I needed to start from scratch and go over everything myself. I was going to ask you to revisit the location...' Zara nodded before she thought. Then she sighed.

'I don't know how I'll be but you're right, you do probably need to start again.'

'DC Smyth and DC Poulson will accompany us. They came down with me as part of the team.' He stood up. 'Tomorrow. Weather permitting. And we'll leave at the time you left and stop where you stopped but we won't spend the night on the mountain.' He looked at her sideways as if to say, 'In case you were wondering'.

***

That night, after everything was washed up and put away in the kitchen —
there had been eight folk in for dinner — Zara sat with Kirsty and George
and a bottle of red wine. Although her friends did not have the bad taste to
make anything of it, the hotel had done handsomely out of the alleged
murder. Kirsty and George might not like it but they could hardly close the
doors; it was their bread and butter and, though time had past, there had
been no diminution of customers, especially when John Muirhouse's room
was freed from police tape. One family had photographed each member in
the John Muirhouse bed.

'Were these his sheets?' asked the granny. Kirsty was unsure whether the
woman wanted a 'yes' or a 'no' answer.

Zara had feared that George might be distressed and it might hinder his
recovery but if anything he seemed more alive, more like his old self. He'd
been going riding on Riga every morning along the forestry tracks and
coming back with a better appetite. When Zara told him about the
proposed reconstruction of the recent Goat Fell murder he was envious.

'Wish I could come,' he said. 'I do miss the mountains. It's different up
there; things seem simpler.'

'Hm', said Zara. 'Let's hope that's how they'll appear tomorrow. We could
do with some "simple".'

'Are you sure you're fit to go?' asked Kirsty.

'Fine,' said Zara. 'And it's not as if I'm going with a stranger!'

Chapter 11   No stone unturned

Zara even took rolls with the same filling. Des had impressed on her he wanted as much fact as possible; he wanted her almost to re-live the experience. Although she thought she had remembered everything, Des told her she would find that retracing her footsteps brought up things she'd forgotten.

They stopped at the bridge where she and Ronnie had had their break. Zara sat where she'd sat and Des sat in Ronnie's place. They'd eaten, DC Smyth and DC Poulson sitting on the bridge, their feet dangling.

'Nobody's passed us today,' said Zara casually.

'Somebody passed you?' Des was straight on to it.

'Three people,' said Zara 'they said something about the weather and... I remember... they asked where the next picnic place was and Ronnie said it was half a mile away and I added, 'By the burger stall.' Smith and Poulson were scribbling notes.

'Did they have accents? Scottish?'

'Yorkshire, I think.'

'D' you know, no one's come forward to say they saw anyone on the mountain. I wonder if we can track these walkers down.'

'We saw them at the top,' said Zara. 'They were climbing the last bit with Muirhouse and Daffodil. They were there to scatter their mother's ashes.'

'Right,' said Des. 'And did they go back down the way they'd come?'

'I don't know,' said Zara. A pause. 'I thought at the time the path was not very busy. I'm sure no one followed us the way we took.' The two DC's stopped writing.

'This is good,' said Des. 'You're remembering things. It's odd what jogs the memory.' Zara rose and looked round for her hat.

'Hat,' she said and told Des about the conversation regarding Rose's hat and the mystery surrounding it. 'We did an experiment,' she said.

'You did what?' said Smyth and Poulson simultaneously.

'I anchored Ronnie's hat under a stone and he very nearly forgot it.'

'So Ronnie Balfour was very interested in the first Goat Fell murder,' said Des.

'He was going to show me the gully; that was part of the trip...' As Zara said the words she was aware suddenly of a possible double meaning. Des shook his head.

'I know,' he said. 'You said that in your statement.'

'You don't think...?'

'...he was going to do you in as well? Who knows? Let's stick to what did happen.'

When they reached the shoulder, Des made everyone stop. He wanted to re-play the meeting between Ronnie Balfour and John Muirhouse. Zara told him where everyone had stood. DC Megan Smyth and DC Bryan Poulson became Daffodil Brown and John Muirhouse. Des was Ronnie and Zara was Zara. She gave them the script as far as she could remember and Des asked her concentrate on recalling inflections in the voices of the two men and their body language.

You decided you were up for it then?' asked Des the actor.

'No' said Zara. 'He was neutral, he didn't sound glad or sorry.'

'So that would fit either a coded message or possibly polite displeasure at Muirhouse's appearance. And Daffodil, can you remember how she looked? Pleased or not pleased to see you? Indifferent?' Zara thought. DS Megan was standing with her head bowed.

'Like that,' said Zara. 'She was quite passive. From the start I felt protective'. Zara suddenly sat down on a boulder. 'Sorry I just remembered she's dead.'

'Okay, Zara. Just rest for as long as it takes. You're doing really well. This is useful. You've no idea.'

Zara was impressed. Her encounters with Des had been many, both social and in the course of what she called her work but which he usually claimed as his. She had never seen him actually engaged in a case. This was a new-age Des with a gently-gently demeanour.

'I would say,' said Zara at last, 'she was totally out of her depth.'

'Right,' said Des. 'Reply, Muirhouse.'

'Yes, we've made good time. Remembered you'd said you were starting at eleven.'

'No,' said Zara. 'He was actually a lot more stilted. Looking back, I don't think he was as calm as he seemed.'

'Explain if you can.'

'That business when something that was only in your head breaks into reality. There was Ronnie. Imagine it if he were part of a plan how you would feel.' Des looked as if he were going to demur but then decided against it.

'You're saying he was thrown by the reality of your presence?'

'Exactly.'

'And Daffodil?' DS Megan looked up when Muirhouse spoke. 'Was that how it was?'

'I see her looking up,' said Zara, 'and you have to remember his height here: she really had to look up. I think I would say her expression was half fear and half admiration. I'd hate to say John Muirhouse had charisma but he certainly has power of some sort.' Des nodded in acknowledgement.

'Anything else you can recall about that particular encounter?'

'Only that the way Ronnie introduced me to Muirhouse and Daffie was quite... natural but the way Ronnie said to Daffodil, "What are you doing here?" sounded like he'd met her before and not just in the pub the night before.'

The day went on, Smyth and Poulson took notes and occasionally, when they weren't acting being Muirhouse and Daffodil, spoke in unison. For Zara it was both stimulating and tiring and when they reached the gully and the rock shelter she was still alert but her body was giving her signs of exhaustion.

Des couldn't help scrutinizing the ground though he knew a thorough search had been made previously. There seemed to be no signs of occupation and no signs that anyone had searched either. The mountains were bare and when the sun was masked by cloud as it increasingly seemed to be, a level of greyness pervaded the scene, hard as the rocks and as silent as the air at dawn.

'It's as if the whole place is gloating,' said Zara, wishing she didn't have to share her chocolate between so many people. 'It knows what happened in 1889 and it knows what happened the other week.'

Smyth and Poulson each took four squares, Des took five. It's just the way it broke,' he said not very apologetically. Then he asked the two DC's to go down into the gully and turn a hawk's eye on the boulder its surroundings and the corrie where Rose was found.

'Just let's not leave any stone unturned, so to speak,' he said to them.

Smyth and Poulson disappeared from sight looking for the best way down. Des continued to scan the ground and the rocks near to where Muirhouse and Daffodil had slept. His face had gone dark with an intensity which might have been frightening had Zara not recognized it as concentration. She sat on a rock and thought. She wondered if she sat long enough an answer would come to her. It still troubled her, the implication that Ronnie had taken part in the crime. She was very reluctant to believe it. There was a shout and both Zara and Des scrambled to look over the edge of the gully.

'We've found some jewellery,' said Smyth.

'Jewellery,' said Poulson a verbal step behind. They were holding something up, carefully. Zara could see Poulson had plastic gloves on. A serious product then.

'It was under a stone inside the corrie,' said Smyth when Zara and Des had climbed down to them.

'We were lifting stones in turn,' said Poulson. Smyth: 'not expecting to find anything.' Poulson: 'but under the twenty-fourth stone, we found these.'

Smyth; 'They may be from before of course.' Poulson laid the transparent bag on a rock. Zara looked and felt sick. Two pendants, one a medallion, the other a heart.

'Ronnie was wearing that,' she said pointing at the medallion. Des turned the bag over to reveal the other side. Somehow the heart had become entangled so it was only possible to see an 'R'. The two pieces would not come apart. It was as if they had been hammered together.

'Balfour then,' muttered Des. Zara looked back at him:

'I shall not believe that,' she said.

'Looks a bit ritualistic to me sir,' said Poulson.

'Me too sir,' said Smyth.

'He didn't do it,' Zara insisted. She moved away. The gully was a noxious place. Maybe there had been a battle fought there centuries ago and the feeling of death had lingered in the corrie. It felt so palpable to her. She could not believe that Laurie had manhandled Rose into such a confined space and piled up stones behind him. It was the act of a mad man. She looked around at the unforgiving rocks and saw the boulder on which Daffodil had ended her life — or so she supposed. Muirhouse had chosen this place. The reason had to be ghoulish. It was difficult to comprehend the mind-set of such a person.

On the way down, Zara talked to DC Megan who sounded quite sensible when she was disengaged from Poulson. Zara hardly spoke to Des. He was so obviously pleased with the day. Apart from the reconstructions having improved his take on Balfour and Muirhouse, she could see that he thought the heart/medallion find was a big coup. She was glad he wasn't talking to her about it. The idea that he had fixated on Ronnie being involved made Zara more certain of the opposite. It wasn't to do with her relationship with Des which was always fraught with contradictions; it was a gut feeling. She thought of Ronnie's parents. No. Their son could not have done that.

Then she thought of other murders where the parents had seemed incapable of producing people who could do such things. She knew she was on sticky ground. However, she could not shift her feeling that she was right.

'Well,' said Des when they had reached the road and the car. 'I don't think we'll be needing your help any further, Zara. Thank you for today. That will be all, unless the DC's have any problems with their notes.'

Chapter XII   Another stone to turn

For Zara the day had been a watershed and she began to look at the whole incident in an entirely different light. Because Des now believed Ronnie to be guilty or at least involved, she felt an overwhelming need to prove him wrong. She spent a lot of time imagining herself into the intricacies of Muirhouse's mind. Having put his profile together, she began to work on the various possibilities of what had happened after Daffie had met her end. She wrote down all the actions she thought Muirhouse could possibly have taken. She knew she had to prove either that Muirhouse was guilty or that Ronnie Balfour was innocent. She began with Muirhouse because of the letters. That there had been a sign of life from him meant that potentially there was something to follow.

She decided she would go and visit his mother in Govanhill. She was not hard to find — a phone number and an address in 192.com. Perhaps she had no reason to hide.

Zara went over midweek on the first boat. She was not going to see Barney or Ben: she was on business and would be back, all being well by four. It was quiet for once at the hotel and Kirsty was happy for her to go though she thought Zara was getting away from the situation instead of going towards it. Zara had been economic with the truth.

She was wearing her investigative journalist's hat and had no qualms about ringing Mrs Muirhouse's bell. It was something she was good at, making people feel she was to be trusted.

Even so, she had taken the precaution of going home and putting on, not exactly a disguise but a set of clothes totally different from those she had been wearing on Arran. She wore heeled boots to alter her height, a suit jacket and she piled her hair up catching it in a comb. Unremarkable black trousers completed her outfit. She went on the bus and left it a stop before Muirhouse's street. She wasn't sure who would be interested but she didn't want to leave a trail. She told herself she would be unlucky to meet Muirhouse, but if she did, she could always run. It was a risk she was prepared to take, though she could think of at least two people who would disapprove.

Mrs Muirhouse answered at the first ring but that was because she had been standing behind her door not because she was nimble.

'Have you come about my John?' she asked, taking in Zara at a glance as someone who was not a social caller.

'I was wondering if you knew where he was,' said Zara, having introduced herself as Susan McFarlane. She stepped into the room in response to the woman's welcoming gesture.

'I've just made tea. Wait a minute.' She plumped a cushion unnecessarily and disappeared into the kitchen. Zara sat down and took in the walls covered in photographs mostly of dogs and children but one or two of the son, John, as a youth, and one of Mrs Muirhouse with a man who did not look at all like John. 'That's my first husband,' she said coming back with two mugs of tea. 'I put in milk but no sugar.'

'Well guessed, thank you,' said Zara. Mrs Muirhouse sat down opposite her and took half a packet of chocolate biscuits from her apron pocket.

'And I daresay you won't say no to a biscuit.' Zara took one. 'And don't worry about crumbs: the Hoover's called Cherry.'

At the sound of her name, a very well-brushed mongrel bounced into the room, came and inspected Zara and then sat down obediently by her mistress's chair.

'I am John's real mother,' said Mrs Muirhouse, 'but I have other children in Australia where my first husband died. I came back to look after my old father. Then I met Muirhouse.' She paused: 'Then there was John and then his sister Robina who died. Muirhouse talked to the dog. He couldn't really talk to people. That's why he married me. He loved the children but he couldn't talk to them. Have another biscuit.' Zara wondered why Mrs Muirhouse was giving her life story unsolicited and in such an incoherent way but she let the woman run on, say what she had to say. 'Who do you think did the murder?' was not the easiest question to broach.

After an image by image tour of the photographs, Mrs Muirhouse settled back in her chair.

'He didn't do it if that's what you're thinking. It was the other fella and John is trying to convince him to plead guilty.'

'Have you been in touch with the police about this?' asked Zara

'John said not to. It would jeopardize the work he was doing,' he said. 'Are you from the papers?'

'I work for the *Evening Times*,' lied Zara.

'We had someone from there the other day,' said Mrs Muirhouse. 'Nice young man it was with almost no hair. I asked him if his head didn't get cold in winter. I offered him a knitted hat I made for my first husband. Muirhouse wouldn't have been seen dead in a hat.'

'Did the man John was trying to help come here?' asked Zara.

'Two nights. He was ill John said. I didn't see him. John said it was best and, to tell you the truth I didn't want to. In fact, I didn't have a choice. John told me about it afterwards. I just heard him helping someone up the stairs. I thought it must be a drunk woman. Not that I hold with drunk women on the premises but John just acts first and then... it's too late. How am I meant to stop him with my arthritis?' Zara nodded.

'I don't know where either of them is at the moment. I said to him, "Don't be going to Arran now, not if you were on the mountain that day. You don't want to get dragged in." The police came round once looking for him but he hadn't been back at that time so I couldn't help them.'

'So from what John said, did you assume he'd been a witness?' asked Zara, thinking of the letters.

'Must've been. Unless Ronnie Balfour made a confession.'

'How did you feel when you knew an alleged murderer had been in your house?' asked Zara, trying to sound like a popular reporter. There was a pause while Mrs Muirhouse digested the question and then she said,

'Well it wasn't really any different from having your granny to stay: you've still got sheets to wash. Muirhouse would have blown a gasket but he's no longer with us, is he Cherry?' The dog did not answer. 'Yes, Muirhouse would not have been at all pleased.'

'So you imagine John is somewhere in Glasgow with Ronnie Balfour?'

'I don't have much time for imagining. It's nothing to do with me. John says not to worry, he'll deal with it, so I'll just wait. I would rather it was all over though.' For the first time Zara sensed a crack in Mrs Muirhouse's defences.

'You'd rather what was all over?' she asked.

'He's started talking about Rose and Laurie again. All those press-cuttings his grandfather passed onto to his dad. What a thing to leave someone! And so then John became fascinated. He got them all out that night he was back. One day I'm going to spring-clean them all into the bin.' She shook her head and looked intently at John Muirhouse senior's photo on the wall.

'What was it that fascinated him?' asked Zara, not sure whether Mrs Muirhouse was wishing to go into details.

'What happens,' she said at once, 'is, he likes to go through his own version of the event. He'll talk as if it happened yesterday. In his mind there is no doubt. Rose — but at that moment the phone rang. Zara sat nervously hoping it was not John Muirhouse. Strangely Mrs Muirhouse did not stir. After the fourth ring the phone stopped.

'That's John phoning from the bus. It means he's on his way here. You'll be able to talk to him after all.' Zara rose to her feet.

'I'm afraid I won't unfortunately, Mrs Muirhouse. 'I've been entertained too long already and I'm meant to be somewhere else in about ten minutes. But if there something he wants to say to me, here's my number,' and she gave Mrs Muirhouse a card with Susan McFarlane written on it and a mobile number underneath. If John Muirhouse was told someone called Susan McFarlane had been there he might just accept it and think less about the identity of the person than if it were a nameless stranger who had to be described.

'Well if you're sure,' said Mrs Muirhouse obviously disappointed at not having an interesting new body to offer her son, instead of a description of a conversation where the visitor had in the event not said very much.

Zara eased herself out of the house as quickly as she could without appearing to hurry. It would of course have been extremely exciting to attempt to pass John Muirhouse in the street. After all he wasn't expecting to see her. But the risk was too great. She had done well and she did not want to jeopardize the information she had. She might even need to go back to the house at a later date.

If he were getting off a bus he would be the opposite side of the road. She kept walking, alert. She had put on a pair of sun-glasses as a precaution and walked as slowly as she could make herself. Suppose she did see him and he her: she would have to bluff it out. She realised now, suddenly, what a huge risk she had taken in deciding to visit Mrs Muirhouse. She almost stopped. This was what Barney complained of: her terrible impulsiveness. Where had she imagined Muirhouse was? She did stop this time and turned to look in a shop window so she could think without moving.

It was in that moment John Muirhouse passed her by within inches of her back, but neither one saw the other.

Chapter XIII   Problematic men

On the train to Ardrossan, Zara sat in a two-seater and put her bag on the seat beside her. Before the train even started, she had taken out her notebook and written down everything she could remember about John Muirhouse, his mother and the rest of the family. Then she studied what she had got.

First, fairly certain evidence that Ronnie Balfour was alive. She realised though, that she had never believed he was dead. This fact threw up the question, where was he now? Zara did not think he was at the Muirhouse's. It might have been an emergency stop-off place but it was too vulnerable to a police search for anything longer term. Where then? If Muirhouse had a car, he might have a garage though it seemed unlikely. Did he have a relative with a garage, a workshop or an allotment with a shed? It seemed to Zara it was relatively difficult to hide a whole live person even in a big city. A corpse was a different matter: you didn't have to revisit it. Zara thought Muirhouse wanted Ronnie alive but she didn't understand why. If she was right, he had to have somewhere where he could check on him, take him food. But a place where Muirhouse's own movements wouldn't be noticed. Possible if you had a trusty mate or even someone who owed you but Zara was willing to bet Muirhouse had neither.

So if not in Glasgow, where? The field was wide. It didn't seem possible, even if he had found somewhere, that he would be able to use it for very long and if you had to move your victim about, eventually even a John Muirhouse would tire. Also, he had said to the police,' Just give me a reassurance that I won't be charged and I'll hand him over to you.' He wanted to hand the guy over. But where would that get him? And was that just a bluff? Was he just buying time when he offered these options? Zara had the feeling there was something she was not grasping here but it was fleeting and she moved on.

What didn't seem to make sense was how the emphasis had shifted from Daffie to Ronnie Balfour. It was as if Daffie didn't count, as if the focus had never been on her. But if Ronnie had been involved, Muirhouse could not have made a fool-proof plan, one he could entirely control. Was that what had happened — a series of random incidents which now Muirhouse had to make appear rational? And, above all, his idea?

***

Walking along the front at Brodick, Zara suddenly heard a car hoot. Des. He stopped beside her.

'Want a ride?'

'Not really,' said Zara getting in. She looked out of the window so he didn't see her face.

'Been up shopping?'

'Aye,' said Zara in a tone that meant 'No and it's no business of yours'.

'What have you been up to then?' asked Des, unperturbed. Zara realised that of course she would have to tell Des what had happened, where she had been. She was furious with herself for not having thought this through.

'Do you have a working kettle at the station?' she said. Des tried not to smile, just drove till they were stopped outside.

Zara decided to tell the bare facts and then see what happened. DC Megan was sitting in.

'Note down anything interesting,' Des said to her. 'Shoot,' he said to Zara.

'Ronnie Balfour spent one night, if not two at the Muirhouse's in Govanhill.'

'How do you know?'

'I spoke to his mother.'

'You went to the house?' Des's eyes had gone very narrow.

'I went to the house.'

'Just knocked on the door as if you were selling insurance?'

'Oh come on Des, I was a journalist from the *Evening Times*. She was pleased. I reckon she doesn't see many people in a day.'

'And?'

'Well, Mrs M. didn't see Ronnie, if it was Ronnie, because he came into the house at night and was bundled up the stair.'

'They weren't...?'

'I didn't get any sense of anything like that. Just that this guy needed a bed. He's not there now. She said she'd told John not to go back to Arran. Not to go getting mixed up with all that, meaning the murder.'

'So you didn't see him, Muirhouse?'

'No but he phoned while I was there, just four rings. She said it was his code. I left then. Didn't

see him on my way back to the bus.'

'Thank God for that!' said Des. 'And two things, Zara. One it would have been helpful if you'd phoned immediately to alert us that Muirhouse was heading home and two, an official warning: just stay out of this.'

'Sorry sir. Slipped my mind. Useful info though, sir?'

'Why Zara, why are you getting involved? I know you were there at the time but this is something else. We are dealing with two violent men and a particularly gruesome death. Have you no sense of looking after your own safety?'

'You may be looking for two men but only one of them is a murderer. Ronnie Balfour had nothing to do with it.'

'That's not how the evidence reads to date.'

'If you're talking about the heart and the medallion, they prove nothing,' said Zara, her voice rising despite the expression of DC Megan who looked as though she thought she might soon have to break up a fight.

***

Back at the hotel, Zara was so quiet Kirsty immediately thought something was wrong.

'I'm just tired,' said Zara. 'I think I'll have an early night.'

'Did you see Barney?'

'He was working.'

'Oh of course,' said Kirsty looking unconvinced. 'Buy anything nice?'

'There was nothing in the shops,' said Zara smiling. 'I bought a new notebook from the pound shop.'

George came in from seeing Riga.

'See Barney then?'

'No,' said Zara.

'Sorry, was that a bad question?' Zara shrugged.

After dinner that evening she sat with them in the kitchen. Zara usually enjoyed this time, chewing the day over, making each other laugh but sometimes Kirsty would use the time to bring things up.

'I know the mountain business is still upsetting you but... can I ask... are you feeling really bad about Barney?' Zara frowned.

'No,' she said at once. 'We're still the best of friends. It's just the marrying business.' Kirsty looked at her. 'What can I say?' said Zara. Kirsty went on looking at her friend and Zara knew she had to tell her what had happened. Otherwise it wasn't the friendship she'd made long ago, when they were at school.

'Shall I go?' said George as Zara let out a long breath.

'Don't be silly George,' said Zara. 'It's nothing that *you* can't hear. It's just that Barney made me an... an un-proposal of marriage and... I accepted.' She shut her eyes.

'A what?' asked Kirsty, cautious. 'An un-proposal?'

'He said he wanted to make it clear that though he loves me and had thought we would marry that he has decided he can't because I would never put family first. I would always be haring off on some mad exploit endangering myself and probably those close to me. We agreed. That's all.' Zara opened her eyes again but could not meet Kirsty's. There was a grim silence.

'I'm sorry,' said Kirsty. George leant forward and patted her arm.

'Poor old you,' he said.

'I can't,' said Zara, 'guarantee I'm not ever going to get involved with things. Life isn't like that. Look at last year. Did I find Ivory's bone by the river? Did I fabricate the connection between Ivory and McKelvie Buildings? I was just doing a journalistic investigation. Same with the Jack Deakin affair. Things come to me. My life's no more in danger than a police officer's but because I'm working for myself I have to take the responsibility and the blame.'

'You can see where Barney's coming from though,' said Kirsty.

'Of course,' said Zara. 'I don't want to hurt anyone. It's not as if I'm going off to climb K2. At least I'm usually doing something that I believe will benefit someone other than myself.'

'But Barney's said "No"?' said Kirsty.

'Barney's said "No",' echoed Zara.

'Would you like to come with me to see if Riga's okay?' George knew Riga was okay but he always went out about this time to have a chat with her.

'Yes, George, I would like that.'

***

Zara could not get to sleep. Disconnected thoughts roamed through her head — mountain, Barney, Ronnie, Ben, Arran, Glasgow, Muirhouse — but Zara could make no sense of them. In the end she reached for the light and grabbed the notebook that was always by her bed.

'What do I need?' she wrote in capitals and then stared at the blank page before her. Much as she enjoyed working with Kirsty and George, it did nothing for her mind and if she were to let go of the Goat Fell murder — not that she'd made her mind up one way or another — she would need some challenging occupation to keep her mind off it. Maybe that was the way through: turn her back on it and see if it went away. She had after all come down to Arran to avoid stressful things. Trying to find Ronnie Balfour was about the most stressful thing she could think of. A matter of life or death. Was it possible to let it go?

She sighed and stared at the blank page again. Words she thought. Obvious. I'll do a series of articles about Arran for the *Evening Times.* Weegee on Arran type thing. I'll work on a proposal tomorrow and phone them.

Having subdued her thoughts, Zara was able to focus on one thing at a time and fell asleep wondering about Ronnie Balfour. Her dialogue with Des had highlighted for her just how differently they were thinking about the case. It seemed to Zara she had to find Ronnie before Des did. She could not fathom what John Muirhouse's game was but she knew it would not be in Ronnie's interest.

In the middle of the night she woke up and was convinced Barney was in the room. He seemed to be hovering by the door. She tried to call out to him to come to her but he refused. She knew it was because of Ben. Then he said, 'When will you ever understand?' and disappeared. Zara sat up and looked hard at the door of the little attic. Slowly she came to and reality seeped into her consciousness. She pulled her duvet over her head and felt very alone.

Chapter XIV   An unlikely protagonist

In the morning, despite her idea about the Arran articles, she decided she needed a day or two to let things settle in her mind but, because of her idea, she was able to think of being a model chambermaid and waitress, to be able to explain to people where the best beaches were and why there were no fish in the sea. She quite liked making wash hand basins sparkle and bed covers absolutely smooth. She could do without the toilets though: they were just something to be suffered.

In the kitchen Kirsty was decorating a chocolate cake and Zara could smell that there were scones in the oven. People were still coming in occasionally for morning coffee and afternoon tea, post the Goat Fell murder. For some reason no one seemed to know that Zara had been the 'other woman' on the mountain so she was quite entertained by the surmisings of visitors who had their own ideas about what had happened and what should have been done.

'The woman heard a terrible scream,' a lady had said to Zara the previous week. 'If it had been me I would have gone to investigate. Wouldn't you?'

'No I wouldn't've,' said Zara, purposely giving the lady the smallest piece of cake she could find. 'I'd have stayed in my bed.'

'You young people have no spunk these days,' the lady replied taking a large bite. 'I'd have done something, I'm telling you.'

'Well,' said Zara. 'If you'd seen as many murders as I have you might've thought twice about it,' and she sailed off before the woman could draw breath.

But today was quiet and by eleven there had only been one couple partaking of scones with cream and strawberry jam.

Zara did not recognize the couple until the woman turned round and smiled at her. Not a happy smile.

'Mrs Balfour, how are you? Have you heard something?' Mrs Balfour regaled Zara with yesterday's story in a version she could hardly believe she'd been party to but she was glad Des had anonymized the situation.

'A reporter had phoned the police with the news that Ronnie had been staying at the Muirhouse's, said Mrs Balfour. 'We're so glad to hear something. I never did believe our Ronnie was lying dead somewhere on Arran.' Mr Balfour looked at Zara quizzically and she wondered if he were thinking: then why are we here, why did we stay?

'I just hope the boy's all right,' he said. 'I didn't like the way the police were talking as if he had been involved.'

'They didn't actually say that,' said Mrs Balfour. 'They just showed us that medallion. It was Ronnie's.' She fell into a silence picking up her scone and putting it down without eating it. 'I don't know,' she said at last, 'if I believe he was there in that house.'

'Because why?' asked Zara.

'Because would he be there if he had nothing to do with it?' Mr Balfour shifted in his chair.

'Unless he was being held against his will,' said Zara. The Balfour's faces told her that this thought had also occurred to them.

'Our other son's in Australia,' said Mrs Balfour. 'He's trying to get home but he's not managed it yet. Something to do with the terms of his contract. He keeps saying that everything will be all right.'

'And what about your daughter? Gina isn't it?' Mrs Balfour looked very cast down.

''I don't know how she's taken it. She's not well and we didn't want to depress her further but we couldn't not tell her... She might have found out and that would have been dreadful. She said that Ronnie made her boyfriend disappear and this was perhaps a judgment on him. I don't think she meant anything bad. She just can't think straight at the moment. She's going to go to a retreat in France and pray for everyone.' Zara couldn't tell what Mrs Balfour thought of that.

'I'm sorry,' said Zara, pouring them both a second cup of coffee on the house. It was hard watching them trying to be brave.

'Do you know about the letters?' asked Mrs Balfour. 'John Muirhouse has been writing letters,' she went on before Zara had time to consider what might be a judicious reply. 'Apparently he's saying he'll tell the police where Ronnie is if they stop hunting him.'

'That could all be made up,' said Zara. 'The guy's an inveterate liar; I can tell you that from when I was...'

'It's okay, Zara. We want to face everything. Every possibility. It's the only way we can think of to help the police cover all eventualities. We just want our boy back.' Zara sat down at their table: there were no other customers waiting.

'Do you think there is any chance he knew Muirhouse? Did he ever say...?'

'The police asked us that. Not that we know of. But of course Ronnie's a man. He doesn't live at home, does he? How would we know who he knows? He certainly never mentioned any Muirhouse. Did he Harry?' she added as if she wanted to be doubly sure.

'Govanhill,' said Zara. 'He never lived or worked there?'

'Never lived there...' said Margaret Balfour. 'Where was it he did that placement when he was doing that community education course? That wasn't Govanhill, was it?'

'No', replied Harry. 'If you remember, it was going to be Govanhill but there was some staffing issue and he got put in Castlemilk instead.'

'So it's unlikely they met then?' said Mrs Balfour. 'I mean how many people are there in Govanhill?' Harry Balfour looked less convinced.

'You didn't mention that to the police then?' asked Zara.

'We only thought of it just now. We should tell them then? Grist to the mill? Maybe Muirhouse has some old score to settle.' Mrs Balfour was certainly not afraid of trying to get to the bottom of things.

Suddenly eight people arrived in three different groups. Zara excused herself and wished the Balfours luck.

'Will you being going back to Glasgow now?' she asked. Margaret Balfour screwed her face up:

'We haven't decided yet,' she said.

***

Before Zara could think again about her Arran articles idea something happened which put it right to the back of her mind: Des received another letter from John Muirhouse.

'So why are you wanting me?' was Zara's first question when she arrived at the station summoned by the D. I. He slapped down the letter.

'Read this and you'll see.' His face was as grim as his voice.

'Dear CID,

'Still no word from you and it's getting near my time for a break. I'd fancied the Greek islands this year but I really don't have the funds. To tell you the truth there are one or two things which are hindering me at the moment. One is I would like to get that assurance from you that I won't be charged. I have access to the man. I've told you this twice. *How many times do you have to hear it?* I need the hot continental sun — I'm a bit of a mad dog, though not of course an Englishman — otherwise I can go slightly loopy. And you wouldn't want that, would you?'

'The second thing is that I am now worried about my mother who is being pestered by journalists. She had a dreadful experience the other day with someone who purported to be from the *Evening Times*. I rang the said newspaper and they said they had never heard of a "Susan McFarlane". Was she a plant of yours? I can assure that another time my mother will not be intimidated and such a person will get short shrift. The dog will bite to order friendly though she may appear.

I do hope your work on the case is progressing satisfactorily. You will have so much expertise at your disposal I can't imagine it will take you long to close in on the killer. You must be anxious that he does not strike again.

Yours sincerely,

John Muirhouse.

P.S. How is that young lady whom I met on the *Waverley*? I understand she is concerned about me. Do tell her I am absolutely A1.'

'Are you seeing veiled threats here, Des?'

'I'm afraid so, Zara. I don't like the way he threatens to strike again and then mentions you in the next breath. I can't think what possessed you to go to Govanhill in the first place.'

'Yes you *can* think: I wanted to get news of Ronnie Balfour and I did. That surely was worthwhile wasn't it?' There was an uncomfortable silence. Zara knew that Des was concerned for her safety because he always expressed this through anger and frustration. 'So when you say about the killer striking again, you're thinking of Muirhouse specifically?' Zara went on.

'I'm thinking of Muirhouse but I haven't ruled Balfour out of the frame yet. We've no reason to.'

'Don't you think he's just being used by Muirhouse?'

'That's conjecture on your part.' Another silence.

'So what are we going to do now?' asked Zara.

'Since when have I had to fill you in on my strategies?' Zara pushed back her chair and left the coffee Des had thoughtfully provided for her untouched.

***

Even though Zara had walked out on Des for not taking her into his confidence she had understood the gravity of the situation and felt appropriately afraid in retrospect. She began to wonder if Muirhouse's mum was a partner in crime not just an innocent woman who wanted to support her son. She thought about the dog and tried to imagine it biting. It had been extraordinarily obedient.

On reflection, hadn't Mrs Muirhouse been strangely casual about Zara coming to the house. Perhaps Muirhouse had described her. Perhaps there were hidden cameras. Zara shivered. Even the chocolate biscuits now seemed to her suspicious.

She rang Barney. She realized as she listened for his voice, that it had been an automatic response to how she was feeling.

'How are you?' he said.

'I'm okay. You?'

'So what's wrong?'

'You think I only phone you when there's something wrong?'

'Zara I know your voice. It's me, Barney. You can't know someone for as long as we've known each other and not recognize when they're upset.'

'Are you coming down this weekend?'

'I could. Me and Ben and Nessie.'

'I'd like that. I need some normality.'

'Ah... Do you want to tell me what's bothering you?'

'It can wait. It's Thursday. Can you get down tomorrow?'

'Yes. You're sure now, Zara?'

'Of course I'm sure. What do you mean?'

'Well, I understood you went to Arran to get away... from me particularly.'

'I wasn't trying to get away from you as a friend.'

'Okay Zara.'

When Zara told Kirsty and George that Ben and Barney and Nessie were coming down for the weekend they exchanged what people call 'meaningful glances'.

'It's not what you imagine,' said Zara.

'And what do we imagine?' asked George.

'I don't know but you're wrong, whatever it is.'

'Okay.'

'Sorry,' said Zara. 'I did a stupid thing. Well, probably stupid.' Her friends waited. 'I'd better tell you.' They looked worried. 'You'll start wishing I wasn't staying at your hotel soon.'

'Zara for God's sake get on with it!'

Zara outlined what had happened in Glasgow and the subsequent letter from Muirhouse, realizing as she did so that she could have been making North Crag a target.

'I'll go somewhere else if you want. It's not fair...'

'You will not,' said Kirsty. 'Just don't go off the beaten track with anyone — except Barney.'

The three of them discussed every aspect of the case till they were exhausted. George especially looked as if he were going to fall asleep where he sat. Kirsty kept telling him to go to bed.

'I won't let you exercise Riga if you don't go now.'

'I could exercise Riga,' said Zara. 'Sometimes,' she added knowing how much George was enjoying it but wanting to ride Riga herself suddenly and if she could be helpful... George said,

'You're welcome to take Riga out any time but I'll stick to my morning routine.'

'Of course George. I wasn't trying to...'

'I know. 'Night.' He left the room after giving Zara a hug.

'It would be good if you could,' said Kirsty. 'Take the pressure off him a bit. He feels he's not being fair to the horse if he doesn't take her out at least once a day so if...'

'I'd love to,' said Zara. 'Galloping is just what I need just now.'

***

Friday morning early Zara got the map out and planned the weekend hoping the dry weather would hold. Ben wasn't difficult to amuse and he prided himself on not being 'one of those boring people who grumble about the weather'.

Zara decided she would propose a trip to Coireann Lochan with the promise of a dip when they got there. Ben would enjoy coming upon the lochan which cannot be seen till you breast the hill. That would be their major trip with a grand picnic after the swim. On the Sunday they could hire bikes again and do Glenashdale waterfall and the Giants' Graves. Ben would be interested because his school had been doing a Bronze Age project that term. Maybe the cycling and the walk would be too much. She'd need to discuss it with Barney first. If they took the bus instead, they would have time for a swim at the jetty before heading back for Brodick and the boat. Also no problem regarding Nessie.

When Zara met them Ben was smiling and enthusiastic.

'Aunty Zara,' he said, 'Dad says we can climb Goat Fell this weekend. Is that right? Will you take us? I've never been and it's fantastic weather and I've brought my camera and Dad says if we come back down Glen Rosa we can swim in the Blue Pool. Isn't that a wonderful idea, Aunty Zara? Will you be able to make us a picnic?' Zara mentally shelved her programme for the weekend:

'Of course, Ben. Brilliant. I'll do a really good picnic. Fingers crossed for no rain.' Because of Zara's chores, they set off about the same time that Zara had started out with Ronnie Balfour, a detail which was not lost on her, the more so because of what Barney had told her in the middle of the night.

Ben had fallen asleep mid-sentence, on the word 'Goat', Barney had told Zara. She and Barney had sat out the back and then they had gone to see Riga. The horse looked amazing silhouetted against his field which was only slowly giving way to night.

'Horses and trees make me feel good,' said Zara.

'More than humans?' asked Barney.

'I can't judge either of them, I think that's what it is. I mean even if a tree doesn't blossom when you expect, you wouldn't dream of being annoyed with it, would you?'

'Couldn't you get annoyed with a horse if it trampled a clump of daffodils in your garden?'

'Why do you pick daffodils? It's not Spring.'

'You know I only know four flower names, Zara.' She took his arm.

'I might have to teach you some more.'

'Why do I need to know the names? It doesn't make the flowers any more beautiful.'

'Not sure about that.'

'Oh my God' exclaimed Barney. 'I'm sorry, I wasn't thinking. How could I have said that! Of course I didn't mean anything by it.' Zara stopped on the road and faced him.

'You've been a bit preoccupied since you arrived, Barney. Is everything all right at work?'

'Yes, yes, Zara. It's not that.'

'But there is something?' Barney looked away. 'Did something happen?' They passed between the yew trees at the back gate of North Crag.

'I'll tell you but not here.'

Zara wasn't sure whether the 'something' was a physical occurrence or a clicking in Barney's mind but she knew him well enough to understand he would take his time with it whatever it was. She wondered fleetingly whether it was to do with the changed status of their relationship. Maybe he thought she wouldn't want to share her bed with him. She realized she hadn't really thought about it. She saw this as an indication that their relationship was relaxed. Whatever else it was she anticipated no embarrassment.

By the time they arrived back George and Kirsty were upstairs. Zara and Barney had some cocoa in the kitchen but still Barney did not tell Zara what was on his mind.

'We could have an affair,' said Zara, leaning in to him as they sat together. He took her hand squeezed it and she put hers on his and in doing so it struck her that neither of their gestures spelled 'affair' to her.

In bed she turned to him pulling his head towards her but he took her hands.

'Zara,' he said. 'I can't. At least not until I've told you.'

'Told me what?' The awful thought struck her that he might be having an affair with someone else.

'I don't know where to begin,' he said and she saw fear cross his face.

'The beginning,' she said. 'I'm not joking,' she added.

'I'm not sure the end wouldn't be better. I don't want you to be more upset than you need be.'

'Barney, I'm getting more upset by the second and if you don't start I shall scream. Just tell it me like a story. You're here for God's sake. Ben's in the next room. I know you're both okay so it can't be that bad.'

Barney sat up as if this gave him more control.

'Okay', he said. 'This is what happened. It was Thursday morning. I was not due in work till eleven, taking some TOIL and I went out with the idea of getting some screws to fix that dodgy panel in the bathroom. It was a beautiful day but breezy. I took my bike and I was wearing that light jacket. What's the matter?'

'Is the detail really necessary? Except I'm really tired Barney but I don't want to fall asleep and miss a salient point.'

'It's significant, the jacket,' said Barney, 'but I'll try to be brief. I mentioned it because there was a woolly cap in the pocket'. Zara looked hard at Barney and wondered if he was going a little insane. She nodded.

'Okay, Barney,' she said trying to sound interested.

'I went along Great Western Road and down Byres Road and it was as I turned into Dumbarton Road that I thought I saw' — his hesitation made Zara's head turn —'John Muirhouse.'

'You phoned the police?' It was Zara's turn to sit up.

'I didn't have my mobile with me.'

'Barney! What a chance! So you missed him?' Well not your fault. You weren't looking for him. No need to beat yourself up.'

'Zara listen. I followed him. I put on my knitted black hat and I followed him. He was walking along quite slowly but not as if he were entirely without motivation.' Zara was fully awake now. 'He turned up that street with the theatre — Cottiers — and then it was too difficult with my bike so I chained it to a railing and went on, on foot. I thought I'd lost him but there he was heading for Hyndland Road.'

'I was fairly sure he hadn't seen me and I thought with a cap covering my hair he would not recognize me anyway, only having seen me that once, that once you remember, here on the steps of the hotel. And momentarily in McDonalds'.

'I remember,' said Zara.

'Unfortunately there were fewer people about. He didn't seem to look behind him but when he crossed Hyndland Road at Novar Drive he scanned right back the way he'd come and he would have seen me. I suppose I hadn't thought through the fact that he's a wanted man.'

'How were you so sure it was him?' Barney thought for a moment.

'Something about the set of his head and one shoulder. It's like he's had an accident and has a weakness which makes his head go just marginally off the vertical.'

God, you're right,' said Zara. 'I know exactly what you mean. And the shoulder sort of compensates downwards, again, just a tiny bit. I've never analysed it before.'

'Apart from that, it could have been someone else entirely. He was wearing a suit.'

'A suit! Are you sure this wasn't a dream you had?'

'I dunno,' said Barney. 'If you never normally wear one, the people you know aren't going to expect you in one, are they? Added to which he was not on home ground.'

'As in Govanhill?'

'Exactly.'

'Go on,' said Zara. 'At this rate I shall need more cocoa or maybe something stronger.'

'This is the nasty bit,' said Barney. 'I don't know if you know but there's a lane behind Novar Drive on the railway side of the street. He turned into it. I was at loss to know what to do. Had he known I was there all the time? A wanted man is going to be on the alert. He's going to be expecting people to be looking for him. I thought I'd just peep round and see if I could see where he went.'

'What was your plan?' asked Zara. 'I don't understand what you thought you were doing.'

'I thought if I saw him going into a house I could take the number and then find a phone. Phone the police.' Zara nodded.

'But?'

'But what happened was,' said Barney, 'I came round the corner and there he was towards the far end of the alley, about sixty yards away. I flattened myself against a bush — I'm really no good at sleuthing Zara — and I peered out. He stood there. I felt he was looking straight at me. Then he took something from the inside pocket of his suit jacket. I couldn't see what it was at first but then it glinted in the sun and then almost the next moment he threw it.' Zara clutched Barney's knee.

'He threw what?'

'He threw the knife. And, Zara, it was such an amazing throw. Like something from the Olympics and it landed beside me. So exactly beside me that I got the message he could have hit me as accurately as expert darts players can hit any number they choose.'

'Do you think he knew it was you?' Zara's voice had gone very small.

'My gut feeling is "yes",' said Barney. 'I'm sorry Zara. I should have known better.'

Underneath Zara's fear at the possibility that Barney had been drawn into the Muirhouse maze, there was a small grain of amusement. Barney, who lectured her constantly about danger, personal and familial, who said he wouldn't marry her because she was too reckless, this same Barney had wittingly thrown himself into the path of the foe.

'What happened then?' asked Zara.

'I must have gazed at the knife — it was actually stuck in the surface of the lane — for more than a second. I was shocked, sort of paralysed, as if the knife had actually pierced me and then, when I looked up he had disappeared. I pulled the knife from the ground — using a piece of string I found in my pocket — and put it in a plastic bag someone had conveniently abandoned.'

'Cool,' said Zara. DI Des will be impressed. Did you manage to phone the police?'

'I went into a shop on Hyndland Road and asked if I could use their phone to tell the police about sighting a wanted man. I didn't realise how I looked with the knife which you could see clearly through the plastic bag. The shopkeeper took one look at me and dialled 999. He went into the back shop so I couldn't hear what he said. I think he thought I was the wanted man giving myself up. When he came back he brought a chair for me and then a cup of tea. He asked if I'd like to put the bag down on the counter.' Zara began to laugh.

'You couldn't make it up,' she said. 'I think I'm going to start writing short stories. You can supply the plots.' Barney managed to smile.

'The police were reasonably quick and didn't spend too much time with me because they thought they might have a chance of running John Muirhouse to ground. There were four of them and they left one to take my statement. Of course I had to explain the links and they phoned Des. I could hear him laughing on the other end of the phone.'

'He didn't tell me,' said Zara.

'You saw him again?'

'Another letter.'

As Zara explained, Barney became grave again.

'What worries me most,' he said, when Zara had finished, 'is the idea that someone with Muirhouse's mind will see our involvement as a big joke; he'll imagine his power has drawn us in. I'm beginning to think he's quite deranged.'

'Deranged possibly but intelligent and skilled enough to avoid arrest,' said Zara. 'I'm not sure I'd back him for a claim of diminished responsibility. I don't think for one moment he would allow that. Sleep,' said Zara. 'Don't worry, the problem isn't going to go away.'

Outside, an owl hooted and Riga pricked up his ears but otherwise all was still and content.

Chapter XV   A beautiful day on the mountain

Climbing Goat Fell was not perhaps the ideal way of distancing themselves from John Muirhouse and his Amazing Puzzle as Zara dubbed it lying in bed the following morning. But there was no going back: Ben was excited; Nessie was excited and it was a perfect day — sun and a small breeze to keep away the midges and the flies.

Zara waited for Ben to start asking awkward questions but he didn't and the first part of the climb was spent testing the males on their lamentable grasp of flora and fauna.

'What's the point of asking children to be enthusiastic about saving the environment when they can't tell a buttercup from a dandelion?' asked Zara.

'Dad thinks all yellow flowers are dandelions,' said Ben who was at least a quick learner.

'I'll teach you and then you can teach your dad,' said Zara.

'Who taught you, Aunty Zara?'

'My dad,' said Zara.

'The one who died picking brambles out in the environment?'

''That one,' said Zara. 'I only had one.'

'Not so lucky then. My friend at school, Fergus, has got three.'

'How come?' asked Zara and Barney together.

'His birth dad, his stepdad and his mum's boyfriend.'

'And that's good?' asked Barney.

'Well it means millions of birthday and Christmas presents but mostly he's at home with his mum.'

'Isn't the stepdad there?' asked Zara

'He's 'out' a lot. Oh look was that a rabbit?'

'A hare,' said Zara, 'See how it leaps along and zigzags.'

Nessie was chasing it without a hope of catching up. She arrived panting at the bridge where they had stopped to wait for her.

'It could have been here where they found Rose's hat,' said Ben suddenly.

'I think it was higher up,' said Zara, glancing at Barney.

'It's all right. Dad and I discussed the whole story. It happened a long time ago I know that.' Behind Ben's back, Barney opened his hands in a what-could-I-do gesture.

'Do you think Laurie did it, Aunty Zara? I don't. I don't think he pushed him, I think he fell. But then it wasn't very friendly to rob him. But maybe he really liked that stripey jacket. Maybe,' Ben looked from his dad to Zara, 'Laurie said to Rose, "I really like your jacket" and Rose said, "If I die, you can have it". Fergus says I can have his play station if he dies.'

'I see,' said Zara. 'Good thinking. It might well have been like that.' They did not picnic at the bridge. Zara did not want to do a re-run of 'before'. Instead they toiled on till they reached the shoulder where Zara and Barney wanted to stop, but Ben wanted to press on to the top and eat the picnic there.

'If you're climbing a mountain, you always have the picnic at the top.'

'You don't have to,' said Zara. 'It's a matter of choice.'

'We did on Holy Isle,' said Ben.

'That's not a mountain,' said Barney.

'Well I'm stopping for a drink and an energy bar,' said Zara. 'You can do what you like.'

Barney and Ben set off and Zara sat for a moment looking back at the crumpled paper effect of the sea and the half circle of Brodick Bay, barely distinguishable in the heat haze. She was suddenly reminded of Ronnie Balfour's remark, 'No fish' in response to her observation of a boat. Both the fish and Ronnie had disappeared. She shook herself. Don't make it a morbid day, Zara, she told herself.

She turned the other way but was immediately hit by the memory of meeting Muirhouse and Daffodil. She jumped up and almost fell off the boulder she had been sitting on and hurried after the others. Shouldn't have left them. Bad move. She tried to go back to Rose and Laurie. Not cheerful but at least nothing to do with her.

There was no getting away from the subject of murder:

'Do you think Rose and Laurie had a picnic at the top?' Ben greeted Zara as she appeared over the last rock.

'According to you, you have to have it there, so I expect they did,' said Zara.

'They might not have had a picnic at all though,' said Ben 'All that way and no food. Not good.'

'They'd probably had a huge breakfast of bacon and eggs and everything else,' said Zara.

'Well so did I but I'm hungry now,' said Ben. 'Perhaps they were starving and that's what made them bad-tempered. Dad always asks me if I'm hungry if I seem to be in a bad mood.' He bit fiercely into a cheese and cucumber roll.

'I think I can see the Paps of Jura,' said Barney. 'Oh! They've gone again.' They argued about what it was possible to see from the summit and then remembered it was all written down at the triangulation point. Zara started to open a big chocolate bar.

'I want the other one,' said Ben.

'We can have that on the way down,' said Zara.

'I want it now,' said Ben.

'Why don't we open both?' said Barney.

'I don't want to open both: I just want the other one!'

'Why are you being so awkward?' asked Zara.

'I'm pretending to be Rose: I'm being moody so Laurie gets annoyed.'

'But you said you thought he'd slipped, Rose, I mean.'

'Well Laurie could get annoyed and when you're annoyed, that's when people make mistakes. Perhaps Rose was thinking about the argument they were having and it made him step too near the edge.'

'I think that might be an eagle,' said Zara. 'Have you got your binoculars, Barney?' He handed them to her not knowing if it were just a ruse to change the subject. Zara looked at the distant shape. It was hovering over north Goat Fell and then it swooped nearer so she had to adjust the lens.

'It is an eagle. Ben, look!' Ben was entranced by the size of the bird. He took his camera out of his rucksack and Zara and Barney held their breath as Ben zoomed in and managed to get a shot before the mighty bird soared away.

'Maybe it was looking for somebody,' said Ben.

'Looking for food, I expect,' said Zara. 'Should we move?' It's quite a way to go if you want to take the Glen Rosa route back.'

'I want to swim in the Blue Pool,' said Ben.

'Come on then,' said Barney. 'We can open the other chocolate after the swim.'

'If we can wait that long,' said Zara.

For most of the way down the Saddle, Ben was occupied with the descent.

'I'm concentrating,' he said to Barney, when his father asked him if he were okay. Nessie was always either behind or in front, sometimes circling groups of boulders to find an easier way. Occasionally the humans had to lift her as her legs were too short to scale some of the rocks.

'Don't fall, Nessie,' said Ben. 'The eagle might get you.' Sometime later he said, 'Maybe an eagle swooped over Rose and he went off balance.'

'So why didn't Laurie say that at the trial?'

'He thought no one would believe him.'

At the bottom of the Saddle, they had two squares each of chocolate and a long drink.

'I've been thinking,' said Ben as they set off down the glen to the Blue Pool. 'I think if I were Muirhouse I would have hidden Balfour on Arran. Like Laurie did Rose.' Zara and Barney were silent. Neither of them had realized that Ben knew so much.

'Who told you about Muirhouse?' asked Barney at last.

'That boy on the beach yesterday. You know how I went along the beach while you two were at the shop? I was standing looking at Goat Fell and this boy came along and said, "Do you know there was a murder up there?" and I said, 'It wasn't a murder, because I was thinking about Rose and Laurie and he said, 'Yes it was and he started on about Muirhouse and Daffodil Brown. And then about Balfour. He thinks Balfour is dead and Muirhouse is just making it up when he says he knows where he is.'

'Where does he get his information from?' asked Zara.

'He says everyone is talking about it. His dad's in the Mountain Rescue. Anyway,' said Ben, as if Zara's question had not been important, '*I* think that Balfour is alive and I think he's on Arran.'

'Why do you think that?' asked Zara.

'Because it's the most unlikely place,' said Ben.

'Are you going to be a detective when you grow up?' asked his father.

'No, I'm still going to be an Olympic high-jumper.'

***

Des, sitting in Brodick police station was at a loss. He had reached the stage where he wished something would happen but he knew this was a dangerous wish because all too often something did happen and though the outcome could be useful in solving the crime, the collateral damage was always undesirable.

Thus, unknown at this time to DI Des, an unpleasant scenario was playing itself out in Glasgow.

It was just after closing time at 'Dot's Flowers' on the Cathcart Road and Dot herself was glad to be finished. The day had started in a flurry with wedding bouquets almost not reaching their destination in time. The child-minder had rung to say she was sending Stuart back early because she was sure now she had the flu and could hardly stand up. Stuart who was four had managed to knock over three buckets of roses before a neighbour had fortuitously popped in and taken the child out of harm's way. Dot was wondering whether Donnie would have remembered to put the steak pie in the oven when a strikingly tall man suddenly filled the space in the small shop.

'We're closed,' Dot said automatically. 'Come back tomorrow at eight.'

'I just want —'

'Please,' said Dot, 'I've done the till and I'm not interested.' The man stood looking at her.

'I forgot my mother's birthday,' he said. 'She loves roses.' Dot began to roll her eyes.

'If I had a fiver for every time...' she began to say.

'Please,' said the man. 'I'll just take this.' He extracted a beautiful bunch of assorted red blooms. 'My mother loves red.' He took out a wallet. 'How much will that be?'

'Seven pound fifty.' Dot gave up. She took the proffered tenner and went to the till. Only when she pressed the key to open it did she wonder if... but then it was too late, the man was at her side deftly removing the float. It's only the float she thought to herself. Keep calm but stupidly she had left the bank envelope beside the till. She had been going to go to the external deposit box on her way home. She and Donnie were saving for a holiday in France. An old school friend had married a French man of all things and gone to live in the Camargue. Dot's sister had said she would come up from Birmingham to look after the shop for a fortnight.

'No!' she shouted as the man's hand encompassed the envelope. 'You can't have that.'

She knew it was a mistake to fight on these occasions. 'That's what insurance is for: you've only got one face,' Donnie often used to say to her. He hated her being in the shop alone when she sent the assistant home early so she could get a particular bus and not have to stand waiting half an hour for the next.

They struggled. Dot had hold of the man's sleeve. He looked at her clenched hand as if in annoyance that some creature should attempt to best him and with a sudden jerky movement he flung her away from him and stumbled over her to the door. He still had the roses. He hardly seemed to register the crashing noise made by Dot's head hitting the edge of a bucket and did not glance back at the picture of a wrong-angled woman buried in roses, blood seeping from an unnecessary wound. He closed the door carefully behind him.

No one noticed the man leave the shop and make his way home, keeping to side streets, roses stashed inside his jacket. He called in at an off-license and bought a bottle of whisky, his mother's favourite.

'Here you are, happy birthday,' he said to her thrusting the roses and the whisky towards her as he came through the front door. 'We can celebrate. I came up on the horses.'

***

Donnie, frustrated, steak pie well cooked, unable to get Dot on the phone, eventually went down to the shop, fortunately deciding to leave Stuart with the neighbour and see Dot first.

Dot wasn't dead. The bleeding, though from a serious wound, was not profuse. She went straight to the operating theatre from the ambulance. Later Donnie went home, threw the steak pie in the bin and tried to explain to Stuart what had happened.

'She's not dead, Stuart,' he kept saying. She's not dead.'

***

The story made the evening news although it was not connected to John Muirhouse until forensics had matched his fingerprints to those on the ten pound note, found on the floor, that Muirhouse had handed to Dot. At this point Des contacted Barney who seemed to have been the last person whom they knew had seen Muirhouse.

134

'Des wants me to reconstruct my encounter with Muirhouse in the light of what the tabloids are calling 'A Bloomin' Assault',' said Barney the next morning.

'What's he going to ask you: 'Was there anything in Muirhouse's stance when you saw him in the lane that would presage an assault on a florist?' said Zara. Ben was out of hearing, walking Nessie in the fields behind the hotel.

'It sounds to me as if he needed money and the assault was an accident,' said Barney. If the woman dies, it will be manslaughter though.'

'Let's hope she doesn't,' said Zara. 'She has a four-year-old son.' She gave an involuntary shiver. Every so often the horrible realization would come over her that she had almost gone up Goat Fell as Muirhouse's companion...

'If he's desperate for money,' said Barney, 'does that mean Ronnie Balfour's alive?'

'What do you mean?' asked Zara. 'Are you assuming they are together? Willingly or unwillingly?'

'John Muirhouse has not apparently been back to his place of work since the murder. To keep on the run successfully, he'll need money.'

'Perhaps he'll hire a BMW and start swanning around with Ronnie Balfour tied up in the back of it,' said Zara. 'What I don't understand, is how he is able to evade the police.'

'Bit like John Laurie,' said Barney. 'He kept it up for two months.'

***

Zara could not get Ben's comments out of her head. She became obsessed with the idea that Ronnie Balfour was on Arran on the 'unlikely and therefore probable' logic that Ben had used. Where could he be hiding if this were the case? She didn't herself believe he *was* hiding but left the possibility in the argument because she could not rule it out.

To deal with 'hiding' first. how well did he know the island? Would there be anyone who would shelter him? How could he hole up in a remote spot? How would he obtain food? It just did not seem likely to Zara.

On the other hand, his leaving. Had he left with Muirhouse, in which case he was involved, unless he had been a prisoner? But how would Muirhouse have managed to conceal a man Ronnie Balfour's size on the boat? Had he had access to a vehicle? Had Ronnie been drugged and secreted under a pile of luggage in a 'borrowed' car?

There was a possibility that Muirhouse had brought a car to the island under a different name. Maybe he had taken a drugged Ronnie to the house in Govanhill under cover of darkness. It was never that dark though in city streets. Had Muirhouse put out a couple of lights to make his job easier?

And did this all argue a grand plan? Had Muirhouse been intending to take Daffodil back with him — dead or alive? If this had been the plan, what had gone wrong?

Having hidden Ronnie in the house in Govanhill, Muirhouse's main concern would be to find somewhere safer. He would know that the police would come looking for him there. What other possibilities were there for him? Surely someone had seen him. Besides herself and Barney, that is. It wasn't as if he seemed to be making an effort to hide.

Barney and Ben went back to Glasgow on the Sunday evening. It was Ben's last week of school and they were coming back the next weekend to spend at least a month on the island. Somehow this had been agreed. All the goalposts had changed. Zara had not said she was going to marry Barney or he her but for reasons too deep to articulate they knew that their 'noes' had become 'don't knows' and they were no longer hostile to each other over that particular subject.

Even though Barney had 'done a Zara' in his pursuit of Muirhouse, Zara did not imagine he would take kindly to her turning detective. Des would be equally displeased. She would just have to wait for developments. If Ronnie Balfour was alive, there would definitely be developments. Zara did not like waiting on the back foot but at that moment she could see no other option.

***

Des's team had not yet been able to question Dot the florist. She was still in hospital and had drifted into a coma after her operation. The doctors were not certain why she was in a coma: the operation had gone well. Donnie and Stuart spent a lot of time sitting beside her and Donnie kept assuring his son that his mother would wake up soon.

There were no leads to be had from the florist's shop other than the matching finger prints. Des had been expecting another letter but none had come. He's good at not doing the expected thought Des. Privately he would have hazarded that Balfour was dead but that was mainly a gloomy gut feeling. On the other hand, he felt Muirhouse was the sort of criminal who liked to play showman. Given long enough he would make some false move because he would be desperate to demonstrate his cleverness.

The team had spent hours trying to work out a possible pattern in Muirhouse's thinking and latterly a possible scenario which would embrace Balfour. They had not succeeded in any way and Dot's assault had confused the issue even more.

But meanwhile in an unknown location, a strange and one-sided dialogue was taking place:

'I don't know why you don't just admit you did it.'

'Because I didn't do it.'

'We all do things we regret sometimes. Well, I don't generally but you are just an ordinary mortal and therefore can be forgiven. It will go much better for you if you just admit it. I'm offering to broker the whole business for you. If you plead guilty, you won't get life and you'll get remission for good behaviour. It's your best chance. I could just turn you in but to tell you the truth I'm sorry for you. In fact, I would go so far as to say I'm beginning to like you.'

'Give me some decent food then.'

'It's a well-known fact that a frugal diet sharpens the mind. I want you to think properly. I'm trying to help you.'

'If I die you will have two deaths on your hands.'

'I'm not going to let you die my friend. Mother said to me, "Keep that young man alive. You must keep him alive".'

'Why did she say that?'

'Because she loves me.'

'You're not making sense.'

'No. You're not making sense. Listen. I'll go over it all again: after the Zara woman had gone back to the tent, we stood talking and I invited you to take part in my little experiment, involving Daffodil. You looked intently at me as I explained and I knew you were interested. But then after I'd finished you shook your head and turned away. I have to admit to being disappointed at that moment but I thought I'd just carry on as planned. I waited five whole minutes to see if you might change your mind and return but when you didn't I went back to Daffodil. Daffodil, a real trooper, so willing to take part. And then, to my joy, you came back and together we sorted the ropes.'

'None of this is true.'

'You were much better at knots than me. We were so careful, making sure to erase all fingerprints and then came the most important part and you, you asked me if you could —'

'I did not. This is all lies. I will never submit to you. You will never make me believe I did it.'

'But we have proof. The marks on her neck. And the police suspect you. They didn't at first but something has made them change their minds. Mother saw it in the newspaper. They are looking for you too. But they'll never find you.' A long pause. 'And of course,' Muirhouse went on, 'there are things in the past which if known, might not predispose a court towards you.'

'What has made you like this, Muirhouse or were you born bad?'

'I believe that every man follows the dictates of his own mind. I do what my mind suggests. I think I look at all sides of the argument logically and then decide. Mother always says it's important to make up your mind and stick to it.'

'And does Mother approve of everything you do?'

'I'm everything to Mother. Everything.'

There was a long pause here. Ronnie Balfour did not know whether he wanted to know the full story which quite likely would not be the truth anyway.

'A violent man, my father, given to strange rages. He would throw objects across the kitchen. The wall beside where my mother sat was pockmarked, riddled with holes. On this occasion I'm remembering he had thrown the toaster. He was a very bad shot and his attempts usually went wide and my mother would just carry on eating or smoking. The dog would sit silently following the trajectory of the missile.

As I said, on this occasion, it was the toaster, and suddenly I could see it was on target and I flung out my hand to deflect it but he had thrown it with such force it took my hand back with it and my fingers were crushed between the toaster and the wall, inches from mother's head.' Muirhouse held up the fingers of his left hand. 'See I have the scars still. I was left-handed till then but my fingers took so long to heal I started using my right hand. Never went back to my left. Mother stood by him of course.' Ronnie Balfour took a deep breath and expelled it slowly. 'I was then beaten up for interfering,' said Muirhouse.

If this were all true thought Ronnie Balfour, I should be feeling more compassion but I'm not. Does this mean it's not true or have I lost my capacity to feel for others? He recalled the faces of his parents and could feel at once pain, for himself and for them. He wondered where they were: he knew they would never give up. It's not the Middle East he thought but I am being brainwashed. Or at least Muirhouse is attempting it. The man had started speaking again:

'I wish you would tell me whether you thought the whole thing up beforehand.'

'What thing?'

'What had Daffodil told you? Can't you understand, I just want to know the story.'

What story? I don't know Daffodil's story.'

The man had gone. He did this: drop in unexpectedly, grill Ronnie for a session and then, as suddenly depart. It made the day more chaotic, totally undependable.

Ronnie focused his mind and went over every single second of his time on the mountain with Muirhouse. He was determined to remember it accurately. He also had a notebook in his boot. In the three weeks of his captivity he had managed to persuade Muirhouse to free his hands; his legs were still tied and he was chained also. He knew he couldn't escape but as long as Muirhouse was ignorant of his notebook he would fill the long nights with an account of what had happened to him. When it was light enough to see. He had no idea where he was nor a clear idea any longer of how many days he had been a prisoner.

Chapter XVI   Spying

Zara had an idea and she thought it would be better to execute it sooner rather than later: she would go to Glasgow and stake out the Muirhouse habitat. She would watch for a couple of days at least. Kirsty said she didn't mind. Her sister was coming up for a visit and she would be willing, Kirsty knew, to do anything necessary. Kirsty thought Zara was going to the mainland to get some respite from the murder. Zara did not disabuse her.

She went back to her flat and looked in her wardrobe for a good disguise. She decided to be a male artist. There were lots of shops in the vicinity of the Muirhouse's. Some looked as if upstairs was used for storage. She would spin a story about sketching different parts of Glasgow. Fortunately, she could draw competently. She would play it by ear. Sometimes things just turned out right. It was time the balance tipped her way.

Zara dressed in some very old jeans a friend had left on his way to Australia ten years previously and an ancient jacket of Barney's with a collar that hid the lower part of her face. She wore Doc Martens and a paint-spattered baseball cap. No hair showing.

Thus disguised, she made to the Cathcart Road. She eyed three possible shops and picked the Asian-run convenience store. A youth of about twenty-five looked up. Zara bought some apples, a large packet of crisps and some bottled water.

'I have a big favour to ask,' she said in her specially gruff voice. The youth looked at her as if to say, 'Okay brighten my day'.

'My name is Jo. I'm an artist and I'm doing a series of paintings of different areas of Glasgow — not just the touristy bits. I notice you have like a storeroom upstairs above the shop. I wonder if it would be possible for me to do some sketches from up there.'

'I'll get my father,' said the youth.

Mr Ram was a stocky fifty-year-old.

'How can I be of assistance to you?' he asked smiling. Zara repeated her request. Mr Ram's smile became even larger. 'I will show you upstairs and you can see if it will do. Very dusty. Very untidy but... you can see for yourself. After, you will come and meet my wife and children.'

Zara followed Mr Ram through a curtain and immediately up some stairs. The room above the shop which was indeed dusty gave a good view of the street.

'Or of course,' said Mr Ram, 'you can go one storey higher and look down on rooftops. You can also see my house from there.'

'Perhaps I could use both?' suggested Zara. 'That is if it is not too much trouble.'

'No trouble at all,' said Mr Ram. 'We are in the world to help one another.'

The second floor was even better. Mr Ram pointed out his house with great pleasure, drawing Zara's attention to a large pine tree in his garden.

'You cannot see the garden but you can see the tree,' he said. 'This is good. I think of it as my house protector.' Downstairs again, Mr Ram led Zara into the rear quarters where she was introduced to Mrs Ram and two very small Rams. Mrs Ram was cooking.

'When we came to Britain, we wanted to start a restaurant but shop easier,' she said. 'So now I only cook for family.' She handed Zara a chapatti filled with vegetables and spices. Mr Ram waved to a chair and Zara sat down.

'Uttam, go and fetch your sketchbook,' said Mrs Ram. Uttam disappeared. 'He is very good but at school he did not do art and now... but perhaps you can help him, as you are an artist. You will know the ropes.' On the ropes more like thought Zara, and it's true what they say about free lunches.

Uttam was away a long time and Zara realized he had gone home for his sketch book. That obedient she thought. She sipped tea and fleshed out her story, now very unwilling to tell lies to such helpful people. She decided to talk about the future rather than make up the past.

'I've been working so hard at my job, my painting has fallen away recently.'

'And what is your job?'

'Unfortunately my employer died and the business was closed. He was a frame-maker and I helped him and dealt with the customers. (This lie was on the back of a summer job Zara had had ten years previously).

'So now your job is?' He didn't let go, Mr Ram.

'I've been doing temp work in offices but I worked so hard I became ill so I thought I would give myself a painting project for a month. My brother is here from Australia and he has agreed to pick up the rent while he's staying.' Zara had forgotten how easy lying was.

'And your brother, what does he do in Australia?'

'He has a vineyard,' said Zara off the top of her head. Why did I say that she wondered.

'You have been to Australia?'

No', said Zara. 'I haven't. Never got it together.'

'I have a brother there,' said Mr Ram. 'First he was in Melbourne, then Sydney. I like Sydney. If I was young again I would go there.' Zara was relieved she didn't have to invent a visit to Australia: it was tough enough inventing a brother.

'I'd better get started,' she said. 'The chapatti was lovely and so was the tea.'

'Shipped direct from my cousin in Assam. None of your floor sweepings here,' said Mr Ram, standing erectly while Zara got to her feet. 'You wish to sketch now?' Zara nodded and headed for the stairs. She remembered Uttam's sketchbook.

'If Uttam wants to bring his sketchbook up,' she said.

'We will tell him,' said Mrs Ram.

Zara found her task on the one hand relaxing and on the other full of tension... Setting up her sketchbook on the portable easel she had dug out of the back of the cupboard at home and sharpening her pencils gave her a feeling she'd almost forgotten. She experienced an anticipation peculiar to the action, an excitement at the idea of connecting with what she saw through the marks she would make on the sheet before her.

She found looking up and down it was easy to keep a small part of her mind alert for any movement from the Muirhouse's. As yet nothing. She concentrated on her sketch. If it turned out half decent it would go a long way to convincing the Rams of her authenticity.

She was just finishing her first attempt at the scene before her when the Muirhouse's front door opened and Mrs Muirhouse came out. At the pavement she seemed to hesitate, looking both ways and then, by divine coincidence, who should come along the street but Uttam. He was sauntering along and did not break his stride. Any sketchbook he might have had was concealed in the rucksack on his back. He passed Mrs Muirhouse and Zara thought perhaps he greeted her — maybe she used the shop — but then she was aware of the woman raising her fist and shouting something. Uttam kept walking. Zara was intrigued but kept on working. Mrs Muirhouse crossed the road and followed Uttam into the shop. Was this luck or good management?

Zara hear Uttam's feet on the stairs. First things first. She smiled at him and he took it for the invitation it was and began opening his rucksack, fumbling with the fastening as if he were in some sort of hurry. He handed Zara one of three large sketchbooks.

Her reaction was vocal. She turned the pages quickly just to make sure there weren't just one or two good pieces of work.

'Uttam these are magnificent. Your Glasgow is Glasgow but it is Indian too. The colours, it's because the colours are Indian. You have the light. They are tremendous. She turned to the second book.

Where the first paintings had been water-colour, the ones in the second book were oils. Some were better than others and Zara could see the guy was challenging himself, trying for more complexity. Most of the pieces had figures in them in bright garments where appropriate. There was a romanticism about them so that the brightness complemented water or the leaves of a very green tree. The result was Glasgow enhanced but believable. When you look at them thought Zara, it's as if you remember somewhere having seen that scene although you know you haven't. She thought rapidly.

'I have a friend in Pollokshaws who has a small gallery. She might take some of these. Also, had you thought of getting printed reproductions?' Uttam's face lit up and Zara felt that if her being there had any meaning it was this.

'Please take them to show her. I would be very grateful.' Zara promised she would, cursing her disguise at the same time. She wondered if she had come across as male or female. She desperately wanted to be herself now. Otherwise, down the line if there were a positive outcome regarding the pictures, she was going to be in a tangle.

Uttam was looking at her sketch. Then back at her. He lowered his voice.

'Why are you really here?'

'What do you mean?' Zara attempted to sound surprised at being asked.

'It's a good cover story but I'm not convinced. I think you want to watch that house.' He pointed across the road.

'Why do you say that?'

'Because they are strange people: I can well believe that someone would be watching them.'

'Forgive me for asking,' said Zara, 'but did the lady who came out of the house under question speak to you?'

'Just the usual string of abuse. She is seriously weird. One day she phones up and asks if "your son who loafs around in the shop" could possibly deliver something and when I get there she opens the door, takes the bag, counts the money into my hand and then says, 'Would you like to come in for some milk and a biscuit? — as if I was six or something! Other times, like today, she shouts, 'Why are you here? Go back where you belong.'

'And what do you do?' asked Zara.

'My father always taught me to be polite to old ladies so I usually just whistle 'I belong to Glasgow, softly you understand.' Zara laughed.

'Good for you.'

'It's just her. No one else. She is on her own. Left over from the empire. You're not CID are you?'

'No but maybe you should be,' said Zara. 'That was a cunning thrust, trying to surprise me into telling the truth.' Uttam looked at her questioningly.

'So if you are telling the truth is there another reason why you are watching the house of the mother of the man who the police are looking for in connection with the murder on Goat Fell?

'Have the police been here?'

'Routinely. Knocking on all the doors but it's likely that even if someone had seen John Muirhouse they wouldn't have said. I haven't seen him for two weeks. On the other hand, she has been buying different things from usual.'

'Really,' said Zara. 'What sort of things?'

'Tins of beans,' said Uttam. Zara fell silent. She was wondering whether she should tell Uttam everything. 'So,' he said, 'is that why you're here?' Zara made up her mind suddenly and told Uttam about her experience on the mountain and how the police suspected both Muirhouse and Balfour and why she wanted to find Balfour. Uttam listened with full attention.

'I could keep watch at night,' he said.

'But what would you say to your parents?'

'I'll say I am inspired by you to do night paintings. It hardly gets dark anyway this time of year. I wouldn't be able to do the whole night but... hey... I think Dad has another CCTV in the storeroom downstairs somewhere. Perhaps we could rig it up.'

'I don't like the idea of you doing things behind your parents' backs.'

'See, if you can get my paintings on some walls, they will be so chuffed they won't notice if you drive a tank through the front shop.'

'Let's see how the next day or two go,' said Zara. 'I just need some new piece of information which leads somewhere instead of nowhere. You promise you won't do anything to draw attention to yourself or the building?'

'Jo, you are the mad one. I'm cool. I'm helping you because I hope you are going to help me. I just want to paint.'

'Are you sure your parents won't think it's odd you sleeping up here?'

'I've slept here before once when we were threatened with burglary. My parents trust me. What's your real name by the way?'

'Zara,' said Zara.' 'I'm sorry. I obviously should just go and get a job at the checkout in Tesco's: I'm rubbish as an undercover agent.'

Zara kept watch for the rest of the day and saw nothing. Meanwhile Uttam had regaled his parents with the news of Zara's promised support and they were so thrilled they would have done anything for her. What Mrs Ram did was make her a takeaway dinner. Plenty for two. Zara phoned her friend with the gallery and went straight round to her flat with Uttam's sketches leaving Uttam painting a night-time picture of the lone protector pine tree for his father.

She was completely happy to leave Uttam watching the Muirhouse building. Even when she woke with a jolt in the middle of the night she did not panic: she was not being warned in a dream, her duvet had merely slipped to the floor. She went back to sleep immediately.

However, at seven the following morning she was wakened by her mobile ringing:

'Uttam reporting,' said a conspiratorial voice. 'I fell asleep at the crucial point but I had rigged up the CCTV and Muirhouse left the house at 02.01 in the company of a very slow-walking man whom Muirhouse had to support. It's all a bit fuzzy and when the car starts you can't see the man at all.'

'Number plates?'

'Yes very clear.' He recited the reg. number.

'I'll be round as soon as,' said Zara. 'Brilliant work.'

But first Zara rang Des.

'You wanting some info on Muirhouse?' Des began to interrupt. 'No time to go off on one, Des. Just get this. Muirhouse was seen leaving his mum's abode at 02.01 this morning in an Astra —she gave the number. Des interrupted again. 'No I didn't say I saw him. I said he was seen. Do you want me to tell you that no animals were harmed in this operation or would you rather get on with telling your traffic people to watch out for the vehicle? No I was not in any danger. I was asleep in bed. Heard of CCTV? Okay Des I'll speak to you later.'

***

No doubt about the fact that it was Muirhouse. The other figure was a blur and there was no certainty it was Balfour but who else was it likely to be thought Zara. Unfortunately, the information might only be useful in that it showed Muirhouse to be in the country and probably up to no good if he were transporting people around at two in the morning. But by the time the police caught up with the vehicle, Muirhouse would probably have abandoned it. Officers would go to the house and Mrs Muirhouse would say he'd dropped in with a drunken mate or some such story. Where was he going? That was the interesting question.

Once again Zara thought about Ben's contention that he would take Balfour to Arran. But, thought Zara, he would hardly go straight there. It would be too obvious. There would be a delay. Perhaps another teasing letter or perhaps the hiatus — even more teasing — of no letter, just silence. But it was over three weeks now since the murder. Perhaps Arran was now a possibility.

All day Zara sketched and watched. Uttam joined her for some of the time and she told him that her friend, who really was called Jo, had been very enthusiastic and wanted him to call round and discuss which paintings might be reproduced. She was willing to back him financially. Uttam demurred at this.

'The money is no problem,' he said. 'My parents will be delighted. They will pay and I can pay them back later.'

It looked like being another dead day but then, about five, who should turn up at the flat but John Muirhouse — on foot. Zara rang the local station. She had already been in touch with them re the CCTV and she'd taken the film to them so it could be properly analysed at the appropriate centre. Zara had the impression Des had been talking to the duty officer about her.

'I've just seen John Muirhouse enter his home,' she said, trying to keep the excitement out of her voice.

'Ah, PC Mac,' came the reply. Zara thought he was talking computer gibberish at first. Then she realized: was that what Des called her to his colleagues: Police Constable MacDonald — not? 'I'll get someone down there right away.' Zara was not convinced but there was nothing she could do. The station was less than five minutes down the road but when the police rolled up ten   minutes later, there was only a short interval between them knocking on the door and leaving again with no prisoner.

Zara watching from upstairs shook her head. The guy certainly had talent. Mrs Muirhouse had come out onto the steps and even from a distance Zara could see she was not looking pleased. There was the fist again. How awful, Zara could not help thinking, to have a baby that grew up to be John Muirhouse. Regardless of whether he was born that way or whether his parents were at all responsible, Mrs Muirhouse had to deal with her son's behaviour, she had to decide whether to be for him or against him. Zara hope she would never be placed in that position. If they were two of a kind, maybe it wasn't so bad. They could approve of each other.

Chapter XVII   Treading Water

Ronnie Balfour was on or rather in a rubbish dump. John Muirhouse had run the Astra smash into the middle of the disused dump and left. The prisoner had nothing to eat but Muirhouse had thrown a bottle of water over onto the back seat. Ronnie had just enough strength to undo it. He recognized the strategy: Muirhouse was trying to wear him down by playing on his nerves. It was not the first time he had abandoned him and it was difficult to know for how long. Ronnie found himself drifting off to sleep and when he woke he could not remember if it was the next day or the day before. Was it two weeks since he was on the mountain? He guessed two, but was it more? He sometimes tried to work out the likely thought patterns of the police. Did they imagine he was dead? Escaped abroad? Or did they know he was a prisoner but were always remaining just a step behind John Muirhouse in terms of information?

When he read his journal, it did not always make sense to him which was worrying. If he were not found soon, he would disintegrate. He thought of people who had endured months of prison, years even, hostages, prisoners of conscience and he could not believe he was being held for no reason except to be part of Muirhouse's plan to get him to plead guilty to the murder of Daffodil Brown. He was not going to do that.

He raised himself from his lying position across the back seat and tried to look in the rear-view mirror. It was difficult and when he saw the face he was shocked. At first he thought it was someone else. This person was pinched and cadaverous with no light in his eyes. I will not give up, he told himself and made the face smile. Someone is looking for me he repeated to himself over and over. Eventually Muirhouse will make a mistake. He pulled out hair and secreted it in a crack in the seats. He spent time fingerprinting as much as possible of the surfaces accessible to him.

After several hours, there were footsteps. Ronnie Balfour was pulled out of the Astra and pushed into another vehicle. Muirhouse did not speak but he did go over the internal surfaces of the Astra with a cloth.

Two hours later the police came by and found the abandoned car. They took some stray fingerprints and they found the hair but by this time Muirhouse was a good hundred miles away.

Zara felt frustrated. She could discover Muirhouse but she could not pin him down. She was not equipped. She was glad Uttam was not the sort of person to have followed Muirhouse on impulse on a bicycle. Something she might have done she reflected. Something Barney *had* done. Very foolish at night with nothing else on the road. Anyone doing that would have been a sitting duck.

She saw no future in watching the house any more. At least she was now fairly certain Ronnie Balfour was alive and that fact seemed to indicate that John Muirhouse had a vested interest in keeping him so. At least for the present. Was he going to become a bargaining tool in a different way? When, for instance, he got the message that the police were not going to agree not to charge him if he gave them Ronnie Balfour. She hated the idea of going back to Arran and waiting. She liked to be doing something but she couldn't think of anything new to do. At the point where she felt her head begin to ache, she took heed of the warning: go back, she said to herself, to a point where some action is possible and look at whether it might be effective.

Maybe, she thought she should talk to the Mountain Rescue people. Even if Muirhouse was not hiding Ronnie Balfour on the island at the moment, maybe he had done previously and maybe there were clues to be picked up. The Mountain Rescue would probably know the good hiding places but then, would they not have been searched already? However, it was something to do. You never knew when one piece of information might lead to another.

Ronnie had mentioned to her the pub where the members of the Mountain Rescue often congregated. Zara persuaded Kirsty to come out with her for a quiet drink.

'Only if you explain your hidden agenda,' said her friend. Zara grinned.

'You know me too well,' she said.

As luck would have it, the first people they met inside the bar were the two men who had been on the mountain when Daffodil had died.

'What y' for?' said the taller one called Tom, recognizing Zara at once. The two women sat down on the barstools beside the standing men.

'Heard anything?' asked Davy not thinking it necessary to explain what he meant. Zara saw no reason not to explain what had been caught on CCTV in Govanhill. 'Do you think the police believe Muirhouse to be a serial killer?' he asked. Zara shivered. 'They're not really pulling out all the stops, are they?' But what can you do? said Davy. He'll be under a large toadstool.'

'Or a raised bog,' said Tom.

'What's a raised bog?' asked Zara and Kirsty together.

'Gases form under the ground from decaying matter and raise the surface leaving a hollow underneath. Cows and sheep fall into them sometimes,' said Tom, 'and are never seen again.'

'I don't know whether to believe you,' said Zara.

'Stranger things have happened at sea,' said Davy. 'Did you ever hear the story of the unsinkable ghosts?' Zara and Kirsty shook their heads.

'It was about fifty years ago, well before you two were born,' said Davy. My uncle told me the story. He was in the RNLI and one night they had a call to go to a small craft someone had sighted through binoculars from the beach at Brodick. It appeared there were two people clinging onto the bow of the boat but in the water. They would not last long even though it was June.'

'You're saying June because it's June now,' said Zara.

'It's a well-known fact,' said Tom, 'that the brain is incapable of telling a story the same way twice.'

'How are you ever going to get reliable evidence then?' asked Zara.

'Maybe you don't want to hear the story,' said Davy pretending to look injured.

'Please,' said Kirsty. 'We're all ears.'

'They launched the lifeboat in Lamlash and motored round to Brodick looking for a small boat on a dark sea. At times the crew thought they heard cries but it was the sound of curlews —'

'Saying, over here, over here,' said Zara. Davy ignored her.

'They circled the bay finding nothing. The man who'd called had sounded very definite. About half a mile out, he'd said. One of the crew knew him for an ex-sailor so they assumed his assessment of the distance would be fairly accurate. They circled again, again hearing cries and this time they saw a boat and two people clinging to it just as the man had described. But as soon as they drew nearer, first one person then the other and then the boat, just disappeared. Sunk you might think but then when they circled again it would re-appear and the crew was convinced of its reality. It wasn't as if it was only one person could see it, it was the whole crew. And the cries of "Help! Save us! For pity's sake", everyone heard them.'

'Then one of the crew threw a long rope towards one of the men on the little boat which was no more than a few spars holding together but the rope seemed to fall straight through the clutching figure. By this time all the crew were afraid but not to be thwarted the man tried again and this time the crew were amazed to see at last the figure seize hold of the rope and begin to pull. And the lifeboat rocked. The men clung to the sides. It was as if their boat had been magnetized by a dark force.'

'Let go of the rope,' the skipper shouted as the vessel careered towards the floating spars. One of the crew managed to wrest the rope from the holder's hand which broke the contact with the wreck and then another member caught it again. They all breathed freely. The sea had an evil look, undulating back and forth as if to hide an awful secret.'

'Explanation,' said Zara. 'There has to be one.'

'They gave it one more try, not wanting to give in to the idea that they were dealing with something not of this world. But when the man throwing the rope was almost pulled into the sea, the skipper decided they would head for home. He could not imagine how he would record the event but he had a strong gut feeling that the safety of all the crew was at risk. Unacceptable risk.'

'So was there a monster under the waves needing fed?' asked Zara.

'You can mock,' said Davy, 'but listen'. On the 5th June 1851, a sailing ship, the *Bonnie Mary* was caught in the Clyde in stormy weather and was heading for the shelter of Lamlash Bay. She never made it. From the shore people watched unable to help. The ship went down with all hands except for two men. The following morning, the sea was calm and there was no wind and the remains of a small boat was seen with two men clinging to it. Although there was a mist that came and went, three men rowed out. They located the boat but it kept evading them and disappearing. When they could see the men they called to them but there was no reply. Eventually they managed to draw alongside. The two men were dead. The rescuers could not understand how they were still clinging to the boat.'

'Rigor mortis,' said Tom.

'They hauled the men into the rowing boat and made for the shore. The wreck disappeared.'

'So it's the spirits of those two men that haunt the bay,' said Zara.

'I think they re-appear in the hope that they will be rescued alive,' said Tom.

'Always on the 5th June,' said Davy. 'Always the 5th of June.'

Talk turned to other things and Zara tried to get Tom and Davy to tell her about good hiding places but they would only tease her and when the two women left their parting shot was,

'Look out for raised bogs!'

'I'm not a sheep,' said Zara.

***

Des called. He'd had an update from the station in Govanhill but he wanted to go over it all again. Still looking for something useful thought Zara.

When she arrived at the station he began by telling her about the abandoned car with evidence in it that Balfour had been there.

'God knows what he's doing to him,' said Zara.

'I don't understand what you mean,' said Des.

'Well it seems to me he's being dragged from one place to another to avoid discovery. Very Muirhouse if you ask me. Most people would find a good hiding place and stick to it but Muirhouse likes to thumb his nose at everyone at every opportunity he can get.' Des looked hard at Zara.

'I don't think you have any basis for assuming that Balfour is a captive. The forensics tell us that both men were in that car but they don't tell us that Balfour was there under duress.'

'If he's not under duress why hasn't he come forward? And, the letters sound as if Muirhouse has the upper hand,' said Zara trying but not succeeding in staying calm. 'I can't believe you think he was in the car of his own free will. Was the evidence pertaining to Ronnie Balfour in the back or front seat?' Des hesitated and then dismissed Zara's question.

'Maybe it's because I'm starting from a different base-line: I'm only using ascertainable facts, not hunches and wishful thinking. As far as I'm concerned, Balfour is still in the frame.'

They faced each other, neither giving way.

'What about the jewellery?' said Des. 'Why was the heart and —?'

'You can't prove how or why that happened. Muirhouse could have planted it as a piece of false evidence.' Zara stood up.

'Wait,' said Des. 'I need you to go over what was seen from above the shop.'

'It's all on the videotape,' said Zara still standing.

'But you saw Muirhouse walking into his house?'

'I saw him and I saw his mother come out when the police were leaving.'

'How can you be sure it was Muirhouse?' Zara let out an exasperated breath.

'I suppose Barney didn't see Muirhouse either. I suppose the two of us are just doing our best to waste police time. You'll be telling me next that I'm in league with Balfour, that he killed Daffodil and Muirhouse is innocent.'

'We haven't ruled it out,' said Des.

Zara left feeling so angry she wanted to throw bricks. Fortunately, there were none in the vicinity. Kirsty had just put the kettle on when Zara entered the kitchen and exploded.

'Okay Zara, okay. I hear you. You're upset. Have a cup of tea and a scone. It's a new recipe. I'd like your opinion. And then you can tell me why Des is such an unintelligent moron.'

After half an hour Zara was still angry but less so. Kirsty was able to say to her that perhaps it was possible to think differently about the Balfour question.

'I can see where Des is coming from,' said Kirsty, 'and I can see where you are coming from too. Your view is based on having spent time with Ronnie Balfour and getting a positive take on him but you can't expect Des to have that perspective.' Zara looked mutinous but said nothing.

'I suppose I'm just worried about Ronnie,' she said. 'I'm going to see Riga.'

Out in the field, Zara put her head against Riga's neck and listened to her. The horse wasn't actually talking to her but she was calming her down. She stood patiently while Zara collected herself. Suddenly she could see that the sun was shining through the trees and she could hear a wren singing. The grass looked unbelievably green and Riga's back was comforting and warm.

By the time she returned to North Crag she was in a much better temper.

'By the way,' said Kirsty, as Zara re-entered the kitchen. 'This came for you. I didn't give it to you before… What is it?' Zara had gone white. She felt for a chair. She had ripped open a rather ordinary envelope and pulled out a piece of paper cut with jagged sides like cartoon lightning on which was written the words, TIME IS RUNNING OUT BUT WHO FOR? Kirsty snatched the paper from Zara's hand. 'My God Zara. You'll need to take this to Des. Do you want me to come with you?'

Zara did not immediately understand why Des did not look surprised when he was shown the paper. He pushed another piece of paper towards her. This was a rough circle but it looked like the same texture, colour and weight as hers. Written round the circle were the words, YOUR SON HAS

NOT MUCH LONGER WRITE TO THE EVENING TIMES AND TELL HIM TO CONFESS.

'Obviously,' Des was saying, 'we need to test for fingerprints but it seems probable we already know the author of both these missives.'

'How are the Balfours?' asked Zara in a small voice.

'Worried as you can imagine. Understatement of course. I did manage to convince them it was probably bluster, just done to stir things up a bit. Muirhouse keeping himself on the front pages.' Zara remembered how John Laurie had written to the papers in 1889. That was after Rose was dead though. And everyone knew that Rose was dead. This time around there was one dead woman and one mystery man who might be guilty or not guilty, dead or alive.

'Very elaborate game if Balfour's guilty,' Zara commented. Des shrugged his shoulders.

'The thing is Zara, we have letters but no leads. Without more evidence we can't prove anyone's hypothesis.'

Zara felt very depressed knowing that the Balfours would be feeling a lot worse than she did.

'The footage,' she said, 'Did they think it was Ronnie?'

'They weren't sure,' said Des. 'It wasn't his jacket. They wanted it to be him of course so they had to try and discount that. It was more difficult for Mrs Balfour than for Mr.' Des told Zara to be especially careful and not to say anything rash or go anywhere dangerous.

'You want me to stay indoors with a crash helmet on?' She knew that at heart Des cared only about her safety.

'Zara, one of them is a psychopath.'

'Just one? Why not both?'

'Zara behave.'

'You're telling me it's possible Ronnie Balfour wrote that appalling note to his parents?'

'It's possible.'

'You're working on a nothing-is-what-it-seems premise?' Des sighed.

'I'll admit to being almost completely unsure of what's happening and where to go next and what the behaviour of Muirhouse, Balfour, whoever is behind these letters means but one thing I am certain of is: Ronnie Balfour is in some way involved.'

'Come on Kirsty. We don't have to listen to this,' said Zara almost pushing her friend out of the room in front of her.

***

'Dad, Aunty Zara is very worried about the guy Ronnie Balfour, isn't she?' Ben and Barney were packing to go to Arran for what seemed to Ben like eternity.

'That's right,' said Barney putting a spare pair of trainers into his rucksack and taking them out again.

'But we don't want her going off and getting captured by someone like Malloch, do we?'

'We certainly don't, Ben. Do you have a plan? You sound as if you have a plan in mind.'

'I was thinking that if we had a programme, we could get her enthusiastic about it and keep her mind off what happened on Goat Fell. We could start it this weekend,' he added looking dreamy.

'Hm,' said Barney.

'You don't think it would work?' asked Ben.

'You know Aunty Zara,' said Barney.' It's a good idea though,' he said seeing Ben's face fall. 'It's worth a try. I don't know whether us being on Arran is a good thing or a bad thing.'

'A good thing, Dad. Of course it's a good thing. You're going to teach me to fish. We're going to learn lots of birds' names and we're going to explore the island inch by inch — that's my programme. We're going to go into every field and up every crag. It will be like bagging Munros and I'll shade the map when we've been to a place so we know where we don't have to go again. Unless we like it so much we want to.'

'Have you worked out the order yet?' asked Barney.

'Not yet. I thought I'd print out some google maps. I can't draw on your ordnance survey map.'

'If you want to work on them on the boat, you'd better do it now then. We're leaving in three hours.'

***

Zara wanted very much to go and see the Balfours who were still staying in the village but, as if by magic, they appeared by the car park later that day as Zara was walking along the Shore Road. She ran down to greet them and they all sat down on a bench to talk properly. Margaret Balfour was dismayed to find Zara had been threatened. She had wanted to write to the *Evening Times* as the writer had suggested but say something completely different.

'I thought if Ronnie was going to see it...' she said.

'But he's not,' said Harry Balfour. 'Muirhouse is just after publicity; another chance to point out that he's one step ahead of the cops.'

'You do believe he's holding Ronnie against his will?' asked Zara.

'Don't you?' asked Harry. Zara hastened to assure him 'yes'. 'That Muirhouse can say anything. He doesn't need us to write to the papers. Ronnie knows we believe in him. Confession! My God.'

'What upsets me,' said Margaret Balfour, 'is the idea that the police have Ronnie in the frame. It breaks my heart to think that anyone could believe that'.

'They have no evidence to rule it out.' Zara found herself quoting Des. 'They don't know Ronnie like you do.'

'We talked to some of the Mountain Rescue people,' said Margaret. 'They said he could have fallen down somewhere and never be found. There's gullies...'

'But he was in that car, Margaret.'

'We don't know when though. Perhaps they knew each other.' Zara could see it cost Ronnie's mother a lot to say this. 'Perhaps before… you know… before this happened, they were in that car and — '

'But don't you think it was Ronnie on the CCTV?' asked Zara.

'I couldn't swear to it,' said Margaret. Zara couldn't think of anything to make her feel any better. She began to wish she hadn't been so impetuous in speaking to the Balfours. The whole business was just too painful.

However, when they said goodbye, it was evident that the couple were glad to have spoken to her.

'We've no one really to talk to who understands,' Margaret Balfour said, 'now Mark has gone back to Australia. He didn't want to but he had to in order to hold onto his job. He'll come back as soon as he can. Something to do with his contract.' Zara nodded.

'How was he feeling?'

'Awful. He totally believes in Ronnie. They were very close. Did everything together, right until they left school. He'll come back as soon as he can,' she repeated.

***

Coming away Zara felt a familiar feeling of helplessness and taxed her mind for something to do, something even a small thing which might help move everyone towards a solution. It was different from last year when she had been up against Malloch: until he had actually kidnapped her, she had never ever felt personally threatened, even though she knew others had thought she was in danger. While she did not want to be bloody-minded — I'll do as I please and look out for myself — she still believed that if she thought hard enough she would come up with a possible action. Safe? Safe-ish perhaps.

She went over all the conversations she had had with the Balfours, Des, Tom and Davy, Barney, Kirsty and George and filtered the content slowly through her mind to see if there was anything that held a spark she could nurture into a flame. But she came up with nothing. She imagined Ronnie in an abandoned car, an abandoned shed, a derelict house but how in the world did she set about finding him?

Zara met Barney and Ben at the boat. All three were glad to see each other though Zara still had to tell Barney about the threatening letter. Ben had told Zara about his plan before they even reached the Shore Road.

'She looked quite glum,' he said to Barney later. 'My idea really cheered her up.'

Ben rushed upstairs as soon as they reached the hotel and unpacked his rucksack placing his maps on the small table under the skylight. He laid out his pencils — a black one for writing the date, a green one for shadowing in fields, a brown one for moorland and a grey one for the mountains.

'I'll have to put flowers in and birds,' he said to Zara and Barney at dinner, 'otherwise the maps are going to look unexciting.'

After dinner they all sat and drew up a list of alternative activities should it be wet.

'It had better stay dry,' said Ben. 'All the things I want to do are out of doors apart from the castle and the museum. There's something else,' he added, 'something I didn't tell you about the plan.' Zara and Barney looked expectant.

'It's the unplanned bit of the plan.'

'Right,' said Barney.

'We've all got a role: we've each got to provide a surprise every day. Yours, Aunty Zara, is easy. You just have to provide a different kind of sandwich or roll every day for lunch. Mine's to decide where we're going but I shan't tell you till we set out and then only in which direction. And Dad, yours is to think up a special surprise every day.'

'Why do I always draw the short straw?' said Barney. 'I thought we were meant to be on holiday. I shan't be able to sleep at night, racking my brains and then when I've thought of something I'll be worrying about whether you'll like it.'

'You'll think of something, Dad. It could just be a bar of chocolate or something.'

'Or something being sweets I suppose.'

'It's entirely up to you, Dad. If you think chocolate or sweets is a good idea, I won't mind. Not fantastically original but we can put up with that, can't we Aunty Zara?'

Chapter XVIII   Surprise Picnic

Somewhere, Ronnie Balfour was being lectured by John Muirhouse:

'I sent your parents a letter. I implored them to write to the *Evening Times* and ask you to confess your crime. They haven't done it. What does that say to you, Balfour? I know what it says to me: Ronnie's parents don't care what happens to him now. They've given up on him. They know he did it but they don't even want to write to him because they are ashamed of the association. How does it feel to be alone in the world? No parents. Brother in Australia. Didn't come back. Why? Didn't want to be associated with a murderer. Who says blood's thicker than water? But then when we are dealing with a psychopath we're not expecting feelings, are we? Why did Daffodil have to die? Are you going to tell me? It would be so much easier for everyone if you would just confess. Time is running out you know. Look how weak you are. You're not going to last much longer. You can't blame me. I did everything I could to make things go smoothly. I tried to save Daffodil but you...'

Ronnie tried not to listen. His body and mind were exhausted. Sometimes he felt delirious which he imagined was a result of virtual starvation. He felt spaced out, not himself. He kept dreaming about being under a hot shower and then eating a meal consisting of... It was difficult thinking about food. If he thought of chips or sausage he almost vomited He had to imagine swallowing something simple and wholesome like thin chicken soup.

He had reached a stage of numbness where Muirhouse's taunts left him cold in his mind but strangely, made his body feel tireder and tireder, as if he were continually receiving punches which, he reflected, he was in a sense. He wished he knew his location. He was at the moment blindfold and could hardly detect if he were outside, in a barn or in a house. He had stone beneath him — an old derelict cottage? — and there was a damp smell but he could not decide whether it was the smell of wet stone or the smell of plants. There was an occasional breeze but whether that was through an open window or just openness, he was at loss to say.

He re-tuned to Muirhouse's voice:

'I've set trip wires up. Anyone approaching this location will seriously injure him or herself,' said Muirhouse with a smile Ronnie couldn't see. 'So don't try and shout if you hear anyone coming. You might kill them as a result and that would be another charge against you.'

***

Zara had a phone call from Uttam. She felt a waft of something positive.

'Hi, how are you? Lovely to hear from you. Have you sorted out which paintings are to be made into prints yet? Have you —'

'Zara listen. Everything is fine for me. Your friend is going to give me space in a group show in September but Zara listen, yesterday I had to deliver some groceries to Mrs Muirhouse. I thought nothing of it, it's happened before often but after seeing him on the CCTV, Muirhouse gives me the creeps and I heard his voice through the open window. I couldn't see him.'

'Did he know you were there?'

'I don't think so. It was all so quick. I heard the words and a big laugh which made me shiver.'

'What words Uttam?'

'It was a horrible laugh like the bad man at the pantomime. I couldn't believe it, that it was Muirhouse, I mean, but then he opened the door. I had my finger on the bell and he opened the door before I pushed it. I nearly fell into the room.'

'What did he say, Uttam?' Zara's patience was almost used up.

'He said, "Mark Linwood" and laughed. I just thought you might like to know. I didn't know if it was important. He just took the bag of groceries and handed me the right money. They always have exactly the right money. His mother laughed too. People usually laugh when they are happy but this was... was more like gloating.'

'Mark Linwood,' Zara repeated the name. 'Doesn't ring any bells. Did you phone the police?'

'Yes, Zara but of course they arrived too late. It was a re-run of the last time. Mrs Muirhouse on the step shaking her fist and cursing them for trying to get her boy.'

'Thanks anyway Uttam. You did the right thing. And be careful.'

'You be careful too Zara. I want you to come to my exhibition.'

'Don't worry. I wouldn't miss it for anything.'

'I'm going to do new paintings for it. Jo says I don't have to, she could just frame what I have but I want to do new stuff.'

'Good for you,' said Zara. 'Best of luck!'

Zara put the phone down slowly. Mark Linwood? Did that mean anything? Mark. Wasn't there another Mark on the periphery of the picture? Ronnie Barbour's brother in Australia. Was it possible he was only Margaret's son, making him Ronnie's stepbrother? But then Mrs Balfour had particularly mentioned how they were almost like twins. Not likely then but it seemed too much of a coincidence: everything was altered if there turned out to be a connection between Muirhouse and Mark, Ronnie's brother. The holding of Ronnie could have been a primary plan and Daffodil some sort of collateral. Zara shook herself: just thinking herself into John Muirhouse's mind brought on a degree of insensitivity she wouldn't have thought possible.

She thought through the possibility of her hunch being correct. There were two paths Muirhouse could have taken. One was a flexible plan that Ronnie might fall in with. Zara had not been present in the pub when the two had met. Maybe they had met on Arran more than once. If they knew each other, had they ever been friends? Or had they been to the same school, shared an interest in sport, gone to the same youth club? Had John Muirhouse had a relationship with Mark back in the past, which Ronnie probably knew about or was it recent and a secret? Had John Muirhouse ever been in Australia? No, the police had said he had never been out of the country. Could Ronnie's decision to climb Goat Fell on the same day as John Muirhouse have been a result of the other's influence? Did he know Ronnie was coming to stay on Arran and if so how? It was all plausible but it was not exactly a mantrap, depending as it did with Ronnie falling in with what John Muirhouse wanted.

Zara thought back to the *Waverley* and how she, having decided to have nothing to do with Muirhouse on the boat had ended up eating ice cream with him and sharing a dolphin experience. Was that the man's special talent — an ability to lure people into situations without them being aware of it?

On the other hand, maybe Muirhouse cast his net wide but put certain key things in place and anticipated success — Zara thought it out — because he took into consideration who he was trapping, leant on their psychological profile and what's more, got a tremendous kick out of being right. The first way of working was mundane depending more on making sure he was in the right place at the right time, the second way depended on his victim making deductions and thereby falling into his trap, you might say, of their own volition. Much more satisfying. The third possibility was, of course, that it had all happened by chance and that Muirhouse had decided to kill Daffodil on the spur of the moment and then thought of capturing Ronnie Balfour.

So what was the point? He had Ronnie. Was he going to use him as some sort of hostage? Maybe he was blackmailing Mark and Mark had not told anyone. I'll kill your brother unless... and furthermore I'll tell your parents it was within your power to save him but you didn't, you just buggered off back to Australia.

It was to be presumed that Mark would be drip-fed the information on Ronnie: how he was failing, how there was not much time. John Muirhouse really seemed to enjoy drawing things out.

Did this Mark Linwood have anything to do with the Goat Fell murder? This was the question Zara fell asleep with, her mind vainly pursuing a connection.

***

Something woke Zara in the middle of the night. At first she assumed it was a noise. She listened but heard nothing untoward. Then she realised there were two words beating a rhythm in her head. Merkland Wood, Merkland

Wood. She could not think why. Merkland Wood was a mile outside Brodick. Not a particularly dense wood, with huge trees and some impassable undergrowth. Perhaps Ben had mentioned it? Or maybe her psychic powers were growing. She drifted back to sleep.

Ben woke up very early the next day and was busy with his maps before he was even dressed. He was excited and accused Barney of looking over his shoulder to second guess where they were going. Taking her cue from Ben, Zara zipped through her chores as fast as she could and the three of them were ready to leave by ten-thirty. Nessie ran round and round the North Crag garden as if limbering up for a marathon.

'Everyone ready with their surprises?' said Ben stowing his maps in the outside pocket of his rucksack.

'My rolls are so surprising you won't be able to eat them,' said Zara. Barney admitted he would have to get his surprise en route. Ben looked dismayed but Barney assured him he knew what he was buying.

Barney came out of the shop with a long plastic bag and he wouldn't let Ben guess what was in it.

'This surprise is for later. After yours and Zara's,' he said, putting the bag carefully in his rucksack.

Ben took them along Fishermen's Walk and then along a short cut, missing the turn-off to the String Road.

'Not uphill today then?' Zara commented.

'You'll see,' said Ben. They went past Duchess Court and round the corner. Zara began to wonder if they were going to the castle grounds but no, Ben kept them firmly on the road.

Eventually they came to a parking space on the shore side of the road.

'First stop,' said Ben. 'Has anyone brought a chocolate surprise or at least a biscuit surprise? We might see some seals here if we sit on these rocks.'

'Does the magic only work if a treat is produced?' said Zara searching for the flapjack she had brought.

They sat on a rock, the sun went behind a cloud and Ben began to look disappointed. No seals. He left them to go nearer the water. There was a cry and they looked over to where Ben had been and couldn't see him. Zara was disconcerted to find that the first image that came into her mind was of Muirhouse pouncing on Ben from behind a rock.

Ben had tripped and fallen, fortunately not in the water. Nessie sat looking on, solicitous. Ben's knee was bruised but it still bent and straightened in the normal way. Barney had arnica in his rucksack.

'That's two things gone wrong and we haven't even started on my main surprise,' said Ben.

'I can't wait,' said Zara. 'You are a very good holder-onto-er.'

'You'll see when we cross the road,' said Ben.

They followed him to a gap in the wall where the top stone had been displaced to make a lichen-covered stile. Once over, they were in the wood.

'Merkland Wood,' said Ben. 'There's a trail and we have to find things.' It was something in the way Ben said it: Merkland Wood. Zara hit her head with her hand. Mark Linwood, no. Merkland Wood, yes. Oh my God she thought, is Ronnie Balfour here? And Muirhouse didn't know she knew? She could not believe the train of events that had led her there. She walked behind and said nothing.

Ben was very excited now they were actually in the wood and pleased that Barney and Zara were showing every sign of being excited too. It was therefore easy for Zara to pretend she was on Ben's quest and let out her feelings of trepidation. She was torn as to what to do next. If she phoned Des he might well laugh at her. If she told Barney, he would insist she phoned Des and then their picnic would be spoiled. On the other hand, they might go deeper into the wood and come upon not only Balfour but Muirhouse. But on that reasoning they might come upon the two men anywhere they might think of going and anyway everyone knows, argued Zara to herself that more accidents happen in the home than outside so they were comparatively safe. She knew also that no one liked that sort of logic. The words 'common sense' came into her mind. I'll give it till we've had the picnic she decided.

'There's curly crooks like unfurling leaves carved on a special rock,' said Ben. 'We have to look for them.' The path they followed was dry and they made little noise. Even Nessie was quiet, busy sniffing, coming and going, in and out of sight. Zara wondered whether, if Ronnie Balfour was anywhere around, Nessie would smell him out. It was possible. They could hear the occasional birdsong and at each sound Zara stopped.

'Why are you stopping, Aunty Zara?'

'I was wondering what that bird is,' said Zara. 'Aren't you spotting birds today?'

'When I see them,' said Ben. 'At the moment I'm looking for crooks.' Progress was slow because every time Ben came to a fallen tree he had to climb up and walk its length but the wood was delightful and they had it to themselves.

Or did they Zara wondered. If Ronnie Balfour was here, would he not be shouting? She started making more noise. It would be just like John Muirhouse to tantalize his victim with the prospect of being found. If he were blindfold with his mouth taped and his legs tied what noise could he make? He would be like those victims of near misses, who, in survival at sea stories, have a ship pass by them at three-hundred feet as they light their last flare.

Zara was behind. She heard Ben shout and she scrambled up a short slope to a clearing. They had found the crooks. Ben was elated. He ran his fingers over the pattern on the stone.

'It's good the way you just find it suddenly,' he said. 'It looks almost as if it grew here.' Barney wondered about having the picnic then but Ben said it was up to Zara because she was in charge of the food surprises.

'Have we to find anything else?' asked Zara.

'We have to find gold,' said Ben, 'and something made of wood.'

'Well should we find the gold first and then have the picnic?'

They set off again, Zara still keeping a look out for possible hiding places. She stopped when Nessie stopped, watching her closely. Ben found the golden rain first and took a photo of the shiny drop-shapes gleaming on their rock while Zara unpacked the picnic. The rolls were various. There were sundried tomatoes and houmous with black olives, cucumber, lettuce and chorizo, and celery with grated cheddar and mango chutney. Ben gave Zara nine-and-a-half out of ten.

'Why not ten?' asked Zara pretending to be disappointed.

'Presentation,' said Ben. 'Mine was slightly squashed and I think you used the same knife for the chutney as you did for the chorizo.'

'I'll try and do better next time,' said Zara,' 'though I have to say, I'm not sure where to go next in the realm of food surprises.'

After they had eaten, Zara felt strangely sleepy and when Barney said they were moving she grunted and lay back on the moss.

'Just coming,' she said. Nessie was beside her probably only because Zara had just shared with her the last bite of her chorizo roll.

She intended to follow immediately but lying back looking at the patterns of the leaves against the sky she found her eyes closing and when she eventually came round ten minutes later, Barney and Ben were nowhere to be seen. Nessie was still there, eyeing the rucksack.

'Where have they gone, Nessie? Do you know? Can you hear them? Which way shall we go?' There was more than one path but Nessie seemed in no doubt and Zara assumed the dog was following the scent of the people she knew. They walked quickly, to catch up but just found themselves deeper in, further from the road and although they were still on a well-defined path, Zara felt lost. She had been looking continually at every tree, bush and rock to gauge whether it would yield a hiding place and as they plunged steeply down, she was intent on not tripping on the many tree roots that crossed the path. They came to a place where a huge tree had fallen and behind it there was a massive overhanging rock which made a cave beneath it which Zara could not see into. She was focusing so hard on the rock that she did not see the stone in her path and fell headlong. She had landed askew, not having managed to use her arms and legs to break her fall, cracking her head as she contacted the ground. She lay for a few seconds regaining her breath and then became aware of Nessie whining.

She sat up and listened. Nothing. Nessie whined again. It was uncanny how spooked Zara felt. The hair stood up on the back of the dog's neck. Zara looked again at the cave-like space obscured as it was by foliage from the huge tree. She thought she saw a movement. Before them was a patch of mud criss-crossed with broken branches.

'Come on,' she said to Nessie. 'Let's investigate.'

Nessie sprang in the direction Zara pointed and then floundered almost completely disappearing. Zara, who had been about to take a step forward, stepped back and by a piece of extraordinary luck caught the strap of her rucksack on a living branch. Thus suspended she leant forward and grabbed the dog.

'Raised bog' were the words that came to her. Davy had not been joking then. Instead of attempting a further crossing, Zara climbed onto the fallen tree having first placed Nessie on top of it. They made their way along its twenty feet and slithered through at the uprooted end to find themselves enclosed in dimness. At one end was a dark hunched shape.

'Ronnie,' cried Zara. 'I can't believe it.' She could not unfasten his shackles but soon dismantled the blindfold and tape round his mouth. It was all too much as she had imagined. He was trying to speak but seemed to have difficulty forming words.

'Food,' Zara guessed. She emptied her rucksack of everything that was left and put a roll into his shaking hands which could only just reach his mouth. Zara was aghast at his appearance. The fine figure of a man with whom she had climbed Goat Fell was now a pallid shadow. He looked like a creature of the moss, unused to sunlight, diminished. Even his voice was weak. He spoke as if it cost him dearly to draw breath.

'How can I get you away from here?' said Zara.

'You have a saw?' He indicated his bound feet and hands. 'And anyway I could not walk.' Zara had to lean towards him to catch his voice. She punched Des's number into her mobile but there was no response. No signal. And nearly out of charge. She almost threw it away in disgust. It wouldn't even take a photo. She stood.

'I'll be back. As soon as.' She would have to find the road quickly and someone with a working mobile. She did not have time to think about Ben and Barney. She arranged the food where Ronnie could reach it. 'It's fantastic to see you,' she said feeling totally inadequate. She turned to go but Ronnie was muttering something. 'What Ronnie? What is it?'

'Daffodil,' he said. 'It must be to do with Daffodil.'

'Tell us later, Ronnie. I'm afraid for you. You're so weak. You can talk later when we have you in the hospital.'

Zara didn't think of Nessie till she found she was panting beside her. She went downhill as the crow flies, towards the sea, shouting Barney's name. It took longer than she expected. Bushes and trees kept tangling in front of her and she stumbled often on the uneven ground.

Once she gained the road she realized she was south of where they had entered the wood. Where were Ben and Barney? Why would they be here? They were still looking for sculpture. She tried her phone again: still no signal. She would need to flag down a car or ask someone on foot but the road was completely empty. She was not sure why she was panicking. It looked as if Ronnie had been left to rot. She started walking towards Brodick.

The first car did not stop. Obviously saw me as a manic hitch-hiker thought Zara. She began to run. Then looking back, she saw a cyclist. She stood in the road and put her arms out to stop him. The young man seemed torn between irritation and alarm.

'Mobile? Do you have one that works? I need to phone the police?' He produced one from somewhere on his bike. Nessie sat obediently on the verge looking expectant. 'I've found him,' said Zara when she got through. She was not speaking to Des. Tell DI Des that Ronnie Balfour is in Merkland Wood. Straight up from the clump of birch trees that were driven into last month. How far from Cladach? About a mile. He's under a rock. An overhang, I don't mean pinned down. He'll shout when he hears you coming but he's very weak. Yes, I could show you. Yes, yes.'

'Would you like me to wait with you?' The young man, having grasped the gravity of the situation was prepared to be helpful.

'It's okay thanks. I'm with friends. I just lost them momentarily.'

'Is it an injury?'

'No, no. It's just...' Zara felt it was all too complicated to explain. 'You've been very helpful but I need to go now. My friends will be looking for me.'

'Are they with the...?' But Zara was off waving, she hoped not too dismissively as she went.

She was thinking she would have to try to do two things: one stay on the road for the police and two, try and locate Barney and Ben. She suddenly thought to look at her phone again. Three missed calls from Barney. He would be imagining her lying injured in the wood. She began to run but it was too hot. Isn't it about time something went right she thought? She no longer felt any elation over finding Ronnie only a curious sense of unease.

Then she saw a kite on the shore, high above the trees. It was a quarter of a mile away but she had the feeling it would be Ben at the end of the string.

'It was my idea, Aunty Zara, when we couldn't find you. I said Aunty Zara will see it and know it's us. We thought you might have gone back to the parking space. You weren't there and Dad looked in his rucksack for something and I saw the kite. I could see it was a kite but still it was a very good surprise.' He stopped because of Zara's face.

She had called to them from her position on the road and although she had heard Ben's every word, when he reached her he could sense that she was not entirely focused on what he was saying. Zara opened her mouth and shut it again. She was trying to think how to tell Barney what had happened without telling Ben.

'Ben,' she said at last, 'would you just stand here for a minute and shout me if you see a police car coming. And flag it down.' Ben was too excited to ask why. Zara moved towards the beach with Barney. 'Found him,' she said. 'He's in a terrible state.'

'But how did you know he was there?'

'Too complicated to explain just now. Police coming. Couldn't get a signal on my mobile or I would have phoned you.' Barney nodded.

'So you need to take the police to the place?'

'Yes. I think it would be quickest.'

'Aunty Zara! There's a police car and an ambulance coming.' Zara scrambled back to the road. 'Who is it for? Did you find —?'

'An injured man,' said Zara. In the woods. That's how we didn't meet. I was following you and then I found the man.' She ran along the road, back to the broken birches.

Barney managed to lure Ben away with the promise of a further surprise back in Brodick and the prospect of more kite-flying on a flatter terrain.

Des jumped out of the car with three of his team; the ambulance drew up behind. Zara re-crossed the road and indicated,

'Here,' she said. 'Straight up from here.'

'You lead,' said Des.

Chapter XIX   An assortment of incidents

Zara was not at all sure she would remember the way. Uphill instead of down, all the trees and bushes showing their other sides. She hadn't considered landmarks in her previous flight. She plunged over moss and boulder hoping she would be right instinctively. Suddenly she saw ahead of her a familiar tree: the one she'd dozed under.

'Nearly there,' she said. Des looked at her and she stared back at him. She knew he was thinking, this had better be good.

In two minutes they were all standing opposite the rocky overhang.

'Don't go forward,' said Zara. 'There's a raised bog or something. I nearly lost Nessie.' Des looked at her again and held his palm uppermost as if to say, So which way? Zara turned to climb the tree trunk:

'We're here Ronnie,' she shouted. 'Are you okay?' She jumped down onto the cave floor, Des followed immediately. They stared around them in the gloom. Zara made to move but Des stayed her.

'Police locus,' he said, 'even if there's no one here', for they could see no sign of Ronnie Balfour at all.

'He was here,' said Zara. 'Half an hour ago he was here. He couldn't have left by himself, he wasn't fit. He couldn't walk. He was tied up. Chained.' Her words fell over one another in justification.

'We need to check the ferries,' said Des. 'Muirhouse must have picked him up. He could be moving him to another location on the island but my guess is he'll have left.' He called the island police to have them look for Muirhouse at the Brodick and Lochranza piers. 'You didn't happen to take a photo, Zara?' Zara muttered something about her mobile not working. She was mortified. Des seemed to be implying that perhaps she had imagined it all. But more than that, she was bewildered by the whole experience: had Muirhouse been in the wood the whole time or was it merely an unlucky chance that he came back just after she had gone?

The police scoured the area for clues. Almost immediately they found trip wires. Zara had not fallen over a stone: wires had been purposely placed in such a way that from whichever direction anyone approached the hiding place they would have encountered them. More disturbing was the 'raised bog'. When Zara told Des about Nessie's experience, he had his men investigate, very cautiously moving dead branches to discover a gaping hole, a pit deep enough to cause death or serious injury. The hole was natural but looked as if it had been enlarged by the removal of rock loosened by the fall of the tree.

Because she had to, Zara explained how she had come to the conclusion that Ronnie was in the wood. Even with hindsight, she still could not be sure that a trap had been laid for her, specifically, from the point when Uttam was called across to the Muirhouse's to deliver groceries. It could have been chance that Uttam had reported Merkland Wood as Mark Linwood. Zara preferred this reading of the situation. She did not like that Muirhouse understood how her mind worked, that perhaps Muirhouse had set his mother to watch for people like Zara, just as she herself had set Uttam to watch for Muirhouse.

'Was this trap in the wood set for you Zara?' asked Des. 'Balfour would maybe have had to listen to your screams.' He fell silent. 'The weird thing about Muirhouse is how he likes to play. His scheme went wrong — it was never fool proof — but then it seems he got a kick from outwitting us. It's one thing to make an escape yourself but to vanish altogether with a grown man who can't walk, that takes talent.'

There were no fingerprints in the hiding place. Des reckoned that Muirhouse had actually wiped and sprayed the surfaces with something that dissolved grease. Scene-of-crime officers would go over it and the surrounding area but the outlook was bleak.

***

Muirhouse had been in the wood fortuitously and had waited for Zara to leave and then, losing no time, lifted Ronnie Balfour into a body bag which had convenient straps and hoisted it like a rucksack onto his back. He left the wood by walking parallel to the shore till he came to a clearing near the road. A car — it would be a mistake to call it his — was waiting in the undergrowth where he had left it. He turned north. He had more than one workable plan depending on how things developed. He drove very fast along the straight but slowed down at corners. He was calm: he felt excitement but he knew he had to contain it, knew it was best to do so.

Approaching the Sandstone Quay in Corrie he cruised looking for the youth he had seen the day before. He had not been definite but he'd said he might have a job for him. To hang around. The guy was unemployed: he'd hung around.

Muirhouse signalled and the figure trotted over.

'I have a job for you. Take this car to Lochranza and get on the next ferry. When you get to the other side there will be a guy waiting. He'll be wearing a blue naval cap and he has a ponytail. Shortish. Liverpool accent.' Muirhouse was enjoying making this up. The young man spoke for the first time.

'I don't know accents, I won't be able to...'

'I'll phone him, He'll recognize you. And the car. It's his car. Got it? Here's the money for the fare and the rest is for you'. Muirhouse handed him a folded bundle of notes. Counting was unnecessary, the youth could see it was more money than he'd had in his hand for a long time. 'Take this.' Muirhouse produced a mobile phone. 'Dial 999 and report a speeding car with this reg.' He wrote down the number.

'What car would that be?' Bobby smiled. 'You mean me? In a minute?' Muirhouse nodded.

'One more thing before you go.' Muirhouse was muttering something about bathroom tiles. The man, nameless as far as Bobby was concerned, took a large bag from the boot. Bobby was still mesmerised by the money and thought nothing of it. Didn't wonder what the man was going to do next. Didn't register consciously that the last time he'd seen a bag like that it had held a drowned man.

It was a lovely motor; he'd said he could drive but he hadn't passed his test yet and he wasn't very good. He was itching to get away before the man realised. He stepped into the car and turned on the ignition. So far so good. He made the 999 call. Gave a location for the speeding car with a grin on his face.

'Okay, no problem,' he said.

'Drive fast,' said Muirhouse.

Muirhouse hardly watched him leave. He didn't really care what the guy did. He'd told him to drive fast so he'd be noticed. He turned his attention to another vehicle. A beat up van he'd seen parked up the day before. Old enough to be hot-wired. He prayed there would be some petrol in it but he wasn't going far. He turned north again but travelled only as far as Sannox. Driving the van into a stand of roadside shrubs so it would not immediately be noticed, he extracted his burden from the back of the vehicle and hoisted it on his back again. In a few minutes he passed the resting place of Edwin Rose and soon he had disappeared down the Glen Sannox path.

***

Bobby was enjoying himself. The car climbed the Boguille with ease and he met no one. He was exhilarated by the time he reached the top and suddenly the image came into his mind of smooth water and the car sailing into it and of him escaping as in a film, the vehicle going to the bottom and himself waiting for it to fill with water before he lunged from an open window and floated to the surface. Beside Lochranza castle. He could do that there. People would find the car with no one in it. He could swim to his mate's house on the other side of the inlet, get dry and go home. His mate would be impressed.

He drove past the distillery and the long straggle of houses, past the youth hostel till he reached the part of the village where you become aware of the water. What should he do if there were people on the grass by the castle? It wouldn't matter. He would be going at such a speed they would just get out of his way. Adrenalin began to pulse through him. He felt his inside breast pocket for the comforting bulge of the folded notes: he did not want to lose those. The castle sat ruined and desolate. Bobby wished some millionaire would turn it into a proper visitor centre with a restaurant. He turned onto the grassy approach. There was one family and one couple strolling to his left. They had no time to look askance as he continued to drive past where people usually parked, drive around the castle walls and maximising his speed, accelerator foot to the floor, plunge, airborne for a moment into the cold water. By the time onlookers had reached the scene, there was hardly a ripple, no sign of the car nor of the mad bad driver.

***

Barney and Ben headed back to Brodick.

'Will the man be all right?' asked Ben as the ambulance passed them.

'I should hope so,' said Barney.

'Will he have to be air-lifted? Will we see the helicopter?'

'I don't know Ben.'

Gradually Barney managed to ease Ben away from the excitement of the afternoon and turn his mind to what they might do next. There was a good breeze picking up. More kite flying seemed to be in order. And ice cream because it was so hot.

'It was odd that a surprise was waiting in the wood,' said Ben. 'Do you think it's true that surprises come all at once like the buses, as Gran says?'

'Very odd,' said Barney. 'Not sure about the nature of surprises though.'

He hoped Zara would be back soon. He did not know what to say to his son. Zara would be exhausted he thought even though she would be overjoyed at finding Ronnie Balfour. She would be pleased she had been right in agreeing with Ben that the man would be on the island. But had it been a total coincidence? Did she stumble upon him up there in the wood or had there been some clue she'd kept from him? He could imagine her wanting to keep the information to herself until she was proved right and also, he thought she would want to avoid worrying him, Barney. He tried to make his sigh inaudible. He had half thought that Zara was being more sensible than usual but he had obviously been wrong.

Ben was hungry and Barney decided they would eat at North Crag and not wait for Zara since he had heard nothing from her since she had set off with the police. (Barney had forgotten her mobile was out of charge). Ben went into the annexe beyond the dining room where there was a pool table. Barney, having arranged for dinner, went upstairs.

He felt conscious of something different as soon as he opened the door to their attic room. Had they left the skylight wide like that? He looked around for evidence of a burglary. Nothing appeared to have been touched. He sat on the bed unsatisfied but cursing himself for feeling paranoid. Just because someone was killed on a mountain, it doesn't mean everyone's after you, he told himself.

Then his eyes fell on a piece of paper, scrumpled in the waste paper basket. He recognized Zara's writing. He lifted it unwillingly. It looked like a page torn from a notebook: '... Ronnie I can't write a letter to you as I don't know where you are. If you would only give me a sign! More and more I feel the need to be... I am so worried. I don't know what I will do if I never... but one thing is certain, I will never forget... If only I were speaking to you not writing...'

Barney sat like a stone. Even his eyes did not move. They remained focused on the words in front of him. His one thought was to leave but how could he go back to Glasgow when he had promised Ben a month in Arran? Lochranza Youth Hostel? Could he lure Ben away from Brodick with the promise of the ruined castle? They could climb up to Coireann Lochan. They could go over on the Claonaig ferry and visit Skipness castle. He started to throw things into his rucksack. He was so intent on what he was doing he did not hear Zara come in.

'He wasn't there, Barney. Muirhouse must have taken him. He must have been watching us in the woods all the time we were there. I'm so...' Zara went towards Barney for a hug but he held her off.

'...upset your lover boy has gone!' If Barney had been in a rational frame of mind he would have registered that Zara's shock was genuine. He looked at the floor and handed her the note. 'I suppose you will say that's not your writing.' Zara snatched the paper from him and took in the purport of the message in a second.

'I didn't write this, Barney. Barney, you don't think I wrote this?'

'Explain it then.'

'I didn't write it Barney. My word should be good enough for you. I don't need to explain myself.'

'Okay, Zara. Look, I'm taking Ben to the youth hostel in Lochranza. We can't leave Arran, I promised him. Later we'll maybe buy a tent and camp in Glen Rosa but I don't want to see you or hear from you. I can see you don't want me and that's it.' Zara held the door handle for support.

'Let's have dinner together at least. Presumably you're not going to tell Ben what you imagine is happening?' Barney shook his head.

They went downstairs. Zara told Ben she had a headache.

'Too much excitement,' said Ben. 'Tomorrow we should have a day on the beach with no surprises.'

Barney saw an opening and explained that there was a late surprise — he and Ben were going to Lochranza for a night or to as Zara was going to be very busy on account of having to make statements to the police. Also Kirsty wanted extra help because the hotel was full. Ben was excited. He had only stayed in a youth hostel once before and was dying to repeat the experience. Barney took Zara's accepting stance as an admission of guilt. In reality, she was too stunned to think. And Ben was there: she did not want to upset Ben. Barney and Ben caught the last bus to Lochranza.

Zara, though she was utterly exhausted, had a restless night. She did not know which awful subject to tackle next. As she turned from one, another rose like a boulder out of the dark. The note had poleaxed her and it wasn't until the middle of the night, when she realised she was not going to get any sleep till she'd at least attempted to solve the mystery, that she left her bed and tried to reconstruct a possible scenario.

The first thing that came to her mind was John Muirhouse and his threatening note: TIME IS RUNNING OUT BUT WHO FOR? How had she managed to forget that? It would be like him to strike in such an unexpected way; to undermine her, divide her energies. Zara became certain Muirhouse was behind the note Barney had found.

She went to her bedside and searched the notebook in which she kept a sort of journal. There was a page torn out. She compared the jagged edges. They fitted. She glanced at the skylight. It was a modern one, quite big enough for an agile man to climb through. And, the roof at the back of the hotel had valleys which would make... Zara suddenly remembered Kirsty had said something about a window-cleaner coming. John Muirhouse would always set things up to make a situation easier for himself. He would enjoy also appearing to Kirsty disguised somehow, to be unrecognisable. What had he done this time she wondered. Shaven head? Fake tattoos? She felt a shiver of fear as she realised he had also taken the trouble to learn which room she was sleeping in.

She compared the handwriting on the note to her own. It was so similar she could hardly believe it. How had he managed that? Even a Muirhouse would need a bit of practice.

She thought back to the day on the mountain. She had had her notebook with her. Was it possible he had stolen a page? The notebook was quite thick — she was halfway through it; she'd had it for months — and spiral bound. It would have been quite easy to leave no trace of a missing page. She started at the beginning and twenty pages in found a place where an unfinished sentence at the bottom of the page was not continued onto the next. She racked her brains to try and recall a moment when Muirhouse could have taken it. When she considered it, there was more than one instance when it could have happened. When they were gathering sticks for the fire. When she was asleep in the tent. That would have been a snip for John Muirhouse.

However, if she was right, it meant he was really thinking ahead, laying in a store of possible tools to use should the need arise in the future. She would need to take the note to Des tomorrow.

She looked at the waste paper basket again. It was almost full. She thought back but could not remember putting stuff into it. She took out a few pieces: they were not her rubbish, just screwed up sheets of tabloids. Muirhouse had been in the room and he had done his job thoroughly.

***

Although Zara was furious with the man's strategy and its effect on her life, having solved the immediate mystery, she managed to fall asleep almost at once and in the morning she went to the police station as soon as she had completed her morning chores.

Telling the story and watching Des's face was a strangely discomforting experience: every word she spoke revealed how she felt about Barney. In the end she had to look down and close her eyes to prevent her tears from falling. And whether from diplomacy — unlikely Zara thought —or because he considered the relationship angle irrelevant, Des's questions concentrated on theft, breaking and entering and, not the least important, the possibility that Muirhouse was carrying out his somewhat generalized threat.

Zara, by contrast, stayed with her angry feelings:

'How could he have known that Barney would react like that? He doesn't know either of us.'

'He's excellent student of the human mind,' said Des 'and anyway we both know by now that he bases his plans on possible outcomes, not probable ones. He enjoys the game, you've said so yourself.'

'I don't know if Barney will ever trust me again!'

'That sounds as if there was something between you and Balfour. You certainly seem extraordinarily interested in his well-being.' Zara thought she detected a suspicion of Des's own jealousy in his words. There had been a time before he was married when they had dated for a few months. They had never left off sparring. If there was any humour in what Des had said Zara failed to see it.

'If you had been on a mountain with someone and shared a tent with them, would you not have a modicum of interest in why and how they'd disappeared? Or is the job making you insensitive, Des?'

Des refused to rise to Zara's bait:

'From where I'm sitting, Muirhouse acted with very serious intent. It's an unusual move. Imaginative you could say. He's possibly chosen the one strategy that might make you back off.' Des smiled. 'Except he doesn't realize quite how bloody-minded you are, how gritty you become in the face of a challenge. But I think the man-trap was far worse: you could have died or seriously injured yourself. We would have had a job tying the whole thing to Muirhouse. He wasn't there. We found no trace of him except the trip wires and there's nothing to tie them to him except the idea that he wanted you tripped up.'

Zara was silent, wrestling with her frustration and disappointment, to have been so near, to have seen Ronnie in the flesh.

'You do believe Ronnie was there, don't you?' Des nodded.

'Yes of course I do but probably mostly because I know you.'

'Do you think it means he's been taken off the island?' Des looked surprised.

'You don't know what happened next? Or at least what we think happened. Or at least what we know...' He ran his fingers over his head which was covered by only a quarter of an inch of hair.

***

The onlookers at Lochranza castle saw nothing but that 'nothing' meant a great deal since they all knew they had seen a gold-coloured car speed round the corner. It had not levitated, there were no twinkling lights in the sky; and it had all really happened. A call to the police resulted in an officer arriving within minutes since a detail had been posted at the Lochranza pier to see if Muirhouse would try and leave by the ferry. An ambulance also arrived at the scene but by that time Bobby had surfaced and was making swift progress in the lee of an anchored boat. Once he was nearly on the sand he pretended he was in a war situation: how to get off the beach with no cover? Pretend to be the only rock? Make a run for it? His friend's house was only fifty yards away. He could see no one but imagined people might be watching the sea for signs of a body — dead or alive. Soon the police might come and investigate this most obvious place to land.

He was longing to take a proper look at what was going on by the castle. Someone would dive down to see if anyone was still in the car — an is-there-a-diver-in-the-house? situation. He grinned to himself. He swam along the shallows keeping his head under water until he was opposite Tommy's mum's cottage. Tommy was also unemployed but his mum was not. Tommy had a boat and a dinghy moored on the water in front of the cottage. Bobby swam to its shore side and pulled it behind him for cover.

He lay for a moment on the sand and then peered round the dinghy to see what was happening.

'What the fuck are you doing man?' Bobby jumped but it was Tommy.

'Just invent some tall grass for me will'y,' said Bobby. Tommy looked round as if maybe some grass might materialise.

'Hang on,' he said. 'Lie low for a minute. I'll be right back.' Bobby lay flat, his face just raised enough to see. He could not make out what if anything was happening. Someone did seem to be swimming around where it was probably thought the car would be but... they would be waiting for some machinery to haul it out. He grinned again. He'd caused some ripples that afternoon.

Tommy returned with paper, matches and a rake.

'There's this rubbish,' he said indicating a pile on the verge. 'Mum's been on at me to burn it for weeks. It's dead garden stuff. Should be easy to get going. Create a bit of smoke.'

'Nice one,' said Bobby, shaking his head. 'Can you hurry though. I'm getting kinda cold.'

In the cottage Bobby had just finished telling Tommy about his escapade when the police arrived and he had to tell it all over again. A man had seen a youth in a beige jacket talking to someone, and then get into a gold car and streak off northwards. They'd phoned the police after they'd watched the car swerve and swerve again to avoid a lamp post. When the officers asked onlookers who had grown in number, if anyone had recognized the driver of the car, someone had suggested Bobby: driving cars fast was apparently a hobby of his. Someone else knew Tommy was his mate who lived, would you believe it, just where that fire was burning on the beach.

***

'Presumably,' said Des, 'Muirhouse wanted us to follow Bobby over to Claonaig while he disappeared elsewhere. But his plans seem to work even when they don't work if you see what I mean. Trust Muirhouse to choose an accomplice with a streak of madness in him.'

'And no leads as to where Muirhouse might have gone?' asked Zara.

'None whatsoever. We have him in Corrie talking to Bobby at 15.59. After that, zilch. Did he leave by car or boat?'

'And Ronnie Balfour?'

'Oh sorry Ronnie was transformed into a body bag full of bathroom tiles according to Bobby, who was very impressed with the subterfuge, not in a very pleasant way I have to say.'

'And where are you now in terms of thinking of Ronnie as a guilty party?' asked Zara.

'Hm,' said Des.

***

Kirsty found it difficult to believe that the window-cleaner had been John Muirhouse.

'I would have thought I would have recognized him anywhere,' she said to Zara. 'I don't like to think of him being in your room.'

'I don't like to think of Barney believing the stuff Muirhouse wrote. How could he?' said George.

'He was in a hyped up mood. We all were. I think he was imagining me coming back here tired and happy; all his sympathy was with me and then he found the false journal entry...'

'I suppose,' said George. 'Poor Ben though.'

'Ben seemed quite happy going to the youth hostel. I wonder if he saw the gold car.'

The next day Ben phoned Zara and gave her a very excited monologue:

'Aunty Zara, the youth hostel's great. I slept in a top bunk and there are some boys here with their dad and they came on a boat — their own boat not the ferry — and guess what? They've invited me and Dad to go across the Mull of Kintyre with them. Sailing! And then we're going to camp near a

186

place called Campbeltown. Wish you were coming too. Got to go now. Lots of love. From Dad as well.'

***

The word 'love' sent Zara off on a different tack. First she mused on the fact that the Goat Fell murder had had an effect on her own love life. How little one can control things she thought. Perhaps there was a love thread entangled in the main story, the part involving Muirhouse, Balfour and Daffodil. For some reason she had dismissed early the possibility of connections between the three of them. This was, she thought because on one level she had been a fourth party and the rest of them had seemed to come together randomly, the way she had.

She thought again of Rose and Laurie, about the two of them spending the night in the same room in Glencloy. Did this have a bearing on what happened later? Had they in fact had some sort of liaison as some people thought? But however you looked at it, whether they had or they hadn't, although it put more puzzle pieces on the table, it didn't make it any clearer whether Rose had fallen or was pushed.

She had mentioned Ronnie Balfour's words, 'It must be to do with Daffodil' to Des who had been dismissive.

'We've been down that route. Dead ends you might say. Parents deceased. A job finding any relatives. Eventually an aunt who insists Daffodil is buried guess where? In the graveyard where Rose is. You didn't hear about it because it was kept quiet. Imagine what a drama the papers would have made of it! No leads in terms of Daffodil having had contact with either Muirhouse or Balfour before.'

Zara had asked if any friends of Daffodil's had come forward. She'd mentioned friends on the hill.

'We tracked them down but they said they hardly knew her. Met her out clubbing one night and it turned out they were all going to Arran but they weren't best mates or anything. We looked up where they went to school and where they'd lived. No matches whatsoever.

Zara cursed herself for not letting Ronnie Balfour say more. Why had she been so damn sure of herself? Did Ronnie know something about Daffodil because Muirhouse had told him or was it because he, Ronnie had been involved? She could not see why Des was so dismissive.

'Do you know where Daffodil worked?' she asked.

'Difficult to piece together. No track record. Not on any books we've discovered. Even the Inland Revenue only has a patchy account of her.'

Zara decided she would have to do some more private sleuthing. She would find out more about Daffodil and also more about Ronnie Balfour. She would take the approach of 'no lead too small'. Now Barney and Ben were not around she would have plenty of time. She swallowed that last thought, she couldn't afford to let it vex her.

Chapter XX Grave news

The next morning Zara had planned to visit Ronnie Balfour's parents again and get them talking, but she was foiled by Kirsty who at breakfast asked her if she would very much mind taking Kirsty's elderly cousin who was staying at North Crag, to Glen Sannox, to see of all things, Rose's grave.

'She's been reading 'Murder not Proven' which you left in the dining room and she's fascinated. I wouldn't ask you but although she's a bit loopy she was very good to my mother when Dad lost his job. She lent Mum five thousand pounds — there were debts that needed paying off — and Mum found out later she'd taken out a loan against her house. She's a good soul and this, believe it or not, would give her a lot of pleasure.'

'Does she know about my minor part in the more recent incident?' asked Zara.

No' said Kirsty

'Of course I'll take her,' said Zara.

'It's her balance,' said Kirsty. 'She finds getting on and off buses a real trial.'

Zara found the situation ironic. Of all places to be going to! But deprived of her own plan of action she rapidly became more enthusiastic, especially when she remembered that Daffodil was buried there too.

Zara and Aunty Vi, as she was called even though she was a cousin, set off straight after lunch. Aunty Vi was wearing a hat which could have been for protection from the sun but which Zara saw as a mark of respect for Edwin Rose.

'You are so kind, Zara, to give up your time to take me and, Kirsty, thank you so much for lending us your vehicle. We don't need anything half this size but I suppose you can't rustle up a small car at the drop of a hat.' At the last moment Aunty Vi decided she needed to go to the bathroom. 'Better be safe than sorry,' she said. 'I'll be back in two shakes.' Kirsty smiled at Vi's receding back.

'You're in for a jolly afternoon,' she said.

In the event, Zara found Aunty Vi more of a tonic than she had expected.

'I love it when the sky is so blue and the leaves so green and there's a little breeze,' she said as Zara started the car and lowered the windows. Zara bit back her habitual retort: nice when you can get it. Instead she took in the trees and realized she'd been so intent on the solution to Ronnie Balfour's plight she had hardly looked at the landscape properly since the murder had happened.

It turned out that Aunty Vi had spent a lot of time on Arran as a young unmarried woman, taking summer jobs just to be on the island.

'I didn't care,' she said. 'My parents wanted me to stick at something and make a career but I lived for the summer. I loved the sea you see.' She stopped. 'Did you notice the heron?' she asked. 'Tch. I always think it's a shame for drivers, having to keep their eyes on the road but I suppose it's for the best.' Zara glanced at her companion but could detect no sense of irony.

She realised they had passed Merkland Wood and were heading for Corrie.

'Then I met Bertie,' Aunt Vi was saying, 'and of course everything changed.'

'Everything?' echoed Zara.

'We were married and we had a little girl, Patricia — we called her Patty and then we moved south with Bertie's work. He got a job in Corby. He was an engineer.' Zara glanced at Aunty Vi again. She had a horrible feeling there was going to be an unhappy ending. I must stop being so gloomy she thought. Murder is really quite uncommon in the whole scheme of things.

'We came back to Scotland when Bertie retired four years ago. Patty married and went to Canada.'

'And Bertie,' said Zara 'does he not want to come on trips with you?'

'Bertie died two years ago. Cancer of course. Patty came back for the last weeks. It was lovely having her. And the doctors said he wasn't in any pain. Just slipped away. We had a good life together. Corrie. Now I worked one summer at the Corrie hotel. They had some rum customers would you believe. I remember a Mr Hoskins. I was thinking of him when I read the murder book. He was from Tooting like Edwin Rose. He was dapper. Not dressed for the country but always getting himself damp and muddy.

"Violet," he used to say, "Would you be so kind as to air my hat? I fear it has become a trifle damp." We really used to take the mickey in the kitchen.' She was silent for a moment. 'I could see him getting pushed off Goat Fell too. There was something about him.'

Zara was saved the necessity of satisfying her curiosity as to the 'something' by their arrival in Sannox.

'My very favourite glen,' said Aunty Vi. 'Those pools. I loved those pools!' They parked and started walking. Vi was fine on the flat but Zara wondered why she didn't have a stick.

'I've been down this lane so many times and I never knew Edwin Rose was buried here.' Zara didn't know if Vi knew that Daffodil was there also but she thought it morbid to bring it up unnecessarily.

Two people passed them going in the opposite direction and then another two. And then no one and nothing but the birds and the sunshine.

'It is really kind of you to give up your afternoon for me,' said Vi again but then they were there at the little gate into a small walled resting place.

They had to look for Rose's grave and when they found it Zara found it hard to reconcile the terrible death with the peacefulness of grass and stone. Lichen covered many of the headstones and some had fallen away as if to demonstrate how life subsides through entropy.

Vi read the words on the stone and seemed very affected by them. Zara wasn't sure what to do. She didn't know Vi and hadn't thought through what she might feel. She hadn't imagined she would take the grave personally.

'I'll just sit on the wall by the gate,' Vi was saying. 'Don't mind me. I'll just sit and have a peppermint. Do you want one?' Zara took one out of politeness and stuffed it in her pocket when Vi wasn't looking.

I'll look for Daffodil's grave thought Zara. New, it shouldn't be difficult to find but maybe there's no headstone yet. Maybe the aunt couldn't afford a headstone. Zara walked methodically round, her head bent so that she almost tripped over a woman kneeling on the grass, obscured by a large stone.

'I'm sorry,' said Zara. 'I'm, afraid I didn't see you.' She followed the woman's eyes which were intent on a pot of flowers she had obviously gathered from the wayside.

'Daffodils of course would have been more appropriate but of course in June...'

'Are you Daffodil's aunt?' asked Zara. The woman nodded.

'And who might you be?'

'I'm Zara. I was the other woman on the mountain.'

'You were!' The woman seemed overjoyed. 'Perhaps you can tell me something then, about that dreadful day?'

'What do you want to know?' asked Zara.

'I don't know. My name's Mary Ann by the way. I don't know what I want to know. I suppose I want to know if there is anything to know.'

Zara gave Mary Ann a blow by blow account of what she had seen and heard, starting from her first sight of Daffodil, standing a little apart from Muirhouse on the shoulder of the mountain. Mary Ann listened, her head on one side keeping her eyes on Zara's. At the end she touched Zara's arm as if in thanks.

'I don't know,' she said. 'It could all have been so different.' Zara imagined Mary Ann was being philosophic and she tried to think of a suitable but un-clichéd reply. But then Mary Ann went on,

'You see, he was wrong for her but she couldn't see it, not that he wasn't a good man and I mean a good man, not just a good man in his way but... You know yourself sometimes you see two people together, they're both good-looking, he's a couple of inches taller than her, when they smile their faces take on a similarity, they've met doing something they both enjoy — dancing, walking, evening class, I don't know — but even in spite of all that you have a feeling it's not right, it won't last — if it even gets off the ground in the first place.'

'And did it?' Zara asked, wanting to get to some specifics.

'Well, you know how these things go. On, off. Will they, won't they?'

'Who?' asked Zara.

'Well Balfour of course.'

'And Daffodil?' Zara had to be sure of what she was getting.

'Yes and then he intervened.' Mary Ann was fumbling in her pocket. 'Would you like a sweet?' She proffered an open packet. Zara took one, inwardly shaking her head. Was the universal energy working on sweet clusters today? 'I have to say I was glad at first but of course it was the wrong reaction. Daffodil was never a particularly independent young person but with a man she just became a cipher. Perhaps it would all have petered out of its own accord but for what happened next...' Zara was becoming aware that Mary Ann was becoming increasingly upset. 'I don't think I can bear to... I'm not supposed to know... and I don't actually know, I'm just guessing...' I live next door by the way, I should tell you that.'

'Next door to whom?' asked Zara. She was wondering if she would remember any of this accurately, it was so confused.

'It's all in the past now, that's what I tell myself and nothing can bring back the dead. What time is it? I'll need to go.'

'We could give you a lift to Corrie or Brodick.'

'I'm going north. Staying with friends in Lochranza. Home tomorrow.' Mary Ann became totally preoccupied with catching her bus.

'What's your other name?' asked Zara desperate not to lose the woman entirely.

'I'm a Brown. Daffodil's father was my brother. Nice to have met you and thank you for telling me about Daffodil's last day.' She was gone and immediately Vi stood before Zara.

'I couldn't help overhearing some of what that poor lady said. Is that true, this is Daffodil's grave? What was a nice young lady doing getting mixed up with the likes of John Muirhouse? How the innocent suffer in this world! Let's go my dear. We'll have some refreshing tea and maybe a cake. Thank you for bringing me but I feel now I shouldn't have asked you.' Zara wanted to contradict her but she couldn't because it would have meant a conversation and she didn't want to overlay her memory with anything else until she had written down what Mary Ann had said.

'You're all right, Vi,' she said, 'I've had a very interesting time.'

***

When Zara and Vi arrived back at North Crag there was a half hour before the dinner experience. However carefully Kirsty planned, she had not found it possible to avoid entirely the feeling of tension that arises when you know your best is not going to be good enough for some people. Zara heard Kirsty offer Vi a 'wee sherry in the kitchen' and she escaped up to her room to write down everything she could recall of what Mary Ann had said and as far as possible, verbatim.

When she entered the room, for a fleeting moment she expected to see Barney there or at least some vestige of him but of course there was nothing, not so much as an empty cheese and onion crisp packet. She beat down the feeling of sadness that began to rise inside her: time enough for that. She was excited, not sure what she had but sure it was something. There was also a seed of doubt. Surely Des would have interviewed Mary Ann. If so, why had he not followed up? Or had he followed up and reached dead ends?

Des had assured her that there would be another hunt for Ronnie Barbour on Arran and of course there had been roadblocks in place after the debacle in Merkland Wood, on the piers and round the island. Nothing had been found as yet, except the van Muirhouse had used to transport Ronnie Barbour to Sannox. It was wiped totally clean of fingerprints but because Bobby had been able to connect it to Muirhouse, the police had searched up the glen with no success. It was as if Muirhouse paid visits from another planet and then whirled away into outer space.

That night the papers made much of the florist's return to consciousness and her total recall of John Muirhouse's face, figure and clothes. All that could be finally counted on though was a witness statement that a man most likely to be John Muirhouse had bought red roses for his mother on her birthday. The florist had been sceptical but when the police had asked Mrs Muirhouse for her date of birth, it tallied.

'I'm sure he paid for them like anyone else. He didn't say anything about knocking out the florist.'

***

Zara phoned Uttam:

'Do you know who lives next to the Muirhouses? Either side?'

'One side is an elderly couple, the McCalls. They're in the shop most days. The other side, it's an old lady.'

'How old?' asked Zara, thinking there might be a generational difference in perception regarding 'old'.

'At least fifty,' Uttam replied. 'I'm not very good at old white women. Sorry. I just saw her go in her house once or twice. I don't think she's there very much. She doesn't come in the shop so I don't know much about her. Not caught the crim yet then, Zara?'

Zara gave a cross-court return: 'How's the painting going, Uttam?'

Not conclusive she thought. Uttam hadn't known the neighbour's name and she didn't want to give him the responsibility of finding out. The Balfours? Did Mary Ann live next door to them? How easy would it be to find out? She would need to go and see them tomorrow. She wished Barney were with her to discuss things. Much as he disliked her involvement she knew he was always interested in the individual logic of people's behaviours. She had often used his brain to bounce her own ideas off.

Although it would have been pleasant to sit and relax with Kirsty, George and Vi, Zara decided she would go and see Des: if she could eliminate some questions, she would be that much further on by tomorrow. If she had been honest, she would have admitted to herself that she was so worried about Ronnie Balfour that she did not think she would be able to sleep but she knew if she thought about where he might be she would go round in unprofitable circles. They all had to face the reality that they had insufficient facts to go on. Zara saw the case being put aside. Other murders would be committed and this one would become a cold case. Ronnie Balfour would become chronically disappeared.

'What now Zara?' Des seemed to be at his most closed and unfriendly.

'I met Daffodil's aunt, Mary Ann, this afternoon. At the grave.'

'And what the fuck were you doing there, Zara? I begin to suspect you of being addicted to dark things.'

'It was a coincidence, Des. I didn't know she was going to be there, —'

'You're the sort of person who would just happen to be near Bedford when the Great Train Robbers were clobbering the driver, you would just happen to have —'

'Des, I'm here to give you information. You may have it already but I won't know that till I tell you.' Des sighed, gave in and indicated with a gesture for her to go ahead.

'Okay. First, a couple of questions. Did Mary Ann tell you of any connection between Muirhouse and the Balfours and Daffodil?'

'She was adamant there was nothing.'

'Adamant? As in protesting too much?'

'I didn't think so.'

'Do you know where she lives?'

She gave her address as Maryhill but she said she had been living in England and had not found a place of her own here yet. The address in Maryhill held up.' Zara had the impression the police had been bored by Mary Ann and had not wanted the Maryhill address to be bogus or shaky.

'What would you say if I suggested she might live next to either the Balfours or the Muirhouses?' Des looked at Zara as if she had perhaps turned into a parrot.

'Come again?'

'Mary Ann said she 'lived next door to him'.'

'To whom?'

'She didn't say, but the name Balfour came up in the conversation which was really more of a monologue. She was upset.'

'Zara, her niece has been murdered.'

'I know but listen, it wasn't just that.' Zara sketched the purport of what had happened that afternoon. 'I definitely thought there was something worth knowing there, something I wasn't being told. I'd go so far as to say she was afraid to say it out loud.' Des yawned. 'You must have knocked the doors either side of the Muirhouses?'

'Of course. The McCalls, an elderly couple lived on one side. The other was in the name of McKenzie but a relative lived there who was away in England during the whole time we are talking about.'

'And her name?' Des shook his head. 'You don't know?'

'The Balfours deny Ronnie knew Muirhouse and the aunt denied Daffodil knew him — or the Balfours. I can't think of a good reason why I should interview them again.' Zara had the distinct feeling that Des knew someone had not quite followed up properly in determining the name of McKenzie's absent tenant.

***

The next afternoon, too late, Des received a call from the mainland. It appeared that there had been a sudden death at the house next door to the Muirhouse's. The deceased was an elderly lady by the name of Mary Ann Brown. The shop across the road had received a phone message asking for something to be delivered but the message had tailed off. Someone had rung back but there had been no reply. Someone had gone to the house and found Miss Brown slumped on a chair.

Des too slumped in his chair when he heard all this. He really wanted to believe it was a coincidence but he had to accommodate what Zara had said the previous day: the woman had been afraid; there were apparently connections between Daffodil and either Muirhouse and/or Ronnie Balfour.

Des found himself looking at his notepad but when he stared at it, it did not look like police notes, more like an attempt at a poem.

'Where ever I look for you, you are not.

To find you, must I stop searching?

Will I come upon you accidentally?'

When had he written this? The middle of the night? Des had never thought of himself as a poet. His last foray into the realm of verse had been for a stag night when his friend, the best man at the imminent wedding had asked him to help with a limerick about the bride, Lydia. He had tried to oblige but nobody had liked the rhyme word 'chlamydia' so he had given up.

He hoped things would become clearer when they had the pathologist's report. Except, in his recent experience, such reports tended to make everything seem more complex. Des doodled around his poem fragment and wondered whether he should have stuck to his childhood ambition of driving a bus.

***

Zara, on the same afternoon, while turning out her pockets found two sweets and out of curiosity examined them both. One was undeniably a peppermint, the other a diabetic lozenge. She wondered idly who had given her which. She couldn't remember.

She thought no more about it till she heard on the six o'clock news about the death of an elderly lady in Govanhill. At first she wondered if she should go and talk to Des again but then decided that if he wanted the benefit of her wisdom he could ask for it.

Nevertheless, her mind went over the previous afternoon with a toothcomb and came to rest on a diabetic sweet. The news report said the police wanted to interview anyone who had spoken to Mary Ann in the last twenty-four hours. It had not said whether the police were treating the circumstances of Mary Ann Brown's death as suspicious though Zara's mind immediately flew to this possibility but after mulling it over for some minutes she could make nothing of it.

In another place, John Muirhouse mused on his next move. He felt it was time for another letter. He was becoming annoyed with the police for not progressing. The game was not fun unless they played their part. He had enjoyed the diversion of the gold car episode but thought he would need to rein Bobby in a little if he were to use him again. A bit of a loose cannon, though he gave him ten out of ten for initiative.

Muirhouse visited Ronnie Balfour who had been on his own for two days, not without food, albeit a repetitious diet of cold beans and water. Muirhouse didn't think the man was anywhere near dead yet but he knew he needed to be careful. He could not understand why the man wouldn't tell him what he wanted to hear.

'You have only to admit it, Ronnie,' he said during one of his attempts at smoothness, 'and I'll let you go. I won't even take you to the police. You can decide that for yourself. Now, another photo for the records'. Muirhouse took several shots. To Balfour it felt as if he were already dead and being photographed by the police — profile, full face et cetera. Muirhouse reluctantly turned off his tape recorder. 'You are going to regret this, I know.'

Ronnie, left to himself again was at first pleased with himself as he always was, for holding out against Muirhouse one more time, but this feeling rapidly gave way to depression and despair. If only he had told Zara more, but he had felt so weak his words just would not come. 'Daffodil is the key' was shorthand for so much. He had not had the strength to tell the whole story but he had hoped Zara would pursue the Daffodil lead. She would surely know about the aunt. He'd had the feeling she was really on his side and had not forgotten him; that her finding him had not been entirely coincidental.

This thought led him to worry that she might have been set up by Muirhouse. It would be like the guy to lure her to the prize and then snatch it away. Anger swept over him and he fought to calm down again; he did not have the strength to waste on such an emotion. Instead he fell to wondering how his parents were and whether they had contacted his brother. Surely. But the police would have contacted him anyway to see if by any chance he, Ronnie, had managed to reach Australia. But wouldn't Mark be doing something if he knew? That's what he should have done: given Zara Mark's contact details. Why hadn't he thought of that? He wanted to kick something but his legs were still tied together.

It was Ronnie who had suggested his brother go to Australia. If he hadn't, Mark would probably be here now. Hindsight was a wonderful thing.

Sometimes he thought he should try reasoning with Muirhouse but he knew from past experience that any reasoning that wasn't Muirhouse's own tended to bring on a fit of rage. He didn't feel equipped to deal with that. He couldn't imagine how Muirhouse could worsen his, Ronnie's, position but he had no doubt he would find a way. Patience was what he needed at the moment, just patience.

Chapter XXI   New hopes

John Muirhouse composed another letter.

Dear CID,

I know you think I am just blustering and trying to annoy you by dangling carrots but I don't think I've got across to you that I'm perfectly serious: I have important information for you about Ronnie Balfour. Why don't I come down to the station with it? It's too complicated. It would not result in the outcome I require. There are more players in this drama than you imagine. You have to admit I know what I am talking about when it comes to drama. What did you think of Merkland Wood? Mission accomplished eh? I bet you enjoyed posting officers at the piers? We'll get him now you thought. But I was a step ahead of you and now you have no idea where I am. Or where Ronnie Balfour is.

I am fighting on more than one front. Occasionally something happens even I had not bargained for but this is what makes life interesting isn't it? I'm sure you will agree that RB is my trump card. I'll get there in the end but we don't want any more collateral damage, do we?

Yours truly,

John Muirhouse.

***

Ben wrote a letter to Zara. It had a Campbeltown postmark.

Dear Aunty Zara,

I am having a fabulous time. I never told you about when we were still in Lochranza, we saw the gold car being lifted out of the sea. It was really exciting. Nobody knew if it was going to be empty or not. I thought the man might have stowed some treasure in it but it turned out there was none. Just an open window. Divers went down to see if they could find anything on the seabed but there was nothing there except some crabs and starfish one of the divers told me. Dad said later he'd heard that the man swam out of the car to the shore because he's alive and well and the police have talked to him. His name is Bobby. I talked to a boy from Lochranza and he said Bobby was asked to drive the car to Claonaig (I think I spelled that right) but he decided it would be more fun to drive into the sea. He thought it was cool. I don't think he meant the temperature of the water. One other thing, the man that wanted the car driven to Claonaig had a very long rucksack with him and said it contained bathroom tiles. What do you think?

Both these letters gave Zara a lot to ponder on. Des had let her see the Muirhouse letter thinking she might just construe it differently from his team. He'd also shown it to the Balfour parents.

Zara saw in Muirhouse's letter the trace of a back story they were not picking up on. Who were the 'other players'? Was the 'important information about Ronnie Balfour' something to do with a past scenario, not what had happened on the mountain? Maybe what happened on the mountain had been a second act. And the collateral damage? Was Daffodil just collateral damage, not the main point after all? Or was Muirhouse referring to the now conscious florist? When she raised these three points with Des — he had after all asked for her input — he was noncommittal. She knew what he was thinking: I can't interview people speculatively. No, but I can, thought Zara.

And Ben's letter. Had Ronnie Balfour been in that sack? Mouth taped? Drugged? She wouldn't put it past Muirhouse to give his victim a shot of something. Was Ronnie then still on the island? Maybe Muirhouse was looking for another episode of cat and mouse.

Zara went to see the Balfours.

'We thought you might have called before,' said Margaret Balfour, 'seeing as you knew how worried we were'. Zara felt contrite and annoyed with herself.

'I'm really sorry,' she said, 'but here I am and I can tell you Ronnie is still fighting'.

'But not fighting fit,' said his father.

'No I couldn't say that.'

'Did he have any message for us?' Zara thought about lying but decided against it.

'I was only with him for a few minutes. I took off his blindfold and the tape round his mouth and gave him my left over picnic.'

'Was he really thin?'

'I'm afraid he was quite thin. And to answer your question, he was too weak to say anything much but what he did say was about Daffodil as if he thought the answer to everything was to do with her. I know you said Ronnie didn't know her but this seems to indicate —'

'She could have known Mark,' said Margaret Balfour suddenly. 'We were only talking this morning about why he went to Australia.'

'Why did he?' asked Zara.

'We don't really know. That's what we were discussing. It was like one minute he was moving down south for a job and the next he had thrown that up and was going to Australia. Better prospects he said.'

'But we were wondering,' said Harry Balfour, 'especially with that mad letter of Muirhouse's, if something happened way back then that's sparked all this off.' Zara nodded.

'But you have no idea what that might have been?'

'No,' said Margaret. 'Ronnie was just the same. He didn't want Mark to go to Australia though ironically it had been his suggestion in the first place. Mark wanted Ronnie to join him there. That would have been great, both of our boys overseas.'

***

Barney was beginning to feel bad about Zara, especially when Ben talked about her as if she were a normal person who hadn't done anything wrong. Barney kept recalling her voice when he accused her. She had looked shocked and at the time he had taken that for guilt at being found out, but thinking about it now he saw it differently: she had been shaken because he had thought that of her. She had been quite clear about the fact that she wanted to go to Arran to sort out their relationship, whether they were going to become committed partners or stay just friends for ever. Her going up Goat Fell with Ronnie had been in line with that. He wasn't so precious he begrudged her time with other people — even male people. He wondered why he had been so jealous on this occasion. Was it that he had come back from the picnic full of good feelings about her, the woman he loved, full of empathy for how exhausted she must be feeling? And then to find that note! It had been an emotional right hook: he could see that now.

He turned on his mobile which he had switched off on leaving Brodick: a shutting of his ears to Zara's act. He was dismayed to find how many missed calls there had been. None granted over the first two days but then a flurry over the last twenty-four hours. The last message was a text: 'Phone me at once when you get this'. Barney phoned.

'Are you okay?' He could never lie about what his real feelings were.

'I need your help,' said Zara. 'Just as a human being if that's all that's on offer.'

'Ben and Nessie included?'

'Absolutely.' Pause. 'Might be dangerous though. Mainly I want you around as sort of emotional back up.' Another pause. 'I know it's a lot to ask.'

'I'll say 'yes' and then you can explain,' said Barney.

'You're going to think I'm batty as usual but I want to explore every single cave possibility on the island. I'm sure Ronnie is still here.' This time the pause was initiated by Barney. 'You don't still think I wrote —'

'I've been giving it a lot of thought. I haven't found a good explanation but I'm not angry anymore and... I trust —'

'Okay. Good.' Zara didn't seem to want to dwell on it.

'So,' continued Barney, 'as long as you understand that I don't want Ben anywhere near a place where Muirhouse might be lurking.'

'Back-up,' said Zara. 'That's what I need. For instance, supposing it was Blackwaterfoot, I would leave you and Ben on the beach and I would go myself to reconnoitre.'

'Vehicle?'

'Piece of luck,' said Zara. 'I was talking to Tom and Davy from the Mountain Rescue again. They're going to give me a list of all the caves they know by the way.'

'Do they know why —?'

'Sort of. I didn't spell it out but I think they had an idea. They think I'm mad anyway but the good news is Tom has an old van he's giving up. He was going to wait till its MOT ran out in a couple of months but he had the chance of a motor that was just what he wanted so he took it. It's all in order and ready to go, so he says I can have the van to run around in. Says it's just scrap.'

'No charm involved then?' Barney was genuinely admiring. Zara had a way of impressing people and getting what she wanted.

It was Muirhouse's letter that had fired Zara's decision to search all caves, the allusion to cat and mouse, another game of, even though she was aware this might be another Muirhouse trap. He couldn't be everywhere at once and Zara was sure he didn't do a twenty-four-hour watch. Part of his torture was to leave Ronnie Balfour alone. Uttam had reported to her that he had seen Muirhouse arriving at the house in Govanhill more than once, both times not looking at all like Muirhouse, once as a window-cleaner and another time as a Jehovah's Witness, complete with tracts. Uttam was suspicious when the Jehovah's Witness was invited in.

***

'I'm glad you're friends with Zara again,' said Ben when Barney announced they were returning to Brodick and North Crag. 'I kept in touch with her by postcard,' he continued.

'Yes well there was no reason for you...' Barney realized he didn't need to confirm his contretemps with Zara. 'She's managed to get a van for us to go about in so we'll be able to explore further.'

'Cool,' said Ben. 'It's always exciting to be where Aunty Zara is.'

'I know,' said Barney, 'and I can tell you now, we are not being enlisted as front-line troops. Definitely, not even reservists.'

'What then?' asked Ben.

'Well I suppose we might be in the area and she might phone us and ask us to do something.'

'Like go and help?'

'No exactly not that. More...' Barney felt he was getting mired in this hypothetical situation ... more like she asks us to... to go and buy some bread or some water.'

'Bread and water,' said Ben. 'Is she going to lock someone up in a prison?'

'Let's wait and see, Ben, but I can assure you, you will be well out of harm's way.'

'Aye aye, Captain' said Ben. Barney could tell he was unconvinced.

***

The pathologist had reported that Mary Ann Brown's death had indeed been related to her diabetes. The contents of her stomach had shown that she had not taken her medication that day and also there was evidence of a major sugar overload. Des felt, given the fact that Mary Ann lived next door or at least had a house next door to John Muirhouse, he had grounds for doing some questioning.

The officers who undertook this found no one at home. There was however a lot of buzzing going on. They broke in and searched the house and became aware of honey dripping through the ceiling at the top of the stairs. The search was temporarily terminated.

The disappearance of Mrs Muirhouse was not deemed in itself suspicious and they hadn't expected her son to be home. The officers asked around but no one was aware that Mrs Muirhouse had gone on holiday or to visit relatives. There was nothing of interest found in the house.

The next day Zara had decided she would investigate the Corrie caves. She didn't really expect Ronnie to be in them, they were much too frequented but she wanted to be thorough. She made the usual picnic with a surprise ingredient. Ben said he and Barney had a joint surprise for when they returned.

It had been a seamless reunion and neither Barney nor Zara had felt they wanted to discuss things. Zara did not want to go near the question of how she felt about Barney and Barney thought Zara far too involved in the murder situation to consider giving time to whether she should spend the rest of her life with him.

But before they could set off — Barney and Ben were sitting in a corner of the dining room waiting for Zara to come with the picnic — a tall figure entered the hall, hesitated and then said,

'Can you tell me where I might find Zara MacDonald?'

'She's behind you,' shouted Ben as Zara appeared from the kitchen. The man turned and Barney saw Zara's face change.

'Ronnie! No it can't be!'

'Mark,' said the man. 'Pleased to meet you. Mum and Dad said I should come and see you. They said you'd seen Ronnie.'

The man standing before her could have been Ronnie except for his rude health and his tan.

'Pleased to meet you,' said Zara holding out her hand. She introduced Barney and Ben and asked Mark if he would like to join them. He declined. He'd just arrived, seen his parents, hired a car. He needed a day to get his bearings. Zara took him aside and told him the plan which involved explaining her perspective. He held up his hand.

'I think this needs longer. I'll come back in the evening if that's all right. I can see time is important but I think I need time before I can understand.'

'There's questions I'd like to ask you too,' said Zara. 'About Daffodil.'

'Daffodil.' Mark echoed the name. 'I don't know what to say about Daffodil.' Zara saw pain cross his face.

Mark went off and for Zara the day was dislocated. She went through the motions because of Ben and Barney, wanting to stick to what she had promised them. At some illogical level she assumed they would not find Ronnie today because now Mark was here, they would find him together.

She left Barney and Ben at Sandstone Quay where, unbeknown to her, Muirhouse had taken Ronnie from the gold car and put him in the beat up van.

Barney had brought fishing rods and he and Ben had 'fished' off the quay with a nil result. This gave them an equal success rate with Zara who found nothing in the Corrie caves. As she had expected. Even so, it was a good day out and by tea-time she felt her relationship with father and son were both in order again.

***

Zara met Mark after dinner while Barney was spending time with Ben before he slept. Zara made coffee and took it out the back. A slight breeze was dealing with the midges.

Zara quickly realized that Mark had an organized mind and liked to have everything clear and understood. She told him her version of the story so far. He listened without interruption.

'Thank you,' he said when she had finished. 'And not just for telling the story. Thank you for being here. Mum and Dad were right, you have a much more coherent picture than the police.' Zara pulled a face.

'I like a challenge,' she said. 'That's about everything except one part of the story which I would rather leave till I've heard your side.'

'My side?'

'The way I see it,' said Zara, 'there has to be a back story to all this and Muirhouse seems to hint at it in his last letter. If you tell me you don't know Muirhouse, I shan't believe you. Even your parents —' Mark stopped her.

'Okay. I'll tell you what I know though I have to say it's the sort of situation where the less you know the better.'

'I'll begin to think you're an accomplice if you start talking in riddles,' said Zara. She had liked Mark initially as she had liked Ronnie, but now she began to doubt her instinct.

'We have to trust each other for Ronnie's sake,' said Mark looking as if he had read Zara's mind.

'Tell me what you know then,' said Zara trying to remain calm.

'It's true,' began Mark, 'Daffodil is an important part of the story.' He stopped and Zara saw the same fleeting expression of pain cross his face as it had done earlier. 'I was in love with Daffodil,' he went on. 'She was working for Muirhouse senior as his secretary. I started going out with her. She didn't tell me old man Muirhouse had a thing for her. I found out by accident and faced her with it, asked her if anything had happened between them. She swore it hadn't but then let Muirhouse senior know my feelings. Things became very nasty and that's when I decided to go to Australia.' Zara waited. 'I was hurt by Daffodil's betrayal, because I could see from Muirhouse's reaction to Daffodil's information that there had been something between them. Now of course I realize she was probably flattered and bamboozled into the liaison: she's not the most independent of women. Wasn't,' he amended. 'Anyway I went to Australia and I'm happy to say I met a wonderful girl called Janine.'

'Australian?'

'Scottish.' Zara nodded. 'We have a little girl, Ninette. Yes, very quick but we haven't regretted anything. However, this is why all this business with Ronnie has been difficult for me. It felt like coming back into the lion's den.'

Zara sat mulling over what Mark had said.

'It sounds as if you were a long way round the spectrum of nasty if you had to go to Australia. Did you fight for Daffodil or just give her up to your rival? Did Daffodil actually prefer Muirhouse?'

'As I said, can we just stick to what's relevant? The main thing is that what happened then makes sense of what's happening now. I was receiving photos of Ronnie — just from the neck up. I don't know how John Muirhouse obtained my e-mail address.'

'He was threatening you?'

'He was threatening me.'

'With what?' asked Zara. 'It sounds as if Muirhouse is threatening both you and Ronnie. Is he playing you off against one another? Did you do something? Can't you just tell me?'

'I can't,' said Mark. 'Look, I thought we could work together but perhaps it's not possible.'

You may be right,' said Zara. It suddenly crossed her mind that she had never wondered about the whereabouts of Muirhouse senior. She wondered why.

Mark doesn't trust me she thought. He can look for his own brother. Why should I care? She was sick of the whole thing. She would forget about the Balfours and the Muirhouses and concentrate on having a good summer, return to the original plan of using the time for what she wanted in her own life.

She stood up.

'Nice meeting you and good luck.' She held out her hand and he took it reluctantly.

'I didn't quite mean —'

'Exactly,' said Zara. 'It's the "didn't quite" that upsets me. 'I prefer "did completely" or "didn't at all".'

Zara saw Mark Balfour out through the front door and went to join the others in the kitchen.

When Barney heard that Zara was giving up on the whole affair he wanted to dance and sing, throw his arms round her and congratulate her as if she had won a prize but he knew her too well, knew she would have mixed feelings.

'How do you feel about it?' he asked, making do with catching her arm and giving it a squeeze. Zara shrugged and occupied herself with the mug of hot chocolate Kirsty had placed in front of her.

'Bit chilly out there was it?' her friend said.

'I don't know,' said Zara. 'I don't know anything and I don't want to know anything. Ever any more.'

'That chilly,' said George.

Chapter XXII   Away but towards

But in the morning everything changed again. When Zara entered the kitchen early to get a map from the cupboard, George was sitting hunched over a piece of paper.

'I found this sort of hung in Riga's mouth. Couldn't have been there long or she would have eaten it.' He proffered the paper which was damp and scrumpled to Zara. It was hanging by a loop of string and read 'cheese = 48526014139701149231. Zara didn't look at it.

'I'm not interested. It's from Muirhouse. The bastard, using Riga.'

'I know but it might be important. It might say where Ronnie Balfour is.'

'Can I see?' Ben had entered the kitchen silently. George passed the paper over.

'Ben, I'd rather you didn't...'

'But Aunty Zara, it's a puzzle and I love puzzles. We can always give the answer to DI Des if you —'

'Well, I need to go and work. I'll leave you two to your Bletchely Park-ing. Okay Alan?' George nodded. Zara left.

'Why did she call you Alan?' asked Ben.

'Alan Türing. Genius codebreaker in World War Two.' Ben's face became very determined.

'We can crack this, Uncle George, I mean Uncle Alan. Can I write it out again so I have my own copy to work from?'

They both sat absorbed, George knowing he should be starting the breakfast. Occasionally he insisted Kirsty should lie in an extra half hour while he made everything ready for 'the big push' which was Kirsty's version of the traditional Scottish breakfast.

Eventually George left his chair and started banging utensils about.

'Don't think your name's Türing after all,' said Ben.

'Well you haven't got anywhere either, have you? Zara's right. It's a waste of time. It's nothing to do with us. I don't like…' He tailed off; he didn't want to say anything that implied any danger.

'… the fact that Muirhouse is involved,' finished Ben. 'I think I've got a clue. Can I use the laptop for a bit?'

Kirsty appeared and slid into her cook role without a word.

'Aunty Zara's birthday is the fourteenth of April, isn't it Aunty Kirsty? Kirsty nodded and flung some bacon into her pan.

'Born '79, same year as me.'

'Aha,' said Ben. He underlined some of the numbers and then turned to the laptop.

***

How ever much Zara tried, she did not succeed in putting Ronnie Balfour out of her mind. She would think she had forgotten and then suddenly a big dark rock would remind her and she would have a pang of conscience. Ironically Barney and Ben were a bit disappointed that Operation Balfour had been called off but if Ben even hinted that some likely place might be investigated, Zara would just put her foot down on the accelerator.

Zara had a phone message from Uttam, the burden of which was that Mary Ann Brown's death was now being treated as murder. A large quantity of banknotes had been found in an old handbag, some of which had been issued only a couple of months before which meant the pile could have been added to recently. Apparently Mrs Muirhouse had been seen knocking on Mary Ann's door earlier in the day of the murder. Another search by police of the Muirhouse establishment had turned up diabetic pills in a bag belonging to Mrs Muirhouse. She was not known to be a diabetic. Of the woman herself, there had been no sign. She had vanished with the same skill her son showed. Zara deleted the message.

***

Meanwhile Des, apparently, had had a breakthrough. At long last the three hikers from Yorkshire, seen by Zara and Ronnie, had been identified. They recounted to the police the conversation they had had with Muirhouse on the summit of Goat Fell. Or rather, what he had said to them:

'Lovely day for it eh? My two mates are just behind. Amazing, you don't see someone for years and years and then you bump into them on a mountain. Would you believe it?' The Yorkshire hikers had nodded and gone on eating their sandwiches. They were two brothers and a sister who had come to scatter their mother's ashes. Goat Fell was her favourite mountain and she'd lived in a cottage with a full view of it.

Because of their serious task, they had registered Muirhouse's hail-fellow-well-met attitude as something they would rather have avoided and although they were certain they had met both Zara, Ronnie, Muirhouse and Daffodil, the only useful fact they could contribute was that the following morning the sister had seen Muirhouse in the Cooperative buying six tins of beans. Zara had said that Ronnie had been fed beans exclusively so Des saw this as evidence that Muirhouse had secreted Ronnie Balfour somewhere on Arran at the outset, until the police had stopped watching the boats.

Just how had he managed to get off the island with Ronnie Des wondered. And how had he got back on again? He supposed it wasn't impossible. You had only to pay a man with a sailing boat. Maybe John Muirhouse had become dapper again and approached someone with a cabin-cruiser in Lamlash. Offered them money. What had he said about Ronnie Balfour? He was blind and deaf perhaps? Why would Balfour submit to being treated like a captive? If Muirhouse threatened to kill his parents? Ronnie knew Daffodil was dead. Maybe... Des began to wonder about connections with the past, denied by the Balfour parents. But what if there was some hold Muirhouse had over Balfour which meant Muirhouse could do what he liked with him? Des sighed. He had a sinking feeling he would profit by talking to Zara again.

He reached for the phone but then thought some more. Mark. The interview he'd had with this brother from Australia had seemed a complete waste of time but he had better go over it once again before speaking with Zara. What was coming into his mind now was the Yorkshire hikers' conversation with Muirhouse: he had apparently referred to Ronnie as someone he knew. Given the description of Muirhouse's mien, Des had almost written off the words as one of Muirhouse's stories, like the one about his mother being in the Brodick care home. But what if they really did know each other? He thought back to his interview with Mark. Mark had not owned any acquaintance with or knowledge of Muirhouse. Had he been lying? Des then remembered that the Balfour parents had communicated with Zara: they had told him as much. And perhaps now Mark had told Zara things he hadn't told Des. He reached for the phone again and counted to ten before dialling the number for the North Crag hotel.

***

In Des's office, Zara told him what she knew in a neutral voice.

'You don't sound very interested, Zara. It's not like you.'

'I'm following your advice for once: not getting involved. It's ironic, isn't it, that just when I decide to leave it all to the cops, they suddenly want my help.'

'I just wanted to know what, if anything, Mark told you.'

'Well, I've told you.' Des sat back in his chair and looked at the ceiling.

'People don't leave for Australia for no good reason.'

'True,' said Zara. 'But maybe he thought his life was threatened. Maybe Muirhouse senior likes killing people too. Is he alive or dead by the way?'

'I assumed he was dead, in that he is never at the Muirhouse abode. Someone's looking it up anyway.' Des looked sharply at Zara who was yawning. She returned his look thinking he was about to remonstrate with her but his voice had softened.

'It's been a burden for you, all this. I can see that. I'm sorry Zara. It's unfortunate you seem to be involved. I feel I have to get your slant on things. Like the Mark perspective. You had valuable information.'

'Well, here's another piece of jigsaw,' said Zara putting the line of numbers and letters that had arrived that morning in front of Des. 'Something right from the horse's mouth' — she explained about Riga. 'Don't waste any of your men on it: Ben's probably cracked it by now.' She left.

I have to find out what he withheld thought Des. And what about Mary Ann Brown? Is she part of the puzzle? Did she know something? He cursed himself for not going over that ground again with Zara. He began to feel stupid and summoned up a picture of his daughter. She didn't think he was stupid. His wife though, he thought she did. She didn't like him talking about his work which was understandable but she had no need to belittle him for not solving impossible crimes. At least Zara... He stopped himself: not a good road to go down. Pam was fine. She was a good mother and a great cook. It was just... well, she didn't have Zara's sense of humour. He reached for his phone and not getting Mark's voice, left him a message.

***

Zara could not help being intrigued by Mark's silence in the face of Des's questioning but she still felt she would stick to her decision to stay uninvolved. The next day she was going on a day trip to Bute with Barney and Ben. Ben had some special reason for wanting to visit Mount Stuart, a stately home belonging to the Marquess of Bute. Zara had a passing interest in the island as the place where John Laurie had met Edwin Rose.

'We shouldn't really be starting from Arran,' said Ben as he walked between Barney and Zara down the pier to the first boat. It was Zara's day off, a day she didn't often claim, but Kirsty had insisted this time.

'No,' agreed Barney, 'it would be a lot easier from Glasgow but we're not in Glasgow.'

'How do we get to Wemyss Bay?' asked Ben.

'Train,' said Barney. 'Then it's thirty-five minutes on the ferry to Rothesay. Then a shuttle bus to Mount Stuart.' Ben skipped twice.

'Good. I like travelling. Getting on and off things.'

'Why is it you want to go to Mount Stuart?' asked Zara.

'Aha,' said Ben. 'I'm not telling you till afterwards.'

'It doesn't matter,' said Zara. 'I've always meant to go. Apart from it being billed as 'Britain's most spectacular Victorian Gothic house', the beach is meant to be 'one of the most beautiful and peaceful beaches in Scotland.'

'Are you teasing me?' asked Ben good-humouredly. 'If you get bored you can just read your book. I'm sure you've brought one with you. You always do. Is it the same one you were reading last summer?'

'I shan't sit with you if you're going to mock me,' said Zara, turning her mouth down.

The three of them stood at the rail till the boat had swept round in a big arc leaving Brodick Bay behind.

'Shall we go and have a cup of something?' said Barney.

'Wimp,' said Ben. 'Just do your jacket up. What's the point of being on a boat and staying inside as if you're in a café on land?'

***

They arrived at Rothesay around eleven o'clock and almost immediately boarded the shuttle bus. Thank goodness something is going right for once thought Zara.

'Let's do the house first,' said Ben, 'because it's not so sunny now but it might get out later.' They paid and joined the group of people waiting to be guided through the ornate and spacious rooms. Zara was trying hard to remain un-enthusiastic as she had an antipathy towards stately homes. She couldn't help remembering, all the time she was looking at exotically painted ceilings and grand marble staircases, that somebody's sweated labour had been expended to supply the money to make the whole shebang possible. It certainly wasn't the sweat of the Marquess of Bute. However, she found she had to live with a contradiction: dirty money had produced extraordinarily beautiful architecture. She decided to look now and analyse later.

But they were only in the second room when it suddenly struck her that there was a distinct possibility that John Watson Laurie and Edwin Rose would have been to Mount Stuart. She fantasised about them strolling from room to room and then saw from the guidebook that the house had only opened to the public in 1995. Even so she thought they might well have walked through the grounds. Or visited the chapel. Mount Stuart seemed to be the sort of place they would have liked to have been seen in. Maybe John

Laurie had sought an introduction to the Marquess. On what grounds though? Made up grounds of course. Maybe an uncle who had met the Marquess abroad and who had asked his nephew to pay his respects.

'Why are you smiling, Aunty Zara? Nobody's said anything funny.'

'It's okay, Ben. Private joke. Just thinking.'

Even though it couldn't have happened, Zara continued to fantasise about Rose and Laurie enjoying the wonders of Mount Stuart. They reached the last room and Zara said to Ben,

'So have you seen what you came to see?'

'No,' said Ben, 'not yet'.

'I bet it's like Munro-bagging,' said Barney. 'Stone columns over fifty feet high or...'

'No,' said Ben.

'Houses with over a hundred windows,' said Zara.

'No,' said Ben, 'you won't get it.'

Food became the main concern till they'd eaten. Then Ben wanted to go to the adventure playground. Zara said she would go to the contemporary art exhibition. Barney went with Ben. Zara didn't really enjoy the exhibition. She couldn't analyse why. Perhaps she was just not in the mood. On the way out she noticed a visitors' book and on an impulse went to look at the comments of others. It was always interesting trying to understand things from someone else's perspective. Intrigued by the number of people who had found the present exhibition 'Awesome', 'the best exhibition in Scotland'— one woman had written: 'my mum who is 92 really enjoyed it as did my grand-daughter who is 4', — Zara turned back the pages looking for something negative. What would Edwin Rose have had to say if he'd been there she wondered. She turned another page and at the top, as if to add special significance, she saw the name Ronnie Balfour and underneath it, with as many flourishes as possible, the name John Muirhouse. The date was two days before the murder.

Zara backed away from the book as if a contagious disease was emanating from it. What to do? She had her press card and also a private detective card but maybe she should try passing herself off as a plain-clothes cop working on the Muirhouse case. She decided to try to breeze through, staying as much with the truth as possible. She approached the reception desk.

'A word, if I might.' Zara smiled, a flicker of conspiracy in her eyes. She could see the woman at the desk was interested, as if she could smell something untoward in an otherwise crushingly boring afternoon. Zara flashed her card hoping the woman would only register 'detective': 'DC Zara MacDonald,' she said. 'I wonder if you could help me or maybe I should speak to your boss?' Zara knew that most people resent even a hint of being thought not capable of dealing with what's on hand:

'I'm sure I'll be able to help you. My boss is actually in a meeting just now.' Zara smiled again.

'I should have phoned ahead but I'm doing my boss a favour. When I told him I was coming to Mount Stuart on my day off, he asked me if I could check something out.' The woman, whose name was Erica, looked interested. 'Well,' said Zara, 'I've checked it out and, on the basis of what I've found, I'd like to ask you a few questions.'

'Fire away,' said Erica, clasping and unclasping her hands like a child with an unopened parcel.

'Two weeks ago,' began Zara, 'two men visited this gallery and signed the visitors' book. I'm wondering if you might remember them'. She showed Erica the page.

'You have photos?'

Damn thought Zara, this is where my acting has to excel itself.

'You know Erica, I wouldn't confess this to anyone but I swapped handbags this morning because I wasn't really in work mode and I went and left the two photos on the kitchen table.'

'What a coincidence,' said Erica. 'I left my sandwiches on the kitchen table this morning. Must be something in the stars. Couldn't believe it when I got here and they weren't in my bag. Tuna with cheese and onion crisps. My favourite.'

Zara held a commiserative expression for as long as she could and then launched into a description of John Muirhouse and Ronnie Balfour.

'Red and white!' I remember. We don't get many like that. I said to Mhairi in the gift shop, you want to watch them. They may be up to something. I actually phoned across. We have a code because obviously you can't say out loud to all and sundry that someone in the gallery is odd or suspicious but we need to warn each other.'

'They were together then?' Erica nodded and then her nod changed to a slow shake.

'I'm not sure about that Muirhouse. He was for ever joshing the other one's arm but the other one, he just stood there. Didn't look upset by it but on the other hand didn't exactly enter into the spirit. The fellow in the white jacket, he was the one with the initiative.'

'Do you recollect anyone else of that name... Muirhouse?'

'No, I don' think so. Never met anyone... Should I have...? Muirhouse... Now you say it, it does sort of ring a bell but we get so many people through. But I do remember something...' Erica bit her lip. Zara didn't know whether she was thinking or deciding.

'I'll tell you what: see two weeks ago that was when my daughter was taken into hospital with acute appendicitis. Knocked me sideways. Thought it was going to burst. I said to Graham, as if we haven't got enough to deal with without that but I know I was actually talking about our Muirhouse because of that missing man in the paper and Graham said it was of no consequence me having seen him, always supposing it was him because it's not a particularly unusual name, because it was before the murder. Graham said the police wanted to know where he was after the murder. He was so adamant I just left it what with Jackie and all. I'm sorry, I've been a bit economic with the truth.' Zara comforted her with a smile.

'The paper you read didn't say that both Muirhouse and Balfour were missing?' Erica was silent for a moment.

'Well yes of course it did and I see where you're coming from: it has to be them: they have to be the two in the book. Oh dear, are we in contempt of court or anything? I'm really sorry, Detective Constable, if we've messed up. It was my husband. He's very private. Hates the outside world to affect his life in any way. He kept saying, "It was before the murder. It's of no consequence".'

'It's okay, Erica,' said Zara. 'Don't worry. I'm just glad to get the information now and of course your husband doesn't need to be involved. He wasn't there; he didn't see them in your gallery or watch them write in the visitors' book. But you could really help us because one of the things we are trying to establish is whether Ronnie Balfour and John Muirhouse knew each other or whether they perhaps only met recently, an acquaintance struck up on holiday or –'

'I would say they knew each other for longer than a holiday but perhaps hadn't seen each other for some time.'

'What makes you say that?' Zara asked.

'Well,' said Erica, folding her arms and leaning forward over her desk. 'Obviously I couldn't hear everything but Muirhouse was so exuberant, like a dog that you wish the owners would put on a lead and I heard him say at one point: "Saw your name in the book and then, see, when I saw your back I thought, there's Mark! But of course it was you, Mark being in Australia." And Balfour replied, "I didn't think I was that like him" and Muirhouse said, "I study these things" and sort of danced in front of him. Balfour looked a bit embarrassed. I wondered if Muirhouse had known Mark or been friends with him and Balfour was being polite to him out of respect for that. I think that's what aroused my curiosity: there was quite a tension between them.' She paused. A very clear memory Zara thought.

'If you're wondering how I remember so well it's because I discussed it all with Mhairi.' Zara nodded.

'This is very useful, Erica. Can you remember anything else they said?' Erica bit her lip again.

'No,' she said eventually, 'but Muirhouse asked Balfour if he'd got married, Mark, that is, and Ronnie said "Yes". That's when I thought one of them's been away somewhere if he doesn't know that.'

'What made you think they might be up to no good?'

'The way Muirhouse picked things up and put them down and asked me questions about different prints and things. You get wise when you work with the general public. People often work in twos. For all I knew, Ronnie Balfour was acting polite and quiet because that was his cover.'

'Nothing missing though after they'd gone?'

'Not a sausage.'

'How did you feel when you heard about the murder?' asked Zara.

'Shocked. I was really shocked. It's not every day you come face to face with a suspected...' She didn't want to say the word. 'I talked about it to Mhairi as I said. We kept looking in the papers and listening to the news but there wasn't much. Muirhouse seems to have kept his trail cold from the start.' Erica did not say this as if she were criticizing the police and Zara stood and thought about how the case must seem from the outside.

'So who do you think did it?' she was putting away her notebook to indicate that the formal part of the questioning was over.

'I'll tell you what I think,' said Erica. 'It reminds me of Rose and Laurie, except of course there was just the two of them and this time here were four people up the mountain.' Zara didn't want Erica to know she'd been one of them.

'You'll be telling me next Muirhouse stayed at the Hydro.'

'But he did,' said Erica. 'I forgot that. I asked him. It's one of those touristy questions: Are you enjoying your stay? Is it the first time you've been on the island? You do it especially when you can see that people don't like the art. At least they go away on a positive note. Unless of course they've got an uncomfortable bed or a room that doesn't face the sea. Well, Muirhouse and Balfour, they were not at all interested in the pictures. They were like people who had wandered in out of the rain. They didn't quite fit. That's why I watched them.' Zara put out her hand.

'Thank you very much Erica. I will report back and you will probably get another visit. From another detective.' Erica looked quite pleased.

'I hope you catch him soon,' she said.

***

When Zara met Barney and Ben she was quite quiet and Ben asked if she'd lost her purse or something.

'No, Ben.'

'Did you have a boring time? You should have come to the adventure playground. I got really hot.' The sun was now a big orange presence. Zara stuffed her jacket into her rucksack.

'Do you feel okay?' asked Barney. Privately he had thought a day out at Mount Stuart might do something to break Zara's serious mood but it seemed to be having the opposite effect.

'All right,' said Zara suddenly. 'I suppose I'll —'

'No, I can guess,' said Ben. 'You've discovered something about the murder.' Zara smiled with her lips. 'I'm right. I'm right,' sang Ben 'Tell us. Tell us.' Barney groaned.

'It wasn't my fault,' said Zara. 'I was in fact bored by the exhibition and I looked at the visitors' book to amuse myself. I had been thinking about Rose and Laurie and wondering if they'd visited Mount Stuart when they were on Bute and then, two weeks back, whose names should I find? Muirhouse and Ronnie Balfour.'

'Phew!' Ben had only recently learned to whistle.

***

They needed to leave to get the bus, the ferry and another bus before they would be back in Brodick. Although it was evening, Zara went round to see Des whose face when Zara slapped down a hastily photo-copied image of the two names in the Mount Stuart visitors' book, showed a mixture of deep interest and exasperation at Zara's evident wayward behaviour.

'It was a pure coincidence. I was on a day out with Barney and Ben. You'll need to get Erica at the gallery interviewed and also visit the Hydro. Apparently Muirhouse stayed there but under another alias so the management didn't pick up from the news that they had had him staying under their roof. I just phoned. Hadn't time to go there but the desk clerk was very obliging — I had flashed my police card at him over the phone.' Des acknowledged Zara's joke with a pursed lip. 'He'd signed in under John Jones and given a fictitious address in Edinburgh. It was definitely him. The clerk described him to a T.'

'So,' continued Zara, 'this makes the Balfour parents either ignorant or devious. It makes Mark Balfour economic with the truth and it ties Ronnie and Muirhouse together for some reason, even if it's indirect, through Mark.'

Des sat back in his chair mentally checking off the points Zara was clarifying by her story.

'It means,' said Zara, 'that the back story is everything. Mark knows it. The fact that he won't divulge it must mean something.'

'His own implication?' suggested Des.

'It makes me think that Ronnie is innocent but that he knows something. Or maybe Muirhouse is playing Mark off against Ronnie.'

'That could be what's happening now but it may have nothing to do with what happened then.'

'Then?' said Zara.

'When Mark found it expedient to go to Australia. I wonder how Muirhouse feels about him coming back.'

'Did you ever find out if Muirhouse senior is dead?'

Yes, he's dead,' said Des.

Have they searched Mary-Ann's loft, by the way?' Zara said suddenly.

'Should they have?'

'If she was killed, she must have known something. There were beans she was not meant to spill. It's like some puzzle where the pieces only fit together one way and have to be assembled in order. I'll have to sleep on it.'

'You're interested again then?' Des didn't smile but Zara knew he was teasing her.

'It's just that my perspective keeps changing. At the moment both Mark and Mary Ann have flashing red lights above them in my mind but I don't know if I need an ambulance or a fire engine.'

Des looked mystified.

'Can't explain,' said Zara getting up and leaving.

The moment of clarity came early the next morning.

Chapter XXIII Be aware of where you are going

'Barney,' she said, sitting up and taking half the duvet off him in her haste, 'Mark Balfour is in danger'.

It was still very early so she texted Des hoping he was awake if not at work as he'd worked late the night before: Is Mark all right? Des phoned back immediately:

'Well Ms Clairvoyant.'

'What happened?' Zara was clutching Barney in her fear.

'Fake accident. Guy's lucky to be alive. Someone cut his brake cables.'

'Were they giving him a warning or did they mean to kill him?'

'Who knows?'

'John Muirhouse?'

'Well possibly but as per usual there's no sign of him and no clues at the scene. Why can't he make mistakes like other people?'

'He will, Des, he will. Was Mark injured?'

'A couple of broken ribs and a punctured lung. He went into a wall. There was grease on the road which hadn't been there earlier. Guaranteed. DC Megan Smyth passed along the same stretch, south of Whiting Bay half an hour before. She noticed a couple of local vans, then a car with one man in it. She didn't really clock him but did notice he slowed down well ahead of her. Then she stopped to look at the lights on the mainland, trying to work out which town was which. Then Mark's car passed her. She got back on her bike and a hundred yards or two further on she came upon the same vehicle crashed. Went into a wall of rock. Out of control.'

'It was a set up?'

'There was a message on Mark's phone: I need to meet you. And a place, quite near where the car was found.'

***

Meanwhile, an old lady on the mainland who had taken a bus southwards was unwittingly drawing attention to herself. She was found after a comfort break at a motorway stop having failed to re-join her vehicle. She seemed deranged and kept repeating the same sentence: 'I should never have left him'. Nobody could work out whether she was referring to a person or a pet, whether she had left under duress or of her own free will. They deduced she had come off the Glasgow bus but suggestions that she might return brought on hysteria.

The police were called. They interviewed a woman far different from the wily person Zara had visited. This woman was broken with a sorrow that overrode any other emotion and any thought that what she said might be taken down and used in evidence against her. A quick perusal of her bag confirmed her as Mrs Muirhouse with an address in Govanhill.

'I should never have left him. What will happen if they find him? It wasn't meant to happen.'

A computer search soon connected Mrs Muirhouse with a certain John and amazingly, it seemed to the police, their northern counterparts were searching the house next door to that of the lady in question at that very moment. Everyone was bemused by Mrs Muirhouse's insistence that John was at home. He can't have moved,' she said over and over again. 'He can't have left me.'

***

Monday morning. Kirsty had run out of mushrooms and Zara had been sent to the co-op for replenishments. Des was in buying mandarin oranges which he ate as snacks since he'd given up chocolate in a fight against an expanding waistline.

'A deranged Mrs Muirhouse has been discovered on the M1,' he said conversationally. Zara raised her eyebrows. 'She keeps saying she should not have left John at home but officers have been to the house and he's not there.'

'Disappointing,' said Zara. 'How is Mark?'

'He's not bad considering. Still not talking though.'

'Hm,' said Zara, trying to decide between open and closed cup mushrooms. She couldn't remember which Kirsty had asked for. 'If you ask me, which you probably weren't going to, I would say that Mark's silence plus the mysterious death of Mary Ann Brown add up to another dead body somewhere along the line.'

'But whose?' asked Des. 'Not Ronnie's? You don't mean Ronnie?'

'No I don't mean Ronnie. I don't know who I mean but it's an easy sum to do: just write down every single person mentioned in the case and eliminate them one by one.'

'Shoot them all?' Des smiled at her.

'Aye right,' said Zara.

***

Later a thought struck Zara and she phoned Des. Has Mary Ann's house been searched?'

'You know it has. The money. They found a whole load of banknotes.'

'Did they search the whole house?'

'I think so?

'Attic?'

Mary Ann Brown's doesn't have an attic.'

'How do you mean?'

'Is English not your first language any more?' Zara put the receiver down quietly. She couldn't be bothered when Des decided to close ranks. She phoned Uttam who answered his mobile at once.

'Uttam. Funny question. Has Mary Ann Brown's house got an attic?

'No.' Uttam's voice was unhesitant.

'Okay, thanks. Painting going all right?'

'Zara listen. It was a "no but". There used to be an attic but joiners came and blocked it off about two years ago. I remember because the job seemed to go on and on and the man doing it came into the shop for food. Mother used to make him chapattis. Mary Ann was extremely specific about what she wanted. It was driving the guy crazy.'

'Thanks Uttam. That's wonderful. I'll speak later. Good luck with the painting.'

Zara phoned Des back. There's a dead body in Mary Ann's attic but access is past the bees' nest in the Muirhouse's. I'll put a thousand on the body or what's left of it belonging to... well I'm not saying. I'll put the name in a sealed envelope and if I'm right...'

'Zara I can't —'

'Look silly then, Des,' said Zara and cut the call.

She didn't know how she was sure but she was. Some puzzles the brain works out without reference to the conscious mind. When she looked at the puzzle completed, it just was right. She phoned Uttam again:

'Sorry to be a bore, Uttam. Could you watch for police arriving at Mary Ann's and then find some excuse to go over, like someone's phoned an order over, and then casually ask if they are searching the attic, Mary Ann's attic that is and tell them about it being blocked off.'

'Mine is not to reason why,' said Uttam. 'I can manage that. There is actually one tell-tale sign. Mary Ann used to go on about it though no one would have noticed it unless they knew what they were looking for.'

'What was that?' asked Zara.'

'A small crack in the plastering where the hatch used to be. Only about three inches long but then it turns a corner making an angle. Hairline though.'

'That should help,' said Zara. 'Let me know how you get on.'

Uttam phoned back half an hour later: the officers had broken through the hatch. He had tried to make himself invisible but had been asked to leave at the point where the first officer up had uttered a gasp at the very odd smell.

'The bitter odour of truth perhaps,' said Zara.

Whether or not it was because Zara sensed the approach of an end game, she began to feel very apprehensive about Ronnie Balfour. If the 'accident' that had come Mark's way was anything to go by, Muirhouse would have no hesitation in finishing Ronnie off if he decided his game required that move. Zara was concluding that, in some way, someone else's move or maybe just their presence had substantially altered the stakes. John Muirhouse now feels threatened by the Balfours she thought. At any point Mark may tell the police what he's refrained from telling them so far. And from Mark's point of view, maybe the game had changed; that or Mark's attitude.

Zara felt a pang of conscience at having abandoned Ronnie. She had sensed no desire on Muirhouse's part to do anything with the man except let him sit in one cave or another until… until what? But now her sense of urgency returned although a small part of her still felt justified in having handed the baton to Mark.

Even so, Zara phoned the Balfour parents to find out if Mark was with them or still in hospital. He was in hospital so she went over to see him. Mark being injured gave her a good excuse to come back into the picture as a support. It didn't sound as if he would be ready for any mission that involved physical exertion any time soon.

Mark was sitting alone in the patients' communal sitting room. His parents had just left. By his expression Zara imagined he was tired of being fussed over.

'So are you going to tell me the rest of your story?' asked Zara after she had ascertained his state of health would tolerate some interrogation. Mark remained silent.

'Would it make any difference if I told you that the police are investigating the attic belonging to Mary Ann Brown at this very moment?' Mark jumped visibly but Zara found his reaction difficult to read. 'You knew Mary Ann? You have an idea what might be in the attic?' Mark passed his hand over his eyes and shook his head. 'Okay, let me put it another way: if it were a dead body whose do you think it would be likely to be?' Mark went pale.

'I don't know,' he said but uncertainly and then collecting himself, 'I've been in Australia for two years.'

'I'm only asking you to guess,' said Zara.

'I really don't know,' said Mark, his voice almost pleading now. 'I have a wife and child to think about.'

'I'm sorry,' Zara began, 'but I don't see the connection between —'

'Perhaps,' Des's voice broke in, his shadow falling across Zara and Mark, 'I can help here. I have the answer to one of your questions Zara. The body of John Muirhouse senior has been discovered in Mary Ann Brown's attic,' said Des into the vacuum. Mark became even paler and Zara looked like someone who had won a bet but wished they'd staked money on it. 'The deceased is in an advanced state of decay but there is no doubt he died of a bullet wound to the head. Thanks for the tip off, Zara but I'm going to have to ask you to leave. I'll be in touch later.'

'One question before I go,' said Zara. Des acquiesced with a resigned nod. Did Ronnie know John Muirhouse before the incident on the mountain?'

'No,' said Mark. 'I knew him but not Ronnie. Why do you want to know?'

'We have evidence that they spent time in each other's company on Bute, at Mount Stuart.'

'Zara,' said Des. 'I don't think — Zara held up her hand. 'I have a witness who seemed to think they had met before that day, that something bound them together.' Mark's face became anxious and ugly.

'Let's keep Ronnie out of this. Take my word for it, my brother did not know Muirhouse except as a bad-timer and only then at the point before I left for Australia. Please. Ronnie is a victim...' Zara looked as if she wanted to continue but Des again asked her to leave. She didn't mind: she had a lot to think about.

***

Back at North Crag, Zara sought out Barney and Ben who were playing pool unenthusiastically in what Ben called the games room. Both their faces brightened as Zara entered.

'Troops,' said Zara, 'the search operation is to resume. Orders the same as before. You will be back-up only.'

'Something's happened,' said Ben. 'Are you going to tell us or do we have to guess?' Zara filled them in. Ben became excited, Barney anxious.

'Do you think you are going to find Ronnie alive?' he asked.

'Yes I think so. An interesting tidbit Des let go the other day. Remember Bobby who drove the car into the sea at Lochranza castle? A shop-keeper reported selling him a dozen cans of beans, a large bag of apples and a dozen rolls. Bobby was embarrassed when the shopkeeper asked if he had visitors. Shop-keeper is a friend of one of the Specials so Des got to know through that. I reckon Muirhouse suddenly decided the death of Ronnie was not something he wanted to have on his hands.'

'Why not?' asked Barney.

'Too complicated, even for him, now Mark is around to be reckoned with.'

'So we start tomorrow?' asked Ben. Zara nodded. 'Did you ever look at Uncle George's and my solution to the Riga puzzle?'

'I'm sorry Ben, I'm afraid I didn't.' Ben shook his head in mock exasperation.

'It's okay, Aunty Zara, I know you said you weren't interested. This is the answer anyway.' He flourished a neat reckoning and Zara saw at once it was the Black Cave down past Kildonan.

'Do you think he'll still be there though?' she said. 'It's days since... And why would he want to tell us anyway?'

'You mean it's a trap,' said Ben trying to hide his disappointment.

'Could be,' said Barney. 'In which case there's no way any of us should go near it. Remember what nearly happened in Merkland Wood, Zara.'

'You think his little plans are mostly about getting me off his back,' said Zara.

'It's his idea of a joke,' said Ben, 'but we have to outwit him. I think it's worth going to the Black Cave. There might be something there that would lead to where Ronnie is now.' Zara suddenly looked at Barney. He knew exactly what she meant: Ben is getting into Famous Five mode. We have to wind back. Ben had noticed the exchange and immediately became huffy. 'Can't we just see if Uncle George and I were right. We could just go a walk. Loads of people walk to the Black Cave. There must be a deeper bit no one knows about.' Zara was silent. 'Well?' said Ben.

'Perhaps,' said Zara. 'Let's see how it looks tomorrow. We could maybe take another tack altogether.'

'What?' said Ben and Barney.

'I'll need to think it through,' said Zara. 'Tell you at breakfast.'

***

The police had found it difficult to make sense of Mrs Muirhouse even after they understood her secret. She would talk about 'John' but they were at loss to know which one she meant. She was extremely agitated and, most uncharacteristically, tears were found drying on her cheek, squeezed, Uttam said, from ducts so rarely used they had almost ceased to be functional. Because Mrs Muirhouse was so unforthcoming, the police were even keener to re-interview Mark Balfour but in the meantime Mark had procured a lawyer and had been advised to say nothing.

It was amazing how few leads there were to pursue. Daffodil, for instance, did not seem to have had any friends and Mary Ann had been her only living relative. Daffodil's previous workplaces had been investigated and, though people remembered her without difficulty, they knew nothing about her private life either in terms of specific relationships or in terms of what might be her typical behaviour.

***

'Right,' said Zara. 'I know what I'm going to do. I'm not really expecting you to join me though.' Barney took in Zara's firm tone and cooled his desire to act protective:

'What had you in mind?'

'I'm making an assumption that Bobby is being used as a messenger, taking food to Ronnie Balfour, if I follow Bobby, I'll get to Ronnie.'

'And how are you going to do that without arousing suspicion?'

'My disguise is so perfect even you and Ben wouldn't recognize me.' Ben was sceptical but knew Zara would be unmoved by anything he might say about it.

'So Dad and I will go to the Black Cave.' Zara looked uneasy.

'Or I could drop you somewhere and pick you up later.'

'But you don't know where you'll be going or where you'll end up.'

'Mm,' said Zara. 'Well, I'm only agreeing because I'm absolutely sure there's nothing there. It is a lovely walk and you can take a picnic but will you promise me you won't go into the cave?'

'But, Aunty Zara, what's the point of going all that way and not going into the cave?'

'It's that or nothing. Barney, you agree surely? You who always think I'm leading Ben into danger. In fact, now I consider it properly, I think it's a thoroughly bad idea. Why don't you go out in canoes or up another mountain? It would be much more fun than a boring old cave. Barney, what do you think?'

But Barney was saved the problem of answering by the entrance of a boy about Ben's age. They could almost have been twins. Ben saw a possibility.

'Hi Peter. What are you doing today? Peter's staying here too,' he said to Zara and Barney. 'With his dad. His mum's gone to England to look after her mum. We met on the beach.'

'We're going to the Black Cave,' said Peter. 'You said it was really exciting —'

'We could all go together,' said Ben. Barney met Zara's eyes over Ben's head. Her eyes and lips spoke resignation. Peter's dad came in. He was tall and thin like Barney and looked genial. Zara felt he was relieved to join forces and lessen the load of listening to his child's chatter and having to answer. This way the boys would always be ahead and the men would be able to talk or not talk as they wished. Zara went to the kitchen to make up rolls for them all.

'How will you know where to start?' asked George who was privy to Zara's plan.

'I met Tom and Davy from the Mountain Rescue yesterday,' said Zara, and got the conversation round to Bobby's escapade with the car and Tom said he'd seen Bobby in an ancient silver Vauxhall — he meant the car was over ten years old. Davy said he'd seen him leave his house in a cloud of dust yesterday. He loves speed. The sea's one thing but...'

'So you're going to drive round the island till you find a silver Vauxhall?'

'Correct,' said Zara. 'I know it doesn't sound like much of a plan. My cover is I'm a trades person I'll be wearing a short red wig and an old pair of Kirsty's dungarees and Doc Martens.' George shook his head. Zara was about to leave when George asked:

'How come Bobby is still driving after the Lochranza Castle episode?'

'Good one, George. You can't put points on a license someone doesn't have? I don't know. I should imagine he is chancing his arm and the police are busy doing other things — like not finding Ronnie Balfour.'

Chapter XXIV Lures large and small

Peter's dad, Max, was driving his son, Barney and Ben to Kildonan and from there they were taking the shore path to the cave. They were armed with large quantities of rolls and Barney promised they would get chocolate and drinks on the way. Max was a lawyer: he liked to listen and analyse and conclude. Small children were mostly outside his box. He got by with his genial demeanour. Everyone just assumed his mind was elsewhere, on his last case or his next one. Barney tried to engage him in conversation as they drove southwards but he appeared to be concentrating very heavily on the twists and turns of the road and he wouldn't go fast over the 'bumps' as Peter called the dips and rises going towards Largymeanoch.

Barney contented himself with looking out over the sea towards Ailsa Craig. So much water, but it was an estuary not the open sea. Facing the Pacific must be... awesome — Barney found himself using one of Ben's current words for 'amazing'.

Having arrived at the Kildonan shore, the boys raced ahead to see the seals, promising they would go no further till Max and Barney arrived. No one noticed a silver Vauxhall and its silent occupant.

'I hope the seals are there today,' said Max sounding unexpectedly human. 'Last time we came, you couldn't even see the rocks.'

'Bad luck,' said Barney. 'Fingers crossed.'

When the two men drew nearer they could see there were many, many seals and Ben and Peter were down clambering over the slippery basalt to get a closer look. They were being extremely quiet not wanting the animals to take fright and slide back into the water. Barney and Max stood on the grassy hillock from which the boys had descended and watched.

Suddenly Peter gave a great shout and there were several loud splashes and waves as the seals sought the safety of the sea. Ben was furious.

'What did you do that for? One, they've all gone now and two, why did you want to frighten them?'

'They're okay,' Peter mumbled, looking to see his father's reaction.

'Come here Peter.' Max beckoned his son with his index finger. Peter bent his head.

Propelling his son in front of himself, Max started walking in the direction of the cave. Barney, assuming he wanted a quiet word, allowed Ben to rummage in the rucksack for chocolate so when they set off again Max and Peter were quite a way ahead. Barney had to talk the seal incident through with Ben to calm him down and the next time he looked up, he could see father and son at least fifty metres apart, Peter in front.

Barney suggested Ben run and catch up with him but Ben was still put out and refused, plodding along beside his father, swiping the grass with a stick he had found.

Max was wishing his wife was there. She always knew what to say to mollify Peter. Max also wished he were at work. Clients could be difficult of course but in the end they always left the office whereas your family... He stopped suddenly realizing he could no longer see Peter.

He screwed his eyes tight shut and then looked again and then reached back past his preoccupation to retrieve his last image of his son. Peter had been standing on a large rock and pointing towards the shore. Peter, assuming he had found the cave, had waved back. Peter was in the cave then, Max told himself and stumped on trying to suppress the feeling of unease that was beginning to take hold of him.

Barney and Ben came up.

'Where's Peter?' asked Ben.

I think he's in the cave.' Ben looked questioningly at his father.

'Let's stay together,' said Barney.

The tide was out so it was easy to gain entrance. The whole place struck Ben as gloomy and chill but he did not want to be disappointed.

'Peter,' he shouted. 'Where are you?' but Peter did not reply. No one spoke. Everyone hunted.

'Maybe he's fallen,' said Max.

'Maybe,' said Barney but when Ben caught his eye he looked away. Ben knew then they were thinking the same thought: it had been a trap. He climbed up to the back of the cave to where Barney stood:

'Muirhouse has got Peter, hasn't he? It was meant to be me, wasn't it?'

'We'd better divide,' said Barney. 'Max, you go on ahead in case he just walked on and we'll stay and explore here thoroughly. Maybe he went up the cliff and will appear back any minute.' He looked doubtfully at the bramble and nettle-infested face above them. 'Doesn't look likely though.'

Ben had squatted down in the remotest depth of the cave he could find and suddenly gave a cry:

'I've found a bean tin!' he shouted. 'Ronnie Balfour was here.'

***

Zara tossed a coin and drove south from Brodick. She had disguised the van by putting an old ladder on the luggage rack and some posters advertising cleaning services on the side of the 'no job too small' variety. This meant she could stop almost anywhere and people would think she was either on a job or having her lunch. She'd painted on North Crag's number but with one digit wrong, hoping this way she wouldn't get any clients. She hesitated on the east side of Kildonan: should she keep to the high road or go down to the shore? Knowing Barney and the others were going that way she decided to stay up. She couldn't quite believe it when she saw the silver Vauxhall nose its way out from the west road down to Kildonan and set off southwards.

She was at loss to understand the game. Unless of course there was no game. It might just be Bobby going about some private business. She wondered if she had been right about Ronnie having left the Black Cave but at Bennan, opposite the cave although a mile inland, Zara reckoned, Bobby's brakes squealed as he took a turn down a farm track. Even with her disguise Zara dare not follow. She did not want to find herself in a cul de sac with Muirhouse if he should be down there. She decided to wait. Bobby had to come back the same way eventually. If Ronnie did happen to be there, she could go and see after Bobby had returned and gone. She pulled off the road a little past the turning Bobby had taken, at a place where trees made the van less conspicuous and then walked back to the track. She would just have to sit in the hedge and wait. She tried not to let in images of Muirhouse meeting Barney and Ben, Max and Peter, but felt they would be protected by their numbers. What could Muirhouse do and to what end?

***

Bobby had the feeling everything was going well. He had been promised a hundred pounds for this job and, although it had seemed daunting when John Muirhouse had given him the brief and warned him not to go beyond it like last time — 'No swims in the car, Bobby!' — what he had been asked to do, now seemed a cinch. He was especially looking forward to the bit where he had to drive to the secret place, a location as yet unknown to him. He really did feel as if he were in a gangster movie. First though he had to lure the boy back to the car. The start, which he had expected to be hard had gone like a dream. Look for a blondish boy around nine with a tall lanky father. There had been a moment when he had doubted: the car had held two sets of fathers and sons. He had followed them on foot till they had reached the seals and then one set had forged ahead. They must be the ones he thought: they looked as if they were on a mission and the boy was so far ahead. If things stayed that way, it would be so easy to talk to him.

He had retraced his steps, driven south and then come down to the cave from above. Found the boy. He sold him a story about his car; how something had loosened the exhaust and when he had stopped and looked underneath, something had fallen off and rolled away. He could see it but he was too big to reach it.

'And then I found you,' he said. 'The answer to my prayers...' Bobby was getting really proud of his dramatic performance. It was so believable that neither he nor the boy saw the holes in the story: why would anyone go towards the shore for help and not the road and why not just drive on a bit so the car wasn't on top of the missing widget?

They had climbed straight up the cliff. The quickest way, Bobby had said. He told the boy he was in a hurry because he had to meet the boat to pick up someone who did not know the island at all.

The boy who said his name was Peter, seemed to enjoy rising to the challenge for the first ten minutes while they were climbing the cliff but when they reached the top and there was no car to be seen, he looked quite panic-stricken. Bobby pretended to be surprised too.

Honestly, it's not far,' he said. 'We'll see it when we're over the next rise.'

'My dad will wonder where I am,' said Peter stopping. 'I didn't know it was going to take so long.'

'Oh dear,' said Bobby. 'I'm really sorry. It really is only another five minutes. I've got an ice-box with ice cream in it in the car.'

Peter's eyes gave him away. Bobby had struck gold.

What's your favourite flavour?' he asked.

'Chocolate,' said Peter.

'You're in luck. You can have as much as you can eat. The next time Peter lagged behind, Bobby promised him a tenner. 'You don't know how much this means to me,' he said, 'you doing this for a stranger. You must have been very well brought up.'

By now Peter felt thoroughly confused. He was so far away from his father and also completely lost. He saw Bobby as a raft to cling to, that and the idea of ice cream which he kept firmly in his mind.

At last they were there. Bobby had to be a bit brisker now: widget first, then ice cream. Peter crawled under the car and found the widget Bobby had carefully placed there.

'A thousand gold stars for you,' he said, copying his step-father now thankfully dead, who had never followed through on any promised reward.

Peter stood by the driver door waiting for the ice cream and the tenner. Bobby made a show of looking in the boot then he hit the side of his head:

'You know what? I must have taken it out at the farm. I was delivering a motor part to them. How stupid can you get?' he said to Peter, grinning. 'Jump in and we'll go and pick it up. It's just round the corner.' Peter's desire for something cool overwhelmed his misgivings. He jumped in. 'Belt up, it's very bumpy,' said Bobby, purposely driving over stones he could have avoided. Peter looked anxious but he stuck it out until they reached the road. Then he asked,

'Where's the farm? I thought you said...' but Bobby crashed his foot down on the accelerator and laughed out loud.

'We're going for a ride,' he shouted. 'Nee-ow!' and he started taking the bends like a racing driver.

***

Zara had been almost asleep. She had tried everything to stay awake — recited all her favourite poems, sung all her favourite songs and was just beginning on naming all the girls in her class in first year at secondary school when she was sprung into full awareness by the sound of a motor bumping along the farm track. Her heart stopped when she saw a blond boy in the passenger seat but because she had first thought, Ben, knowing it was not him, did not diminish her fear. Bobby has taken the wrong boy she thought, stabbing Des's number into her phone.

***

On the beach, Max was steadily losing his mind. Barney and Ben did their best but there was very little they could say to make him feel any better. Before John Muirhouse they might have said it was impossible to get off the island without detection but now... Max had phoned the police and not answered their questions very well. They had asked where he had last seen Max and suggested he might be in the sea. This idea upset Max even more. He felt sure he would have seen Peter approach the water but then in his imagination he saw him there disappearing under the waves.

Ben looked at his father in a 'know-what-I'm-thinking kind of way. Barney shook his head imperceptibly but Ben's lip's set in a firm line. He was reaching the same conclusion as Zara.

'I wonder where Zara is,' he said as a code message to his father. 'You should phone her and tell her Peter's missing.'

'They're sending someone,' said Max.

Neither Ben, Barney or Max thought Peter had gone straight up: if he had been abducted they imagined he would have been taken up the Shannochie track further along. But wasn't it more likely he had slipped and fallen into some hidden hollow? Their minds wanted to believe this but their fear took them to worse places.

***

Bobby's foot was on the floor, Peter had become white-faced, his hands gripping his seat, eyes closing and opening as each bend came hurtling towards them with Bobby's melodramatic turns of the steering wheel. They were approaching the Gaire Slip where on the off-shore side a concrete wall attempts to limit further landslide and on the shore side there is a drop of two hundred and fifty feet into the sea, when Bobby registered the oncoming police car. He was coming out of a left-hand bend and the sight of the car momentarily stopped him righting the steering wheel. The next thing he saw was the wall; he wheeled sharply away but bounced off the concrete ricocheting across the road to the edge of the drop, the vegetation slowing him sufficiently to keep all but his front wheels on the ground. The engine stalled. Even Bobby's mind took in the impossibility of backing off and making a getaway.

It was difficult to gauge what was preventing the car from falling, poised as it was between the two elements of earth and air. Peter struggled with his door handle but the door was jammed. Bobby could open his door but only six inches.

All at once he began to realize what he'd done: it was one thing to ride into the sea in a car on his own but... He stared at Peter in surprise: he might have killed the boy. At this point Peter, subconsciously registering the change in Bobby's emotional temperature, started to cry.

'I want my dad,' he wailed. 'I helped you with your car and you didn't even give me my ice cream!'

The words 'I'm sorry' were in Bobby's heart but couldn't quite reach his lips so full was he of all the events, how one thing had led to the next but it was becoming a confusion in his mind. He had just been trying to carry out the task he'd been set. He had no idea why Muirhouse wanted the boy. It

hadn't entered his head he might want to harm him. He hadn't thought —
except about the money. He was saving up for his dream car. And now...?
Maybe he would never be allowed to drive again. He wondered whether he
would go to prison for kidnapping. For that was what it had been, he could
see that now.

He wondered why he had never thought about that possibility. He thought
about John Muirhouse and hated him. He banged his head on the side of the
car and Peter who had stopped crying, frustrated at the lack of reaction,
started again in desperation. Bobby thought again about escaping but there
was something about his right leg: it didn't seem to be obeying his brain.

***

Meanwhile, Zara had contacted Barney and offered to meet them all where
the farm track ended. She had to convince him there was a route up the cliff
quicker than going all the way to Shannochie.

'That's the route Bobby must have taken,' she said, 'to have come past me
with Peter. By the time they all met, Des had informed both Max and Zara
that the boy was safe. They were waiting at the Gaire Slip for Max.

Chapter XXV   Who believes whom?

Back at the hotel Barney and Zara were very subdued.

'I can't think how I let Ben talk me into going to the Black Cave,' said Barney.

'Yes you can,' said Zara. 'It was the Max and Peter addition that made it all seem safe to us but ironically for Muirhouse, it's that that made his plan founder. I wonder if he was going to hold Ben, had he managed to capture him or whether he was just going to give us all a fright.'

'He's certainly done that,' said Barney. 'I shan't dare let Ben go anywhere on his own now.'

'How did Muirhouse know you were going to the cave on that particular day?'

He only had to post Bobby there, say, from ten till five. The guy's unemployed remember and not that bright. He'd probably do it for a tenner a day. Muirhouse is clever enough to know we would likely be intrigued by his coded message.'

'I can't believe I put Ben in such danger.' Barney buried his head on his arm and Zara knew he was hiding tears.

'If you feel bad,' she said, 'how do you think Max feels, his own boy going missing on his watch. He knew nothing. As far as he was concerned Peter just ran ahead the way children do. He must be feeling dreadful.'

Max and Peter had not been seen since the return to the hotel. Zara thought Max was trying to avoid them.

'I don't know what to do,' she said Barney. 'I feel really devious: we knew there was a possible trap and we didn't warn them.'

'But Zara, we thought the trap was for us. We didn't reckon on the Bobby factor.'

'We should have done,' said Zara.

'I expect Des will have told him, at least something,' said Barney. 'He would have to reassure him Bobby wasn't a kidnapper on the loose.'

'Wasn't he?' said Zara.

***

John Muirhouse himself was only a little perturbed at the failure of his plan. He had so many plans: he knew some would work. His latest one was about to come to fruition.

***

Although Zara's strategy of following Bobby had been useful she knew that that course of action was no longer possible: Bobby would not be driving anywhere for a long time. Back to searching caves she thought.

After the failure of the police in their last big push, Des had told Zara that the case seemed to be going cold. They had had a huge number of police out. They reckoned they had searched every nook and cranny on the island: no sign of Ronnie Balfour. Zara's simple explanation was that Ronnie had been moved to Argyll perhaps — or maybe another island — for the duration of the search and then moved back as soon as it was over.

Zara had also been thinking about Mount Stuart and what bearing it had on John Muirhouse's operations. Her mind went back to John Laurie and Edwin Rose. Had John Laurie planned to kill Rose from the moment he met him on Bute or was Laurie, like Muirhouse, just good at taking advantage of opportunities when they presented themselves? As it was, Rose and Laurie knowing each other already certainly coloured one's perspective when one tried to decide on the motives of either party. Who met whom where? Was it chance or deliberation? But the truth in the latter case was as hard to come by as in the former.

***

Thursday. Zara met Des in the middle of Brodick.

'How is it going?' she asked. Des shrugged. Zara could tell from his expression that things had moved on. Tell me,' she said. 'Something's happened, hasn't it?'

'You were wrong,' said Des.

'Me?' said Zara in mock surprise. 'About what?'

244

'It was Ronnie Balfour.'

'What was Ronnie Balfour?'

'Zara don't be obtuse. It was Ronnie Balfour that murdered Daffodil Brown.'

'Don't be ridiculous, Des.' Des looked at her in a way that brought her up short. Zara's mind went over the possibilities that could have led Des to be so sure. 'He's confessed?' she said.

'In his own fair hand,' said Des. 'He's explained exactly how he did it. How he met John Muirhouse on the Isle of Bute and saw how he could entice him into being an accessory. He painted a picture of some fun they could have up the mountain if they could get a couple of girls to play ball. Ronnie said he could get a girl called Zara' — Des narrowed his eyes as he looked at Zara — 'even said he'd swap Zara for Daffodil if Muirhouse fancied her. Muirhouse had at some point told him the story of the Waverley expedition. But because Muirhouse had seemed to be content with Daffodil, you were side-lined and left in the tent. In the middle of the night, Ronnie Balfour heard Muirhouse's pre-arranged signal. You heard it too and together you went to investigate. This was an extra cover to make Balfour look as if he were on Daffodil's side. You were encouraged to go back to the tent.'

'Meanwhile,' Des went on, 'Daffodil had been bamboozled into being tied up. She was told she was taking part in an ancient Celtic ritual. All John Muirhouse did was to provide a rope. Neither Muirhouse nor Balfour quite knew what was to happen next but Balfour somehow managed to get Daffodil to the edge of the cliff and tie the rope to a boulder but in such a way that he, Muirhouse could easily step on it thus allowing the rope to unwind and take Daffodil over the cliff to the boulder below where she was found...'

'But that didn't kill her?'

'Remember the fingerprints round her neck were Balfour's?'

'Yes but they were from the earlier incident, when we were trying to simulate what might have happened to Edwin Rose.' Zara waited.

'In his own words,' said Des, '"I gave a great cry and rushed as fast as I could down to the boulder. I placed my thumbs on Daffodil's neck exactly where I had placed them before. Muirhouse was not familiar with the terrain and by the time he reached the boulder, the deed was done".' Zara looked hard at Des.

'I'm sorry, she said,' 'it's very neat but I don't believe a word of it. That confession was done under duress or... no, I think Muirhouse just made it up. If it were true and Muirhouse knows where Ronnie is, why doesn't he tell you? How come I found Ronnie in the cave in Merkland Wood?'

'We've only your word for that, Zara.'

'You'll be telling me next that I was an accessory!'

'Zara, there is no evidence.'

'I saw him.'

'That's uncorroborated. And if it happened, how do we know he didn't just set it up?'

'And his pale face was just make-up and he starved himself to look as if he were at death's door? Des, you have to be joking.' Des put on his 'patient' voice:

'I know it must be a shock for you to imagine that this person you shared a tent with is a murderer and I don't deny that there is a lot of contradictory evidence but...'

Zara who had climbed into Des's car for privacy now leapt out and slammed the door after herself. She had a horrible picture of Ronnie in prison saying over and over, in a re-run of John Laurie's story: 'For the brutal murder of Daffodil Brown, I'll never take the blame.'

***

Zara turned towards the North Crag but after a few steps, turned again in the direction of the guesthouse where the Balfours were staying. As she would have expected they were not in good heart. When Zara saw them she realized she had imagined they would not have believed the confession — but they had.

'Our Ronnie,' said Margaret Balfour, leaving the obvious words unsaid. Her husband just shook his head.

'But I'm sure, I'm still sure he didn't do it,' protested Zara. 'Why do you believe in a piece of paper?' The Balfours were too far gone into gloom to hear her.

'It's his handwriting and there's his fingerprints on the paper. They can even tell by the amount of sweat whether the writer was in a state of fear. He wasn't.' Zara sighed out loud. 'And Mark, he seems to have been mixed up with this other death.'

'John Muirhouse senior?' asked Zara. Margaret nodded. 'Apparently it happened round about the time Mark went to Australia.' Zara remained silent: one son was bad enough but to have reason to imagine that both your children had been responsible for a murder each...

But when Zara thought about it, it was that that made her even more certain she was right, that there was no way Ronnie Balfour had killed Daffodil Brown. Even the machinations with the rope smacked of John Muirhouse — unless all boy scouts of that era had learned the same techniques, Ronnie and John both.

'Was Ronnie ever a boy scout?' she asked. The Balfour parents looked bewildered. 'I'm thinking about the rope,' said Zara. 'John Muirhouse did a fancy trip-wire up in Merkland Wood when he trapped me into looking for Ronnie there.'

'The police say Ronnie could have set all that up,' said Harry Balfour. It was as if, having crossed a line into believing his son's guilt, nothing was going to persuade him otherwise.

'He never was a boy scout,' said Margaret Balfour.

Zara was in two minds. She wanted to comfort the Balfours but she couldn't comfort them on their terms because she did not believe their son was a murderer. She tried one last time:

"If he's the murderer,' she said, 'why does he not just give himself up? What's stopping him?'

'I wish I knew,' said Harry. 'We've put a letter in the paper telling him to do just that.'

'You did what?' Zara was horrified.

'That's what it asked, his letter of confession: 'Let me know you know' and it said which paper to phone.' Muirhouse tricks thought Zara. Des kept that bit back. She was suddenly furious with Muirhouse, with Des, and with Margaret and Harry Balfour.

'Don't you realize how hurt Ronnie will be when he discovers you don't believe in him? This is just Muirhouse being cruel. Don't you see, it's a false confession? Muirhouse probably threatened Ronnie with your death if he didn't sign his name to it.' Both Balfours had changed colour.

'But what makes you so sure you are right?'

'Why do you think Muirhouse attempted to kill Mark? — It was a demonstration: if I can do this, I can do that.' Zara stood up.' I'm sorry if I've upset you but...' The words choked her. She ran out of the gate and down to the road turning by the big wooden house to find the shore. Reaching Fishermen's Walk, she slowed down: one thing was obvious: she had to find Ronnie before John Muirhouse went completely insane.

***

Zara couldn't find Ben and Barney but then remembered they had gone out kayaking. George and Kirsty were talking to some guests who wanted to give them a detailed account of their previous day's trip to the Holy Isle.

'We saw a monk,' she heard the woman say, as if she were talking about some animal in a safari park. Zara went to her attic room with a mug of coffee, took out her notebook and started to review the whole situation.

The pictures Zara drew and the words she wrote down helped to pacify her mind. They showed her what she did and didn't know. Her focus was on trying to get into John Muirhouse's mind. First there was the murder of Daffodil Brown. What was the motive there? John Muirhouse had not been in love with her. Had he done it to pay out Mark who had been? But what was so wrong about being in love with someone that it merited a killing? Mark Balfour did seem to be a lynch-pin in the whole affair. Whatever had happened to make him go off to Australia had been extremely significant. Something he wanted to forget. Something he wanted everyone to forget. Had he killed John Muirhouse senior? If so, under what circumstances? If so, would he risk coming back to Scotland to have it possibly raked over and brought to light?

Zara went back to John Muirhouse. Why was he holding Ronnie? He was like a cat playing with a mouse. But was it the right mouse? Perhaps he had wanted to interrogate Mark but made do with his brother, involved his brother as a further retaliation on Mark. And was all this in honour of his father or was he just mad? He was clever but madness and cleverness are by no means mutually exclusive thought Zara.

All the business of holding Ronnie could be seen as the delaying tactics of someone who was not certain what to do next even though Muirhouse's behaviour and strategy tended to look deliberate and purposeful. And perhaps he had been thrown by the arrival of Mark, who seemingly was prepared to put himself in the hot seat for Ronnie though he didn't seem to be making much progress in finding him. Maybe Muirhouse's shot across the bows had weakened his determination.

Muirhouse seemed to want to threaten all the Balfours. Was it a case of threaten or be threatened? If the whole point was to shut people up what was it that was being withheld by whom and for what reason? Did reason anyway have any relevance in the present situation?

Zara sat thinking for a long time. In the end she came up with two possibilities and three lines of action: one, to establish a working relationship with Mark; two, to try and talk to Mrs Muirhouse and three, to find Ronnie. Not in that order.

Chapter XXVI Little movements on different fronts

Bobby was seething with rage. He was not a killer and he felt he'd been made to look like one. He was not... he wanted to say he was not a child abductor but the facts stared him in the face. The facts and then John Muirhouse's grin which was the grimmest Bobby thought he could imagine. Why ever did I trust him, he asked himself? His mother had always said that money wasn't everything. He had wanted to suggest that this was usually said by people who had it but answering his mother back was not something he had learned to do. She wasn't here now. John Muirhouse was here though, in a manner of speaking and Bobby had trusted the colour of his money. He began to feel guilty. Then remorseful.

He remembered the little talk Muirhouse had given him before this latest escapade. Looking back, he saw he should have taken it a lot more seriously, realized the significance of what the man was saying. 'If things don't go as planned and you do get picked up,' Muirhouse had said, 'say nothing. They can't make you speak. Whatever you do, don't plead guilty'. He had followed Muirhouse's advice and now he was in a prison being held on remand until his trial. Muirhouse had not contacted him. Where was the cake with the sawblade inside? Bobby smiled bitterly to himself. He knew he didn't believe in fairy-tale escapes but the thought of Muirhouse doing nothing to help him fuelled his anger. He thought about changing his plea. It would mean dropping Muirhouse in it. Was that why the guy had told him to keep his mouth shut? Bobby didn't think about consequences: the idea of making trouble for Muirhouse seemed a good one. The next time someone came to his cell he told them he wanted to see his lawyer.

***

That afternoon when Ben and Barney came back from kayaking, Zara filled them in on what was happening. There was no pretence now about keeping things secret from Ben: he had been too nearly involved. He would never again be content with not knowing things. They were all quite stunned at the outcome of the 'Black Cave Event' as Ben insisted on calling it, although it had not happened at the Black Cave. Barney kept re-running the day, seeing Ben being inveigled into Bobby's car instead of Peter.

'You wouldn't have done that, would you, got into a stranger's car?'

'Don't worry, I wouldn't have gone a step further without the ice cream. No chance.' But though Ben joked, Barney and Zara knew that he realised the gravity of the situation. He'd only seen Peter once since the incident. He was remarkably unscathed but still shocked at what had happened to him. Father and son were leaving, cutting their holiday short. Going back to mum who was flying up to meet them.

***

Barney agreed guardedly to be back up for Zara in her continuing search for Ronnie Balfour but on a much more restricted basis: he and Ben would undertake to be an anchor in the village nearest to where Zara was exploring but on no account was Ben going anywhere near any prospective danger zone. Barney could not quite see why Zara thought she was going to succeed where the police had failed in their last very exhaustive search but the fact that he did not think she would be successful made him more willing to underwrite the plan: he didn't think she would be in much danger.

Zara herself was acting from 'dogged', the toothcomb approach. Eventually she thought, she had to turn something up. If she had been right about Bobby servicing Ronnie as prisoner and Bobby was now out of the running, John Muirhouse must be taking his place and visiting more regularly. Muirhouse, however he may appear, is human she thought: he has to make a mistake sometime, even if it is only giving us another coded message.

But before she embarked on her search, she sought out Mark Balfour to see if there was any small piece of information she could glean which would help her in her understanding of John Muirhouse's mind. She couldn't imagine what Mark was doing apart from recuperating. The hospital in Lamlash would be bemused, Zara thought, if they knew Bobby's injured leg and Mark's broken ribs had been initiated by the same person. What was Mark feeling about his brother? How had the disastrous encounter with the Muirhouse machine been set up in the first place? If Mark had a past history with Muirhouse, why had he not realised the likelihood of a trap? Then she chided herself: pots and black kettles.

Zara eventually caught up with Mark in the Ormidale where he was having a lunch-time drink.

'A word in your ear,' said Zara. 'Same again for him and a ginger beer and lime for me,' she said to the barman. Mark followed her to a corner of the room without asking any questions. The place was quiet. 'How are you doing?' Zara thought it best to start friendly.

'My ribs are still sore if that's what you mean,' he said, 'but probably making more progress there than with the other business'.

'That's what I wanted to talk about,' said Zara.

'I imagined you would.' Mark didn't crack a smile.

Things have changed since we last spoke. I was wondering whether joining forces, or at least pooling information might not be a bad idea.'

'What information have you got?' No change of tone. Keep calm Zara, she said to herself, he is worried about his brother.

'Well nothing new but —'

'— a lot of speculative rubbish designed to make people even more anxious than they already are!' She was unprepared for this outburst.

'Sorry? What do you mean?'

'My parents. You've really upset them, suggesting Muirhouse is threatening to kill them. Fucksake, what a stupid thing to say. They've not slept for weeks now without pills. They don't know whether to stay here or go back home. The confession was the final straw and then while they're trying to come to terms with the fact that their son is a murderer, you come along and put another spanner in the works.' Zara was flabbergasted. She realized she had not considered what Mark's take on the confession would be.

'You believe he killed Daffodil?' There was a long silence. Then,

'I don't want to believe it but what about the evidence?'

'Let's look at possible motives for Muirhouse setting this up,' said Zara. 'For instance, you were in love with Daffodil, how does that affect your feelings towards Ronnie as a possible perpetrator?' Another silence.

'You mean Muirhouse is trying to alienate me from Ronnie so I stop looking for him?'

'Well?'

'Yes. Could be.' Mark's face changed. Zara waited. 'You know, I feel relieved. What you say is possible. I think I was just carried away by the awfulness of the idea of... I should have known better.' He drained his glass. 'You wanting another of those?'

'You're all right,' said Zara.

When Mark returned with another beer, he placed a bag of nuts in front of Zara as if to compensate for not buying her a drink. She began to like him a little better.

So', she said, feeling it was now possible to engage with him on a putative rescue bid, 'maybe you could tell me where you are with all this and whether you have any plans to progress.'

'My last plan didn't really work out,' he said at last managing a smile with one corner of his mouth as he patted his ribs.

'But do you understand Muirhouse's game plan? Why he's holding Ronnie? What might make him let him go?' Again a long silence.

'I'm sorry, I still don't want to tell you what I know.' He looked at Zara not in a hostile way but desperately.

'So,' said Zara again, 'if you gave me information, you would lose control. It's the sort of information I would be compelled to use in a way that makes you afraid, afraid of the consequences?' Mark nodded. 'You know who killed Muirhouse senior?' Mark made to get up. 'No Mark. Please. I won't go there if you'd rather not but isn't there anything you can give me?'

'To tell you the truth, Zara, apart from what I can't tell you, I know nothing. I certainly have no idea how Muirhouse's mind works.' Zara looked closely at him and believed what he said. A blank then. He was not going to be any use, either, in an action that might end up physical. He looked pained every time he breathed. Even so, it was good to know they were not in conflict.

***

It had been impossible for the police to conceal from Muirhouse a search involving so many officers. While the police had been searching the island, Ronnie had been secreted not far away, on the peninsula of Kintyre. Deep in the woods. It had been easy leaving the last Arran cave: Muirhouse had promised Ronnie he would be freed. He had been feeding him up and had actually allowed him to wash.

And it had been easy for John Muirhouse to worm his way into the confidence of a Lochranza boat owner. An old man whose windows he had cleaned to sparkling; John Muirhouse sporting a blond wig and some very dirty overalls. His friend, he had told the old man, was dying of cancer but loved fishing especially at night. Could he borrow the boat one evening and bring it back the following day? He had asked the question in advance so he could move fast if need be. Of course the old man said 'yes'. He had even watched the progress of the 'cancer-ridden' friend down the jetty and onto the boat and felt glad in his heart that the man was fulfilling what was probably a dying wish.

'Just do as I say,' Muirhouse had instructed Ronnie and Ronnie had done so. He was tired; he imagined freedom and could not any longer be bothered to add up the detail, to wonder why the boat trip would be involved. It had taken him some time to realize that Muirhouse's apparently kind offers of tea from a flask had been an opportunity for sedating him but he had more than once caught himself thinking, what does it all matter, thereby slipping unconsciously and completely into Muirhouse's control.

Until the day Muirhouse had triumphantly showed him a newspaper headline: 'My son is a murderer'. Underneath was a confession in Ronnie's writing. The part of the letter asking for an acknowledgement had been a Muirhouse add-on, undetected by the police because of the man's calligraphic skills. Somehow Ronnie had not factored this in, what the confession would do to his parents. He had focused solely on saving them, on preventing Muirhouse from carrying out his threat to kill them. He knew he had to resist the tea Muirhouse brought but it was hard because he was so thirsty. Muirhouse, he was sure, put extra salt in his food, to make sure he was thirsty enough to drink any liquid that was put in front of him.

Ronnie had however taken heart from the advent of the extra food: you don't usually feed up people you are going to kill. On the rare occasions when the sedation had worn off but Muirhouse had not appeared with a new prescription, he tried to think out what was motivating his captor. Something had changed: there was a reason for the increased food. He wondered if Mark was back over — Muirhouse had stopped taking Ronnie's photo — and if there was an engagement going on there. He wondered if Zara MacDonald was still on the island and whether if she were, she was doing anything to help him. He had been amazed to see her that day but, coming back to reality after being placed sedated in Muirhouse's rucksack, it seemed more like a dream than a real event. He was sure she would have alerted the emergency services but Muirhouse had come almost as soon as she left. He must have been lurking there, spying on the whole event. It was impossible to imagine how the police could fail to catch the guy so consistently but, thought Ronnie, there are serial killers who manage to put away several people before being caught and some who are never caught or only after many many years.

When his mind reached this point of morbidity he had to drum up all the positivity he could muster, recall the seaside holidays of his childhood, Saturday visits to the Art Galleries with his father, his granny's kitchen. He still had his journal in his boot though he had not been able to write in it for many days. Consequently, he had completely lost count of the time.

***

Bobby was in gaol in Kilmarnock. He felt very isolated. When he was being held overnight on Arran he had felt safe: he was still on home ground. Now he felt cut off, though, he thought I'm cut off wherever I am. Nowhere is near Australia.

When Bobby was eighteen his parents had announced there were going to live there. 'Dad's got a job,' his mum had said. 'We'll make lots of money and come back and buy a house on Arran.' Bobby had wanted to go with them but they quite obviously had not wanted that. He realized they'd waited till he couldn't go down on a form as a dependant. He had no other known living relatives and the back house where he was living hardly graced the label 'house', damp and falling to pieces as it was. It belonged to 'Aunt

Marion' who for some mysterious reason elected to count as a friend of his mum's and she let him stay on there. She spent most of her time in Spain now. He cut the grass and pruned the hedges. She hardly ever asked for rent. His parents sent photos back and seemed to be doing all right but they never sent money even though they knew Bobby didn't have a job. He thought about his modest ambition — fast cars apart — of becoming a swimming instructor. He supposed he wouldn't even be able to do that now. Except perhaps he could teach adults?

***

Zara thought for a long time before deciding she would try visiting Mrs Muirhouse again. First she would have to find out where she was. She didn't ask Des because she didn't want him to know she was thinking of making the contact. She rang Uttam. He was full of enthusiasm about his new paintings and the support he was getting from her friend in Pollokshaws. Eventually she brought the conversation round to the Muirhouses and discovered that Mrs Muirhouse had returned from hospital the previous week and was back living in her house on her own.

'That's what she says when you take messages over,' said Uttam. 'I'm on my own now. Obviously John, her son, doesn't count. I suppose he dots in and out. Not the same as a reliable corpse in the loft!'

Zara didn't know whether Mrs M. had even been present at the death of her husband but if not, she imagined she would have to have been present soon after. Whose idea had it been to place the body up there? Had it been done in order to hide the death? Was it just good luck that Mrs M. had been amenable to guarding the body or had she relished the idea of a long secret? Zara wondered how Daffodil's aunt had been paid off and who had thought of putting the body in the next door loft and sealing off Mary Ann's access and opening up an entrance on the Muirhouse side. It was the Muirhouses' natural job to deal with the body but, unless they had killed Muirhouse senior, why would they need to hide him?

And Daffodil's aunt? She had seemed as principled a person as one might meet. Why would she have consented to having a corpse in her loft? Had she been involved by accident and therefore become a natural choice? Or perhaps she hadn't known. Perhaps she had been persuaded that her loft was dangerous and needed to be sealed off. Full of bees for instance which could not be moved.

Zara felt excited. She knew she should have felt wary and afraid but she was too focused on her mission for that. John Muirhouse would have to be keeping a close eye on Ronnie Balfour now he didn't have Bobby to do it for him. Where was he she wondered. Amazing to maintain two hiding places… Or was he now holed up with Ronnie? On the island or off?

***

Ben had what he felt was a secret lead. When he and Barney had gone to the Black Cave, Ben had found an empty bean tin but the beans were not Heinz or the co-op but a brand he had never heard of. Even though it seemed a bizarre thing to do he had started asking for the brand by name in every food shop they went into. When Barney had accused him of doing it for a laugh, he said it was a school project. Barney had looked at him disbelievingly.

'You're right,' said Ben, 'it's not a school project, it's a Ben project. Okay? It's not exactly dangerous, is it, going into a shop and asking for a particular brand of beans?' Barney had had to agree.

The day Zara went to Glasgow to see Mrs Muirhouse, Ben persuaded Barney to take him to the King's Caves.

'I want to see the carvings on the rocks.' Barney was pleased It was a good walk with a focus and he liked Ben to have a reason to be enthusiastic. Ben rejoiced: Barney had swallowed the bait. All Ben had to do was to ask for ice cream when they arrived in Blackwaterfoot and he would be able to check out the shop.

He stood where he could see most of the shelves and scanned them. He knew shopkeepers didn't like young people getting too close to the goods. He wanted to avoid drawing attention to himself. Fortunately, there was a customer ahead of him talking. He scanned for a second time, the customer was moving to the door…

'Yes?' said the shopkeeper.

'Ice cream please,' said Ben.

'In the freezer,' said the woman. He noted she didn't say it as if she thought he was stupid. He was feeling excited: he had just seen one tin of the right brand of beans on a shelf near the door. He chose a cornetto for himself and a choc ice for Barney.

'Do you have any more of those beans?' His voice, he couldn't help it, had gone into a higher register. The woman smiled. Ben thought she was covering her curiosity.

'Funny thing. Those beans were marked down. Even then I couldn't sell them. Suddenly they start going. Did you want that last tin then?' It was fifty pence marked down from seventy-eight. Ben nodded. When the full tin joined the empty one in his rucksack he felt like a real detective.

***

Bobby was quite surprised when his friend Tommy came to visit him at the gaol. He had been thinking he had no friends at all. It was odd how seeing Tommy started his brain working.

'Have you seen my Aunt Marion?' he asked looking Tommy straight in the eye. 'Is she worse? The doctor didn't seem to think she would pull through this time. I need to know if... you know...'

'You think they would let you out for the funeral?'

'Well I hope it doesn't come to that but...'

Tommy knew Aunt Marion was not a real aunt and he didn't understand Bobby's drift. He hadn't heard that the old lady was ill; hadn't thought she was back from Spain and he didn't know if Bobby was just being a wishful thinker or whether he thought a death could be cooked up. Why though? He presumed Bobby wasn't expecting him to kill off the old lady himself. Tommy had never done anything outside the law but the two of them had been pals since primary school and he felt a loyalty to him because of that. There would be nothing illegal about letting him know if 'Aunt Marion' had died, if in fact she had. His mind sped ahead. He felt there was a point to all this but he couldn't see it. He knew he mustn't ask. He tried being circumspect.

'Your pal been by? The one you were doing work for?'

'No,' said Bobby. Tommy picked up Bobby's disappointment.

When Tommy reached home he went onto Facebook and put the situation to a couple of his friends. One called Snorkelbuddy replied from the Maldives:

'Don't do more than he's asked.'

The other said:

'He's in prison: the likelihood is that if he wants you to do something it will be iffy. Sorry to sound sensible. Bigbruv.' Reassured, Tommy forgot about the mission altogether. After all, if the old woman did die, he could just send Bobby a postcard. If it seemed like a good idea at the time.

Chapter XXVII Zara makes some visits.

When Mrs Muirhouse opened the door to Zara, Zara thought she didn't look surprised. But maybe if you kept a corpse in your loft for years and years, you would become immune to surprises. There was no question she did not recognize her. She gestured to her to come in and sit down. Zara looked round for the dog.

'It's dead,' said Mrs Muirhouse. 'The day after my John...'

'I'm sorry,' said Zara automatically. There was a pause and then,

'They won't let me bury him yet. John I mean, not the dog. After all this time and they won't...'

'I suppose it's sufficiently unusual for them to want some questions answered,' said Zara. 'Hard for you though.' Mrs Muirhouse suddenly looked at Zara as if she were a complete stranger or as if she couldn't quite remember if she were friend or foe.

'I'm the journalist,' said Zara, unwilling to fake anything at this stage. 'I came to ask after your son.'

'Not seen him,' said his mother. 'I told him but he took no notice.'

'Told him what?'

'Would you like a cup of tea? It's not been made long.' Mrs Muirhouse picked up her teapot and swirled the contents round.

'Thank you,' said Zara. Mrs M. stepped through to the kitchen closing the door behind her and after some clattering returned with a china cup and saucer.

'Tastes better from a proper cup. Mugs...' She shook her head, 'No biscuits, I'm afraid. I only bought them for the dog.' Zara sipped her tea and wondered what to say next. She glanced at Mrs Muirhouse intermittently: the woman seemed lost in her own thoughts.

Suddenly she began to talk. Zara felt it was as if she had had to open a sluice gate and let something out.

'It was a terrible thing and nobody's fault at all. The gun just went off.'

'Whose gun?' asked Zara in a small voice.

'Bang. Just one bullet. That's all it took. Of course they got the wrong man. It was the other man who was meant to die.'

'Who...?' began Zara.

'And then, would you believe it, the woman from next door came round. I ask you. "Is there anything wrong?" she said. "I thought I heard a gunshot". I don't know why I went to the door. Nobody stopped me or I suppose they thought I would be able to put off anyone who was asking questions. To tell you the truth, Mary Ann was all right. I'd lent her a pie dish the week before and, you won't credit this, but as I was going to the door, part of me was thinking it'll be Mary Ann with my pie dish back. Well it was her but no pie dish. She stood there and tried to look past me and someone rushed past and unfortunately their hands were covered in blood and she cried out, "Oh dear oh dear" — I can hear her now — "is somebody dead?" Well you can imagine, I had to drag her in, otherwise she'd have gone straight to the police.'

Zara gave Mrs Muir house her full attention: she didn't want to break her flow.

'We told her it was an accident and we were sending for a doctor. "Not the ambulance?" she said. She wasn't stupid. She asked if someone had been cleaning the gun. Then John said, "I was showing the firing mechanism to a friend. I didn't realise the gun was loaded." Mary Ann looked as if she didn't believe him. "Whose gun was it?" she asked. "My father's," John said, quick as quick. My John, John senior, never had a gun in his life.' Zara nodded but did not believe her.

'Then John, my son, said, "Mum, make us all a cup of tea while we wait for the doctor." He'd recovered himself. I could tell he wanted me to make sure Mary Ann didn't get into the room with the body, so I suggested she come and help me with the tea. We all needed tea. So Mary Ann and I were in the kitchen when we heard a ring at the door and John's voice saying, 'Come in doctor' and then mumbles. After about twenty minutes — I took some tea through but Mary Ann and I had ours in the kitchen —John came through and said his father was away in an ambulance. "I didn't hear an ambulance," said Mary Ann. "Must have been that noisy kettle," said John. Mary Ann looked sceptical. "Pour me another cup," said John, "although I could do with something stronger." "I would have thought you would have been away with the ambulance," said Mary Ann in that dry tone of hers. John said he'd go over shortly. It was just over at the Victoria. Said he'd wanted to make sure I was okay. He asked Mary Ann if she'd stay with me.'

'Of course she said "Yes" and we sat for a couple of hours till John came back. His face was really strained.' He said, "I'm sorry Mum but he's definitely gone" and he came over and held me against his chest which wasn't like him to be demonstrative but your father doesn't die every day, does he?' Zara shook her head. 'Anyway Mary Ann went home then but before that John came up with a good thing. He's so clever when he gets going. "Not the right time to say this probably but you know the conservatory you wanted to build out the back? Well it was only the old man who opposed it. Mum and I don't mind." Mary Ann's face was a picture: she was torn between wanting to jump for joy and feeling she had to stay solemn. And then John said, "And what's more we can probably help you with materials. Dad knew someone who has just gone bankrupt and there's all these conservatories going at knockdown prices". Well, you can imagine, Mary Ann was ecstatic. I've never seen anyone leave the home of a dead man so happy.'

***

Zara came away pleased but unsatisfied. She was not sure what she had learned. After the revelation about the conservatory and some detail about how it got itself built, Mrs Muirhouse had suddenly clammed up. Zara had tried asking small questions which she felt would sound insignificant but it was as if Mrs Muirhouse had become deaf. The interview was at an end.

'Let me know if you hear where John is, my son that is. Never was a good idea both of them having the same name.'

On the train, Zara took out her notebook and wrote down everything she could remember. She included gestures, the way Mrs Muirhouse had sat, her expressions, her pauses, everything that might help towards forming an understanding of what had happened on the night John Muirhouse senior died.

Zara saw John Muirhouse's plan for the disposal of the body as characteristic: he was a master of circumstance, able to use what was to hand to fashion himself a watertight operation. If Mary Ann Brown had not knocked at his door he would not have been able to ask her, later, if he could store something in her loft, just temporarily. The needed door from the Muirhouses to Mary Ann's could easily have been facilitated during the building of the conservatory.

The conservatory, it transpired, had happened almost overnight. Fortuitously Mary Ann had acquired the requisite planning permission already and was only delaying because Muirhouse senior had gone round and shouted at her, making her think she had to wait for his appeal. Even after the conservatory was built, things kept arriving which would make it more comfortable. They were excused on flimsy pretexts — of a couple of wicker loungers with luxuriously plump cushions: 'You'll need two chairs for when Mum comes round for a cocktail'. Mrs Muirhouse had never previously set foot in Mary Ann's house and only once after it, to christen the chairs.

Zara could see that, to Mary Ann, the conservatory was a beautiful bribe she just could not bring herself to turn down: she was in the predicament before she knew it, suddenly an accessory after a crime. Zara was not certain that Mary Ann had even clocked that she was storing a body at first. After all, John Muirhouse wouldn't have said, By the way, can I store my dad in your loft? It would have been done in such a way that Mary Ann would have sounded very rude and inappropriate if she'd mentioned it. Why should a large coffin-like box actually be a coffin? Her education had not prepared her for such an eventuality.

But later, it appeared, for some reason Mary Ann had become more suspicious or maybe felt guiltier. A horrific thought came into Zara's mind: supposing Daffodil's death was a threat gone wrong? Supposing putting Daffodil in danger, had been a way of warning Mary Ann to say nothing about the body?

Zara thought about the Muirhouse predicament. While it was quite possible to break up a body — especially one that had been dead for some years — and put it in a sack with weights, drive to a quarry or a bridge over a deep river and drop it in, you might not want to do that with your own father. Even though Zara did not have any evidence for thinking John Muirhouse was fond of his father, there did seem to be a family bond. He could have been deferring to his mother's wishes to keep him. Zara wondered whether Mrs Muirhouse had ever gone up to the loft to commune with her dead husband. She couldn't imagine it. The woman was overweight and looked as if her eyesight was failing. Access to the loft was by a narrow not very stable-looking stair. But if this were so, that Mrs Muirhouse never went up there, wouldn't it have been easier for John Muirhouse to get rid of the body and pretend to his mother that it was still there? And had John Muirhouse managed to concoct a funeral? The more questions you asked the stranger and more complicated the whole situation appeared.

***

Bobby's friend Tommy was slightly surprised when he heard that Bobby's Aunt Marion had had a heart attack and that she was in the hospital in Lamlash. He thought about it not really wishing to get involved but eventually, for his own peace of mind, he decided to visit her on Bobby's behalf. If he knew better how the land lay, he would be able to make up his mind more easily if he had to fulfil his promise to let Bobby know about any possible death.

Aunt Marion did not look well. Tommy went at visiting time with a bunch of sweet peas he had picked from his mother's garden. He'd even taken a jam jar to put them in.

'Bobby asked me to come and see you,' he said as a way of testing what she knew. She immediately shook her head.

'That boy. I don't know. He's not so much bad as stupid. He'll be the death of me.' She sighed and flung her head back on her many pillows.

'I visited him in Kilmarnock,' Tommy offered.

'That was good of you,' Aunt Marion returned. 'Maybe I'll visit him myself soon.' Privately Tommy didn't think so. 'I was only back from Spain a couple of days. I don't know.' She lapsed into silence but kept her eyes on Tommy who didn't know whether to look back or focus his attention on the bare walls. 'If anything happens to me, you must let Bobby know.'

'I will,' said Tommy. It sounded to him as if someone else had answered.

'I've told the doctor. There shouldn't be any problem.'

'Good,' said Tommy though he had no idea what she was referring to.

Walking away from the hospital he felt he hadn't gained much. If anything he considered himself absolved from further action. I'll just wait and see if the old biddy dies he thought. If there's something I need to do, perhaps someone will tell me.

***

While Zara didn't feel her visit to Mrs Muirhouse had been wasted, it hadn't brought her any nearer finding Ronnie Balfour. Where was the unturned stone she wondered. Who had she not talked to? Who knew something, some small thing which would move the situation towards a finishing point?

Zara went to her notebook and found her list of people involved in any way with the whole business: she realised she had never spoken to Bobby. Would there be any future in visiting him in gaol? She thought not. He would hardly be able to speak, even if he wanted to about the matters which interested her. She remembered the drowning car story. Hadn't Bobby had a friend he'd gone to when he came out of the water? It took her two phone calls to find out Tommy's name.

'Evening drive to Catacol,' she said to Barney and Ben.

Zara left the two of them on the beach and went into the Catacol Bay Hotel where she had been assured she would find Tommy.

'I'll be very quick,' she said.

'Will she be safe in there?' asked Ben.

'I think so,' said Barney. Although one never knows with Zara he thought to himself.

Zara walked straight up to Tommy at the bar, recognizing him by his red hair and spectacles from the description she had been given on the phone.

'I wonder if I could have a word, Tommy. Zara MacDonald. I'm the woman on the mountain. The other woman.' For a moment he looked wary but to him her face presented no threat.

'What are you drinking?' he said politely.

'Be my guest,' said Zara signalling to the barman. They carried their drinks to the window. There was a voluble group between them and the bar which lent them some aural privacy.

'What's all this about?' asked Tommy.

'Look,' began Zara, 'let's talk direct. Your pal Bobby was well shafted by John Muirhouse. He wouldn't be awaiting trial now if he'd managed to avoid getting involved with him'.

'I know that,' said Tommy.

'I'm looking for Ronnie Balfour.'

'You plain clothes or what?' Tommy looked worried.

'No, no. I've already said, I was the other woman on Goat Fell. The one that didn't —'

'I can see that.' Zara wished she could say something to make the guy lighten up.

'That's why I'm interested,' she went on, 'because I was there, even though I didn't know till afterwards'. Tommy nodded slowly, looking like someone who very much wanted to check his watch but who had decided to go on being patient. 'I really want to find Ronnie Balfour and I'm stuck. I'm wondering whether Bobby told you anything that would be useful.' Tommy let out a long sigh.

'What sort of thing?'

'Anything,' said Zara. 'Sometimes people have information but they don't realize it. Have you been to see Bobby?'

'He didn't talk about John Muirhouse.' Zara waited. 'Well he wouldn't would he, not in prison visiting. Guys standing around listening to everything you say.'

266

'So what did he talk about, Tommy?' Tommy allowed his mind to go back to the prison visit in detail.

'Well as a matter of fact, I did ask him if... I said, the guy you were working for... whether he had been to see him and Bobby said "No". Sounded annoyed, like disappointed.' Zara nodded.

'So what else?'

'He kept on about his Aunt Marion who isn't his real aunt but she owns the back house Bobby stays in. She sort of stands in for his mum a bit.' Tommy told Zara about the parents buzzing off to Australia. 'So then he says to me, "You must tell me if Aunt Marion's going to die" and says he wants to go to the funeral. But the funny thing is we didn't know she was ill. But then I hear she's had a heart attack and ...' He stopped. 'I sort of know her too, being Bobby's pal. So I go and see her in the hospital and she says, "You must tell Bobby if..." Zara nodded again her mind racing. 'I'm not sure if this all adds up to anything,' Tommy added. Zara could see he was warming to the task.

'Another drink?

'You're all right,' he said. 'I've got my motorbike.'

'He's lucky to have a friend like you,' said Zara. Tommy blushed.

'We go way back,' he said.

'You say you don't know how what you've said adds up but if you were to guess?'

'If it was a film or something you mean?'

'Yes, if you like.'

'I'd say it was odd them both talking about funerals and needing to know the other one knew if you know what I mean.'

'If it was a really corny movie Bobby would be planning an escape and using the funeral as an opportunity,' said Zara.

'But Aunt Marion wouldn't be in on something like that,' said Tommy.

'No? Well, you know her.'

'Not in a million years.'

'Then Aunt Marion's heart attack is a divine coincidence then — just a manner of speaking, I'm not being religious or anything.' Zara was quick to notice Tommy's eyes look confused. 'Do you think,' she went on, 'that Bobby would think about escaping?'

'He's that mad,' said Tommy.

'It sounds to me,' said Zara, 'he was sussing you out. Perhaps he sees you as having a role...'

'Harbouring a... I don't think I...'

'Did you not hide him before?'

'That was different,' said Tommy. 'He'd only driven a stolen car not kidnapped a child.'

'You wouldn't help him then?'

'You think I should?' He squirmed in his seat as if he could get the problem to go away.

'We might be able to sell the idea to the police, that he could be used as a decoy, lead the police to John Muirhouse.' Tommy smiled for the first time.

'Now we really are in a film,' he said. Zara grinned back at him.

'Okay, let me put it like this. If Bobby should make a break and contact you, could you let me know?'

'Wouldn't you have to tell the police?'

'Tell the police what?'

'Okay,' Tommy replied after a long pause.

'Have you any ideas about where Bobby might hole up if he had no one to help him?' Pause.

'Aunt Marion has a beat up caravan which is completely covered in brambles and stands at the corner of a field or what used to be a field, overgrown now, willows fifteen foot and birch. Don't suppose anyone thinks about it much. No one passes it. It's very small. We used to use it as a den when we were younger.' Zara noted something sad in Tommy's eyes as if he were remembering a time when life was less complicated.

'So Bobby wouldn't need to spell out to you that's where he'd go? He'd expect you to know.' Tommy didn't answer.

'Thanks,' said Zara. She knew she had a deal.

***

'What's the next move?' asked Ben when Zara reached them. He and Barney had started building a fort of large pebbles but Ben had decided to make it into an armchair. The arms kept falling off. Fortunately, the tide was coming in so the project could be left without anyone having to lose face.

'The next move is... well we could walk back to Brodick over the Boguille and then have fish and chips.' Ben didn't blink.

'I'd rather go south and then cut across the moor onto the String. But I'd like to go in the van because I'd rather have my fish and chips tonight.'

They went back to the van and Zara drove off in Ben's direction. They sped past Pirnmill and Whitefarland and a big house on the left.

'What's that funny-shaped black and white house?'

It belongs to one of the land owners,' said Barney.

'It's a big house for one land owner.'

'They have people to stay and take them shooting.'

'Do they know John Muirhouse?' asked Ben.

'Not that sort of shooting,' said Zara.

'You mean like paintball guns?

'Oh look,' said Barney, 'to change the subject a moment, there's some cave-y things over there you could check out sometime, Zara.'

'Let's go now,' said Ben. 'Let's go and find Ronnie Balfour again!' Zara speeded up. 'Please!' Ben thought he might find an empty tin to match the one he had found in the Black Cave.

Zara only slowed to turn off onto the moor road.

'Can you see the standing stones?' she asked Ben. He picked up the binoculars they'd had the foresight to bring.

'I think I can,' he said. Zara stopped the van in a layby and they all looked but Ben was the only one who could see them.

***

The next day Zara was wondering whether to phone Des when he phoned her.

'I hear you've been acting police officer again.'

'What do you mean?'

'Visiting the Muirhouse domain.'

'Well she did talk. Bet she told me more than she told you.'

'Is it worth sharing?'

'It won't help you find Ronnie Balfour.'

'There's something about your voice that tells me you have more information than you are letting on.'

'You accusing me of withholding —?'

'Okay. I'm about to go out and purchase a cappuccino. Suppose I get two would you be free to meet me? I'll be sitting on a bench looking out to sea.'

'Well If I don't make it, I'm sure you'll manage to drink two.'

Zara felt as if she'd been caught on the back foot. It would now be more difficult to bring things up casually. Things like Bobby's possible gaol break. She wanted to discuss it with Des but it was pure speculation on her part though if she mentioned it, Des would assume she had evidence. She did not want to have the initiative taken away from her should a situation arise where she could use it. However, Des did not come empty-handed, though he reported his information rather than showing it to Zara as hard copy.

'We've had another letter from J.M.'

'And?'

'Very short and compared with the previous ones: a strip of paper about ten inches long that says,

"Time is running out for Ronnie Balfour."'

'So what's new?' said Zara with a calmness she did not feel.

'I don't think he's on the island, do you?' Zara hadn't been expecting that question.

'Your men couldn't find him you mean?'

'I don't suppose we managed every single nook and cranny but it was quite comprehensive. He would have had to take Ronnie across the interior —'

'— at night in a sack,' added Zara 'I admit it seems unlikely but how do you know he didn't get wind of the search and take Ronnie off for its duration? How do you know he's not brought him back?'

'I don't,' said Des. He sounded weary. 'I'd love to close this one. I mean, rather than have it become a cold case.'

'It won't become a cold case,' said Zara. Des held out his hand for Zara's cardboard cup and standing up threw first one then the other into a nearby litter bin.'

'Are you sure you've told me everything about the note?' asked Zara, feeling desperate.

'Difficult to make a mistake about seven words on a strip of paper.'

'The strip,' Zara persisted, 'can you describe it?' Des thought for a moment or two, respecting Zara enough to give her question time. His face suddenly altered:

'Now you mention it, one thing. At the ends, the strip seemed to have glue stuck to them.'

'But it was one long strip? Was the glue on the same side at each end?'

'I can't be sure to be honest. I'll get back to you on it.' He sighed audibly as if he were thinking, surely the case can't rest on the position of a dab of glue. 'I just assumed he'd re-used a piece of paper which happened to have glue on it.'

'Let me know,' said Zara. 'Thanks for the coffee.'

***

Zara came away from her rendezvous with Des quite excited. The discussion, trivial though it had seemed, had stirred up her thoughts about John Muirhouse and his love of codes and secret messages. It occurred to her that he might have left a calling card at each place he had hidden Ronnie Balfour in. He liked games. To test this, she would need to revisit the Merkland site and the Black Cave. She thought back. Where had John Muirhouse taken Ronnie Balfour after Merkland? Where would I take him she wondered. It had all been planned, with the trip wire: he must have known exactly where he would go next. Somewhere near but not too near.

She would need to consult Barney but she thought it would be safe for them all to go. She didn't think Muirhouse would use the same place twice. It would be fun for Ben looking for some clue and then if they found one, looking for another in the next cave.

***

When Des arrived at the station he went straight away to look in the production bag containing the strip of paper. He put his hand to the phone to tell Zara what she wanted to know when it started to ring. A girl was lost in the mountains: her parents feared kidnap and murder. Her friends said she had gone off by herself saying she was meeting someone at Cladach. No one knew who this person was. The girl had not been seen for twenty-fours hours. Had the Goat Fell murderer struck again was the question on everyone's lips as pleas for information went out on the airwaves.

While Zara was mildly irritated by Des's apparent forgetfulness, she put it to the back of her mind. She was fired up with her idea of a Muirhouse pattern. Barney cautiously agreed on her plan and that afternoon the three of them plus Nessie set out for Merkland wood, Zara equipped with both camera and binoculars.

Barney and Zara were both amused when they found Ben packing his empty bean tin in his rucksack. It was ensconced in a clear plastic bag.

'What is this, Ben? What are you collecting now?'

'Just something,' said Ben. If he had been asked to justify himself, he would have said, 'You keep information from Des so why shouldn't I keep information from you?' But he said nothing although he was jubilant about the opportunity to look for evidence that Zara's plan presented.

This time round Zara had no difficulty finding the rocky overhang but nevertheless they approached the place carefully, Zara scanning the area from a distance to assess whether Muirhouse was not by some ill-fated chance engaging in some new nefarious scheme. No traps, nothing. They stood in the green grey gloom and tried to scrutinize every square inch of rock below and above. Ben took another look at his bean can when he thought the others were otherwise engaged.

'Found something for your tin?' Barney joked.

'Not yet,' said Ben.

He really wanted to find another tin so that he could be the cunning detective for once but he could see that he was going to draw a blank. He went outside the cave, climbed into the fallen tree and took out his tin in private. He thought hard about what a real detective might do. Zara was busy taking photographs of what might or might not be meaningless hieroglyphics on the rock face. If there were any matches somewhere else, it would be relatively easy to spot them by comparing images. Barney hunted the ground for the tiniest possible piece of evidence — a stick hammered into the earth perhaps, a seemingly random placement of pebbles.

'If there was a trail,' Ben said to himself, 'what would be its purpose: to say we were here? For what reason? You haven't caught up with me yet?' He shook his head. One thing a trail might do he thought was to eliminate places to look: the more they found, the less places to search. But then if they ended up with only one place left, would that be the trap?

'Keep thinking outside the box,' he said to himself. He went back to his original quest of finding another tin. Again he pulled his own out of the rucksack. The label was slightly torn and he suddenly realized that the label could represent the tin: he wasn't necessarily looking for a tin but perhaps for a much smaller more hideable item. Where would you put a label, folded or rolled maybe? He began to examine every crevice he could find. Nothing. He was hit by a wave of disappointment but he kept quiet. Aunty Zara would just keep going he thought but I do need some more information.

'Aunty Zara,' he said, keeping his voice neutral, 'where exactly was Ronnie Balfour sitting when you found him?' Zara went and crouched in the exact spot to show Ben and then got up and went on with what she was doing. Ben crouched in the place and looked round. Just when his knees began to tell him to change position he had an amazing idea. Being in Ronnie's position he had suddenly become Ronnie Balfour and he realized that it had been Ronnie Balfour who was leaving a trail, who had left the bean tin and that meant any other tin or label would have to be nearby otherwise it would have been outside the prisoner's reach.

He looked round hardly daring to breathe and after a long minute when he was about to give up he caught sight of a tell-tale yellow signal. He pulled a piece of paper from a crevice in the rock beneath his feet. A bean tin wrapper:

'Look what I found, Aunty Zara!' Ben could not contain himself any longer.

Zara treated Ben's find with due respect.

'It's the same wrapper as... Ben, where did your first bean tin come from?'

'The Black Cave,' said Ben, as casually as he could.

'And you didn't tell us?'

'It could have belonged to anyone. It was at the low tide mark. I had to find another to make a trail.' Zara's face broke into a big smile.

'That's great work, Ben. Clever old you, finding something no one else could find.'

'The tin may have got into the sea while people were looking and then got washed back in,' said Ben modestly. 'But, Aunty Zara, look, there's writing on his wrapper I can't decipher, but do you see what it all means? We're following a trail left by Ronnie Balfour, not by John Muirhouse.'

'You're right,' said Zara. 'It's an I woz here trail.'

'Will you have to tell Des?' Ben asked, wondering if his prize was going to be snatched away.

'We'll see,' said Zara, looking at her watch. 'I think we have time to look at one more likely place.'

'Where's that?' asked Barney.

'Glen Sannox. I have a hunch that's where Muirhouse might have taken Ronnie after he was here.'

They all ran through the wood as if they had no time to lose.

'Don't drive too fast,' said Barney as Zara swung out from the carpark onto the Corrie road, 'we're not expecting to find him today, only maybe his footprint.' All the way to Sannox Ben recited,

'I had, I haf, I hag I haj, I hal...'

What Zara had in mind was the old barytes mine on the hill to the north side of Glen Sannox. One could see the entrance from the path but people were not encouraged to go there. It had a truly abandoned look about it.

It was still the middle of the afternoon when they set out past the cottage with roses and the high thorn hedges, past the gate to the wee graveyard where both Edwin Rose and Daffodil were resting now. They came through the big gate across the path and into wider country, an expanse of bracken-covered hill, Suidhe Feargas up to the right, looking so near but a stumbling mile or so away. Cioghe na-Hoy to the left, glowering down, a small cloud encircling its summit.

At her first sight of the mines, Zara took out her binoculars.

'What are you expecting to see?' asked Barney.

'Don't know,' said Zara. 'The unexpected perhaps.' Ben asked to look, hoping to see another eagle but he could only see sky, he said, handing back the instrument and running on ahead. The adults plodded on, Zara feeling sure there was some sort of path that led towards the mine. Every few yards she would stop and look through the binoculars.

'Just being careful,' she said when Barney waited for the nth time for her to catch up. 'Here', she said suddenly, 'I think this is where we turn.' She took up the binoculars again and scanned the horizon and then the mine entrance. Nothing. But she felt edgy.

The path did not take long. Ben was excited by the mine and Barney and Zara were relieved that it was blocked up a few yards in. They resumed the same tasks they'd undertaken in Merkland. Zara photographed the walls, Barney studied the ground in a random, anxious way and Ben looked for tins and labels. Nessie did her own private exploration.

Ben soon gave up on the mine. He had taken seriously the new theory Zara had explained in the car, about John Muirhouse possibly using the hiding places himself. John Muirhouse was not chained up but he might still eat beans and the tins might be further afield.

Ben began to range in semi-circles from one side of the mine mouth to the other. He found a stick to poke through the undergrowth. It was hard work but he thought John Muirhouse might have flung a tin a long way thinking someone might look for it.

At the point where Ben shouted, 'Nessie!' Barney shouted too. Zara reached Barney first. He had discovered a patch of earth which looked as if it had been recently scraped but there were tiny bits of burnt stick round about. Somebody had had a fire. Ben came stumbling back with a new tin he'd taken from the dog. It had been crushed by a foot before being thrown away. No label and the top had been taken off neatly with a tin-opener. The tin was blackened on the outside.

They all sat and looked at the two tins and the label. After a minute or so Ben said,

'I know what the message says now.'

'What?' asked Zara.

'I hate cold beans!' It seemed very obvious in retrospect.

'What makes you so sure, Ben?' said Barney.

But at that moment Zara gave a cry and fumbled for her binoculars.

'I saw him,' she said. 'Up on the skyline, coming down Suidhe Feargas. I'm sure it's him. We must go. Ben get your tins into your rucksack. We'll have to stay on his blind side. He might well guess it's us, the three of us. They all looked around anxiously to see if they'd dropped anything. Ben had probably flattened some bracken but there were deer about and a wind which could equally have been responsible. Barney kept looking back and asked once for the binoculars but he saw nothing and nobody.

'Are you sure you saw someone, Zara?' Zara was punching Des's number into her phone.

'Of course I'm sure. We need to get off this hill. It's too dangerous.'

'I never thought I'd hear you say that,' said Barney.

Chapter XXVIII   A break for two people

Things were going extraordinarily well for Bobby. By chance he learned from another prisoner, Rod, who had a relative on Arran, that Aunt Marion was very ill and not expected to recover. Bobby had found in Rod an unexpected ally after an incident in a creative writing class where Rod had been sneered at by a man with bright orange hair. Bobby had written an exercise on 'what I would like best' and included, a sentence saying 'for Rod and I to be friends'. He also said that he would like to escape from his prison. The teacher was naïve enough to think he was speaking metaphorically. Rod heard it as a message. When they went to the exercise yard Bobby was not aware of Rod brushing up against him but when he reached his shared cell he found a universal key stuck to the inside of his prison shirt. Had the guy been a magician in a former life or was he just a natural? Okay thought Bobby I can get out of my cuffs if need be but where do I run to? Even if I could get through the gates, I'd be in my prison gear…

But because of the help Bobby had received over the key, he relaxed and waited for whatever might happen next. He grinned to himself. Perhaps he would get to Arran before Aunt Marion died. Go and surprise her at the hospital.

His first plan had been to evade the guards on his journey back from the funeral. Rod had told him that the transportation business was contracted out to a firm who had a reputation for negligence but the more Bobby thought about it the more he considered it would be more of an adventure to make the break before Aunt Marion died. She had been good to him. He wanted to say goodbye to her. But however hard he thought he could not come up with a plan.

And then good fortune smiled on him: Rod told him a prisoner was being moved to Greenock. It could be arranged that Bobby went in his place. This seemed a tall order to Bobby but Rod had just shrugged his shoulders.

'Just be ready at twelve noon,' he said, 'and I'll do the rest. The other guy is easy and it won't look like his fault: the transport guys will get the blame. All you have to do is evade them somehow and then make yourself scarce. You needn't send me a postcard.'

Bobby could not imagine what was going to happen but at eleven forty-five the fire alarm sounded. All the prisoners' doors were opened and the men were ordered into the exercise yard under close scrutiny. Rod wasn't there. Bobby wondered whether the fire had been started by him and then had got out of control but suddenly a strange prison officer appeared and walked straight up to him.

'You. Now. You're leaving. Your gear's waiting at the door. Hurry.' Bobby followed him through the deserted prison. It had all happened so quickly and the prison officers on duty had been pre-occupied with a prisoner who had freaked out, shouting over and over again,

'Fire! Fire! Mind your backs!'

At the entrance, Bobby picked up the bag that was waiting and was hustled outside to a van with two security men. The strange prison officer signed various sheets with a flourish.

'One less to worry about,' he said cheerfully, waving his hand at the smoke issuing from the back of the building. Then Bobby was in the van and away.

***

The police failed to apprehend John Muirhouse. So what's new thought Des. He wondered whether Zara had indeed seen him or whether she wasn't becoming obsessed and hallucinating his image. He went back to the real business of the day: finding the missing girl.

***

Zara was pleased with what the three of them had discovered at the mine and with what they concluded afterwards: that Ronnie Balfour was given cold beans but Muirhouse had his hot.

'I hope he didn't eat hot beans in front of Ronnie,' said Ben. 'That would have been torture.'

Now Zara wanted to investigate other possible hiding places. There were for instance the big pink rocks between Pirnmill and Machrie that Barney had pointed out a few days before. But she excluded the possibility of exposing Ben to a possible meeting with Muirhouse. She went cold when she thought of how close they had been to him at the mine. I'll need to go myself she thought and have Barney and Ben as back up but far away, Machrie tearoom say, out of sight. She planned her expedition carefully. First they would all go on a picnic to the Standing Stones on Machrie Moor and then at some point she would slope off. She would have to say she was going to investigate something. She would have to promise to be careful. She could watch the rocks for a while to see if there were any signs of life before venturing anywhere near them. She might even strike lucky and find Ronnie Balfour again. She screwed up her face. Not very likely. More and more she was beginning to feel that Ronnie was not on the island but that Muirhouse was hanging around to give the lie to that notion.

She wondered fleetingly about the strip of paper and why Des had not got back to her about it but then ceased to wonder when Kirsty told her that evening that the girl was still missing. Zara was momentarily confused. She realized she had not quite taken on board that the girl was thought to be missing on Arran. She had shut it from her mind, refused to connect it with John Muirhouse. However, she could see now that Des would be preoccupied and his short laugh when he'd heard the story of Zara's sighting was now explained.

Perhaps it was a foolhardy thought but she tended to go by her instinct and in this case, she felt John Muirhouse had enough on his plate without getting involved in murdering someone else. However, there was a niggling doubt in her mind and because of this she took to bed with her Jack House's Murder not Proven.

***

It is not far from Kilmarnock to Greenock and Bobby presumed he would be taken by a designated route, probably one without shops and pubs or even petrol stations. Somehow he had to get his gaolers to stop somewhere before the prison gates of Greenock closed him in. The two security officers, he had noted, were young and possibly not very experienced. Unfortunately, he could not see out of the van, had to rely on his ears to determine whether the country was urban or rural. He was aware he did not have long and he realized he would have to take an initiative. If he waited for them to stop for a burger he might just wait...

He had undone his cuffs with the key. Now he went through the bag he'd been given exiting the prison in Kilmarnock and put on the enclosed clothes, replacing his prison clothes on top of them.

To make them hear above the noise of the engine he had to bang on the connecting wall between him and the cab. His plan was to make them think he was in dire need of medical attention. He wished he'd thought to wheeze a bit as he was getting into the van. An inhaler. That's what he would say. He needed his inhaler from inside his bag. He would sit as if cuffed, and while hopefully one officer looked in his bag, he would fly past the other and make off. He banged monotonously on the steel panel and then with fury and rhythm as if he might be having an epileptic fit. After what seemed like ten minutes, Bobby felt the van slow down and then stop. He put himself in a foetal position and began to twitch.

He could tell from the way the doors banged that the guards were disgruntled. Perhaps, he hoped, unsure of what to do. He could hear them talking but could not make out the words. Then, one half of the door was flung open and a voice said,

'What is it? It had better be good.'

'Can't breathe,' whispered Bobby. He indicated his bag with his held together palms. 'Inhaler,' he said and went on twitching. The guy who had spoken started fumbling in Bobby's bag. He was in Bobby's path. With a cry between a wheeze and a scream Bobby rolled towards him his eyes showing whites only, a trick he had learnt as a child which always frightened his mother. Out of the corner of his eye he saw the man recoil and lose his balance. In that moment Bobby propelled himself forward, landing awkwardly, but on his feet. He saw a piece of clear road ahead and shot off.

Back at the van, the second guard helped the other to his feet but by the time they looked round, Bobby had disappeared.

He was not sure where he was but was glad to find it was a dilapidated area and as soon as possible, he dived into what looked like a disused garage and took off the prison uniform. Holiday person he thought, feeling in the pocket of the shorts to make sure of the money that he'd felt there earlier

— Rod was a star! Arran. First Aunt Marion and then, John Muirhouse. He had not allowed himself to think about the man but now he was free, thoughts of revenge flooded through him. He would... he would... he was not sure what but somehow things had to be evened up. He would find a way.

***

For Zara everything was going to plan, the standing stones, Machrie tea-room. She looked at her watch. She needed to observe the caves in a good light. Couldn't afford to make a mistake. Take a man for a shadow.

She left the car about a mile from where she was going, off the road and obscured. She wore a baseball cap and boots which made her walk differently from usual. If Muirhouse caught sight of her he wouldn't immediately guess it was her. There was always such a chance element in these situations however much you tried to protect yourself. It could be that just the measures you took would be the ones that tripped you up and worked against you.

But she saw no one as she progressed along the shore, purposely avoiding the road but keeping her eyes on the pink rocks which glowed in the afternoon sun. Eventually she found a good natural hide and settled down with her binoculars to reconnoitre. She thought she would watch for an hour and then take the risk. The wind blew in little gusts and the weeds around her rattled their seed pods. She was in danger of being mesmerized by the afternoon and had to force herself to stop following a wheeling buzzard out looking for its supper.

After fifty minutes she could wait no longer. She had seen nobody approach the cliffs. Hardly a vehicle had even passed along the road. It was not in the least bit spooky. She walked through the field gate and set off towards the giant excrescences which formed an uneven cliff parallel to the road.

She came in on a slow curve. There were sheep but they made no noise. She could hear her own feet on the grass but there was nothing she could do about that. A solitary dragon-fly rushed past her and she jumped and then shivered realizing she was afraid even though she had been telling herself she wasn't.

The first four rocks yielded no appreciable caves but the fifth concealed a dry though dank-smelling area though with no signs of human habitation. She plodded on keeping an eye all round for a sudden intruder. The next rock was similar and the next. She began to lose her fear but only because she began to doubt her theory: she was wrong she thought. John Muirhouse had never been here. There were only two more rocks and approaching the first she almost fell over a sheep which baa'd at her as if to say mind where you are going but, absurdly she felt reassured. John Muirhouse wouldn't kill me with a sheep looking on she thought. Then she thought I'm losing it... I'm... but then she saw the last cave and knew at once that John Muirhouse had been there. Not only had been there but she felt was even now using it as his residence.

But he wasn't there now. She took a swift look around the field and entered the gloomy space. Muirhouse had become lazy. There were tins lying about and the remains of a fire. At the back was a pile of bracken which had obviously been lain on but there was something else which to Zara was over-riding proof that this was the enemy lair. She stood still and inhaled deeply. She had smelled that smell before and her brain connected it to Muirhouse though she had never registered it till now. She thought back to her encounters with the man — the Waverley, the mountain. Strange. It couldn't be a faint aroma if she had picked it up outside and if she had not noted it, it must have been because she hadn't associated it with him. It had to be the mountain. She closed her eyes and pictured the evening round the fire. Either she must have connected the smell to the mountain itself, a particular plant perhaps or... Suddenly she remembered John Muirhouse going to his rucksack and retrieving a package. He'd opened it and shaken into the pot...What? Spices? She hadn't found out. The question had been on the tip of her tongue When Ronnie had begun to tell a joke and by the time he had delivered the punch line, Zara had forgotten the package. She now recalled the particular taste of the beans. She had been taken with the thought that not many people would have taken spices on a camping expedition but she had said nothing. Someone she had known better she would have teased but not John Muirhouse.

And the same smell was here. Curry-ish she thought now. She poked about at the back of the cave and dislodged a carrier-bag half-hidden behind ferns. In it she found an unwashed pot: the smell was undisputable. Tut tut she smiled to herself, the guy's getting really lax.

She glanced out of the entrance and saw the buzzard again. Something about its flight disturbed her and she felt the need to depart. Mission nearly accomplished. She had only to reach her car but now she was possessed by that dread that overtakes you when you feel your luck can't last another minute. The sun was still shining. The afternoon appeared unchanged but Zara's insides registered something else. She could hardly stop herself from breaking into a run. The buzzard circled again and let out a mournful crake. She reached her car.

In seconds she was on the road back to Barney and Ben. In minutes a tall figure strode through the gate into the field. He too looked about him but seeing nobody made for the last cave.

***

Bobby had managed to take a bus to Ardrossan. His only purchase had been a baseball cap not unlike the one Zara was wearing and some sunglasses. He was counting on people not recognizing him because they wouldn't be expecting to see him. He was hoping too that the chaos caused by the fire might create a delay in any searching that might ensue. It would be confusing too that it wouldn't be him that was reported as escaping.

In the event, the two guards, after a desultory search, made their way to Greenock as they were only a mile or so from it, and confessed their story there perhaps finding it easier to tell people that the escapee was probably quite near at hand, if only they looked for him.

But Bobby knew none of this and managed to board the three-twenty ferry in the back of a truck belonging to an acquaintance. Since he also used this method on his arrival in Brodick, no one saw him at either end. His luck held: he saw no one else he knew, bought a few things to eat in the co-op and headed to Lamlash via Corriegills and Dun Fionn. Once in the woods, he sat and ate most of what he'd bought. Escaping makes you hungry he thought. Then, so does being a prisoner — he wasn't thinking of himself but of Ronnie Balfour.

Even before Muirhouse had dropped him in it with the kidnap, Bobby had begun to turn against the man. He hated delivering those tins of beans. He hated seeing this wreck of a man tied up. Muirhouse had told him not to speak to him.

'I shall know if you have,' he'd said looking Bobby straight in the eye. Bobby didn't understand what he meant but he felt sufficiently intimidated to keep quiet. He didn't want his source of money to dry up.

He hid what remained of his food in a hollow stump — he had decided to return the same way — and finding a dry-ish bed of leaves, he fell asleep. He was tired but he also needed the dark.

He woke about nine, refreshed and buoyant. He lay for a minute or two thinking about what was ahead of him and realized with a jolt that he had completely forgotten that he had been in the hospital very recently with his trapped leg after the car crash. He had not been there long as miraculously his leg had been uninjured. Maybe no one would recognize him. Maybe he should dirty his face a bit. A false name and a lot of confidence — that would have to be it.

By the time he reached the hospital, most of the patients would be in bed asleep. He had not sorted in his mind how he would get into the building. He realized he might have to rely on lucky timing. This bothered him. He liked to be in control of all the circumstances. He would anyway have to creep right round to find out where Aunt Marion was. He imagined she would be in a room on her own. Perhaps if he could locate an office or nurses' room there might be an open window. The only other possibility was a staff member going out of a fire door for a smoke. He shook his head. Not reliable enough.

He walked fast, not because he wanted to reach his destination but because he was full of nervous energy.

The kitchen he thought. A window open in the kitchen would be a likely thing. He wasn't particularly afraid of meeting anyone once he had achieved his purpose. He put a lot of faith in his running ability. Even so, he recognized the fact that the hospital was a place where they might look for him if and when they started looking. First you try to get out of somewhere, then you try to get in he thought. Is this what life had come down to? He thought about his lost ambition. Aunt Marion was one of the only people who had ever believed in him. He had to see her. The awful thought struck him that she might already be dead. There was the hospital ahead of him. It had too many lights. It was going to be impossible. He went forward despite this.

Suddenly it occurred to him. How could he have been so stupid? He would get in through A&E. Something bad but not that urgent. A suspected fracture? They would most likely have to get hold of a doctor. Bobby would be sat in the waiting room. He could leave there to go... to the toilet if asked, and snoop about till he found Aunt Marion. It wasn't as if he were looking for someone in the Glasgow Royal Infirmary. There were no endless corridors in Lamlash Memorial hospital.

He put his finger on the bell and then took it off again and backed away round the corner. He needed a lump or bruise to convince. He hunted around till he found a stone and holding his breath he brought it down on his shin. The pain was intense: he hoped he hadn't actually broken anything. He went back to the door, rang the bell and limped in.

The nurse looked at him enquiringly.

'My leg,' he said 'I tripped over a root I think, coming out of the woods. I think it might be broken.' A wave of nausea came over him and he was aware, as he began to faint, of the nurse clutching his arm and leading him to a chair.

When he came round he was in the waiting room. So far so good. The nurse was saying the doctor was on his way. She was asking him if he had hit his head. He started to say 'no' but then changed it to 'I don't know'. Then he realised he'd better be a bit more lively or the nurse might decide he could not be left alone.

'I think it's just my leg,' he said. 'It was getting dark. I should have started back sooner.'

The nurse took his details all of which were false. He used a friend's name and address in Glasgow and said he was staying at a campsite in Lamlash; that his pals were in the pub but if and when he could get hold of them one of them, would pick him up — a local with a car. He didn't think this part of the story mattered since he intended to have left before the doctor even arrived.

At last the nurse left him. His skin had produced a wonderful bruise and he sat with his leg on a chair, a glass of water at his side. After about a minute, he peered round the door. He could see the nurse in the reception office. Her back was turned: the corridors were empty. He set off, still limping naturally, in the direction he remembered from his previous visit. He hoped doors would be open. He did not want to frighten anyone. The worst that could happen would be finding a stranger awake and having them ring their bell. He looked for a broom cupboard to disappear into should the need arise. He heard a door ahead open and then a voice saying,

'Okay, Mr McKenzie, you go to sleep now. I'm sure the tablets will be working.' The door closed. He heard feet, had time to dodge into a corner and hope that the nurse would be looking ahead. He held his breath and closed his eyes as if this might make him invisible.

The second door was ajar. Bobby crossed his fingers. If only this door could have Aunt Marion behind it! He stole up to the crack and pushed gently. No response from inside. He pushed a bit harder and then quickly put himself through. The bed was opposite him A figure propped up on many pillows stared back at him.

'Is that you Bobby? You've come? I can't believe it. That's wonderful. Is it really you? I came back from Spain to see you and you weren't there. And then I had to...' She stopped speaking as he approached. He sat down on the bed and took one of her hands. There was so much he wanted to say but he didn't know where to start. 'I heard you were in prison but I didn't believe it and I was right because here you are. I'm so pleased to see you. I wanted to tell you I'm leaving you...'

'No, Aunt Marion,' Bobby interrupted. 'You can't die.' He found a huge choking lump in his throat. It was an unfamiliar feeling and he did not know what to do with it. He put his other hand on top of hers. 'Aunt Marion, I wanted to tell you, thank you, for everything. I haven't been a...' he wanted to say 'a good person' but he could not shape the words. 'Thank you.' Aunt Marion smiled.

'I'm going to leave you…' Again her voice trailed off. Her eyes stayed on his for several seconds and then the lids slowly closed. Bobby extricated his hand gently and stood up. He approached the door with trepidation, opened it silently and peered out. Nobody. He walked along the corridor, saw the toilet and decided to pay a visit to give credence to his disappearance. As he came out he met the nurse from reception.

'I wondered where you'd got to. The doctor's here. Come along now.' This would seem less suspicious than his former plan Bobby thought. With luck he would be found to have no fracture and maybe, in an hour or so if he had to have an xray, he would become a closed incident.

'Sorry to bother you, doctor,' he heard himself saying.

'It goes with the territory,' the doctor replied cheerfully. 'Would you like to tell me what happened?'

***

The next morning Zara received a phone call from Bobby's friend Tommy.

'I don't know if you know but Bobby's Aunt Marion is dead.

'How do you know?' asked Zara. There was a hesitation at the other end.

'Inside information. I'll only tell you if you don't ask who told me. It might cost them their job.'

'Okay,' said Zara.

'Apparently she had been failing this last week and nobody expected her to last more than a day or two. She had been muttering about Bobby and a nurse had actually told her he was in prison. Fortunately, she refused to believe it. She woke up at about six this morning and said, "I've seen Bobby. I can die now. Everything is in order. Then she just died.' There was a silence. Zara was recovering from Tommy's uncharacteristically long speech.

'I see,' she said. 'Thank you.'

'It seems she was hallucinating. Like she actually thought Bobby was there.'

'Ah,' said Zara. 'Why wouldn't she think he was there if she didn't believe he'd been in prison?'

'Well, I suppose it wasn't visiting hours. She said he'd come in the night when she was asleep. Just appeared, sat on the bed and then left. That not what ghosts are meant to do?'

'Do you believe in ghosts?'

'No. Not really.'

'But you've had no word from him?'

'I didn't say I'd tell you if I had.'

'No, of course you didn't. Sorry. Well, thanks again and Tommy?'

'Yes?'

'If there's anything else you feel you can tell me...'

'Yes, Zara, I will.'

Zara felt reassured by the fact that he had used her name. She was puzzled. She didn't think Tommy had seen Bobby, didn't believe he was just happening to keep that a secret. She was inclined to believe the hallucination story until the phone went again and Des said,

'You won't have heard. Bobby's escaped from Kilmarnock.'

***

Meanwhile at an undisclosed location, John Muirhouse was having one of his customary chats with Ronnie Balfour:

'I'm tired. You're tired. Can't we just finish this? All you have to do is admit what happened. You know you are guilty but no-one serves life these days and you, with no previous — and I'm sure you'd be able to get social workers and psychologists saying what a wonderful chap you are — you would probably get a minimum sentence. I can't see what's stopping you. I really can't. I would like to know. It intrigues me. Me, an intelligent person, unable to make sense of you.' He shook his head. 'If you're not going to play ball I might have to break your leg accidentally and then leave you here.

Untied of course. I need to get back to my life, such as it is. You've no idea what a disturbance you've caused, killing Daffodil. Mother's not been well ever since and I've not been able to look after her because I've been looking after you.'

To all this Ronnie Balfour turned a deaf ear. He had heard it or words to the same effect for so long now. The bean diet was upsetting his stomach. He tried to eat, knowing it was necessary — it was how he knew he was still sane — but he suffered cramps every night, even after John Muirhouse started allowing his legs freedom for a few minutes each day.

'Just a taste so you remember what it's like, knowing it could be yours, like that' — he snapped his fingers — 'if you just say the word.'

***

When Bobby had arrived at the overgrown caravan he found a tin opener and some tins of soup lying on top of a wooden chest he remembered from many years ago. Scrawled on a scrap of paper held down by a tin were the words, 'Open to find treasure'. Inside were bread, butter and jam, teabags and dried milk and a tiny camping stove with a full canister of gas. Also a small pan, a plate, a knife, fork and spoon. Matches. Bobby almost felt there must be a God.

'Ah Tommy,' he whispered to himself as he grabbed the pan and went out to get water from the burn that had found its hidden way through the scrubby bushes nearby.

Bobby had not expected a welcome party. He was sharp enough to know that unnecessary visits could attract attention, even in Pirnmill. He might not have long to execute a plan and he didn't know yet what that plan was going to be. He bit his lip hard as he thought.

HIs eyes fell on the wooden chest and he grinned in spite of his situation. Treasure. That had been one of their favourite games, playing out a fantasy and then opening the box. Years later he had asked Tommy one night in the pub if he had ever believed in the magic they had tried to weave. Tommy had looked into the bottom of his pint and muttered, 'Sometimes'. They had had a great laugh over it.

Bobby's mind ruminated over other things they'd done and he suddenly remembered the matchbox tree. It was about a quarter of a mile away, an old ash with a trunk that had been struck by lightning and yet survived. In the resultant hollow they had left messages for each other, matchboxes wrapped in dock leaves. Bobby dismissed the idea forming in his mind and ate his soup but by the time he had devoured a quarter of the loaf and three mugs of tea he was convinced he would find a message from Tommy in the tree.

The light was fading as he set out but it would not take him long. He hoped Tommy would have some useful information for him. Possibly about John Muirhouse. He picked his way carefully through the inevitable brambles that had grown over what had used to be a path. Everything was either much higher or fallen down. The thorn trees that had stood together like two old men were now both half-hidden in the undergrowth. He found the ash.

It must have come down in a storm and some time ago for its trunk was rotten and insects had made it their home, mushrooms decorating the now horizontal branches. There was nowhere here to place a matchbox. Bobby was suddenly overwhelmed by the present just as, a few minutes before he had been overwhelmed by the past. Stupid bastard he thought. You are not six now. Whatever made you think... and he turned and started back, wanting all at once to gain the safety of the caravan.

Walking along he watched the ground: it was easy to trip here. He didn't look up until he turned the corner which would bring the caravan's location into view. And then he froze: someone with their back to him was standing at the door. In a split second he eliminated Tommy and John Muirhouse: a stranger then, and he flung himself towards them, thinking, whoever they were, surprise was his only weapon against them. He grasped an arm and pulled it back in a half nelson. The face that turned to him was Zara's. They hadn't met but he knew this, had heard about her, seen her around.

'Oh sorry,' he said. 'Really sorry,' he repeated as she rubbed her arm.

'Can I talk to you?' asked Zara. 'I'm Zara MacDonald.'

'I know,' said Bobby opening the caravan door. 'You'd better come in.' She went before him into the gloom.

'Tea?' he said. He didn't smile.

'You're all right,' Zara replied sitting down on one of the rusty rectangular cushions which formed the eating area.

'How did you find me?' Bobby asked.

'Don't worry... I just used my head. Nobody told me except Tommy said it was well hidden. Let's say I was lucky.'

'Are you going to turn me in?' Zara looked at him. He didn't look untrustworthy. That was her gut feeling. One that might easily be overridden by ascertainable facts.

'Probably not,' she said. 'Do you know where John Muirhouse is?'

'No but I'd like to.'

'He's been camping in one of those pink sandstone caves near Pirnmill.'

'He had Ronnie Balfour there at one point.'

'Well Ronnie isn't there now but I'm sure that's where Muirhouse is hanging out. I was there today.'

'Were you?' Zara noticed Bobby look interested but she could not read why.

'Are you thinking of doing any more work for him?' He looked at her as though he thought she had to be joking. 'I wondered if you'd be interested in joining me in a plan.'

'What's that?' He sounded neither interested nor uninterested. 'I want you to get in touch with Muirhouse and say you are available for work. If he takes you on, all you have to do is give me a location where you'll be meeting him.'

'And you'll tell the cops?'

'The cops might well be involved. At some stage,' Zara allowed.

'What about Ronnie Balfour though? If Muirhouse is lifted, he won't speak and Ronnie will be mouldering away some place with no-one to bring him his beans.'

'You had many conversations with Ronnie?'

'Yes and no. I was told not to but… I felt sorry for the guy. Muirhouse is a complete cunt. Sorry,' he added automatically.

'I hear what you're saying,' said Zara. 'Obviously it would be better if we could find Ronnie first.'

She suddenly remembered the strip of paper and made a mental note to phone Des about it.

'Do you need anything?' she asked. 'You won't have anything with you.'

'I'm okay,' Bobby said.

'Like a new mobile?' Zara had one in her hand. 'Not that communicating with people would be a very good idea for you with the cops after you as they will be.' He held out his hand.

'Might be useful in an emergency,' he said.

'You know how to contact John Muirhouse?'

'Yup.' He wasn't going to tell Zara how.

She rose to her feet.

'I'll look forward to hearing from you. I'm available twenty-four-seven: don't worry about spoiling my sleep. I have a feeling Muirhouse will be delighted to have you for his minion again but we probably haven't much time.' Zara was at the door.

'Tommy phone you then?'

'Yes.'

'You heard I was at the hospital?'

'I heard your Aunt Marion had an hallucination.' Bobby almost managed a grin. 'Lucky for you,' said Zara, 'that the staff bought that'. Bobby nodded. Zara left.

***

She retrieved her vehicle and drove to the top of the Boguille, parking in a lay-by from where she could see the whole chain of the mountains on her right. It was easy to look at them and imagine they held secrets on purpose, that they were both malevolent and beneficent. It was difficult to see them as having no power at all.

Des answered at the second ring.

'You never told me about the glue,' said Zara.

'Zara, I've had more important things on my mind.'

'Missing girls, missing men, it's a hard life, Des, but can you just answer the question?'

'Opposite sides,' he said and then relenting, 'I was about to phone you when I got the call about the missing girl. She turned up by the way. On Islay. People just move about without mentioning it to their nearest and dearest. "I didn't think you'd be worried, I'm over eighteen," they say.'

'I'm glad,' said Zara. 'I never thought it had anything to do with Muirhouse.'

'Nor me,' said Des.

'Any more messages?'

'Nope. I do wish things would take a turn.' Zara resisted the impulse to tell Des her plan. She wasn't even going to mention the gaol-break if Des didn't. 'Quite clever of our Bobby to escape from Kilmarnock. I have to hand it to him.'

'No leads?'

'His aunt is dead. He'd mentioned he would want to go to the funeral. He would have been able to but... he'll hardly turn up now... on the island.'

'Maybe John Muirhouse taught him some disappearing tricks.'

'Well, it's not strictly my bag. He didn't disappear from my patch.' Zara felt bad.

'I'll let you know if I hear anything useful,' she said closing the call.

She sat looking at the view and thinking about the strip of paper. Supposing it did mean something? It apparently arrived unglued but this didn't mean it was unglued when Muirhouse put it in the envelope. If it had been glued, surely there was a message there: a circle and the words 'Time is running out for Ronnie Balfour.' Zara frowned and looked at the mountains again. The Castles with the Witches' Step and Goat Fell behind. Goat Fell where it had all started. Zara remembered her instinct to re-read Jack House's book. The mountain's in there somewhere if I could only think where. She thought about the strip of paper, the glued ends being on opposite sides of it, making a Mobius strip. Continuous surface... a jibe from Muirhouse meaning never-ending? And in the characteristic Muirhouse mode — with a twist in it. Full circle. Suddenly she had it. Ronnie Balfour was back in Coire nam Fuaram where he had started. A chill crept over her. Did Muirhouse's words on the strip mean he had been left up there to die? But how could he have got him up there? He couldn't have carried him. But John Muirhouse was both determined and fit. He thrived on doing the impossible.

Even though it seemed unlikely, Zara felt compelled to go and make sure. Not feasible to go up the mountain now. Too dark and the way even in daylight difficult to find. She would need to go back to North Crag and get the right clothes and supplies. She would have taken Barney but not Ben: the sight might be too gut-wrenching. She would have to go alone. She was sure she would find Ronnie there. But the letter and the strip of paper had been sent days ago now. She hoped she would be in time.

***

As soon as Ben was in bed, Zara told Barney, Kirsty and George of her suspicions.

'Shouldn't you tell the police?' said George at once. 'If what you say is true, you may cost Ronnie Balfour his life if you wait till morning.'

'He may not even have water,' added Kirsty.

'Des will think I'm off on one,' said Zara. 'It's a stab in the dark to him. And he hates me being right.'

'Surely he doesn't let that cloud his judgment?' Barney was not being sarcastic. 'Exactly how many days is it?'

'Six.'

'And how many days is it you can go without water?'

'Seven.'

'And that's for someone fit not someone who's been existing on beans for weeks', said Kirsty. Zara went silent.

'Okay,' she said. 'Compromise. I'll phone the Mountain Rescue and say I met someone who was setting out for Coire nam Fuaram this afternoon who said he would see me in the pub tonight... I've phoned round his friends and no-one's seen him.'

'Why haven't the friends phoned?'

'They think he's out for a Sunday walk. No idea of the terrain. City people. Already too drunk to bother too much. Don't worry I can make it up.'

Zara went out of the kitchen to make the call. She returned after five minutes.

'That's that then. All in hand. Police have to know of course but I gave a false name. There's no reason to connect the call with me. I told them the guy seemed to be a bit of a nutter. Interested in rural murders. Doing a PhD.' Barney put his hands in a slow clap.

'Well done Zara. Full marks for restraint.' He smiled at her with a special smile that she interpreted as meaning he felt she was becoming someone he could feel more sure about.

***

In the caravan, lit by a solitary candle, Bobby pondered on his next move. Ideas were swimming round in his head but he knew that any plan he had might be knocked off course by whatever John Muirhouse had to say. In the end, he just punched in the guy's number which he had committed to memory. He was answered on the first ring.

'I was wondering if you had any work. He didn't bother saying anything about his escape. It was obvious and anyway he felt sure Muirhouse would have heard.

'Yes there is. You know where the money is. Buy food from the usual place and bring it to destination seven.' Sometimes Bobby felt a lot older than John Muirhouse.

'I want paid up front.' There was a minute hesitation before Muirhouse said,

'Of course.' In that hesitation lay the recognition that he knew Bobby was trying to wind him up.'

'Tomorrow. I'll be there tomorrow,' said Bobby. His heart beat louder than he had ever heard it. He wondered whether to phone Zara but he didn't want to. It would be giving up power too quickly. He felt he could plan better if he were in control. He wanted to find out what was going on. Who was at destination seven? Muirhouse, Ronnie or both of them?

Chapter XXIX Back to the mountain

At two a.m. Zara woke to her alarm vibrating, stole out of bed, grabbed her clothes and went to dress in the bathroom. Her jacket and boots were in the cupboard downstairs. She took a powerful head torch from its place on the kitchen shelf, stashed some food she had prepared earlier in her rucksack, checked she had her mobile and set off shutting the back door silently behind her. She met no one though she took the precaution of taking short cuts where she could, avoiding the road till she came out just past the Glen Rosa bridge. From there she walked in the shadow of the trees past Duchess Court until she reached Cladach. She turned left towards Goat Fell.

She was not in danger of meeting any of the Mountain Rescue team because she had not phoned them. While she was sure she was going to find Ronnie Balfour, she did not have the nerve to risk the scorn of the team should she be wrong. On the other hand, she had not felt she could risk leaving Ronnie longer than necessary: she had no idea when time was going to run out on John Muirhouse's calendar.

***

Shortly before midday on the previous Saturday, the following conversation had taken place at the secret location where Ronnie was being held.

'Right, your time's up. Are you going to stick to your confession?'

'No.'

'Everyone believes you did it, your parents, your brother... even Zara MacDonald. I sent a message to Zara MacDonald. Well, to Des which is virtually the same thing but neither of them understood it. You should be more careful in choosing your friends, Balfour.' Ronnie flinched inwardly, at each name. He could not bear to believe it but he did not know how good Muirhouse was at faking handwriting.

'This is your last chance. If you don't agree I shall have to carry out plan X. I'm not going to kill you but I'll leave you here and I shan't come back and, just in case you think you can crawl away from here, you will have an accident which will prevent you.' Ronnie shut his ears: he'd heard similar threats so often in the last few weeks.

'What's the date?' he asked. Muirhouse told him. 'You've been on the run for two months then, just like John Laurie. I reckon it's your time that's up.'

'But unlike John Laurie, I have a ticket, two tickets actually, one for me and one for mother. I'll be leaving in a couple of days. I never did like the climate in Scotland.'

'Spain is it or South America?' asked Ronnie. Muirhouse smiled, showing his teeth.

'Do you really want our last conversation to be about my holiday destination? Except it's not a holiday, it's forever. You may have noticed, small talk is not my forte.' There was a silence where the outside seemed to reach in and engulf the two of them as they sat there.

'I would like an explanation. Why not let me die knowing what's in your mind? I cannot understand why you think you can make the murder stick to me.'

I've already talked it over with one of the best lawyers in Scotland. He thinks I have a very good case. And anyway, you do know. You know it's a matter of family honour: you are defending your brother: I am defending my father.'

'That's rubbish,' said Ronnie.

'The point is, I did not kill Daffodil Brown. You did.'

'That your last word?'

'It is.' Ronnie was finding it hard to keep his voice firm. Muirhouse looked his victim in the eye as he spoke.

'Well then on your own head be it.' Ronnie had heard the menace in Muirhouse's voice and he turned his head away as if to ward off a blow. Muirhouse then stabbed him in the thigh with a hypodermic needle. When after several seconds Ronnie passed into unconsciousness he untied the ropes that bound him and dragged him to the entrance. Here he made a wall of stones over which he draped Ronnie's body as if the man were trying to clamber out. Anyone listening on the outside would have heard nothing but the sound of a single stone — intentionally dropped — and Muirhouse's footsteps leaving. Ronnie stirred but did not come round. The footsteps turned in the direction of Corrie.

***

Zara stopped only once on her path up the mountain and then not because she felt tired but because she felt she should pace herself. She tried to push away the idea that she would not be able to find Coire nam Fuaran. She was fairly sure she could find where she and Ronnie had camped. She would have to find it. She could shout. Ronnie would hear her and then it would be easier. She remembered clearly standing outside the tent and looking to where Ronnie was standing talking to John Muirhouse on the edge of the Coire. Why should it be difficult?

The moon came out occasionally, allowing Zara to progress along the path at a reasonable speed and gain the shoulder. It was after this that confusion might set in. She prayed for the moon to be on her side. While it was out the landscape was weirdly beautiful and though for her this was a well-trodden path, everything looked unfamiliar, as if the rocks had re-arranged themselves since she was last there.

It was when she found the place where she and Ronnie had camped that she became full of foreboding. Although the moon graced the scene with a bluish light which threw the rocks into sharp relief, she could not determine at all where Coire nam Fuaran was. She was not even sure of the direction. She could not stumble around for hours in the hope she might come across it. She felt like giving up. She could go back to the hotel now and get into bed with Barney and quite likely he would not even know she'd been gone. Then she saw Ben's face: it wore an expression of complete and utter disappointment. Okay she thought. I will have to stumble around for hours. Come on feet. Take me there.

She chose a direction randomly and walked what she felt was the number of yards she had covered on the night to reach Ronnie Balfour and John Muirhouse. Nothing. She was on the edge of a precipice. She sat and thought. After a time, she remembered climbing a big rock and looking down, seeing... the sheltering overhang in which Daffodil had spent her last

300

hours. If I could find that rock. She looked around. Behind her was such a rock but there was no way of climbing it. Perhaps I was on the other side she thought. She made her way round it, having to go several yards to circumvent the unclimbable but there on the other side, the rock looked familiar: she could see the foothold she had used. She climbed up.

And then it was clearer. She could see the overhang and she could... she thought she could see the lip of the awful black chasm in which the unfortunate girl had met her death.

'Ronnie!' she shouted 'Can you hear me?' But there was no reply. Why am I so sure Muirhouse isn't there as well, she wondered. Because I don't want it to be so, she replied to herself, mentally thumbing her nose at any opposition. She set off again treading carefully, no mistakes to be made so near the goal. She reached the edge and looked over. She could see the corrie where John Laurie had allegedly hidden Edwin Rose and where she felt Ronnie had been hidden at the beginning of the trail.

'Ronnie,' she shouted again. Her torch beam did not reach. She might as well save her breath and go down.

She picked her way over the rough ground to the place where the police had descended. She felt she was going so slowly, each footstep a conscious effort to find a safe foothold. She made herself calm. A few more minutes. Then she was at the bottom and making straight for the corrie, still looking at the path till she was brought up short.

The first she saw of Ronnie was the top of his head. It was at an odd angle and, to one side she saw a chafed arm and a hand. The other arm was half-hidden by a large stone. Another step revealed his torso and then she gasped. Blood. Tentatively Zara picked up Ronnie's right wrist to find a pulse. Relief flooded through her. It was weak but it was there.

The blood had come from his right leg but it was obviously from a vein not an artery. Otherwise the guy would have been dead, Zara reflected. She felt pleased with herself as she took out a bandage she had taken from Kirsty's first-aid box earlier. Although the bleeding had stopped she made the bandage quite tight in case the flow should start again if she moved him at all.

As far as she could see there were no other injuries so she decided to push Ronnie's upper body back into a position where he could breathe more easily. She did not think she could get him into the recovery position. As she moved him he groaned and his eyes flickered.

'Ronnie, it's me, Zara,' she said. 'You're safe. You're going to be okay.'

Ronnie went quiet again and lolled his weight against Zara's body. It felt like a dead weight. Even to her unprofessional eye she thought he looked dehydrated. She attempted to give him a little water from the bottle she had with her. It was impossible; he was not conscious enough.

But what was she thinking of? She must phone Des and he would organize a helicopter. If that were faster. It would be faster. She took out her phone. Would Des be there? He didn't work twenty-four seven. It would possibly be one of the locals. It was the mainland. She'd forgotten the routine. Progress: you could no longer speak to someone who would know the geography of where you were talking about.

'I need a helicopter at Coire nam Fuaran, on the Isle of Arran,' she added she thought, helpfully.

'What's your name?' asked the neutral voice at the other end.

***

For some reason Ben woke very early and decided to go for a walk. He knew Barney would worry to find him gone so he wrote him a note and stole into the bedroom to put it on his dad's pillow He was just about to leave when, in the growing daylight, he glimpsed a white sheet of paper on the bedside table: '2 a.m. Gone to get Ronnie. Don't worry. Zara xxx'

'Dad!' Barney was awake at once.

'Are you okay, Ben? What is it?' Ben thrust the note into his hand. Barney pulled on his clothes and together he and Ben went down to the kitchen where they took rolls and a flask of tea and another of water and Barney left yet another note, this time for Kirsty and George.

Only as they left the hotel did he phone Zara. She didn't answer. Barney thought it must be a lack of signals. He asked Ben to keep trying.

They took Zara's van. Barney couldn't understand why Zara hadn't taken it herself and started walking from Cladach. Once there, they started up the path.

'Shouldn't you phone Des?' said Ben who was having to run to keep up.

'Probably but Zara might kill me if I did and that would not be a good outcome.'

'She didn't phone the Mountain Rescue did she, last night?'

'I don't think so. We were naïve. She was too calm. She wouldn't have been that calm unless she had a plan of her own.'

Barney didn't know exactly why he was hurrying so fast but his legs would not slow down. His thoughts were like a conveyor belt: Zara, Ronnie, Muirhouse, Zara. Endlessly.

'I think after this I'll be fit enough for the Goat Fell race,' said Ben. Barney slowed momentarily.

'I'm sorry Ben.'

'You're just worried, Dad, I know. I'm worried too but I think she'll be safe.'

'Why do you think that, Ben?'

'I just think she will. But I also think it's important we get there. For some reason.'

***

Zara sat with Ronnie. He had opened his eyes again and seemed to be trying to speak but no words came.

'It's okay, Ronnie. Save your breath.' She tried again to give him water but then he lost consciousness again. She looked at the time. Fifteen minutes gone. She thought they'd said half an hour but she wasn't sure now. She was nervous. Had they really understood the word 'helicopter'? She had an awful fantasy they might be sending an ambulance to a Nam Fuaran Avenue somewhere on the mainland. The police officer had asked for landmarks. Zara had almost laughed out loud.

'I'll wave,' she'd said. 'It's where the Goat Fell murder happened.'

'But that was in 1889,' said the officer after a pause.

'The second Goat Fell murder,' said Zara. Then her phone cut out and she could not get a signal after that.

She rummaged in her rucksack and found a white plastic carrier bag. If she put her arms in it, it would make a good flag. She wondered about going to the top of the cliff but she didn't want to leave Ronnie who was cold to her touch although she had put her jacket over him. His pulse was there but very weak and his colour was no colour. His body was heavy against hers but she didn't want to move away: she felt she was giving him some warmth. She wished the helicopter would hurry up as her feet were going to sleep. Because she couldn't move she felt she had to. She eased one leg and stretched it but as her knee retracted it hit the water bottle, knocking it over and spilling it. She cursed herself for not having replaced the lid.

'Drink,' said Ronnie suddenly and clearly. 'I need something to drink.' His eyes opened and stayed open.

'Ronnie, I'll get you some tea.' The tea would warm him Zara thought, turning to her rucksack again. Tea. She had brought tea. Surely she hadn't imagined that. No, of course it was there. She undid the flask and poured. There was barely half a cup left. Zara felt like throwing it away she was so exasperated with herself. What had she been thinking of!

'Here,' she said to Ronnie. 'Drink this. It's all there is I'm afraid.' He took a sip and seemed grateful but then grimaced.

'Too hot,' he said faintly. 'My leg.' and he passed out again.

Thirty minutes. Zara tried her mobile. What's keeping them she wondered. No signal. She looked at the sky, then back to Ronnie. His colour was even worse. I wish I knew more about first aid she thought. I wish... Maybe it would be better if she went out to where she could see the path passing the corrie, see, for that matter, other parts of the mountains where, who knows, there might be a lone climber with water, or, even better, a knowledge of first aid. She tucked her jacket around Ronnie and, having removed her binoculars, made a pillow for him out of her rucksack.

'Don't you dare die while I'm away,' she whispered. She picked up the bottle in case she found a water source nearby.

She climbed back up to the top and looked to left and right. No one. No solitary early morning walkers drinking in the dawn. A wind blowing and no sign of the sun. Where was the helicopter? She took up her binoculars and scanned the horizon. Then she scanned the mountain. She was about to give up when she saw a dot and then another, then both of them disappeared. She kept the binoculars trained. Luck turned at last? Two people! They had to have something useful. She began to shout and wave. Their response was instant: they immediately started heading towards her but it wasn't until the smaller one shouted 'Zara' that she realized it was Ben and Barney.

Zara didn't stop to wonder how they came to be there, she rushed towards them:

'Have you got water?' she shouted. Barney withdrew a bottle from his bag.

'I thought we'd never find you,' he said. We've been searching for the corrie for ages.'

'Ronnie's in the corrie. I think he's dehydrated and he has a broken leg. Not tied up though.'

They diluted the tea with water till it was tepid. Ronnie drank it and seemed to revive but the pain in his leg was obvious.

'The helicopter is coming,' said Zara. 'I promise you. Please hang on.' Barney diluted more tea.

'Thank you,' said Ronnie. 'You are very kind. I'm so pleased to be here. Thank you very much.'

'He's not really seeing us,' said Ben. 'I think he's … what is it called when you… I know, delirious. I think he's delirious. I think he thinks we're someone else.'

'I didn't do it,' said Ronnie. It wasn't what you think. I was…' But Ronnie's small voice was at last drowned out by the noise of the helicopter.

***

Zara was sleeping the sleep of the just even though it was five in the afternoon. She woke to a light patting on her shoulder.

'Zara?'

'Go away whoever you are. I have to sleep. If the house is on fire, I'll burn.'

'Zara, any chance you could talk to Des. He wants a first-hand account of what happened: how you found Ronnie, whether he said anything.'

'Said nothing. Used my common sense. Strip of paper. Full circle. Back to the...' Zara was asleep again.

'She won't wake up properly,' Barney said to Des who was being regaled with cake in the kitchen. She says he said nothing and that it was the strip of paper. She muttered something about 'full circle, back to the...'

'Mountain! Of course.' Des made a face which held in it a mixture of chagrin and admiration.

'She's very clever at working things out, isn't she?' said Ben.

'She is indeed,' acknowledged Des. 'No doubt about it. So, one part of the business cleared up. Once Ronnie Balfour has got his stuckie, we'll see about charging him.

'Charging him?' Barney repeated. 'But he isn't...'

'I've got a written confession on file.'

'But that was made under duress!'

'That's not what the handwriting experts say. They can tell you these days not only what you had for breakfast but what you were thinking of having for lunch.' Barney, who had been feeling elated, fell rapidly into a gloom. He didn't want to have to tell Zara that particular news.

***

Bobby picked up the food and made his way to Destination 7. He used an old motor scooter which at the moment seemed a safer bet than a car. He could wear a helmet and thereby become virtually unrecognizable. And a scooter was easier to hide than a car.

'I'm going to be here on and off till the other business is cleared up,' said John Muirhouse when Bobby appeared. There were no congratulations on his escape, no hint of pleased-to-see-you. Bobby added this to his list of things he disliked about John Muirhouse: he wasn't a person, more a machine.

'Am I to feed Ronnie Balfour as well?'

'That won't be necessary.'

'Someone else doing that then?'

'I said' — meaningful pause — 'it won't be necessary. Now, the next lot of food you'll need to buy…'

'I don't really like going into shops at the moment.'

'If you can't do it legally, you'll have to find another way, won't you? Otherwise I can't pay you.' Muirhouse put his hand in his pocket and kept it there. Bobby felt like a person who can see a cake on a plate but isn't being offered it. Then he thought harder and realized he had to play ball or at least appear to, in order to keep the most options open.

'Okay. I expect I'll find a way. You'll be here then, tomorrow? Or do I wait till the next day?'

'Bring me a newspaper when you come.'

'The next day?'

'Yes.' Said Muirhouse. Bobby looked round the apology for a cave.

'You could do with a telly. 'S quite lonely.'

'Go on now, home.' Muirhouse cut him off, handing him a fistful of change and a couple of tenners. 'I'm not intending it to be a permanent residence. And I've camped in a lot worse places.' Bobby turned on his heel and left, checking first to see if there was anyone about. Muirhouse did not speak again.

Now Bobby had money in his pocket he felt like a drink but he couldn't go into a pub without being recognized. His only recourse was to find Tommy and Tommy might not want to be found. He would have to go back to the caravan and wait. Maybe a bit of telepathy would bring a can of beer.

He left the field, found the scooter and turned northwards. He hated the caravan at that moment: it represented safety but also loneliness. He didn't want to be alone with his thoughts. He needed a plan and he couldn't think of one. Muirhouse always uses circumstances he thought. He somehow turns what's happening to his advantage but my problem is nothing is happening and I can't take initiatives without the danger of someone rumbling me.

He tried to make toast on the calor gas flame but only succeeded in dropping the slice of bread onto the burner and putting the flame out. Antarctic, no he thought to himself. K2, no. I'm not really cut out for adventure. He wondered about phoning Zara. He should tell her about John Muirhouse's movements. But what would she do? He didn't entirely trust her. He sat with his head in his hands till it became dark and even his own silhouette vanished into the shadows.

He must have dozed off because he didn't hear Tommy till he was standing in front of him with a pizza in one hand and a can of beer in the other.

'Go on. Take it. It's real. It won't stay hot for ever.'

'Tommy!' Bobby fell on the pizza as if he had not eaten for days. 'Some day I'll make it up to you.' Tommy took the seat opposite his friend and pulled the ring on his own can.

'Well pal, you can do that the day after tomorrow if you like. My uncle's asked me to fertilize a field down Machrie way. For some reason it has to be that day. He's borrowing a tractor, you see, because his own has a problem. I've got to do something else. Something I can't shift. Trouble is I promised my uncle.' Bobby frowned.

'I've never driven a tractor before.'

'Bobby, a tractor drives itself. It's easy. You can drive a car, you can drive a tractor.'

'But your uncle will know it's not you.'

'No he won't. He won't be there. I'll get the keys off him. The fertilizer will be in sacks in the field. I'll be able to drive the tractor to the field. Then you take over.' Bobby thought about it. Was this somehow the opportunity he was looking for?

'What field exactly are you talking about?'

'You know the one with the pink caves? Bobby's heart stopped momentarily.

'Yes,' he said.

'Well, it's not that one but the one to the south of it.' Bobby tried to speak calmly:

'So what is it you are going to do that's so important?'

'An interview for a job. In a garage. Other uncle put in a word. Could be an apprenticeship type thing. The two uncles don't get on.'

'I see what you're saying,' said Bobby. He licked his lips. 'Okay. I'll do it. I just turn up and you give me the keys, right? Just turn on the engine and she goes? That easy?'

'Pretty well. Thanks, Bobby. Cheers.' They touched cans and drank.

After Tommy had gone, Bobby phoned Zara.

'He's going to be there the day after tomorrow.'

'Right.' Zara didn't sound as collected as Bobby remembered her.

'You okay?'

'We found Ronnie.'

'Alive?'

'Yes. Just about. He's in a critical condition. Dehydrated and very weak. That bastard Muirhouse had broken his leg so he couldn't even try to get away. As if he had the strength.'

'Left him untied?'

'I suppose it made it look as though he was not being kept there by force.'

'Kept where?'

'Coire nam Fuaran.' Destination One thought Bobby. Then to Zara:

'You going to get the police to close in on Muirhouse.'

'I haven't thought it out yet. Thanks for the tip though. You okay yourself?'

'Aye,' said Bobby. 'I'm fine.'

'Let me know, Bobby, if there's anything else... and Bobby, take care.'

'Okay,' said Bobby closing the call, reflecting that Zara was probably a nice person like Aunt Marion.

Chapter XXX   Endgame

Zara was having a leisurely coffee when the post arrived. A letter was an unusual occurrence. Her mother? Not Barney, he was here. She examined the handwriting and recognized the unrecognizable hand of John Muirhouse. Inside was a single sheet of lined paper, torn from a notebook: If you want Ronnie Balfour, he is all yours. A map reference followed and then the solitary word, Tuesday. Tomorrow thought Zara. She asked Ben to look up the map reference. As she had surmised, it was for the pink sandstone caves.

First she decided it was a trap. Muirhouse knew that if anything would lure her to a specific spot it would be the idea of finding Ronnie. But then she realized that the letter had been posted on Saturday when Muirhouse must have thought Ronnie was still on the mountain. Her body went cold. Was his plan to fetch the body — having calculated it would now be just a body — to the sandstone caves and leave it for Zara to find? What would happen then? Would Muirhouse appear and gloat? What would he do when he found that Ronnie was not in the corrie? Zara reckoned the knowledge would not improve his mood.

Des was away now in Crosshouse hospital waiting for Ronnie to be well enough to answer questions. Maybe he would be back tomorrow. She couldn't ask Barney to help her. He would be horrified that she would even think of keeping the rendezvous. Bobby. What about Bobby? She just needed back up in case things went wrong. He was as capable of phoning for help as the next person. But you have no idea what Muirhouse has in mind, her survival brain said to her. His logic is not your logic. His ways are cruel, psychopathic. Why not leave the rest to the professionals? Let Des blunder his way through to a conclusion.

That's not fair said another part of her mind. You know perfectly well Des is a good detective. Running him down isn't helpful to you just now.

Give me one good reason, said Zara's adventurous side rhetorically, why it would be a good idea to fall into another Muirhouse trap.

Because it's there, the answer came back. Zara tried to stifle it but it wouldn't go away.

To quieten Miss Sensible, Zara phoned Des and told him about the letter.

'Don't go near it,' said Des predictably.

'Chance of apprehending John Muirhouse?

'It looks very nasty to me... If he's willing to tell you where he is.'

'He doesn't say that, he says Ronnie Balfour will be there.'

'But we know he isn't.'

'I know Des.'

'I imagine when he finds you've spoilt his plan he'll be angry and that probably means violent. I'll send some undercover men.'

'He'll be watching. He'll be undiscoverable. If he's in the cave —'

'You think he won't be there? Won't he want to vent his anger on you when he finds out Ronnie's in the hospital?'

'I know.'

'So you won't go?' Silence. 'Promise me you'll let me know before you do anything rash?'

'Okay, Des.'

***

Des was not the only one who was worried about what Zara might do. Ben had been keeping a close eye on her, afraid she might decide to sneak off again in the middle of the night. He'd been alerted by her asking him to find the map reference in the letter. She'd tried to confuse the issue by asking for map references for Merkland, the Sannox mine and Coire nam Fuaran as if she were trying to establish a pattern but why now when Ronnie was safe? Ben deduced she wanted to confirm that the map reference was the pink caves. He made a show of looking them up but he almost knew them by heart now. If Zara was going off to the pink caves, he was going too. If anyone had asked him what he was going to be when he grew up now, he tended to say 'detective' and it seemed reasonable to him to start practising. He had been going to the library and looking at books about cold cases. He did not attempt to take the books out; didn't want people to think he was morbid. He just liked trying to solve problems.

Another factor that was driving him was the miniature tape-recorder George had given him the other day. George had come across it in a box in the attic. He'd said jokingly,

'Just think if Edwin Rose had been wearing one of these there might be no mystery at all about the Goat Fell murder. Ever since, Ben had wanted an opportunity to use the machine to help catch John Muirhouse. He had bought batteries with his pocket money and practised hiding the recorder next to his skin and seeing how far away from a speaker he could be and still pick up. It was a good machine. George said it had been given to him by someone who used to be a spy but Ben had not believed him. He was now wearing it all the time in case he had to rush off suddenly in pursuit of Zara.

***

Zara did not have a plan except she knew she was going to the pink caves. She didn't know how she was going to get away from Ben and Barney but then salvation came in the shape of a phone call from Barney's mother. An uncle from Canada was visiting. Could Barney possibly come to Glasgow just for lunch? He needn't bring Ben. The uncle was a bit deaf, had never met Ben and was in Glasgow for a picture postcard conference. Barney could not see any way out. Ben said he was going to the farriers with George and Riga and then he was meeting a friend on the beach. He knew Zara's mind would be set at rest. He had noted a certain expression on her face which he knew from experience meant she was planning something. He was about to tell George he wouldn't come with him when George told him the shoeing of Riga had been postponed. He didn't tell Zara. Consequently, his only problem was secreting himself in the back of the van whenever he saw Zara making preparations.

It was about eleven o'clock. Zara had finished her chores:

'Going somewhere boring,' she said to Ben.

'Can I come?' he said to allay her suspicions: it was what he would normally have said.

'No Ben. Anyway I thought you had things to do.' Ben nodded wondering desperately how he could get Zara away from the van long enough for him to get into it without being seen. Fortunately, all of them had a habit of leaving things like picnic rugs, bags, balls and racquets in the back so he knew he could easily make a nest.

He jumped from one foot to the other and then turned as if to go back into North Crag.

'Oh Zara, Kirsty asked me to ask you if you knew where the dustpan had got to.'

'Tell her it's in the cupboard in the hall.'

'She's looked there.' Zara parked her bag on the passenger seat and went back inside.

'Bye Zara,' shouted Ben as he waited for her to disappear. By the time she came out he was completely hidden. Two seconds later they were on their way. Zara had the radio on so it was easy for Ben to change position, which he did frequently. Forty minutes he said to himself. I should be able to get through forty minutes. He was sure Zara was going to the pink caves.

***

John Muirhouse had not intended to revisit the corrie where he had left Ronnie Balfour but he had found the impulse too strong to resist. He had to know that his strategy was intact and if it were not, he had to adjust his next moves. When he discovered that Balfour was no longer in the corrie on the mountain, a black fury overwhelmed him. He picked up rocks and hurled them from him like a giant at war. Then he sat down with his head in his hands and tried to think but his head was a solid mass of the unmoveable and the unnameable. When he thought of banging it on a rock he stood up. Walk he told himself. Walking leads to thinking.

He had once read a book called 'Self-control and the Control of Others' written by an ex-Nazi prison camp officer, Heinz von Klink and it was often this writer's words that came to him in times of need. As he walked he became calmer. It was obvious that his prisoner had been rescued. It would have been on the Scottish news but his radio battery had run out. He cursed himself: 'A true soldier leaves nothing unprepared that can be prepared.' (Klink) He wondered if Balfour was dead and smiled to himself. Whoever found him would have had a shock, the shock he had cooked up for Zara MacDonald. Had she been the one that found him? He felt disappointed that the hide and seek was over. He saw Zara as an opposing warrior and wondered what he could do now to... impress her? No he realized, he did not want to impress her, he wanted her to understand. To do that he would have to explain a few things. And then what? Reluctantly he began to consider a new plan, one where he would be the only winner.

***

When Zara arrived opposite the field, having hidden the van half a mile away, she saw no one. This was because John Muirhouse was secreted on the cliff, on top of the caves in a place from which he could view all comings and goings. He knew Zara would come and he had positioned himself early to be there first.

In the next field a lone man was driving a tractor backwards and forwards spreading fertilizer. Muirhouse was pleased. The noise was good cover. There were no sheep today in what he thought of as his field. That was good too. Sheep were so unpredictable and might get in the way of what was happening.

Des's undercover men had driven past the field without realizing it was the one they wanted. They continued to drive south in an unmarked car. Muirhouse saw the car but thought nothing suspicious about it.

***

Ben had waited five whole minutes before raising his head. He caught sight of Zara just as she left the road for the beach, having come round a bend which put her in view of the caves. Ben stretched, checked his tape-recorder and then darted over the road to the shelter of the profuse weeds and gorse that lined the shore. It was easy to follow Zara. She did not once look behind, seemed by her walk she was certain of not being watched. But then she stopped suddenly and Ben could see she was searching for something in her rucksack. Binoculars. Of course. Ben wished he had some too. The sun was behind her: there would be no glint from the glass for the wrong person to pick up. Ben felt anxious. He had never seen John Muirhouse but he fully expected him to be at least six foot four with huge hands and feet. Even so, part of him wanted at least to glimpse Ronnie Balfour's persecutor.

***

Zara was not sure what to do next and this was because she could not fathom what was in John Muirhouse's head except that he had an agenda that included her. What would I like she thought to herself: to get the story of what happened when John Muirhouse senior was shot. But she could hardly knock on the door of the cave as it were and ask the son. She tried to think it all through in a different way. She realised that even if John Muirhouse knew Ronnie was missing from the corrie, he would not know who had found him. The police had not given that out. Therefore... But Zara could not think of a 'therefore'. She felt that the man must be feeling desperate, sick of sending messages, sick of hiding. What would I do if I were him she wondered. Ticket to South America or a shot in the head. One thing's certain, he's not going to turn himself in. She considered everything she knew about John Muirhouse. What would be the thing that would draw him out? She was fairly sure he was there somewhere but she could not be certain he was in the cave. It looked very uninhabited to Zara even though she could not see into it. Somewhere John Muirhouse was sitting thinking. It was a stand-off: a game that was stuck. A game. That's what she needed.

Quickly she wrote on a piece of paper — my first letter to John Muirhouse she thought — 'I would like to hear your story. What happened to your father? Why did you kidnap Ronnie Balfour?' And then for badness she wrote, 'Time is running out for you John Muirhouse'. She wrapped the paper carefully round a stone, folding it to make a parcel. It was the best she could do. But where to aim it? To get it into the cave, she would need to go into the field unless... If she got into the field with the tractor, she would be screened by the scrubby trees along the wall between the two fields. She felt oddly supported by the tractor man. John Muirhouse wasn't going to kill her in full view of a witness. Was he?

316

She moved along the beach until she was level with the wall. Then she crossed the road and, she hoped, disappeared from sight. If Muirhouse thinks he's seen me, what does it matter? He'll know I'm around soon enough. It only took her seconds to reach a vantage point from where she could throw her stone. Even if it fell short, Muirhouse would see it and she was certain he would not be able to resist seeing what it said.

The tractor man was at the other end of the field: she could hear him rather than see him. She reached a small clearing against the wall and ran towards it like a bowler. The stone left her hand and rose in a beautiful parabola, falling about four feet in front of the cave Zara had visited. She waited. Almost immediately, the bushes on the cliff parted and John Muirhouse jumped. First onto the cave rock and then onto the ground. He ran to the stone and picked it up and read the note. Zara watched him. His face did not change. He sat down on a boulder near the cave entrance, hands linked behind his head. He's telling me he isn't going to shoot me thought Zara. My move.

***

Meanwhile Ben had wormed his way round the other side of the field with the caves, having seen where Zara had gone. He had decided to climb the cliff and hide in the bushes. As he moved, he kept his eyes on where he'd last seen Zara. He saw the stone arc through the air and guessed who had thrown it. Then he saw John Muirhouse emerge and jump. Ben swayed slightly. I could have gone there, where he was and stumbled over him he thought. Anyway, he's not there now and if I go there I'll be able to see everything that happens and if they speak... He touched the recorder to make sure it was still in place.

No one saw Ben climb the cliff. Zara was intent on watching John Muirhouse. She took a deep breath and walked through the connecting gate. She took up a position thirty yards away, facing him but with a thick bush she could just see over between them. Muirhouse was wearing a very fitting short-sleeved t-shirt and close-fitting trackies. She deduced he would not be carrying a gun.

'Come a bit closer,' said that very recognizable voice. 'I don't want to have to shout.'

317

'I've got very good hearing,' said Zara.

'Perhaps you would like to look inside the cave first.'

'Why would I want to do that?' Zara balled her fists to try to stop herself from trembling.

'Might have someone you know here...' Zara stopped breathing: if it wasn't Ronnie Balfour... Barney was on the mainland... Ben? He must be bluffing. 'Don't worry. I haven't harmed him. He's a good lad. Just using him as a bit of a hostage against you phoning the police. This is my plan. I tell you the story and then I leave. You do nothing for twenty-four hours by which time I'll be on a plane to a place that has no extradition treaty with the UK. If you don't keep to your side of the bargain, something will happen to you or to someone you love.' The word 'love' sat awkwardly on Muirhouse's tongue. 'I don't have to tell an intelligent person like yourself that you don't have to be beside a fuse to detonate it. Speaking metaphorically of course.'

***

Ben from his hideout above them heard the whole conversation. Slowly he eased himself out of the bushes and stood up. He had to take the risk to let Zara know he was okay, that Muirhouse was bluffing.

'And you'll give me ...' She could not bring herself to say his name.' When you've told the story.'

'Who would have thought you would agree to barter the lad for a story. Muirhouse threw back his head a laughed. At that moment Zara caught a movement above the cave. She looked down again, not wanting to draw attention to the spot. Her heart thumped loudly. Could it possibly be Ben and how one earth had he got there? Then she heard his only authentic-sounding bird noise and she was not only convinced but reassured. It was all Zara could do not to cry out. She hoped Muirhouse would read her change of expression as normal for someone faced with this sort of challenge.

'So,' Muirhouse was saying, 'do you want a sight of Ben, just so you know he's okay.' Zara knew she couldn't call his bluff but she felt it would be unconvincing if she didn't seem to want to look.

'No, Muirhouse. How do I know you won't make me a prisoner as well if I get the other side of you? I'm not coming any nearer to you.'

'Okay. I don't suppose Ben enjoyed hearing that, but on your own head be it.'

The two protagonists were so focused that they had not noticed the tractor man leave his field and start his comings and goings at the side of the field they were in.

'I'm not armed,' said John Muirhouse. 'Do come a little closer.' Zara dodged ten yards to another bush.

'This is as far as I'm coming. Give me your story.'

'Well,' said John Muirhouse, 'first you must realize how privileged you are that I'm telling you all this, rather than the police. I just feel it's a waste of a good tale if I leave and nobody understands how clever I was.' Zara stared back at him. 'I'll be brief. I'd like to get away on the four-forty boat.' Zara nodded.

'Okay. The first story is called 'My Father's Death'. My father engaged Daffodil Brown as a p.a. and then fell in love with her. My mother did not know. Never knew. Does not know now. He took Daffodil out numerous times and she liked it because he had money and she was just an ordinary girl. But he was old and naturally she was more attracted to younger men. She made eyes at me more than once but as far as I was concerned she was spoken for. Enter Mark Balfour whom she met through my father. Some business deal or other. She fell in love with Balfour and of course kept it secret. She wanted to juggle the two men. After all, between them they gave her everything she needed –money, status, sex, adventure.'

'When Mark Balfour found out what was going on through some chance word of Daffodil's, he was extremely angry. He came to my father's office which was in the house, with his brother and Daffodil. I think he wanted Daffodil to choose between them. Daffodil had confessed her betrayal to my father and to Mark. Father always kept a gun in his desk. Ammunition separate of course. However, from the time of Daffodil's confession, he had kept the gun loaded. I don't know what was in his mind. Maybe Daffodil had given him to believe Balfour was dangerous. She was a bit of a fantasist was Daffodil: it made up for her naivety.'

'There was an argument. Raised voices. I heard them from an adjoining room where my mother and I waited. Dad and Mum and I were going out to dinner. I left mother and went to see what was happening. As I opened the door my father pulled the trigger of his gun which failed to fire. Immediately Mark Balfour pounced and wrested it from my father's hand. Then he turned and pulled the gun on my father shouting, "Let's see if this chamber is full of duds shall we?" Again the trigger just clicked. I was about to throw myself at Mark Balfour but Ronnie was nearer. As his body made contact with Mark's, Mark failed to let go of the gun and it fired hitting my father in the heart. By the time I had checked my father's pulse the Balfours had gone.'

'They were not going to tell anyone what had happened. Daffodil was a different kettle of fish and needed dealing with but the first question was what to do with father. I told Mother that Dad was being taken to hospital. "He will come back to me, won't he?" she said. And I promised her that.' Here Muirhouse paused and Zara had a fleeting spark of compassion for him but his face remained hard and she immediately went back to staying alert.

'You will be wondering,' he went on, 'how we explained the gunshot wound. My father's gun was old and unreliable. The family could substantiate that, having seen him misfire at rats and pigeons. He'd never kept it loaded before though, to my knowledge. What we told the police was that Mother and I had been in the office trying to hurry him up to go out to dinner. It was Mother's birthday; that he'd opened the drawer for something else and Mother had noticed it. "Shouldn't be there, John," she said. "It's not loaded," he said. He was such a good liar but this time it went against him. She grabbed the gun and cocked it and smiled like it was a game. She always believed what he said, you see.' John Muirhouse had gone so much into his story, Zara was beginning to believe it herself.

'She aimed at his head and pulled the trigger as he shouted, Nancy!'

'And everyone bought the story?'

'It was an accident. There was no time to get the gun from Mother. I think they believed us because it was so bizarre.'

Zara suddenly became aware that Ben was signalling to her. The message seemed to be that there were two people approaching and that she mustn't let on. Des's under-cover men?

'How did you avoid the body being buried?' she said.

'I had a very cunning plan. I asked the undertaker to make two coffins, one of which would be my mother's.' Zara was wondering how the two police officers were able to get near without being seen. 'The coffins were identical. The morning of the funeral, the body was at the house in the front room which we never use, lying in the coffin. It had been viewed through the previous day. The other coffin had been stored in the garage at my request. At the point where we were meant to leave, I told the undertaker that an important wreath had been left at the undertaker's office — a relative had mistaken the instructions. I insisted the undertaker go back for it. I said I'd rung the minister and the funeral could be delayed as it was the only one that day. Daffodil's aunt made tea for the undertaker's assistant in the kitchen and while the coast was clear Daffodil and I took out the body and substituted stones wrapped in heavy cloths. Screwed the lid down again and transferred my father's body to the other coffin. Fortunately, they were much of a size, my parents. Ironically, it was Daffodil who looked after Mother during this time. Persuaded her to have a little rest in her bedroom. Not difficult. Her legs had been playing up.' Zara kept her eyes on John Muirhouse.

'After that everything was easy. The undertaker buried the pile of stones which the minister sent solemnly to eternal rest.' He stopped as if he were expecting applause.

'Very neat,' said Zara as neutrally as she could. The tractor was still there in the background. She wished there was a way of telling the driver what was happening. 'And the reason you persecuted Ronnie? The reason you had to be so complex about it? The reason you had to kill Daffodil?'

'I did not kill Daffodil.'

'You set it up. However it happened, it would not have happened if you had not set it up.' John Muirhouse looked irritated. Zara tensed up.

'Okay, I concede that,' he said.

For some reason Muirhouse had begun to move, not towards Zara but clockwise as if there were both standing on the perimeter of the same circle. Zara was forced to move clockwise too in order to maintain her distance. She could not move back, the ground was too marshy, she was afraid of getting stuck.

'Hold on,' Zara shouted. 'That's only half a story. Did you persecute Ronnie Balfour for revenge? Was killing Daffodil and putting the blame on Ronnie just for revenge?'

John Muirhouse was still moving. Zara had no option but to move onto the marshy ground. She could hear the tractor but it was no help. She could not take her eyes off John Muirhouse. She took another breath.

'My guess is that at some point you thought you would feel safer if Daffodil couldn't speak. Maybe she didn't need a new conservatory.' John Muirhouse folded his arms and stopped walking. Zara was frozen on tufts of marsh grass. She needed to look down to take any more steps but she had to keep watching John Muirhouse.

'Story number two,' he began. 'The Daffodil question. After the murder of my father, Daffodil continued to see Mark Balfour. I suppose the Balfours thought they had won in a way. It was not clear which way things would go if the case ever came to trial. Best leave it. A trial was not going to bring my dad back.'

'But as time went on, knowing Mark Balfour and Daffodil were happy began to eat away at me. One day I woke up and decided I'd had enough. I let Mark Balfour know that if he didn't leave Daffodil alone, I would make sure he had to. Funny how easy it is sometimes to get someone to take a plane to Australia. But best laid plans and all that. What I hadn't anticipated was Daffodil's reaction to Mark's sudden departure the reason for which was kept secret, even from Ronnie who really did know nothing. I know this from various conversations I've had with him over the last two months. His brother convinced him that since the gun had gone off accidentally when

Ronnie was actually trying to prevent a shooting, then he did not have to feel guilty. After all the Balfours had not introduced the gun into the situation. Mark had inveigled Ronnie into going to the office with him and Daffodil. They were on their way to somewhere else. Something Daffodil said, makes me think she and Ronnie hadn't actually met before that night. She said, "Wow, you and Ronnie are very alike, Mark, aren't you?" He'd told Ronnie that Daffodil wanted to give her boss a message. But I suspect that Daffodil may have known about the gun and tipped Mark off. Which means the gun situation might have been engineered. For all I know my father said to Daffodil, "If that guy threatens our relationship, I'll kill him". Far from being an innocent party...'

The tractor was very near, maybe only twenty yards away. It was becoming harder to hear John Muirhouse's voice.

'So what did Daffodil do to upset the apple cart?' shouted Zara. John Muirhouse took a step towards her. She stepped back automatically and almost lost her balance, her foot now firmly anchored in the marsh.

'Daffodil started — you have to understand she wasn't how she appeared on the mountain, all soft and pliable. No. Now my dad had stopped being her money-pot and she didn't have the stimulation of Mark Balfour, she decided to try blackmailing me as a way of assuaging her grief. She became a loose cannon.' Zara had no idea whether she could believe any of this.

'However,' Muirhouse went on, 'what made everything happen the way it did was 1889. I know Mother told you about mine and my father's great interest in the case of Rose and Laurie. When Daffodil became a problem, I suddenly had the brilliant idea of setting up a similar situation but with added extras to suit my purpose. So I followed 1889 in some ways but deviated in others. Partly I wanted explore the theory of accident, whether a serious intention on one person's part can influence the chaos of everyday life so much that the desired event comes to pass. Coincidence? Call it what you like. Meeting Ronnie on Bute, that was good luck. He was wary of course, of my attempts to seem friendly, but perhaps thought I was holding out an olive branch. My phone call to Daffodil to ensure she would be on the island at the right time, that was planning. If you are adaptable and resourceful, it's amazing how you can make things happen the way you want them to.'

'How did you persuade Daffodil to go up the mountain?'

'Easy. I told her I was going up the following day with Ronnie whom I had met by accident in Bute. I had spoken to Ronnie, as you know, in the pub. I took advantage of him. I was affable but not too friendly. When I heard him tell his pals he was going up Goat Fell I just chimed in with a 'May see you up there'. He looked confused but remember, as we know now, he really knew very little about the whole situation and he was probably bewildered but not wanting to make an issue of it in public. Anyway, I suggested to Daffodil I might be able to help her get to know him. One brother is much the same as another to that kind of girl. At worst she might get news of Mark.'

'But how did you persuade her to be tied up?'

'Heard of rohypnol?' He moved a step closer. 'Look, why don't you come and see Ben, just to humour me? I've done what you asked and told you the story but I'd like a picture to remember when I'm away out of the country.'

'Because I don't trust you,' said Zara. The tractor. The noise was so loud, Zara had to look round. It had changed direction and was bearing down on John Muirhouse but he was intent on Zara. He took another step. Zara couldn't. John Muirhouse's grinned as he realized Zara was stuck. He began to move towards her.

Ben took in the scene from his perch on the cliff.

'Look out!' he shouted as loudly as he could. John Muirhouse heard something and turned away from Zara but directly into the path of the tractor. The tractor came on. The last expression Zara saw on John Muirhouse's face was a mixture of terror and disbelief. When she looked down all she could see was a hand: the rest of the man was under the tractor tyre.

Zara didn't wait. She ran as best she could, leaving her trapped boot in the ground, towards Ben who was scrambling down the cliff.

'Did I do the right thing, Aunty Zara? It was to stop him getting to you. But I had to warn him, didn't I, even though it was John Muirhouse?'

'You did... you were amazing. And the bird call, that was...' She hugged him tightly. She wanted to say it probably it probably saved my life but she felt the situation appeared quite serious enough.

Police officers had sprung up as if from nowhere. They were questioning the driver of the tractor. One officer approached Zara.

'I'll come to the station,' she said. 'I have to get Ben home now.' She raised her eyes to those of the tractor driver. Bobby. She was surprised and yet not surprised. She wanted to convey something. 'I'll catch you later,' she said in an undertone.

'Not unless you visit the gaol you won't,' said one of the officers.

'Okay,' said Zara. 'That's fine.' She waved to Bobby who looked resigned rather than defiant.

***

Later Ben was overjoyed to find that his tape would be used in the writing up and closing of the case concerning the second Goat Fell murder.

***

Ronnie Balfour, when completely recovered, brought Zara a rosebush called Mountain Queen to be planted in George's garden. He said he could not thank her enough so he hoped the rose would do it for him over the years.

***

Tommy told Zara that Aunt Marion had left the whole cottage and back house to Bobby. Bobby's version of the event at the caves was that he had come to Zara's rescue but his brakes had failed...

***

When Barney returned from Glasgow he could not believe the game was over. It was a long time before he got the story straight and allowed his admiration to outstrip his misgivings about Zara and Ben's behaviour.

'No pressure,' Barney told Zara, 'but I'd like to rewind on what I said about not wanting to marry you.'

'You've realized I always act for the best?'

'I've realized I can't be sensible about you.'

So where does that leave us?' asked Zara.

'It leaves you with a decision to make.'

'I'll give it some serious thought,' said Zara.

About the author

Zara on Arran is Cicely Gill's second detective novel. The first 'Ivory' is set in Glasgow.

Cicely has lived on Arran for over 40 years. Besides novels, she writes plays and poetry. She is married with two children and four grandchildren.